當代英語用法指南
Modern English Usage Guide

蘇秦 著

晨星出版

序言

《當代英語用法指南》對文法學習者或教學者頗有助益，不僅是可供單一詞條或主題查閱的文法工具書，也是適合逐章研讀的文法學習書。本書適合預備全民英檢、多益、托福、雅思、學測、指考、統測或公職等考試的讀者研讀，也適合英語教學者或英語文字工作者查閱語法。當然，本書更適合有意提升英語文法能力的職場人士進修使用。

本書的文法論述採取「定義明確、條理分明、題材周延、首重當代用法、真實語料」等文法知能建構策略，幫助讀者循序漸進培養文法實力、穩紮穩打累積文法戰力。

定義明確方面，本書明確定義重要文法語詞，幫助讀者奠立文法主題概念基礎，奠定文法學習的基礎。例如關於「受詞」的相關定義：

1. 動詞受詞：

接受動詞所示動作，或感官上接受其影響的對象為受詞。及物和授與動詞必須與受詞共現語意才完整。

1.1 格位：及物動詞，無論限定或不限定，都能賦予右側伴隨的名詞受格格位，使其具備受詞功用。例如：

■ I'm sorry for bothering you.
很抱歉，打擾你。

1.4 受詞的移位：

1.4.1 前移：強調受詞時，受詞前移至主詞左側，形成句子第二焦點。

■ I can never leave music.
= Music, I can never leave it.
我離不開音樂。

> **說明** 由於歷史演進與民族交流，中文也常出現受詞置於主詞前面的語詞，例如「草坪請勿踐踏。」、「蛋糕放哪裡？」或是「飯吃飽了嗎？」。

1.4.2 後移：移至受詞補語右側，受詞空缺可填補 it。

■ Bella makes it a rule to practice playing flute one hour a day.
貝拉習慣每天練習長笛一小時。

序言

題材周延方面，本書對於任一題材都能清楚而周延地完整表述，以使讀者充分掌握主題相關重點。例如「介系詞獨立構句」部分，本書除了明確說明介系詞獨立構句的用法，還依序列舉所有的可能結構，例如：

介系詞獨立構句：介系詞 with/without 引導獨立構句，說明句子原因、條件或附加狀況，形成介系詞獨立構句，搭配名詞/代名詞/現在分詞/過去分詞/不定詞/形容詞/副詞/介系詞片語等語詞。另外，介系詞獨立構句與主要子句的主句不一致。

6.1 with/without 主詞名詞片語

■ The pilot died from an air crash, with his son yet a toddle.

= The pilot died from an air crash, and his son was only a toddle.

飛行員死於空難，他兒子才剛開始學走路。

6.2 with/without 主詞形容詞片語

■ Don't talk to others with your mouth full.

= Don't talk to others if your mouth is full of food.

不要滿口食物還要跟別人說話。

6.3 with/without 主詞副詞片語

■ The giraffe was drinking water, with its head down.

= The giraffe was drinking water, and its head was down.

長頸鹿喝著水，頭往下低。

6.4 with/without 主詞介系詞片語

■ A leopard climbed up to the tree, with a warthog in its mouth.

= A leopard climbed up to the tree, and it held a warthog in its mouth.

獵豹爬到樹上，嘴巴咬著一隻疣豬。

6.5 with/without 主詞不定詞片語

■ With nothing to do, the workers killed time playing mahjong.
= Because there was nothing to do, the workers killed time playing mahjong.
無事可做,工人打麻將消磨時間。

6.6 with/without ＋主詞＋分詞片語

6.6.1 現在分詞

■ The female fox went hunting, with its cubs staying at the den.
= The female fox went hunting and its cubs stayed at the den.
狐狸母親出去打獵,小狐狸留在洞穴。

6.6.2 過去分詞

■ The suspect was brought in, with his hands handcuffed behind his back.
= The suspect was brought in and his hands handcuffed behind his back.
嫌犯被帶上來,雙手被銬在背後。

條理分明方面,本書除了明確定義語詞,詳盡說明要點之外,還能清晰統整內容,提供讀者有效學習路徑。例如有關不定詞、動名詞與分詞等非限定動詞的時態與語態類型皆以表格清楚而周延地介紹,例如:

不定詞的語態:不定詞有主動與被動語態,主動語態不定詞有簡單式、進行式、完成式、完成進行式等,被動語態不定詞只有簡單式與完成式。

時態	主動語態	被動語態
簡單式	to ＋原形動詞	to be ＋過去分詞
進行式	to be ＋現在分詞	
完成式	to have ＋過去分詞	to have ＋過去分詞
完成進行式	to have been ＋現在分詞	

動名詞的時態與語態：動名詞有主動與被動語態，各有簡單式與完成式。

時態	主動語態	被動語態
簡單式	V-ing	being 過去分詞
完成式	having 過去分詞	having been 過去分詞

分詞的時態與語態：現在分詞有簡單式、完成式、被動語態，過去分詞只有簡單式。

現在分詞	主動語態	被動語態
簡單式	V-ing	being 過去分詞
完成式	having 過去分詞	having been 過去分詞

過去分詞	主動語態	被動語態
簡單式	過去分詞	—

首重當代用法方面，本書所述題材都是當前重要英語測驗出題焦點，或日常生活、職場、新聞常見用法，凡是過時或當今英美人士罕用的用法，雖然常見於若干文法書籍，但本書皆不予列入，例如下列句子中的用法皆屬舊式用法，不會出現在本書：

（×）There is nothing but helps us move on.

（×）The patient felt so much the more tired for getting more sleep.

真實語料方面，本書除了首重當代語法之外，例句則以故事導向，事件報導、依據事實及真實情境等原則編寫，引導讀者於愉悅的閱讀中學習當代語法：

■ If you want to take a selfie in public, don't get caught!
你若要公開自拍照的話，不要被發現。

■ Being caught cheating during test, the student was cited with a 1st Level Demerit.
學生被抓到考試作弊，記了一支大過。

■ Even when a snake has its eyes closed, it can still see through its eyelids.
蛇即使閉上眼睛，牠也能透過眼瞼看物體。

　　時值《當代英語用法指南》付梓之際，本人除了感謝晨星出版社給予出版機會之外，還要感謝

　　摯友—CNN iReport 記者 Tony Coolidge 協助校閱，確保本書合乎當代用法的標準。另外，還要感謝先前提供本人文法寫作機會的幾家出版社，由於這些寶貴的文法論述經驗，本人才有信心為廣大英語學習者編寫本書。

　　本書如有疏漏或不妥之處，尚祈專家先進及讀者不吝指正。

蘇泰

2014 年鳳凰花開時

序言

In my experience and observations, many books, and even tests, in Taiwan are unreliable resources for modern usage of English language. There is much taught to students that one does not hear in conversation these days.

Foreigners will feel strange when they hear the archaic or outdated grammar or vocabulary used. Suchin has compiled a valuable resource for English language learners to be able to improve their English abilities and stay up-to-date. The context of the content is based on common everyday situations, and there are many things the reader can learn about the world, just by using this book.

Enjoy the learning experience, and treasure this book.

Tony Coolidge

試讀推薦序

　　我是一名高中學生，一開始對學英文充滿恐懼，總覺得英文就是「背」，尤其面對克漏字測驗時，要先看懂文章，才有頭緒回答問題，接下來要作答的問題又更多變了，一篇文章中，可以考單字考片語考時態考文法，並且需要由前後文去判斷答案，因此更是一大難關，也常常是得失分的關鍵！

　　但是經由了這本書，我學到了許多解題的技巧，藉由前後文的詞性便能選出正確答案，迅速提升了英文能力，在國中時便通過了全民英檢中級，英文也不再是困擾！這本文法指南的一大特點便是，內容豐富、條理分明，運用淺顯易懂的句子讓讀者透徹理解，並採用漸進的方式幫助我們一步一步構築英文深厚基礎，累積實力，分析全民英檢、多益、學測、指考……等等的大考題型，不僅僅是對考生有所助益，對於上班族或是有意進修者更是合適，著實是英語教學書籍的最佳選擇！

台南女中　許珈嘉

　　升上高中後才發現，國中與高中教的英文著實有很大的落差，讓我一度對學習英文感到恐懼，加上自己在解題速度方面總是慢了別人一些，相形之下，自己也愈來愈沒有信心，某天無意間讀了這本文法書，才發現原來其實英文也可以很容易就上手！

　　這本文法書中，將完整的文法結構做系統式的整理，並用一些表格等做對照、加以說明，使得文法更淺顯易懂，給予像我這種理解力較差的學生很大的幫助，自己讀起來也不會太吃力。由於近幾年的考題趨勢，大考閱讀測驗的文章是愈來愈長，在面對如此長的文章，該如何正確答題得高分呢？這本書涵蓋的範圍不僅僅是針對學測，像是升大學必備的英檢及多益，藉由這本文法書會教你許多解題的訣竅，讓你在英文這個科目上事半功倍，成為你考試的最佳利器，它真的是本很棒的文法書！

新化高中　陳柔伊

試讀推薦序

　　從小學開始在學習英文的過程中，各級老師幾乎都告訴我們學好英文的不二法門，就是要多背、多聽、多講。但是在國內缺乏可以經常使用英語的環境，要我死背英文單字，再套上看似無邊無際的文法結構，對我而言，學好英文是一件相當痛苦的事！

　　在學校考試，翻譯及克漏字測驗，特別令我最頭痛，不僅要先了解句子的時態，還要知道句子的意思，才能寫出正確的答案，讓我對學習英文幾度退縮！

　　自從拜讀蘇秦老師這本書之後，讓我茅塞頓開！我從許多淺顯易懂的文法及句法規則，重新建立學習英文的信心；無論是閱讀或是解題，只要能藉由前後文的詞性，便能做出正確的判斷與解答，英文不再是我頭痛的學習科目，反而讓我對學習英文產生更大的興趣，造就我英文能力突飛猛進。

　　這本書是我看過最好的文法書，裡面不僅內容豐富，而且整理得非常齊全，最重要的是可以讓學習者破除學習瓶頸，奠定更堅實的基礎，並快速累積英文的實力，書中還有增列各種測驗的題型分析，對考生或自學英文人士都有相當大的助益，是一本非常值得推薦的好書。

台南一中　李崇正

目次

目次

目次

目次

目次

目次

目次

第8章　語氣

第9章　形容詞

第 10 章 副詞

目次

第 12 章　連接詞

第 13 章　子句

目次

句子的基本成份

◆ 1-1 主詞

就邏輯而言，主詞是動詞描述的對象，句子談論的主題；就結構而言，主詞是句子的必要成分，主詞位置不可留空，即使語意上不須主詞，仍需填補。

■ The volcano has been ejecting ash for three days.
三天來，火山不斷噴出熔岩。

■ The manager chaired the meeting this morning.
經理主持今天早上的會議。

■ What you said is just absolutely stupid.
你說的話簡直俗不可耐。

■ It seems to be raining this afternoon.
今天下午似乎會下雨。

1. 主詞的格位：

限定子句主詞具主格性質，限定動詞賦予主詞位置的語詞主格性質。

■ You seem to have drowned a couple of times.
有幾次你幾乎要溺斃了。

■ She has decided to breastfeed her baby after birth.
嬰兒出生後她決定餵母乳。

■ Look at the story about the woman who is breastfeeding her pet dog.
看看給自己寵物狗餵母乳的那位婦人。

2. 主詞的形式：

凡名詞性質的語詞皆可扮演主詞角色。

2.1 名詞片語

■ Buffalos never sleep.
水牛從不睡覺。

■ Apes eat meat regularly.
人猿每隔一段時間就會吃肉。

■ The book is selling very well.
書賣得很好。

2.2 代名詞

■ It costs a lot to buy a house in Taipei.
在台北購屋所費不貲。

■ Such is life.
這才是生活。

2.3 the ＋形容詞／分詞

■ The rich are not always generous.
有些富人一點也不寬厚。

■ The wounded have been sent to the hospital.
傷者已送往醫院。

■ The living need to make a living; however, the dead don't.
人活者就得謀生，往生了就不需要。

2.4 填補主詞

■ There are many bushes and bright colorful flowers in the park.
公園裡有許多灌木和色彩鮮明的花朵。

■ It's necessary to learn one or two foreign languages.
學習一二種外語是必要的。

> **說明** 不定詞片語結構龐大，移至補語 necessary 右側，主詞位置以 It 填補。

■ It's important that the lesson should be interesting.
課程有趣很重要。

說明 that 子句結構龐大,移至補語右側,主詞位置以 It 填補。

2.5 不定詞

■ To see is to believe.
眼見為憑。

■ To teach is to learn.
教學相長。

■ To live is to enjoy life.
生活就是享受生命。

說明 固定用法的不定詞主詞不需變換為填補主詞句型。

2.6 Wh-to V

■ When to start is the next issue.
什麼時候出發是下個議題。

■ How to solve the problem is the most important part.
如何解決問題是最重要的部分。

說明 除 why 之外,疑問語詞搭配不定詞片語,構成名詞片語,扮演名詞角色。

2.7 動名詞

■ Keeping early hours is good for health.
早睡早起有益健康。

■ Driving and drinking is never recommended.
絕對禁止酒駕。

2.8 名詞子句

■ Whether you will come or not is up to you.
你來不來自己看著辦。

■ What you have done means a lot to the team.
你的所作所為對團隊意義重大。

2.9 介系詞片語

■ After lunch would be fine with me.
午餐過後我可以。（備註：午餐過後我有空了）

■ From now till next Friday is a considerable amount of time.
從現在到下星期五這段時間相當充裕。

2.10 引句

■ "Thank you." was all the woman said.
婦人只說了聲「謝謝」。

3. 主詞的省略：

3.1 祈使句主詞指涉明確。

■ Please tell us whether you may accept the offer.
請告知是否接受報價。

■ Thank you for your close cooperation with us in making the arrangements.
感謝您與我們密切合作協議。

3.2 引介句當形容詞子句

■ The number of the spelling mistakes there are in the composition is awful.
這篇作文拼寫錯太多了。

説明

1. 引介句：

■ There are spelling mistakes in the compostion.
這篇作文拼寫錯太多了。

2. 關係代名詞省略。

4. 主詞與動詞的語意關聯：

以句子結構而言，主詞為動詞語意完整的必要成分，二者須伴隨出現。以語意關聯而言，主詞除了是動作產生者，還有許多其他可能的語意關聯。了解主詞與動詞的語意關聯，對於句子組成成分的鋪陳，能夠賦予結構之外的連結脈絡。

4.1 動作產生者：即動作執行者。

■ The accountant cashed the check at the bank.
會計在銀行兌現支票。

■ White blood cells will attack germs in the body.
白血球攻擊體內細菌。

■ The machine will reverse the direction in which it spins.
機器會反向運轉。

4.2 受事者：被動語態中受動作影響的主詞。

■ The vase was broken to pieces by the janitor.
管理員將花瓶打破，碎成一地。

■ The proposal has been rejected by the committee.
委員會駁回提案。

4.3 主題主詞：連綴動詞描述的主詞。

■ The bacon smelled really skunky.
燻肉聞起來很臭。

■ The beef noodles tasted just fine.
牛肉麵嚐起來很鮮美。

■ The hostel is located in the south of town.
旅館位於鎮上南方。

> 說明 搭配連綴動詞以表示位置的主詞又稱為定位者主詞。

4.4 經驗者：搭配感官或情緒動詞的主詞，體驗動詞影響的對象。

■ I saw a skunk on the stairs.
我在樓梯上看到一隻臭鼬。

■ She was excited to see her sister again.
再次看到自己的姊姊，她興奮極了。

4.5 起因者：影響受詞的主詞

■ The Internet has turned the world into a global village.
網路使世界成為一個地球村。

4.6 工具：達到結果的工具，常搭配介系詞 by, in, with。

■ The screwdriver opened the door to the shelf.
螺絲起子打開書櫃的門。

■ The presentation was made in English.
這項演出是用英文發表的。

5. 主詞的移位：

主詞常因尾重原則或語意強調而前後移位。

5.1 後移：

5.1.1 搭配虛主詞

■ It's interesting to play a chess game.
下西洋棋很有趣。

■ It seems that Leo is not suitable for his new job.
里歐似乎不適合他的新工作。

■ It's amazing that the snake's heart is still beating in the palm of his hand.
他手掌上那顆蛇心仍在跳動, 真是令人驚奇。

■ There are more than 3,000 species of insects on Earth.
地球上有三千多種昆蟲。

5.1.2 移至述語動詞右側

■ They are still alive, the mother meerkat and her husband and their children.
狐獴爸爸和媽媽及牠們的小孩仍然活著。

5.2 前移：強調主詞的主題語意時，主詞移至句首，空缺以代
　　名詞填補。

■ Prof. Lin recommended the website. It must be very informative.

林教授推薦的網站，內容一定非常豐富。

= The website Prof. Lin recommended, it must be very informative.

網站是林教授推薦，那內容一定非常豐富。

◆ 1-2 受詞

接受動詞所示動作，或感官上接受其影響的對象為受詞。及物與授與動詞與受詞共現語意才完整。

■ The farmer caught a big rat.
農夫抓到一隻大老鼠。

■ My host lady is teaching me cooking.
我的寄宿家庭女主人教我烹飪。

■ The music comforted me.
音樂撫慰著我。

1. 動詞受詞：

1.1 格位：及物動詞，除了過去分詞，動詞賦予右側伴隨的名
　　詞受格格位，使其具備受詞功用。

〔主動詞〕

■ I don't trust him.
我不信任他。

〔主動詞〕

■ Leo forgot to invite them.
里歐忘了邀請他們。

〔動名詞〕

■ I'm sorry for bothering you.
很抱歉，打擾你。

1.2 形式：名詞性質的語詞都有受詞功用。

1.2.1 名詞

■ Doing yoga is good for health.
做瑜珈有益健康

■ The movie starred a huge cast of very talented young actors and actresses.
電影卡司陣容龐大，都是才華洋溢的年輕男女演員擔綱。

1.2.2 代名詞

■ Let them go.
讓他們過去吧！

■ Believe it or not.
信不信由你。

1.2.3 不定詞

■ I hope to take a trip to various countries in Africa.
我希望去非洲不同國家旅遊。

■ The government planned to build a crematorium in that area.
政府計畫在那地區興建垃圾焚化爐。

1.2.4 Wh – to V

■ Tell me what to do.
告訴我怎麼做。

■ I wonder who to put the blame on.
我不知道該如何責備。

■ I don't know how to assemble this machine from scratch.
我不知道如何從頭組裝這部機器。

■ Could you please tell me where to rent the car for a cheaper price？
麻煩告訴我到哪裡租較便宜的車子？

1.2.5 動名詞

■ I really regret saying that now.
要是沒講那件事就好了。

■ Bella continuously practiced playing the flute.
貝拉持續練長笛。

1.2.6 名詞子句

■ I doubt whether this is true or not.
我懷疑這是不是真的。

■ We believe the mountain climber is still alive.
我們相信登山客還活著。

1.2.7 填補受詞 it：受詞結構較受詞補語大時，受詞常移至受詞補語右側，受詞位置以 it 填補。

(1) 受詞為不定詞

■ I think it really incredible to raise a python at home.
我想在家養蟒蛇真是令人難以置信。

(2) 受詞為動名詞

■ I found it quite difficult learning a foreign language.
我發現學習外語相當困難。

(3) 受詞為名詞子句

■ The program makes it possible that one day we can travel to the past.
這項計畫使時光旅行讓我們回到過去有可能成真。

1.3 受詞與動詞的語意關聯

1.3.1 受事者：主詞為動作產生者時，受詞為受事者受詞。大多數受詞為動詞受事者

■ Salmon lay eggs upstream.
鮭魚在上游下蛋。

■ The hen is hatching her chicks.
母雞在孵小雞。

說明

1. 受事者若是主詞創造或產生的事物，受詞為受創造者。

■ God created the world.
　神創造世界。

■ Edison invented electricity.
　愛迪生發明電。

■ Beethoven composed many symphonies.
　貝多芬寫了很多交響曲。

2. 受詞為地方場所，且動作已完成，這時受詞為位置標示者。

■ The CEO visited the factory last week.
　執行長上星期訪視工廠。

■ The young students climbed Ah Li Shan.
　年輕學生們爬阿里山。

3. 受詞為約定成俗而不需明示的受事者，可省略。動詞會因受詞省略而變成不及物動詞。

■ Bella enjoys singing (songs).
　貝拉喜歡唱歌。

■ Hank drank (wine) a lot last night.
　漢克昨晚喝很多紅酒。

■ The old man is addicted to smoking (cigarettes).
　老先生有菸癮。

1.3.2 經驗者：受動作影響而產生感官反應的受詞為經驗者

■ I love sports.
　我熱愛運動。

■ The cartoon amused my brother.
　這部卡通讓我哥哥很開心。

■ The learning activity interested children a lot.
　學習活動讓小孩感到很有趣。

1.4 受詞的移位

1.4.1 前移：強調受詞時，受詞可前移至主詞左側，形成句子的第二焦點。

■ The house owner raised the Tibetan Mastiff.
　= The Tibetan Mastiff the house owner raised.
　屋主飼養西藏獒犬。

■ You made what a wonderful Jack-O-Lantern!

= What a wonderful Jack-O-Lantern you made!

你做了一個好漂亮的南瓜燈籠。

■ I can never leave music.

= Music, I can never leave it.

我離不開音樂。

■ I have never met a fortune teller I can believe.

= Fortune teller, I have never met one I can believe.

我從沒遇過可信的算命師。

說明

1. 強調受詞的主題語意時，受詞移至句首，空缺以代名詞填補。

2. 由於歷史演進與民族交流，中文也常出現受詞置於主詞前面的語詞，例如「草坪請勿踐踏。」、「蛋糕放哪裡？」、「飯吃飽了嗎？」。

1.4.2 後移：受詞結構龐大時，可移至受詞補語右側，受詞空缺可用 it 填補。

■ Most people take it for granted to speak Taiwanese in Taiwan.

大多數人認為在台灣說台語是理所當然。

■ Bella makes it a rule to practice playing flute one hour a day.

貝拉習慣每天練習長笛一小時。

■ We must take many factors whose influences are still not well understood into consideration.

= We must take into consideration many factors whose influences are still not well understood.

我們必須考慮許多不明的影響因素。

說明 虛受詞 it 也可用於表示已知的指涉事項，不具語意的受詞填補功用。

■ Beat it !　　少管閒事！

■ Damn it.　　該死！

■ Take it easy.　　放輕鬆。

■ I can't stand it any more.　　我再也受不了。

■ Now you have done it.　　跟你說過不要這麼做。

2. 授與動詞受詞：

2.1 直接受詞：授與動詞的受事者為直接受詞，指涉對象為人、物或事。

2.1.1 人

■ They offered me a good deal.

他們給我一個好價錢。

■ Tom gave himself a new nickname.

湯姆給自己取了一個新綽號。

2.1.2 物

■ Don't feed your Shih Tzu too much food with high amounts of yeast.

別餵你的獅子狗太多添加酵母的食物。

2.1.3 事

■ I will gave the suggestion some consideration.

你的建議我要多加考慮。

2.2 間接受詞：接受直接受詞的對象為間接受詞，通常是直接受詞的目標、來源、受益者。結構上，間接受詞形式為名詞片語、代名詞、to/for 介系詞片語。值得注意的是，名詞形式的間接受詞不一定都可代換為介系詞片語。

2.2.1 目標：間接受詞為直接受詞的目標時，介系詞片語搭配 to

■ Mrs. Lin brought me some maple candy.

= Mrs. Lin brought some maple candy to me.

林太太帶了些楓糖糖果給我。

= Mrs. Lin brought some maple candy for me.

林太太幫我帶了些楓糖糖果。

■ Leo lent me some money.

= Leo lent some money to me.

里歐借給我一些錢。

說明

1. 間接受詞 me 是直接受詞 some money 的目標。
2. 另一分析是將介系詞片語視為間接受詞。

■ Please pass me the salt.

= Please pass the salt to me.

請把鹽遞給我。

★ 間接受詞為直接受詞的目標的授與動詞：

advance 預付	forward 轉寄
award 頒獎	give 給予
deal 給與	grant 承認
hand 繳交	loan 借
lease 租借	mail 郵寄
leave 遺留	owe 欠
pay 支付	send 寄
read 閱讀	take 拿取
rent 租	tell 告訴

2.2.2 受益者：間接受詞為直接受詞的受益者時，介系詞片語搭配 for

■ Hank bought Bella a bunch of roses.

= Hank bought a bunch of roses for Bella.

漢克買一束玫瑰給貝拉。

■ Please reserve me a table for two tomorrow.

= Please reserve a table for two for me tomorrow.

明天請幫我預留一張兩人桌。

■ Mrs. Lin prepared a big meal for her family.

林太太為家人準備豐盛的一餐。

說明 perpare 無名詞形式的間接受詞結構。

■ Gina wrote an email to Mr. Lin.
= Gina wrote Mr. Lin an email.
吉娜寫一封電子郵件給林先生。

【比較】Gina wrote an email for Mr. Lin.
吉娜幫林先生寫一封電子郵件。

★ 間接受詞為直接受詞的受益者的授與動詞：

book 訂	build 建造
fetch 去拿	find 找出
order 命令	paint 油漆；畫
cash 兌現	cook 烹調
get 得到	keep 持有
pick 選擇	save 挽救
cut 切；剪	secure 保衛
make 製造	design 設計
set 放置	mix 混合
spare 分讓	buy 買

2.2.3 來源：間接受詞為直接受詞的來源時，介系詞片語搭配 from

■ I borrowed a large amount of money from my brother.
= I borrowed from my brother a large amount of money.
我向我弟弟借了一大筆錢。

3. 介系詞受詞

3.1 格位：介系詞會賦予其右側名詞受格格位，因此介系詞受詞為受格格位。

■ How about you?
你呢？

■ Don't talk about it now.
現在不要談這個。

3.2 形式

3.2.1 名詞片語

■ Out of sight, out of mind.
出乎意料

■ It's about five kilometers from the station to the museum.
博物館到車站大概五公里。

3.2.2 代名詞

■ I heard from him two days ago.
我兩天前得到他的消息。

■ The town is a place in which we can forget ourselves.
這鎮是個能夠令人忘我的地方。

■ He is the man to whom I talked just now.
他是剛剛和我談話的男子。

3.2.3 不定詞：介系詞性質的 but, except 可搭配不定詞。另外，含介系詞的片語動詞搭配「Wh-to ＋ V」語詞時，可將「Wh-to ＋ V」重新分析為介系詞受詞。

■ The central bank has few options except to keep in terest rates low.
中央銀行讓利率一直維持在低點。

■ The boy did nothing but make an apology for what he did wrong.
男孩只能為自己所做的錯事道歉。

> 說明 「nothing but」搭配的原形動詞為省略 to 的不定詞。

■ I am thinking about how to deal with the case.
我一直在思考如何處理這件事。

3.2.4 動名詞

■ How about going to the pub after the party?
派對後要不要去夜店？

■ I have been looking forward to seeing you again.
我一直期待再次見到你。

3.2.5 形容詞：for 搭配形容詞 good, dead，形成副詞性質的介系詞片語

■ Nobody wants to be left for dead.
沒人想要被置於死地。

■ We will miss Paul Walker for good.
我們永遠懷念保羅・沃克。

3.2.6 副詞

■ There's a convenience store near there.
那附近有一家便利超商。

■ Black-faced spoon bills will return from abroad soon.
黑面琵鷺很快將從外國返回。

★ 其他搭配副詞的介系詞片語：

at home　在家	from somewhere 從某個地方
at last　至少	out of here　離開
at once　馬上	over there　在那裡
before long　馬上	since then　從那時
from there　從那裡	up to here　到這裡

3.2.7 介系詞片語：時間或空間訊息的介系詞片語可當介系詞受詞。

■ The bunny hopped to a spot behind the tree.
兔子跳到樹後面。

■ Blood came out between the teeth after Steve was hit in the mouth.
史蒂芬撞到嘴巴後，牙齒流血了。

■ Copies of the handouts will not be available until before the meeting time.

會議前才拿得到資料。

3.2.8 名詞子句：少數介系詞可搭配名詞子句當受詞。

(1) 搭配感官動詞的 like 介系詞片語可搭配名詞子句當受詞。

■ The hotel room smelled like there was a gas attack.

飯店房間聞起來像遭到瓦斯攻擊。

■ The food tasted like it was overheated in a microwave.

食物嚐起來像在微波爐過度加熱。

(2) 「How about」搭配 if 子句，表示徵詢。

■ How about if we meet after work in the bar?

下班後我們在夜店聚一下怎樣？

(3) except 搭配 that 名詞子句

■ I appreciate the film except that it is too long.

除了片子時間太長，我很欣賞那部影片。

(4) 含介系詞 to 的片語動詞搭配名詞子句當受詞，該名詞子句可分析為片語動詞的受詞。

■ We looked forward to the time that we could meet the author in the workshop.

我們期待能在研習會遇到那位作家。

■ When it comes to whether students should take a part-time job, they hold different views.

一提到學生是否該打工，他們持不同意見。

3.3 介系詞受詞與動詞的語意關聯：介系詞片語提供動作或事件的相關訊息，介系詞受詞與動詞的語意關聯十分明確，例如：

目的	for, with a view to	結果	into
目標	at, to, toward	反對	against, over

受益者	for	支持	for
陪伴	with	肯定條件	in case of
分離	from, off	否定條件	but for, for fear of
關於	about, on	工具	with, in, by

3.3.1 陪伴

■ The giant panda baby enjoys being with its mother.
圓仔很喜歡和媽媽膩在一起。

3.3.2 關於

■ The columnist committed a comment on the policy.
專欄作家發表政策評論。

3.3.3 受益者

■ The government provided food and clothes for the sufferers.
政府提供食物和衣服給受難者。

3.3.4 分離

■ The caretaker isolated the patient from his family and friends.
看護將病患和家人、朋友隔離。

3.3.5 反對

■ Abraham Lincoln debated against Stephen Douglas in the 1858 US Senate campaign.
亞伯拉罕・林肯於 1858 年參議員競選活動中與史蒂芬・道格拉斯爭辯。

★ under 搭配不含限定詞的名詞通常表示該名詞的被動狀態，at 則表示主動狀態，例如：

主動狀態	被動狀態
at work 工作中	under construction 建造中
at play 正在玩遊戲	under control 控制中

at table　用餐	under negotiation　協調中
at random　隨便	under discussion　討論中
at will　任意	under suspension　暫停

3.4 介系詞與受詞的遠距關係：介系詞引介受詞，二者應相鄰連接，但下列情況呈現二者遠距關係。

3.4.1 疑問句

■ What project are you working on?
你在執行什麼工作？

3.4.2 形容詞子句

■ The candidate whom I voted for won the election.
我投票支持的候選人贏得選舉。

3.4.3 強調句：

■ What I think of when I get home is each of my students.
我回家後就想著我的每一個學生。

3.4.4 被動句

■ Has the sales report been turned in?
銷售報告交了嗎？

3.4.5 不定詞

■ The case is easy to deal with.
這案子很容易處理。

3.4.6 動名詞

■ The website is worth referring to.
這個網站值得推薦。

◆ 1-3 補語

補充說明主詞或受詞狀況而使動詞語意完整的語詞為補語，句子的必要成分。

1. 主詞補語：

補充說明主詞狀況的語詞為主詞補語。

1.1 位置

1.1.1 連綴動詞之後

■ The world has become a global village.
世界已變成一個地球村。

■ The sunset looks fantastic from the lake.
湖上的落日太美了。

1.1.2 述語動詞之後

■ The bathroom smelled awful, like a mildew smell.
廁所很臭，像黴菌的味道。

■ The plane was hijacked by terrorists, full of passengers.
滿載乘客的飛機遭恐怖份子劫持。

1.1.3 句首：即倒裝句，造成主詞與動詞詞序變換。

■ Contraband goods are in the bag.
= In the bag are contraband goods.
走私物品在袋子裡。

■ Those who are contented are happy.
= Happy are those who are contented.
滿足的人是快樂的。

■ Leo was so tired that I fell asleep soon after dinner.
= So tired was Leo that he fell asleep soon after dinner.
里歐好累，晚餐後就睡著了。

■ The weather was such that the activity had to be postponed.
= Such was the weather that the activity had to be postponed.
天氣這麼差，活動得取消。

1.2 形式

1.2.1 名詞片語

■ George Washington was the first US President.
喬治・華盛頓是第一位美國總統。

■ The Tasmanian Devil is the largest carnivorous marsupial in the world.
袋獾是世界最大的有袋肉食動物。

1.2.2 代名詞

■ It's me.　　　　是我。
■ That's her.　　　那是她。

1.2.3 不定詞

■ The aim is to complete the detailed plan.
目標是完成詳細計畫。

■ The grocery store seemed to be closed.
雜貨店似乎要打烊了。

1.2.4 動名詞

■ My hobby is collecting stickers.
我的嗜好是收集貼紙。

■ The team ended up losing the game 62-58.
結果該隊以 62-58 敗北。

1.2.5 分詞片語

■ This question is confusing to me.
這問題一直讓我很困惑。
■ Leo was excited about his date with Bella.
里歐對於能和貝拉約會感到很興奮。

1.2.6 形容詞片語

■ The idea sounds great to me.
對我來說，這主意聽起來很棒！

■ The pink dress looks nice on you.
粉紅色洋裝穿在妳身上很好看。

1.2.7 副詞片語

■ I'm just looking around.
　我就到處看看。

■ Mr. Lin is not in now.
　林先生現在不在。

1.2.8 副詞子句

■ That's since you got divorced.
　從你離婚開始。

■ It's because someone else is about to leave.
　因為有其他人要離開。

1.2.9 介系詞片語

■ I was in the dormitory this morning.
　今天早上我待在宿舍。

■ The sunrise looks like a watercolor painting this morning.
　今天早上的日出看起來像一幅水彩畫。

1.2.10 名詞子句

■ The answer to our problem is that we need more expenditure to finish the task.
　問題是我們需要更多經費來完成任務。

■ The point is that you cannot disprove the existence of God.
　問題是你無法否認神的存在。

2. 受詞補語：

補充說明受詞狀況的語詞為受詞補語，不完全及物動詞的語意必要成分。受詞補語形式如下：

2.1 名詞片語

■ Do you think Mr. Lin a good writer?
　你認為林先生是個好作家嗎？

■ Many people consider Edison a genius.
許多人認為愛迪生很大方。

2.2 原形動詞

■ Let me do it.
讓我來吧。

■ Mom had me not stay out late.
媽媽叫我不要晚歸。

2.3 不定詞

■ I would guess the model to be in her early twenties.
我猜模特兒才二十出頭。

■ The coach forbade his players to talk during practice.
教練禁止球員練習時交談。

■ The doctor instructed me to go on a diet.
醫生要我節食。

■ The police urged the kidnapper to release the child.
警方催促綁匪釋放小孩。

2.4 分詞片語：現在分詞表示受詞的主動狀態，過去分詞表示被動狀態。

■ The salesperson kept his client waiting for over an hour.
銷售員讓客戶等了一個多小時。

■ The investigator noticed the door unlocked to the bar.
調查員注意到門沒鎖。

2.5 形容詞片語

■ The connoisseur pronounced the painting miraculous.
鑑定家斷定畫作價值不斐。

■ The manager found it never easy dealing with tough customers.
經理發現奧客很難擺平。

2.6 副詞

■ The chairperson declared the meeting over.
主席宣布會議結束。

2.7 介副詞

■ Could you please pick the magazine up?
麻煩將雜誌撿起來。

■ We have decided to put the meeting off until next week.
我們決定將會議順延到下週。

2.8 介系詞片語：通常表示位置或身分（搭配介系詞 as）

■ The passenger left his umbrella on the bus.
乘客將雨傘留在巴士。

■ Some people describe the man as (a) good-for-nothing.
一些人形容那名男子一無是處。

第2章 名詞

名詞表示人、生物、事物等名稱，是數量最多的詞類。名詞的主要特徵為搭配限定詞及有單複數、性別、格位區分。

◆ 2-1 名詞的數

名詞有單數與複數二種。普通名詞有單數與複數形，形式常因單詞或語意而有所不同。其他名詞次分類的複數形多屬特定用法，端視語意而定。

1. 單複數同形的單字：

aircraft　飛機	carp　鯉魚
cod　鱈魚	deer　鹿
falls　瀑布	fish　魚
headquarters　總部	innings　賽局
means　方法	moose　駝鹿
oats　燕麥	offspring　後裔
remains　遺物	salmon　鮭魚
series　系列	sheep　綿羊
species　物種	squid　魷魚
trout　鱒魚	works　作品集

★ –ese／-ss 字尾的國民名稱也是單複數同形

burmese　緬甸人	chinese　中國人
japanese　日本人	portuguese　葡萄牙人
vietnamese　越南人	swiss　瑞士人

2. 普通名詞的單複數形：

單數	複數
arm 手臂	arms 武器
letter 信件	letters 證書
stair 一級梯子	stairs 樓梯
term 期間	terms 措辭
tropic 回歸線	tropics 熱帶

3. 抽象名詞的單複數形：

抽象名詞	複數抽象名詞
attention 注意	attentions 殷勤
authority 權威	authorities 當局
custom 顧客	customs 關稅
damage 損害	damages 賠償金
force 武力	forces 軍隊
good 好的	goods 商品
honor 榮譽	honors 優等
look 看	looks 相貌
manner 方式	manners 禮貌
mean 意指	means 手段
pain 疼痛	pains 千辛萬苦
regard 正式	regards 關於
saving 救助	savings 儲蓄
time 時間	times 時代
work 工作	works 工廠

4. 常以複數形呈現的單字

earnings 耳環	folks 民謠
jeans 牛仔褲	odds 賠率
scissors 剪刀	shorts 短褲
troops 軍隊	pants 長褲
guts 勇氣	spectacles 眼鏡
pajamas 睡衣	trousers 長褲

5. 複合名詞的複數形

5.1 主要語意或動作執行者的名詞形成複數形

brides-to-be 待嫁新娘	editor-in-chief 總編輯
Passers by 過路人	man-eaters 吃人的動物
runners-up 亞軍	woman-haters 善妒的女人
hangers-on 隨從	son-in-law 女婿

5.2 不含名詞的複合名詞在字尾加 -s

call-ins 撤回	checkups 核對
drive-ins 釘入	forget-me-nots 勿忘草
grown-ups 成年人	hand-me-downs 傳家之寶
has-beens 過時的人	stand-bys 袖手旁觀
close-ups 特寫	hang-ups 懸掛
go-betweens 中間者	take-offs 脫去

◆ 2-2 名詞的性

　　根據語意，名詞的性有陽性、陰性、通性、中性等四種。兼具陽性與陰性的是通性，即雙重性別，中性無性別區分。人稱代名詞、反身代名詞與所有詞等須與指涉名詞在性別上一致。

陽性：指男性或雄性高等動物。

陰性：指女性或雌性高等動物。

通性：可指涉男女性的人或雄雌高等動物。

中性：低等動物、植物、無生命的事物或概念。

■ He is my husband. His name is Leo Lee.
他是我先生，名字叫李里歐。

■ Mrs. Lin devoted herself to children's education.
林女士致力於兒童教育。

1. 陽性與陰性名詞對應出現

1.1 無性別字尾綴詞的性別對應組：

陽性	陰性
bachelor　單身漢	spinster　老處女
boy　男孩	girl　女孩
brother　兄弟	sister　姊妹
father　父親	mother　母親
gentleman　紳士	lady　淑女
husband　丈夫	wife　妻子
king　國王	queen　皇后
man　男子	woman　女子
monk　和尚	nun　尼姑
nephew　姪子	niece　姪女

陽性	陰性
sir　先生	madam　女士
son　兒子	daughter　女兒
uncle　叔叔	aunt　嬸嬸
wizard　男巫	witch　巫婆
work　工作	works　工廠

1.2 含性別字尾綴詞的對應詞組：

抽象名詞	複數抽象名詞
actor　男演員	actress　女演員
divorce　離了婚的男人	divorcee　離了婚的女人
emperor　皇上	empress　皇后
inheritor　繼承人	inheritress　女繼承人
hunter　獵人	huntress　女獵人
waiter　服務生	waitress　女服務生
duke　公爵	duchess　公爵夫人
god　上帝	goddess　女神
host　男主人	hostess　女主人
prince　王子	princess　公主
steward　管家	stewardess　女管家
hero　英雄	heroine　女英雄
fiance　未婚夫	fiancee　未婚妻

1.3 性別語意的複合名詞組：

陽性	陰性
landlord　房東	landlady　女房東
mailman　郵差	mailwoman　女郵差
policeman　警察	policewoman　女警
salesman　銷售員	saleswoman　女銷售員
manservant　男僕	maidservant　女僕
male student　男學生	female student　女學生
male cousin　堂哥	female cousin　堂姊
male nurse　男護士	female nurse　女護士
boyfriend　男朋友	girlfriend　女朋友
baby boy　男嬰	baby girl　女嬰

1.4 高等動物的性別詞組（高等動物通常都有通性名詞，有些陽性與通性名詞同形。）：

通性	陽性	陰性
cat　貓	tom cat	tabby cat
cattle　牛	bull, ox	cow
chicken　雞	cock, rooster	hen
peacock　孔雀	peacock	peahen
turkey　火雞	turkey cock	turkey hen
deer　鹿	stag, hart	hind
dog　狗	dog	bitch
duck　鴨子	drake	duck
fox　狐狸	fox	vixen

通性	陽性	陰性
goat　山羊	he-goat billy-goat	she-goat nanny goat
horse　馬	stallion	mare
lion　獅子	lion	lioness
leopard　豹	leopard	leopardess
pig　豬	boar	sow
sheep　綿羊	ram	ewe
tiger　老虎	tiger	tigress

2. 通性的人稱名詞：

adult　成人	baby　嬰兒
cousin　堂哥	infant　嬰兒
in-law　姻親	orphan　孤兒
person　人	relative　親戚
child　小孩	parent　父母
inhabitant　居民	spouse　配偶

3. 陰性的名詞。

■ The moon is full and bright. She seems to give me a smile.
月亮又圓又亮，似乎在對我微笑。

■ The antique car costs a lot. She's like an elegant lady.
骨董車價值不斐，就像一位優雅女子。

■ The Titanic sank to the sea floor, but people will remember her forever.
鐵達尼號沉到海底，人們會永遠懷念這艘船。

◆ 2-3 名詞的格

格說明名詞與其他詞組間的語法關係,包括主格、受格、所有格。主格與受格形式一致,所有格有字尾變化。

1. 主格:

限定子句主詞為主格,限定動詞賦予主詞位置的語詞主格性質,使具主詞功用。

- The dolphin can't breathe under water.
  海豚不能在水面下呼吸。

- The kangaroo can't move its back legs independently.
  袋鼠不能自由移動後腳。

2. 受格:

動詞或介系詞受詞位置的語詞為受格。及物動詞與介系詞賦予受詞位置的語詞受格性質,使具受詞功用。另外,及物過去分詞右側的名詞無格位性質,因為過去分詞不能賦予格位的性質。

- In the Second World War, the USA invaded Tulagi.
  二次大戰期間,美國入侵圖拉吉島。

- We carved the pumpkin into a jack-o-lantern.
  我們將南瓜刻成燈籠。

3. 所有格:

表示所有者的名詞為所有格,共有「s'＋所有格」、「of＋所有格」、「雙重所有格」三種類型。

3.1 s' 所有格:表示所有者之外,所有格與名詞構成的名詞片語還可表示一個事件,描述主詞(所有格)與動作(名詞)之間的語意關聯。

3.1.1 單數名詞＋'s

- the manager's office　　　經理辦公室
- Leo's roommate　　　里歐的室友
- goat's milk　　　羊奶

說明 有些含所有格的名詞片語演變為更為普遍的複合名詞，例如
「goat milk」就較「goat's milk」常用。

★其他例子：

bear gall 　熊膽	marten fur 　貂皮
alligator leather 　鱷魚皮革	snake blood 　蛇血

3.1.2 s／ss 字尾的單數名詞＋'s

- Dickens's novels　　　　　狄更斯的小說
- Moses's law　　　　　摩西律法
- Jesus's disciples　　　　　耶穌的門徒
- Socrates' wisdom　　　　　蘇格拉底的智慧

3.1.3 s 字尾的複數名詞＋'

- the students' affairs　　　　　學生事務
- athletes' dormitory room　　　　　選手宿舍房間

3.1.4 字尾不是 s 的複數名詞＋'s

- children's hospital　　　　　兒童醫院
- men's room　　　　　男廁所

3.1.5 複合名詞最右側＋'s

- the passer-by's wallet　　　　　路過行人的皮包
- someone else's opinion　　　　　其他某人的意見
- the editor-in-chief's duty　　　　　主編的責任

3.2 of 所有格：表示生命體的所有關係或描述名詞間的關係。

3.2.1 表示所有者與所有物的關係

- the mane of the horse　　　　　馬的鬃毛
- the sting of the bee　　　　　蜜蜂的刺
- the roof of the hut　　　　　小屋的屋頂
- the ventilation of the attic　　　　　閣樓的通風裝置

3.2.2 表示人或事物的特質

- a man of wisdom　　　　　　智者
- a leader of ability　　　　　　有能力的領袖
- a woman of humble origins　　出身卑賤的女子
- a man of royal descent　　　　出身皇族的男子
- a man of London　　　　　　倫敦人
- an angel of a girl　　　　　　天使般的女孩

3.2.3 表示名詞是受事者受詞

- the driver of the truck　　　卡車司機
  = The driver drove the truck.
- the writer of the column　　專欄作家
  = The writer wrote the column.
- the composer of the symphony　交響曲作曲家
  = The composer wrote the symphony.
- the author of the science fiction book　科幻小說作者
  = The author wrote the book of science fiction.

3.2.4 表示名詞的同位語

- the town of Cambridge　　　劍橋鎮
- the match of soccer　　　　足球比賽
- the language of Mandarin　　中國話
- a charge of sexual harassment　控告性騷擾
- a crime of fraud　　　　　　詐欺罪
- the University of Edinburgh　愛丁堡大學

3.3 雙重所有格：「of ＋獨立所有格/所有代名詞」的結構為雙重所有格，搭配名詞形成名詞片語。值得一提的是，名詞的數目與限定條件不拘。

- a friend of the CEO's　　　執行長的一位友人
- any colleague of mine　　　我的任何一位同事
- that client of my uncle's　　我叔叔的客戶
- these neighbors of Mr. Lin's　林先生的鄰居
- some friends of my cousin's　我表弟的一些朋友

★比較：

■ a portrait of the artist's

  1. a portrait drawn by the artist ／ a portrait belonging to the artist

  藝術家的一幅素描

  2. a portrait representing the artist

  藝術家的素描

■ Hank is a student of the artist.

  = Hank is a student who studies under the artist.

  漢克是藝術家的學生。

3.4 所有格的適用情況

3.4.1 說明所有者/所有物的關係

■ Leo's teacher	里歐的老師
■ my sister's instructor	我妹妹的導師
■ he cat's litter tray	貓砂
■ the dog's collar	狗項圈

說明 人稱代名詞所有格也可表示所有者/所有物的關係。

■ That's my new cellphone.

  那是我的新手機。

■ You will give up your right to remain silent.

  你將放棄緘默權。

3.4.2 說明整體與部分的關係。

■ the owl's ears	貓頭鷹的耳朵
■ the fish's fin	魚翅
■ the moon's surface	月球表面
■ a tree's root system	樹根系統
■ We hear with our ears.	我們用耳朵聽。

說明 述及身體部位時，代名詞所有格通常不譯。

3.4.3 所有格表示名詞的來源。

- Ben Johnson's poem
  = poem written by Ben Johnson
  班 · 強森的詩

- Kelly's message
  = message sent from Kelly
  凱莉的訊息

- the proposal made by them.
  他們的提案。

3.4.4 描述名詞的用途或性質

- busker's license　　街頭藝人執照
  = license for a busker

- women's room　　女廁
  = room for women

- a traveler's check　　旅行支票
  = a check for travelers

- the family's support　　家庭支柱
  = the support from the family

3.4.5 國家、城市或場所的狀況。

- Taiwan's advantage　　　　台灣的優勢
- Paris's style　　　　　巴黎的風格
- the US's nuclear weapons　　美國的核子武器
- the world's population　　世界的人口

3.4.6 時間或距離的量

- four hours' flight　　　　四小時的飛行
- ten minutes' walk　　　　步行十分鐘的距離
- today' s newspaper　　　　今天的報紙
- a week's funeral leave　　一週的喪假
- two meters' distance　　　二米的距離

3.4.7 度量衡的數量

■ a yard's width　　一碼寬度

　　= a width of a yard

■ five meter's height　　五米寬度

　　= a height of five meters

■ fifty kilogram's weight　　五十公斤重

　　= a weight of fifty kilograms

■ two liters' capacity　　二公升容量

　　= the capacity of two liters

■ five thousand dollars' worth　　五千元價值

　　= the value of five thousand dollars

3.4.8 主詞與動作的關係：句子結構的名詞片語。名詞與人稱代名詞所有格用法一樣。

(1) 所有格是事件主詞

■ the spy's death

　　= the death of the spy

　　= The spy died.

　　間諜之死。

■ the student's failure

　　= the failure of the student

　　= The student failed.

　　學生被當。

■ the CEO's absence

　　= the absence of the CEO

　　= The CEO was absent.

　　執行長缺席。

(2) 所有格是動作的執行者

■ I deleted Leo's email by mistake.

　　= I deleted the email that Leo sent by mistake.

　　我誤刪了里歐的郵件。

■ I have not received his text.

= I have not received the text he sent.

我還沒收到他的簡訊。

■ Would you mind my turning off the fan?

= Would you mind if I turn off the fan?

你介意我關掉電扇嗎？

■ Bella insisted on his　him wearing a suit.

= Bella insisted that he should wear a suit.

貝拉堅持他要穿西裝。

(3) 所有格是名詞所示動作的受事者

■ the animal's release

= the release of the animal

= The animal was released.

動物獲得釋放。

■ The panda cub's birth

= the birth of the panda cub

= the panda cub was born.

小貓熊出生。

■ I have no idea about his transfer to Liverpool.

= I have no idea that he was transferred to Liverpool.

我不知道他調到利物浦。

■ Danish people pay a lot of attention to their education.

= Danish people pay a lot of attention to the way they are educated.

丹麥人很重視他們的教育方式。

(4) 名詞是動作的受事者。

■ the manager's decision

= the decision of the manager

= The manager made the decision.

經理的決定

■ Their application has been approved.

　= The application they submitted has been approved.

　他們提出的申請案已核准。

3.4.9 獨立所有格：所有格指涉言談已知對象或一些建築場所名稱時，名詞可省略，這種名詞缺項的所有格為獨立所有格。

■ This scooter is Bella's, not Cindy's.

　輕型機車是貝拉的，不是辛蒂的。

■ I stayed overnight at my uncle's (house).

　我在叔叔家過夜。

■ Jack bought a bunch of roses at the florist's (floral shop).

　傑克在花店買一束花。

■ I went to the dentist's (clinic) this morning.

　今天早上我去牙醫診所。

> 說明 所有格代名詞包含所有者與所有物，所有物為中心詞，決定動詞單複數。所有格代名詞可扮演主詞、受詞、補語，也可構成雙重所有格。

【主詞】

■ This is my book. Yours is over there.

　這是我的書。你的在那裡。

【受詞】

■ You do your job, and I'll do mine.

　你做你的工作，我做我的。

【補語】

■ What is yours is mine.

　你的就是我的。

【雙重所有格】

■ This is no fault of mine.

　那不是我的錯。

◆ 2-4 名詞的分類

依據語意，名詞分為普通、集合、物質、專有、抽象等五類。

1. 普通名詞：

普通名詞是指人、動物、植物、時間、空間等名稱，另外，一些動作名稱的名詞也是普通名詞。普通名詞搭配限定詞形成名詞片語。

■ The dolphin is a mammal.
海豚是哺乳動物。

■ All the hemp is grown for animal feed.
所有大麻都以動物食用為種植目的。

■ Each attendee has to pay an admission fee.
每位出席者都要付入場費。

2. 集合名詞：

集合體的名稱為集合名詞，表示單數或複數形的集合體或組成個體。

〔組成個體〕

■ The people there are really friendly.
那裡的人都很友善。

〔複數集合體〕

■ Sudan is a country that consists of many peoples.
蘇丹是個多元民族的國家。

〔集合體〕

■ My grandfather joined the army at the age of 16.
我祖父十六歲從軍。

〔單數集合體〕

■ An army is approaching from the northeast.
一支部隊正從東北方接近。

〔複數集合體〕

■ Many armies hire color blind people to serve in certain tasks.
許多軍隊雇用色盲的人從事一些任務。

> **說明** committee 為主詞時，美式英語常搭配單數動詞，而英式英語則是搭配複數動詞。

■ 1.The committee has voted to plant new trees in the park.
（美式英語）

■ 2.The committee have voted to plant new trees in the park.
（英式英語）

委員會投票通過在公園種植新樹木。

★具複數集合體形式的集合名詞：

class 班級	committee 委員會
family 家人	fleet 艦隊
team 團隊	crowd 群眾
nation 國民	band 樂隊

■ There are thirty classes in this school.
這所學校有 30 個班級。

■ Many families moved to the community last month.
很多家庭上個月都搬進這社區。

■ The clergy are opposed to homosexuality.
牧師反對同性戀。

■ The police were searching for the drug dealer.
警方搜查毒販。

■ These old cattle are being treated in a humane way.
人們以人道方式善待這些老牛。

★ 表示組成個體的集合名詞：

audience 觀眾	crew 組員
people 人	public 大眾
jury 陪審團	cattle 牛群

3. 物質名詞：

表示材料、食物、天然物質、化學元素等名稱的名詞為物質名詞。物質名詞無複數形，但表示限定時，搭配定冠詞 the。

■ There's a little oil left.
那裡還剩一些油。

■ The steam looks like rocket exhaust.
水蒸氣看起來像火箭廢氣。

■ The cheese smells like something dead.
起司聞起來像東西壞掉。

■ Oxygen is a chemical element with symbol O.
氧氣的化學元素符號用「O」表示。

■ The soap is made from 100% natural ingredients.
這塊肥皂是由百分百天然原料製成。

3.1 部分詞：物質名詞計量時，搭配表示單位的部分詞

3.1.1 度量衡單位：

a foot of linen　一尺	a gram of gold　一克黃金
a catty of pork　一斤豬肉	two yards of cloth　二碼布
ten gallons of oil 十加侖石油	five liters of water 五公升水
a pound of cheese 一磅起司	three ounces of beef 三盎司牛肉

3.1.2 容器：

a bag of sugar　一袋糖	a can of soda　一罐汽水
a cup of tea　一杯茶	a bowl of rice　一碗飯
a glass of wine　一杯酒	a spoonful of vinegar 一湯匙醋
a bottle of soy sauce 一瓶醬油	a tube of toothpaste 一條牙膏

3.1.3 形狀：

a bar of soap　一塊肥皂	a cake of ice　一塊冰
a grain of sand　一粒沙子	a loaf of bread　一條麵包
a lump of clay　一團黏土	a piece of wood　一片木材
a slice of meat　一片肉	a drop of honey　一滴蜂蜜
a sheet of paper　一張紙	a strip of land 一塊帶狀土地

3.2 有些物質名詞可形成複數形，但語意不同：

物質名詞	複數形物質名詞
airs　矯揉造作	airs　高傲架子
cloth　布	clothes　衣服
paper　紙	papers　文件
rag　抹布	rags　破爛衣服
spirit　心靈	spirits　心情
water　水	waters　水域
wood　木頭	woods　木林

4. 專有名詞：

表示人名、稱謂、地名、機構、語言、國家、書報雜誌、星期、節目、月份名稱的名詞為專有名詞，首字母必須大寫。

■ The Bible was written in Greek and Hebrew.
聖經是希伯來文和希臘文寫成的。

■ Mr. Suzuki was born in Tokyo in September 2, 1980.
鈴木先生於 1980 年 9 月 2 日在東京出生。

4.1 專有名詞的普通名詞用法

4.1.1 星期名稱可搭配不定冠詞 a 或複數形

■ The incident happened on a Monday.
事件發生在某個星期一。

■ Mr. and Mrs. Lin go to church on Sundays.
林氏夫婦週日上教堂。

4.1.2 表示姓氏家族時，搭配定冠詞 the 及複數形

■ The Lins are moving to Hong Kong.
= The Lin family is moving to Hong Kong.
林氏一家人要搬到香港。

說明 the ＋複數形姓氏可代換為「the ＋姓氏＋ family」。

4.1.3 表示某一位、共幾位、第幾位的人，搭配不定冠詞 a/an、複數形、序數

■ A Mr. Chen is waiting for you downstairs.
有位陳先生在樓下等你。

■ There are two Leos in my office.
我辦公室有兩位里歐。

■ The woman is the second Mrs. Lin.
那位婦人是第二任林太太。

4.1.4 表示類似名人或地方，搭配定冠詞 the

■ Leo is the Mozart of today.
里歐是現代的莫札特。

■ Fred wants to be the Bill Gates of Taiwan.
弗雷德想成為台灣比爾蓋茲。

■ Shanghai is the New York of China.
上海是中國的紐約。

5. 抽象名詞：

表示性質、狀態、心理、學科、疾病、科學等抽象概念的名詞為抽象名詞。

〔特質〕

■ Honesty is the best policy.
誠實為上策。

〔狀態〕

■ I felt a sharp pain in the left side of my chest.
我左胸感到劇烈疼痛。

〔心理〕

■ It is difficult to cope with grief when we are hurting.
當我們受到傷害時，悲傷總是難以處理。

〔學科〕

■ Leo majored in psychology in college.
里歐大學主修心理學。

〔疾病〕

■ My grandfather died of malaria.
我祖父死於瘧疾。

5.1 抽象名詞與冠詞的搭配：抽象名詞無複數形，但表示特指或具體範圍時，可搭配冠詞。

■ The trial is not fair at all.
判決一點也不公平。

■ Leo's advice was a great help to me.
里歐的建議對我幫助很大。

■ I was encouraged to get a good education.
我受鼓勵要接受好的教育。

■ They share a common knowledge of computer operation basics.
他們分享電腦操作基本知識。

5.2 抽象名詞的修飾用法

5.2.1 形容詞：抽象名詞搭配 all, of, itself, full 等語詞，表示同語意的形容詞片語。

■ The CEO is a person of importance.

　＝ The CEO is an important person.

　執行長是重要人物。

■ Linda would be of great help to the team.

　＝ Linda would very helpful to the team.

　琳達對團隊大有助益。

■ The information is of no use to anyone else.

　＝ The information is not useful to us.

　這訊息對任何人都沒幫助。

■ Suddenly, the woman was all anger.

　＝ Suddenly, the woman was anger itself.

　＝ Suddenly, the woman was very angry.

　婦人突然發怒。

5.2.2 副詞：介系詞＋抽象名詞：含抽象名詞的介系詞片語等同於情狀副詞。

■ I'm sure they had a talk in private　privately.

　我確信他們私下談過。

■ I ran across my ex-wife by accident　accidently.

　我意外遇到我的前妻。

■ The shooting guard broke the rule on purpose　purposely.

　守門員故意犯規。

◆ 2-5 具名詞性質的語詞

1. 數量詞

■ The CEO is already in his seventies.

　執行長七十多歲了。

■ One percent is one out of every hundred.
　一百分比是一百分中之一。

2. 形容詞

■ Let bygones be bygones.
　過去就讓它過去。

■ As sick as she was, Linda went to work as usual.
　雖然生病，琳達仍然去工作。

■ The economic situation went from worse to worst.
　經濟情勢每下愈況。

■ The living will die one day.
　活者終將過去。

■ Leo is able to deal with the impossible.
　里歐有能力處理不可能的事。

　說明 冠詞搭配形容詞，構成名詞片語，表示群體現象。

■ You are really a dear.
　你真是個好孩子。

■ There was an awkward calm in the air in the building.
　大樓充滿著詭異的寂靜氣氛。

3. 副詞

■ Leo revealed the hows and whys of the event.
　里歐揭露事件的來龍去脈。

■ My Chihuahua fell down from upstairs just now.
　我的吉娃娃剛從樓梯摔下來。

■ As always, Dr. Lin made the rounds of the wards after the meeting.
　一如往常，林醫師總在會議後巡視病房。

4. 動詞

■ Could you give me a call lift?
你能打電話給我 送我一程嗎？

■ Let's go for a drink swim walk.
我們去喝一杯 游泳 散步？

■ Leo made a deal with the company.
里歐和公司妥協。

■ It's a major scientific breakthrough.
那是科學界的重大突破。

5. 不定詞

■ The aim is to reduce the patient's anxiety.
目標是降低病人的焦慮。

■ It took me few hours to download the latest version of Internet Explorer.
我花了幾小時下載 Internet Explorer 的最新版本。

6. 動名詞

■ Raising a pet is like raising a child.
養動物就像養小孩一樣。

■ My grandfather has quit smoking for years.
我祖父戒菸好幾年了。

■ Global warming might lead to snakesas long as buses.
全球暖化可能使蛇變得像公車一樣長。

7. 分詞

■ Dave decided to leave his beloved.
戴夫決定離開他的摯愛。

■ Tony is living with his intended now.
湯尼與他的未婚妻同居。

■ The court found the accused guilty of the charge.
法院判定被告有罪。

8. 介系詞片語

■ After the meal is the time to drink tea.
  = The time after the meal is the time to drink tea.
飯後適合喝杯茶。

■ A man threw a shoe at the lecturer from among the crowd.
群眾中有名男子將鞋子丟向演講者。

■ My son has been having stomach trouble since after Christmas.
我兒子聖誕節過後肚子就一直不適。

9. 名詞子句

■ What made the ship disappear is still a mystery.
船消失的原因仍是個謎。

■ They fear the change in the weather might affect their cherry tree in full bloom.
他們怕天氣變化可能影響到櫻桃的開花。

◆ 2-6 名詞的功用

1. 句子組成成分

1.1 主詞

■ Time and tide waits for no man.
歲月不饒人。

■ The blue whale can produce the loudest sound of any animal.
藍鯨能發出動物最大的聲音。

1.2 受詞

1.2.1 及物動詞受詞

■ My dog is tasting the meat.
我的狗正吃著那塊肉。

■ Polar bears actually have black skin.
北極熊的皮膚實際上是黑色的。

1.2.2 介系詞受詞

■ I've loved you from the moment I saw you.
我對妳一見鍾情。

■ The town of Tambun in Perak is famous for pomelos.
霹靂州的怡保市以文旦聞名。

1.3 補語

1.3.1 主詞補語

■ The Jack fruit is a tropical fruit.
波羅蜜是熱帶水果。

■ Leo hopes he will make a lawyer in the future.
里歐希望將來當律師。

1.3.2 受詞補語

■ The man professed himself a unitarian.
男子聲稱自己是一神論者。

■ Many customers found the company a bad business.
許多客人發現這家公司是無良企業。

1.4 副詞

■ The accident happened this morning.
意外發生在今天早上。

■ The suspect was detained the day before yesterday.
嫌犯前天遭到收押。

1.5 同位語

■ Don't misspell the word "Mississippi".
不要拼錯「Mississippi」這個字。

■ The celebration will be held next Sunday, May 10.
慶典將於下周日五月十日舉行。

1.6 連接詞

■ The moment I entered the kitchen, I smelled something unusual.
一進到廚房，我就聞到不尋常的味道。

1.7 稱呼語

■ Class, attention, please.
全體同學，請注意。

■ Ladies and gentlemen, lend me your ears.
各位女士先生，請聽我說。

2. 修飾功用

2.1 修飾形容詞

■ The crocodile is ten years old.
鱷魚十歲大。

■ The meat is five centimeters thick.
這塊肉有五公分厚。

2.2 修飾副詞

■ Women live five years longer than men.
女人活得比男人久。

■ The shuttle bus arrived thirty minutes late.
接駁車晚抵達三十分鐘。

2.3 修飾介系詞

■ My niece's birthday is three days away from today.
從今天算起三天後是我姪女生日。

第3章 代名詞

代替名詞性質的詞組的詞類為代名詞。

◆ 3-1 人稱代名詞

人稱代名詞有數─單數、複數，格─主格、受格、所有格，性─陽性、陰性、中性之分。

人格	主格	受格	所有格	所有代名詞	反身格
我	I	me	my	mine	myself
我們	we	us	our	ours	ourselves
你	you	you	your	yours	yourself
你們	you	you	your	yours	yourselves
他	he	him	his	his	himself
她	she	her	her	hers	herself
它	it	it	its	its	itself
他們	they	them	their	theirs	themselves
一個人	one	one	one's	──	oneself

1. 功用

1.1 主詞

■ She married a rich guy.
她嫁給有錢人。

■ It looks like rain today.
看起來今天會下雨。

■ He and I won't attend the meeting.
我和他不參加會議。

■ You and I can work on the project together.
你和我可以一起執行任務。

說明 為表示禮貌，第一人稱常置於其他人稱之後。

■ Poor you！ 你好可憐！
■ Lucky him！ 他好幸運！
■ "I truly appreciate the film." - "Me too."
「我真的很欣賞這部影片。」—「我也是。」

說明 口語中，省略句的主詞常用受格。

1.2 受詞

■ Many people reject him.
許多人排斥他。

■ Toasts to you.
敬你。

■ I'd like to talk to her.
我想和她說話。

1.3 主詞補語

■ Oh, it's me.
喔，是我。

■ Who is it? It's I me.
哪一位？ 是我。

說明 主格當主詞補語是正式用法，受格當主詞補語則是口語用法。

1.4 同位語

■ Only two fools, you and me, went to school on Christmas.
只有你和我這兩個笨蛋，聖誕節還去學校。

1.5 稱呼語

■ Hey, you, get out of here.
嘿，你，閃一邊去。

2. 特別的語意用法

2.1 we：包括自己的群體

■ We all need to work hard.
我們都需要努力工作。

■ We are looking forward to your response.
我們期待您的回應。

2.2 you：泛指一般人，等同於 anyone, everyone

■ You need to be responsible for yourself.
你要為你自己負責。

■ You cannot drive and drink at the same time.
你不可酒後駕車。

2.3 they

2.3.1 泛指某些人

■ They don't allow me to photograph here.
有人不許我在這裡拍照。

■ They are going to shut the store down.
他們即將關店。

■ They speak Portuguese in Brazil.
在巴西的人講葡萄牙語。

■ They raise milkfish in south of Taiwan.
台灣南部飼養虱目魚。

2.3.2 指稱團體，商業英文中常以 it 或 you 指稱公司行號。

■ The company has its own testing department.
那家公司有自己的檢測部門。

■ We are looking forward to your reply.
我們期待貴公司的回覆。

◆ 3-2 反身代名詞

複合不定代名詞結構，指涉句中前述的名詞，因此，不可扮演主詞，所在的子句必須出現先行詞。

1. 反身代名詞的功用

1.1 及物動詞受詞

■ We enjoyed ourselves during the camp.
營隊期間我們很開心。

■ The single mother devoted herself to raising her children.
單親媽媽專心養育孩子。

1.2 介系詞受詞

■ The woman was beside herself with joy.
女子欣喜若狂。

■ I find Leo has the habit of talking to himself.
我發現里歐有自言自語的習慣。

1.3 主詞補語

■ Bella is not quite herself today.
貝拉今天反常。

■ Amy did that to show her true self.
艾咪那樣做是為了展示真實自我。

說明 反身代名詞當主詞補語時，可搭配形容詞以說明主詞狀態，結構為「所有格＋形容詞＋ self」。

1.4 同位語，副詞性質，表示強調，可置於主詞後面或句尾。

■ I myself can do it.
　　= I can do it myself.
　　我自己就能做到。

◆ 3-3 不定代名詞

　　指涉不特定對象的代名詞為不定代名詞,應與指涉語詞的數或人稱一致,因此有人稱與數的限制。

1. 分類

1.1 依肯定或否定語意:

肯定	否定
all another any anybody anyone anything both each enough either everybody everyone everything more most one other several some somebody someone something	neither nobody none nothing no one

★ n- 是否定字首,表示 no, not。

neither ＝ not either

none ＝ no one,語氣較 none 強烈。

never ＝ not ever

1.2 依數的性質

單數	複數	不可數	不可數/複數
another other anybody anyone anything everybody everyone everything somebody someone something each either one	few a few many a great many ones others several	much little less least	any some a lot a great deal a great amount all enough half more most

★ many, much, few, little 有比較級，具形容詞特徵，是雙詞性語詞。

★ one, other 具複數形式：ones, others。

1.3 依是否兼具限定詞

兼具限定詞			不具限定詞
前限定詞	中間限定詞	後限定詞	
all both	any some each enough much several	another either few little many more most neither other	anybody anyone anything everybody everyone everything nobody no one none nothing somebody someone something

★ every, no 是限定詞，不具不定代名詞。

2. 指稱

指稱是名詞對人、事、物的指涉，常因不同的語言情境而有不同的指稱，例如：

【泛指】

■ There's a python in the river.
河裡有一條蟒蛇。

【定指】

■ The python was attacked by millions of ants, with its body full of them.
那條蟒蛇遭到幾百萬隻螞蟻攻擊，佈滿全身。

2.1 泛指：不定代名詞單獨存在會置於名詞前時，不定代名詞或名詞片語為泛指。

■ Several were absent today.
今天有幾個人缺席。

■ All need to sign up for the workshop.
所有人都要報名研習。

■ Most children like to watch cartoons.
大多數小孩喜愛看卡通。

■ All members need to pay an annual fee.
所有會員都要繳年費。

2.2 定指：all, both 是前限定詞，搭配中間限定詞時為定指。另外，副詞用法的 all, both 表示強調，也是定指。

■ Both my dogs are missing.
我的兩隻狗都不見了。

■ All the workers have to work overtime tonight.
今晚所有工人都得加班。

> 說明 most 是後限定詞，不可置於 the 前面。

■ They all　both got hurt a lot.
他們都傷得很重。

■ You have offended them all　both.
你冒犯他們了。

2.2.1 搭配 of 介系詞片語，強調限定範圍時，名詞片語為定指。

■ Many of the patients need to be transported to other health centers.
許多病患須轉診至其他醫護中心。

> 說明 複合不定代名詞不可搭配「of ＋介系詞片語」，但 any one, every one, some one 等可以。

■ Can any one of you volunteer to give blood?
你們有誰要自願捐血。

■ Every one of us is able to operate the machine.
我們每個人都能操作機器。

■ Some of them is acquainted with some of you.
他們之中某個人和你們其中某人熟識。

2.2.2 one, other 搭配限定詞 the 時表示定指。

■ I have two cell phones. One is HTC's flagship smartphone; the other is Samsung's Galaxy Y.
我有二支手機。一支是 HTC 旗艦機，另一支是三星 Galaxy Y。

■ I have three roommates. One is from India, another from Korea, and the other from China.
我有三名室友。一位來自印度，另一位來自韓國，還有一位來自大陸。

■ There are four lions at the zoo. One is a male, and the others, females.
動鹿園裡有四隻獅子，一隻公的，其他都是母的。

■ Some of the books were written in Tagalog, and the others in Catalan.
一些用加祿語寫的，其餘的都是用加泰羅尼亞語寫的。

【比較】：Some were written in Tagalog, and others in Catalan. （泛指）
一些書是他用加祿語寫的，一些是加泰羅尼亞語寫的。

■ I will pick the ones I think are best.
我挑出我認為最棒的那些。

■ The coat with fur collar is nearly 25% more expensive than the one without.
有領子的外套較沒領子的大約多出四分之一價錢。

3. 不定代名詞與述語動詞數的一致

不定代名詞指涉不可數名詞時搭配單數動詞，指涉複數名詞或代名詞時，常因語意或習慣而有多種搭配情況。

3.1 all 表示整體概念時搭配單數動詞，表示每一個人時搭配複數動詞。

■ All is full of love.
一切都充滿愛。

■ All are welcome.
歡迎每一位。

3.2 each 表單一指稱，everybody/everyone 表二者以上。「each + of 複數名詞」搭配單數或複數動詞。

■ I am raising two puppies together now, and I feed each a few times daily.
我現在同時養兩隻狗，每隻一天都要餵食幾次。

■ There are many goats on the farm, and I feed everyone every morning.
農場有許多山羊，每天早上每隻都要餵。

■ Each of the religions has have its their own views on death.
每一種宗教都有獨特的死亡觀。

3.3 either, neither 搭配單數動詞，「either, neither + of 複數名詞」搭配單/複數動詞；「either of you」搭配複數動詞。

■ Either is fine with me.
二者任一我都可以。

■ I texted Leo and Peter, but neither has replied.
我傳簡訊給里歐和保羅，但沒有一個回我。

■ Neither of the animals is ~~are~~ viviparous.
這二種動物沒有一種是胎生的。
= Either of the animals is ~~are~~ not viviparous.
這二種動物任何一種都不是胎生的。

■ Either of my parents is ~~are~~ British.
= Only one of my parents is British.
我父母中有一位是英國人。

■ Each of the beagles has ~~have~~ long ears.
每一隻米格魯都有長耳朵。

■ ~~Have~~ Has either of you seen the aerial photography documentary "Beyond Beauty: Taiwan From Above?"
你們二位有誰看過空拍紀錄片「看見台灣」？

3.4 any of you 搭配單數或複數動詞。

■ If any of you has ~~have~~ questions, we will answer them.
如果你們有任何人發問，我們會回答他們。

3.5 「none ＋ of 複數名詞」搭配單數或複數動詞，強調否定語意或搭配 almost 時用複數動詞。

■ None of the dogs has ~~have~~ been neutered.
這些狗都沒有結紮。

■ None of the owners are allergic to animals.
飼主中沒有人對動物過敏。

■ Almost none of the students are native speakers of Japanese.
學生中沒有人的母語是日語。

4. 不定代名詞的所有格與受格

4.1 為避免性別爭議，複合不定代名詞常搭配 they／their／them。

■ Everyone has to take their own responsibility.
　每個人都必須付自己的責任。

■ Nobody ever expects themselves to be laid off.
　沒有人希望自己被解雇。

■ Everyone expects they will obtain their bonus.
　每個人都期待領到紅利。

■ Did anybody bring their raincoat with them?
　有人帶雨衣嗎？

4.2 each 詞組所有格為 their，one 則是 his/their。

■ Each child should complete their task as scheduled.
　每個孩子都該按時完成工作。

■ One should do his　their best forhis　their own business.
　每個人都該做好份內事。

4.3 other 或複合不定代名詞可加「's」形成所有格。

■ Somebody's briefcase is left in the luggage carrier.
　有人的公事包留在手拉車上。

■ I deleted a MySpace blog comment on someone else's profile.
　我刪掉一則是針對別人檔案的留言。

■ The police have checked the other's profile.
　警方已檢視另一人的檔案。

■ We need to care about other's benefits.
　我們應顧及他人的利益。

5. 不定代名詞的同位語用法

all, both, each 可當名詞或人稱代名詞的同位語，表示強調。

■ They all are dog lovers.
　他們都是愛狗人士。

■ It's all bullshit!
一派胡言！

■ They both agree with one another.
他們彼此認同。

■ They each had a coupon for a free round of bowling.
他們每個人都有保齡球免費優惠券。

6. 不定代名詞與形容詞子句的搭配

複合不定代名詞及 all, other, the one 等都可當形容詞子句先行詞。另外，不定代名詞可搭配補述用法的關係代名詞，表示關係代名詞的指涉範圍。

■ To all who died on 9 11.
致所有死於 9 月 11 日的人。

■ Make sure the one you ordered online fits you perfectly.
要確定你線上訂購的商品完全合適。

■ Try to keep your account safe from hackers or others who might try to steal it.
全力保護你的帳號不受駭客或其他可能竊取者的攻擊。

■ I found someone who is able to do interpretation in those languages.
我找到某位能夠口譯這些語言的人。

■ The conference was attended by over 100 experts, several of whom were very young.
一百多名專家出席會議，其中幾位非常年輕。

■ Africa has a variety of sign languages, many of which are language isolates.
非洲有各式各樣的手語，其中許多是孤立語言。

■ There are two surveys, one of which is a simple random sample and one of which is not.
有二種調查，一種是簡單隨機抽樣，另一種則不是。

7. 不定代名詞之間的搭配

述及不定代名詞的部分範圍時，仍可以不定代名詞表示。

- I'll take some of both.
  這兩個我都取一些。

- Only one of all was alive.
  全部只有一人生還。

- Only several of many are listed below.
  全部當中只有幾件列表如下。

- Some of others are just those who are passionate about Andre Ruei.
  其他人之中有一些對安德烈・里歐十分著迷。

> **說明** another, other 可分別搭配限定詞 one, each，形成 each other（彼此），one another（互相），表示二者或二者以上指涉的關係，一般稱為相互代名詞。

- The two parties are far from each other on some ideas.
  兩者間的一些想法南轅北轍。

- We both deserve each other's love.
  我們都值得彼此的愛。

- They usually complain about one another.
  他們經常彼此埋怨。

- Friends can be more supportive of one another's identities.
  朋友能夠對彼此更加認同。

◆ 3-4 指示代名詞

指示代名詞表示指定的人或事物，結構上，代替名詞語詞或句子。指示代名詞包括 this, that, these, those, so, such, same, the former... the latter... 等。

1. this, that, these, those

1.1 功用：

1.1.1 this, that, these, those 可當主詞、受詞、主詞補語，this, these 指涉距離較近事物，that, those 指涉距離較遠事物。

■ This is a caiman.

這是南美短吻鱷。

■ That's my niece, Leona.

那位是我姪女，里歐娜。

■ These are pears from La La Mountain.

這些是拉拉山的梨子。

■ Those are recycled products.

那些是回收產品。

■ It isn't that.

不是那個。

■ Do you accept that?

你接受那嗎？

1.1.2 that 代替前述不可數名詞或事件， those 代替前述複數名詞或事件，those = the ones。

■ The climate of Keelung is different from that of Pingtung.

基隆的氣候和屏東不同。

說明 that 不可指人，the one 才可指人。

■ The foreigner I met at the party is not the one who is teaching you French.

我在派對遇到的外國人不是教你法文的那一位。

■ The typhoon caused more than US$ 5 million in damage. That's really a big loss.

颱風造成超過五百萬美元損害。真是一大損失。

■ The peaches in Taiwan are much bigger than those in England.

= The peaches in Taiwan are much bigger than the ones in England.

台灣的桃子較英國的桃子大的多。

1.1.3 this, these 代替下文所述語詞，this 另可指前述事件。

(1) 下文所述

■ Tony left me to these words, "Now or never."
湯尼留給我以下這些字「勿失良機」。

■ This is what the crocodile will do. It will pull the prey into the water and wait for it to drown.
這是鱷魚要做的動作，將獵物拖入水中，然後等待溺斃。

(2) 前述事件

■ I am going to swim across the Sun-Moon Lake again. This is so exciting.
我將再次泳渡日月潭，那真是刺激。

① that, those 可搭配形容詞子句。

■ *"What does not kill us makes us stronger." = That which does not kill us makes us stronger. - Friedrich Nietzsche (The Twilight of the Idols, 1899)*
那些打不倒你的困難讓你更堅強。- 尼采《偶像的賢者，（1889）》

■ Heaven helps those who help themselves.
= Heaven helps the people who help themselves.
天助自助者。

2. so

so 當指示代名詞，指涉前述動詞片語或名詞子句。

■ A：I will delete the file soon.
我很快就會刪掉檔案。

B：Please do so. = Please delete the file soon.
就這麼做。

■ A：Will the koala recover its health?
無尾熊能康復嗎？

B：I hope so. = I hope the koala will recover its health.
但願如此。

■ A：Does the hippo need amputation?
河馬要截肢嗎？

B：I'm afraid so. = I'm afraid that the hippo needs amputation.
恐怕要。

■ A：Stay at home and do your homework.
待在家裡做功課。

B：Why? I want to go out with you. Because you said so.
= Because you said "you can go out with me."
為什麼？我要跟你出去。因為你說我可以跟你去。

★一些可搭配指示代名詞 so 的動詞：

believe　相信	imagine　想像
expect　期待	suppose　認為
guess　猜想	think　想

3. such

such 當指示代名詞，扮演主詞、受詞、主詞補語等角色。

3.1 主詞

■ Such is the fact.
事實是如此。

■ Such being the case.
既然如此。

■ Such is the case with me.
我的事情是這樣。

3.2 受詞

■ In her autobiography, Bella talked about her family, childhood, marriage and such.
在自傳中，貝拉談到她的家庭、童年及婚姻等等。

3.3 主詞補語

■ The man's statement was such that the judge allowed him to be released.

【倒裝】 Such was the man's statement that the judge allowed him to be released.

男子做這樣的陳述，結果法官准他獲釋。

> 說明 such 當主詞補語時，常搭配補語子句以表示結果，這時 such 可移至句首，形成倒裝。

4.same

same 當指示代名詞，扮演主詞或受詞。

4.1 主詞

■ The same is the case with my parents.
我父母也是一樣的情形。

■ The same will be done with pdf files.
pdf 檔也是一樣。

4.2 受詞

■ He shrugged his shoulders and smiled, and I did same.
= He shrugged his shoulders and smiled, and I shrugged my shoulders and smiled, too.
他聳聳肩，笑一笑，我也是。

■ The prosecutor checked the files and found the same.
檢察官檢視檔案，發現無誤。

■ Please find enclosed check for same.
= Please find the check which is enclosed with the letter as already mentioned.
隨函覆上前述的支票。

4.3 一些指示代名詞 same 的慣用語詞：

- Same to you! = The same to you!　　　你也是！
- all the same = just the same　　　都一樣
- Same here. = Me, too.　　　我也是。

5.the former...the latter...

表示「前者…後者…」，可扮演主詞、受詞、所有詞等。

- The tsunami and the earthquake are both disasters. The former usually comes along with the latter.

  海嘯級地震都是重大災害，前者通常伴隨後者而來。

- I love both sports and music, but I prefer the former to the latter.

  運動及音樂我都喜歡，但我喜歡運動更甚音樂。

◆ 3-5 疑問代名詞

疑問代名詞代替句中名詞或事件（what），形成直接或間接問句。what, which, who, whose, whom 等為疑問代名詞。

1.what

詢問事物、事件、身分、職業、國籍或宗教，what 語詞可扮演主詞、受詞、主詞補語、限定詞等。

1.1 主詞

〔事物〕

- What will happen next?

  接下來會怎樣？

- I am not clear what happened then.

  我不清楚那時候發生什麼事？

〔身分〕

- What is Mr. Lin? He's a well-known scholar on Middle Eastern affairs.

  李先生是誰？他是知名的中東事務專家。

〔國籍〕

■ What is the lecturer, English or Canadian?
講者是哪一國人，英國或加拿大？

〔宗教〕

■ Linda is a Buddhist, but what is her fianc？
琳達是佛教徒，他未婚夫呢？

1.2 受詞

■ What did you say?
你說什麼？

■ What's the weather like?
天氣怎樣？

■ In what year did the Chen family move to the US?
陳家哪一年搬到美國？

■ What about this proposal?
這份提案怎樣？

■ In what place did you find your umbrella?
你在哪裡找到雨傘？

〔間接問句〕

■ Just tell me what I need to do next.
告訴我接下來我要做什麼？

說明 "What about" 詢問意見，通常搭配名詞片語。

1.3 主詞補語

■ What is the price?
價錢多少？

■ What do you think is the best way to solve the problem?
你想解決這問題的最好方法是什麼？

〔間接問句〕

■ Could you tell me what your plan is.
　麻煩告訴我你的盤算？

說明 what 問句可搭配插入語「do you think」，詞序不變。

1.4 限定詞：連接人或事物，形成結構較大的疑問代名詞組。

■ What time is it?
　現在幾點鐘？

■ What　Which musicians do you admire?
　你景仰那些音樂家？

■ What size shirt do you wear?
　你穿幾號襯衫？

■ I don't know what country the foreign student comes from.
　我不知道外籍學生來自哪個國家。

■ What else would you like?
　你還要什麼？

2.which

詢問範圍中的人或事物，答句為直述句。which 常搭配名詞（這時 which 為限定詞），或表示範圍的 of 介系詞片語。which 語詞可扮演主詞或受詞角色。另外，which 也有限定詞性質。

2.1 主詞

■ Which is my name tag?
　哪一個是我的名牌？

■ Which of the animals belongs to the cat family?
　哪一種動物屬於貓科？

2.2 受詞

■ Which do you like better, rice cake or rice pudding?
　你較喜歡哪一樣，年糕或碗粿？

■ Which are you fond of?
你喜歡哪一個？

2.3 限定詞

■ Which one do you think is better?
你覺得哪一樣較佳？

■ Which one will you take, the blue one or the red one?
你要買哪一件，藍的或紅的？

■ Which sector are you interested in?
你對哪一領域有興趣？

■ Which items did you have in mind?
你想到哪幾樣？

■ Could you please show at which stop I need to get off?
麻煩告訴我要在哪一站下車？

■ Which country did the teacher say Tina is from?
老師說蒂娜來自哪一國家？

說明 which 問句可搭配插入語，詞序不變。

3. who

詢問人的姓名、身份、關係，無限定詞用法，但可搭配副詞
else，詢問「還有誰」。

■ Who is your new physics teacher? Mr. Suzuki.
你的新物理老師是誰？鈴木先生。

■ Who's the man with punk hair? He's my cousin.
留龐克頭的男子是誰？他是我表弟。

■ Who else is there in the playroom?
還有誰在遊戲室？

〔間接問句〕

■ I don't know who the girl with a pierced nose is.
我不知道穿鼻環的女孩是誰。

4.whose

詢問所有者，扮演主詞、受詞、主詞補語。另外，whose 具有限定詞性質，搭配人或事物。

4.1 主詞

■ Whose is the most expensive?
  誰的最貴？

■ Whose cell phone is ringing?
  誰的手機在響？

4.2 受詞

■ Whose did you find? I found Tom's (keys).
  你找到誰的？我找到湯姆的（鑰匙）。

■ Whose seat did you take?
  你佔了誰的座位？

4.3 主詞補語

■ Whose pug is this?
  這是誰的獅子狗？

■ Whose hat is this?
  這是誰的帽子？

5.whom

受格性質，只當受詞，置於句首或 who 問句中。非正式用法常以 who 代替，但與介系詞共現於句首時，不可以 who 代替。

■ Whom　Who will you vote for?
  你要投票給誰？

■ Who sues whom　who for what?
  誰要告誰？事由是什麼？

■ Who will coordinate with whom　who?
  誰要和誰搭配？

■By whom was the music performed?

是誰演奏音樂的？

◆ 3-6 關係代名詞

引導名詞缺項的形容詞子句的代名詞為關係代名詞。關係代名詞兼具連接詞與代名詞功用，填補形容詞子句名詞的缺項，並連接形容詞子句與主要子句關係代名詞分為單詞關係代名詞、複合關係代名詞、準關係代名詞等三類。

1. 單詞關係代名詞：

who, whom, whose, which, that 為單詞關係代名詞。

先行詞	主格	所有格	受格
人	who　that	whose	whom　that
動物、事物	which　that	少用	which　that

1.1 功用

1.1.1 主詞

■The guest who　that stayed overnight here last night is an archaeologist.

＝ The guest staying overnight here last night is an archaeologist.

昨夜在這裡過夜的客人是一名考古學家。

■The river which　that flows through the city of Paris is the Seine River.

＝ The river flowing through the city of Paris is the Seine River.

流經巴黎的河流是塞納河。

■ The earthquake, which occurred last night, was the largest in Taiwan for over a century.

= The earthquake, occurring last night, was the largest in Taiwan for over a century.

昨夜發生的地震是台灣一世紀以來震度最強的。

說明 主格關係代名詞引導的形容詞子句可縮減為分詞片語。

■ Sean is the only one of the attendees who comes from Ireland.

尚恩是出席者中唯一來自愛爾蘭的。

說明 關係代名詞會因先行詞後位修飾語而與先行詞產生遠距關係，因此易與先行詞混淆，例如：

■ Leo is one of the students who failed in Syntax last semester.

里歐是上次句法學被當的學生之一。

■ The textbook of law that I am studying was written by Prof. Lin.

我正在讀的法學教科書是林教授所寫。

1.1.2 受詞

■ The applicant whom I interviewed was so impressive.

= The applicant I interviewed was so impressive.

和我面談的應徵者令人印象深刻。

■ The position which that I applied for was administrative assistant.

= The position I applied for was administrative assistant.

我申請的職務是行政助理。

說明 前無介系詞的受格關係代名詞可省略。

■ I'm looking for someone with whom I can share real love.

我一直在找尋能夠分享真愛的人。

說明 前有介系詞的受格關係代名詞不可省略。

1.1.3 主詞補語

■ Judy is no longer the willful girl who she used to be.

裘蒂不再是以前那樣任性的女孩。

■ *"I am who I am today because of the choices I made yesterday." - Eleanor Roosevelt*

「*因為我昨日的選擇才有今天的我。」— 羅斯福*

1.1.4 受詞補語

■ Mr. Wei is not the brilliant entrepreneur who people thought him to be.

魏先生不是人們所想的顯赫企業家。

1.1.5 所有詞

■ The muskrat is an animal whose fur is very suitable for fly fishing lures.

麝鼠是一種毛皮極適合做毛鉤的動物。

■ The warehouse of which the roof was destroyed by the storm has been repaired.

因暴風雨而損壞的倉庫屋頂已修妥。

說明 whose 較少用於先行詞為物品的情況。

1.2 單詞關係代名詞的用法限制

1.2.1 that

(1) 先行詞包括人與事物時

■ They are hired to protect the residents and buildings that are in the remote village.

他們受雇保護偏鄉居民及建築物。

(2) 先行詞含序數詞、形容詞最高級或 only, very, next, same 等語詞

■ I'm still the same guy that I used to be.

我還是老樣子。

■ The longest snake that exists today is the Reticulated Python.
現存最長的蛇是網紋蟒。

■ Neil Armstrong was the first man that walked on the Moon.
尼爾・阿姆斯壯是最先步行於月球的人。

■ The next interviewee that I communicated with was Roberto Baroni.
我下一位交談的面試者是羅伯特・巴羅尼。

■ *"Man is the only creature that consumes without producing."- George Orwell*
「人類是唯一只有消耗，而不事生產的生物。」— 喬治・歐威爾

(3) 限定用法中，先行詞指涉形容詞子句主詞補語，不論人或事物，限用 that，但常省略。

■ My Harley is still the fascinating motorcycle (that) it used to be.
我的哈雷機車還是如以前那麼炫。

■ The village is no longer the conservative place (that) it was before.
這村子不再是以前那樣封閉的地方。

1.2.2 which：補述形容詞子句不搭配 that。補述用法中，先行詞指涉形容詞子句的主詞補語，述及人的職業、背景、特質時，限用 which，且不可省略。

〔地位〕

■ Dave seems like an excellent fund manager, which he is.
戴夫是一名優秀的基金經理人，這就是他的成就。

〔職業〕

■ The man sounds like a fortune teller, which he is.
聽起來男子像個算命師，實際上他就是。

〔背景〕

■ The guy talked like a native of the United States, which he is.
那人談起話來就像個土生土長的美國人，他真的就是。

〔特質〕

■ Andy is very active in adventure sports, which his twin brother is not.

安迪熱衷於冒險運動，他的雙胞胎弟弟則不然。

1.2.3 who：先行詞為人稱代名詞或 he, she, all, one, any, anybody, any one, no one, everybody 時，限用 who。

■ *"Anyone who has never made a mistake has never tried anything new."- Albert Einstein*

「任何未曾犯錯的人就是從未嘗試新事物。」—阿爾伯特·愛因斯坦

> 說明 不定代名詞若不指涉人，例如 all, any, anything, none, nothing, little, everything，關係代名詞多用 that。

■ There's still much that we can improve upon.

我們還有很大改進空間。

■ Is there anything/something that I can get you?

有什麼我能幫你買的嗎？

■ Here is all that I can say about my new microfilm.

這是我對新拍的微電影的介紹。

2. 複合關係代名詞

複合關係代名詞兼具先行詞與單詞關係代名詞功用，引導名詞子句或副詞子句，包括 what, whoever, whomever, whosever, whichever 等。

2.1 引導名詞子句

2.1.1 主詞

■ *"What is done is done." ="The thing that/which is done is done." - Oscar Wilde*

「木已成舟。」— 奧斯卡·王爾德

■ Whoever reaches the goal first wins!

= Anybody that who reaches the goal first wins !

誰先達成目標，誰就贏。

■ Whichever of these sniffer dogs completed the course fastest wins.

哪隻緝毒犬最先完成課程，誰就贏。

2.1.2 受詞

■ My Dachshund eats whatever I feed it.

= My Dachshund eats anything that　which I feed it.

我餵我的達克斯狗什麼，牠就吃什麼。

■ Whomever　Whoever you recommend will be hired.

= Anybody whom　who you recommend will be hired.

你推薦誰，就雇用誰。

■ You may choose whichever you prefer.

= You may choose any, no matter which you prefer.

= You may choose any, regardless of which you prefer.

你較喜歡什麼，隨你挑選。

2.2 引導副詞子句

■ Whatever happens, stick it out.

= No matter what happens, stick it out.

= Regardless of what happens, stick it out.

無論發生什麼事，堅持下去。

■ Whoever is nominated, we will all be on the same side.

= No matter who is nominated, we will all be on the same side.

無論提名誰，我們都支持。

■ I don't care to join you, whoever you are.

= I don't care to join you no matter who you are.

= I don't care to join you regardless of who you are.

不論你是誰，我都不介意加入。

3. 準關係代名詞：

特定狀況或句構中才具關係代名詞功用的連接詞為準關係代名詞，包括 as, than。

3.1 as：指涉限定或補述形容詞子句的主詞、受詞、主詞補語。

3.1.1 限定用法：搭配含 as, same, such 等語詞的先行詞。

(1) 主詞

- As many volunteers as those who come will be admitted.
  來的每個志工都會被接納。

- There are such stories as may inspire the minority children.
  有能夠激勵弱勢兒童這樣的故事。

(2) 受詞

- You may obtain as much subsidy as you require.
  你需要多少補助金額，你都拿得到。

- We will face the same situation as we did years ago.
  我們將面臨與多年前同樣的情勢。

(3) 主詞補語

- The cell phone is no longer the same as it used to be ten years ago.
  手機不再與十年前所使用的一樣。

- The building is just as it was in Japanese Colonial Period.
  該建築物如同日本殖民時期的樣貌。

3.1.2 補述用法：先行詞無語詞限制，形容詞子句多表肯定語氣，不須置於先行詞右側。

(1) 主詞：形容詞子句搭配連綴動詞，指涉主要子句所述內容。

- The humanitarian is wearing a fur coat, as is ironic.
  那名人道主義者穿著毛皮外套，真是個諷刺。

- They reached the final agreement, as was expected.
  他們達成最後協議，如預期一樣。

- As stated above, cancer is not an incurable disease.
  如上所述，癌症不是絕症。

(2) 受詞

■ The chapel was not, as you suppose, designed by Tadao Ando.
這小教堂不如你所認為是由安藤忠雄所設計。

說明

1. 句意：You suppose that the chapel was designed by Tadao Ando.
2. as 子句置於否定主要子句中間，表示主要子句的肯定語意。

■ The dish was, as you guessed, not made by an aboriginal chef.
這盤子不像你所認為的是原住民酋長做的。

句意：You guessed that the dish was made by an aboriginal chef.

■ As everyone knows, the python is not poisonous.
如同大家所知道的，蟒蛇無毒。

說明

1. 句意：Everyone knows that the python is not poisonous.
2. as 子句置於否定主要子句前面，as 子句與主要子句所述一致。

■ The official wasn't involved in the scandal, as many people were told.
如同許多人聽說的，官員未涉及醜聞。

說明

1. 句意：Many people were told that the official was involved in the scandal.
2. as 子句置於否定主要子句後面，表示主要子句的肯定語意。

(3) 主詞補語：as 子句中的 be 動詞可移至主詞左側。

■ The cake tasted very fresh, just as it looked appeared.
蛋糕嚐起來很新鮮，和外觀一樣。

■ It is the most excellent thoroughbred, just as it seems.
牠感覺上就是最優秀的純種馬。

■ The little panda bear is very adorable, as are its parents.
圓仔很討喜，和牠父母一樣。

3.2 than：含比較語詞的先行詞搭配準關係代名詞 than，僅用於限定用法。

■ Don't feed your dog more food than is really needed.
不要餵食過量的飼料給你的狗。

■ We usually make more calls than are really required.
我們打的電話量常比真正需要的量還多。

【比較】**副詞子句**：Men make fewer calls than women do.
男人打的電話比女人少。

■ Leo answered fewer questions than was required.
里歐回答的問題比要求的少。

【比較】**副詞子句**：Leo answered fewer questions than I thought.
里歐回答的問題比我想的還少。

■ There are more rip-offs than was reported.
= There are more rip-offs than what was reported.
搶劫的案件較報導來得多。

> 說明 than 當形容詞子句主詞時，述語動詞與先行詞的數與人稱可不
> 一致。

◆ 3-7 代詞

代替句子組成成分的語詞為代詞。

1. 名詞：

代名詞為句中名詞組的代詞。

■ This is Mr. Suzuki. He's my advisor.
這位是鈴木先生，他是我的指導教授。

■ A: Would you like tea or coffee?
你要茶或咖啡？
B: Both.
都要。

> 說明 名詞性質的不定詞、動名詞或介系詞片語可以 it, that, this 當代
> 詞。

■ Leo likes to do tai chi and meditation, but I don't like it.
里歐喜歡太極和打坐，但是我不喜歡。

■ Peter is addicted to playing online games, but it is not my cup of tea.
彼得沉溺於線上遊戲玩上癮，但那不是我喜歡的事。

■ The snake came out from behind the bathtub. That is where it hid.
蛇從浴缸後面出來。那是他躲藏之處。

2. 動詞：

一般助動詞與情態助動詞皆都當動詞組的代詞。

■ I have been to Beijing, and Leo has, too.
我去過北京，里歐也去過。

■ My parents went to church this morning, but I didn't.
今天早上我父母去教堂，但我沒去。

■ Gina was surfing the Internet, and her roommate was, too.
吉娜在上網，他的室友也是。

■ Hank will resign next month, and Bella will, too.
漢克下個月要離職，貝拉也是。

3. 形容詞：

常見代替副詞的代詞有 so, the same 等。

■ A: It is chilly cold outside now.
現在外面很冷。

B: It's so in here, too.
裡面也是。

■ A: I'm feeling worried about the result next week.
我擔心下星期的結果。

B: I'm feeling the same.
我也是。

4. 副詞：

常見代替副詞的代詞有 then, there, so 等。

■ My family moved to Taiwan in 1998, and I was born then.
我家於 1998 年搬到台灣，我是那年出生的。

■ I studied university in Taipei, and I met my wife there.
我在台北念大學，也在那裡遇見我妻子。

■ My coach arrived at the gym on time, and so did I.
我教練準時抵達體育館，我也是。

5. 全句：

常見代替子句的代詞有 it, this, that, which, so 等。

■ A: The manager has been laid off.
經理已遭解雇。

B: I can't believe it that.
我無法相信。

■ My proposal has been accepted. This is so nice.
我的提案通過了，真棒。

■ Leo won first place, which allowed him to get a scholarship.
里歐贏得第一名，這讓他獲得獎學金。

■ I will reach my goal; I really think so.
我要達到目標了。我真的這麼認為。

第4章 限定詞

限定詞置於名詞前面，扮演標示名詞片語界線的指示詞角色，功用為限定名詞，不同於形容詞的功用為修飾名詞。限定詞依出現位置分為前置、中間、後置等三類，其中以中間限定詞最重要。

> 說明 單數可數名詞必須搭配限定詞。

◆ 4-1 限定詞

1. 前置限定詞：

all	such
both	what
double, half, twice（倍數詞）	only
a third (of), three quarters (of)（分數詞）	

★分數詞為前置限定詞，結構是「基數＋序數」，基數為複數時，序數為複數形，例如：

one fifth	五分之一	two thirds	三分之二
three fourths	三分之四	four fifths	五分之四

2. 中間限定詞：

a, an, the（冠詞）	either
this, that, these, those（指示詞）	neither
my, your, his, her, our, their, its（所有詞）	enough
no	what

any	which
each	whatever
every	whosever

★ this, that, these, those 等指示詞與名詞的單複數必須一致。

this buggy　　這部運輸車　　these buggies　　這些運輸車

that camera　　那台相機　　those cameras　　那些相機

3. 後置限定詞：

one, two, three（基數）	other
first, second, third（序數）	several
next	much, many, more, most
last	few, fewer, little, less
any	which
each	whatever
every	whosever

★ many, more, few, little 等具比較性質，兼具形容詞性質，屬於雙性語詞。

★ 後置限定詞不具排他性。例如：

several other guests　　　　幾位其他客人

many other members　　　　許多其他會員

◆ 4-2 限定詞的排列

1. 前置 - 中間

■ all these persimmons　　　　這些所有的柿子

■ such an old moon guitar　　　這樣的老月琴

■ three quarters of the expense 　　四分之三的經費
■ twice a month 　　每月二次
■ only this moment 　　只有這時刻

【例外】my only son 　　我的獨生子

2. 中間 - 後置

■ my fifteenth birthday 　　我的十五歲生日
■ those two street performers 　　這二位街頭藝人
■ my first two days off 　　我休假的前二天
■ their next two projects 　　他們接下來的二份工作

說明 前置與中間限定詞具排他性，不同接連出現。
【誤】my this book 　　【誤】no every car

3. 前置 - 中間 - 後置

■ all my other credit cards 　　我所有其它的信用卡

◆ 4-3 冠詞

演變自形容詞的冠詞是最重要的限定詞，明確表示名詞的泛指或指定的語意性質。冠詞分為定冠詞、不定冠詞、零冠詞等三種。

1. 定冠詞：

the，連接母音為首的單詞或表示強調時唸〔ði〕。

1.1 搭配指定、已知或易於推知的名詞。

■ Here comes the bus.
公車來了。（易於推知的名詞）

■ The foreigner is teaching me Spanish.
那位外國人教我西班牙文。（單數普通名詞）

■ The residents in the community are very diverse.
社區居民非常多元（複數普通名詞）

■ The liquid in the tube is mercury.
管子裡的液體是水銀（物質名詞）

■ The boy wants to be the Schweitzer of Taiwan.
男孩要成為台灣的史懷哲。（專有名詞）

■ The committee are meeting tomorrow at 10 A.M.
委員會明天早上要開會。（集合名詞）

1.2 宇宙唯一的物體

■ The sky is clear.
天空晴朗。

■ The moon moves around the Earth.
月球繞著地球運轉。

■ Pluto is the farthest planet from the sun.
冥王星是距離太陽最遠的行星。

說明 表示當下的特徵時，sky, moon, sunset 可搭配不定冠詞。

■ There's a clear sky and a full moon over the lake.
清澈天空及圓滿明月高掛湖上。

■ I saw a red sunset while driving along the countryroad.
我沿著鄉間道路開車時，看見一抹火紅落日。

1.3 最高級修飾語

■ Neptune is the nearest planet to the sun.
海王星是距離太陽最近的行星。

■ The sailfish can swim the fastest in the water.
旗魚在水中的游泳速度最快。

1.4 序數

■ The Lins lives on the seventh floor.
林氏一家住在七樓。

■ The Yankee fell behind but made a comeback in the last inning.
洋基隊原本落後，但在最後一局逆轉勝。

範圍不確定時，敘述可搭配不定冠詞。

■ They voted for a third time to prevent a government shutdown.
為防止政府關閉，他們投了三次票。

■ Jack thinks very deeply but does things without a second thought.
傑克思慮頗深，但做事不多考慮。

1.5 同類總稱

■ The platypus is a mammal.
鴨嘴獸是哺乳類動物。

■ The lotus is an aquatic plant.
睡蓮是水生植物。

■ Hollywood is home of the stars.
好萊塢是明星的家。

■ The tachograph is a useful tool.
自動迴轉速度計是有用的工具。

■ The aborigines are the only real Taiwanese.
原住民是唯一真正的台灣人。

說明 不定冠詞搭配單數名詞或名詞複數形都也表示同類的總稱。
■ A frog is an amphibian.
= Frogs are an amphibian.
青蛙是兩棲動物。

1.6 方位名詞

■ Cars drive on the right in London.
在倫敦，汽車右側行駛。

■ Zurich is located in the north of the country.
蘇黎世位於國家北方。

1.7 與水有關的地理名詞或船舶名稱

- the Pacific Ocean 太平洋
- the Gulf of Mexico　　墨西哥灣
- the Caspian Sea　　　裡海
- the Sun Moon Lake　　日月潭
- the Tamshui River　　淡水河
- the Suez Canal　　　蘇伊士運河
- the Titanic　　　　　鐵達尼號

1.8 複數形山脈或群島名詞

- the Alps　　　　　阿爾卑斯山
- the Philippines　　菲律賓群島

1.9 國家、組織、團隊或報章雜誌名稱

- the United States　　美國
- the Red Cross　　　紅十字會
- the United Nations　聯合國
- the Economist　　　經濟學人
- the New York Yankee　紐約洋基隊

1.10 建築物或公共場所

- the British Museum　　　大英博物館
- the Palace Museum　　　國立故宮博物院
- the Statue of Liberty　　自由女神像
- the Globe Theater　　　環球影城
- the Children's Hospita　兒童醫院
- the Sydney Opera House　雪梨歌劇院

1.11 搭配形容詞或分詞，表示特定的群體、事物、概念等。

群體	事物	概念
the blind	the possible	the right
the deaf	the impossible	the good

群體	事物	概念
the unemployed	the ordinary	the true
the dying	the unknown	the wrong

■ Make the impossible possible.
讓不可能變為可能。

■ the True, the Good, the Beautiful
真・善・美。

■ The rich are not always happier than the poor.
有錢人並沒有比窮人快樂。

■ The handicapped elevator is reserved for the disabled.
殘障電梯保留給殘障人士使用。

1.12 表示年代

■ I was born in the 90s.
我出生於 90 年代。

2. 不定冠詞：

a, an, an 用於首字母為母音的單詞前面。

2.1 搭配不特定的單數可數名詞。

■ I bought a scanner yesterday.
昨天我買一部掃描器。

■ The guy is really a villain.
那傢伙真是個惡棍。

2.2 表示 one，搭配單位的數量詞。

■ The maternity outfit costs a hundred dollars.
孕婦裝值一百元。

■ The chapel is a kilometer away from the station.
小教堂離車站一公里遠。

2.3 表示 each／every, per

■ Their presidential room costs ＄2,500 a night!
總統套房一晚 2,500 美元。

■ The inspector makes an inventory once a month.
督察每月盤點。

2.4 表示 the same

■ Birds of a feather flock together.
物以類聚。

■ I don't have much of an opinion of my boss.
我和我老闆意見不合。

2.5 搭配姓名，表示某位、某人作品或與某人相同特質的人。

■ I'm sure it's a Blake.
我確定那是布雷克的作品。

■ My cousin is a Conan Edogawa.
我表弟是江戶川柯南。

■ There's a call from a Mr. Lin waiting for you on the office line.
內線上有一位林先生在等您。

2.6 國籍、民族、政黨、宗教的一員。

■ Mr. Suzuki is a Japanese.
鈴木先生是日本人。

■ My roommate is a Hakka.
我的室友是客家人。

■ Mr. Lin is a Republican.
林先生是共和黨員。

■ My fianc e is a vegetarian.
我的未婚妻是素食主義者。

2.7 物質名詞的特指狀況或類別時，可搭配不定冠詞。

■ A warm sunset greets a still evening.
溫和的落日迎接一個靜謐的夜晚。

■ There is a light rain falling.
正下著一場毛毛雨。

■ Medoc is a very nice wine.
梅鐸是一款醇釀紅酒。

■ Diamond is a precious stone.
鑽石是一種珍貴礦石。

■ This morning, a heavy snow was falling.
今天早上大雪不斷。

3. 零冠詞：

零冠詞就是冠詞缺項，通常用於泛指或慣用語詞。

3.1 搭配泛指的不可數名詞

■ Silence is gold.
沉默是金。

■ Knowledge is power.
知識就是力量。

3.2 搭配球類運動名稱

■ They are playing volleyball.
他們在打排球。

■ Soccer is the national sport of Brazil.
足球是巴西的國家運動。

3.3 泛指三餐或季節名稱

■ I don't normally eat anything between dinner and breakfast the next day.
晚餐到隔天早餐之間我通常不吃任何東西。

■ Spring is the season between winter and summer.
春天是介於冬天及夏天間的季節。

3.4 指涉唯一職務的名詞

■ arbitrary rule of the king.
國王的獨斷統治

■ We elected Mr. Lin as chairperson of the assembly.
我們推舉林先生當大會主席。

3.5 介系詞片語表示行為概念時，名詞搭配零冠詞

■ He went to bed very early when in jail.
入監服刑時，他很早就寢。

■ Jack went to church before he came to the office today.
傑克今天進辦公室前先去教堂。

3.6 平行結構的名詞

arm in arm　肩並肩	face to face　面對面
day and night　日以繼夜	side by side　並駕齊驅
from coast to coast　全國地	top and tail　全部

■ We need to work on the project step by step.
我們必須按部就班執行工作。

■ Some animals can tell right from wrong.
有些動物能夠分辨對錯。

■ They walked hand-in-hand as they hung out in the street.
他們手牽著手在街上散步。

■ Some residents live from handtomouth on government pensions.
一些民眾靠政府救助金餬口。

動詞

◆ 5-1 動詞的結構

就構詞而言，動詞分為單詞動詞、複合動詞與片語動詞等三類。

1. 單詞動詞

不與其他單詞共同構成的動詞，又分為字根動詞與派生動詞二種。

1.1 字根動詞：不含動詞綴詞的動詞，動詞中以字根動詞數量最多。

■ Care kills a cat.
憂慮會致命。

■ Theyceasedfire temporarily.
他們暫時停火。

■ Please don't drink and drive.
請勿酒後駕車。

■ Red deer feed on grass in themeadow.
赤鹿以草為生。

1.2 派生動詞：相對於字根動詞，包含綴詞的動詞為派生動詞。派生動詞的黏接綴詞可能是動詞字首、字尾或其他詞素。

1.2.1 黏接字首

■ The student misused the phrase.
學生用錯片語。

■ A good owner would never mistreat his pet.
好飼主絕不虐待自己的寵物。

■ The sponsors outnumbered the audience.
贊助人數量超過聽眾。

■ Some consumers under value the product.
某些消費者低估產品。

■ Don't overload your van.
不要讓你的廂型車超載。

■ The server has been disconnected.
伺服器已斷線。

■ The mechanic unpacked his tool box.
技工打開工具箱。

1.2.2 黏接字尾

■ It is a carbonated drink.
那是碳酸飲料。

■ We need to heighten the fence to keep our dogs in.
為了圈住小狗，我們必須加高圍牆。

■ Mrs. Lin has diversified the investment across a large number of securities.
林太太買進很多股票以分散投資。

■ The government managed to modernize the country's communications system.
政府設法將國家的通訊系統現代化。

★常黏接於動詞的綴詞：說明：常黏接於動詞的綴詞：

co- 共同	pre- 在…之前
counter- 反對	re- 重新
dis- 否定	trans- 橫穿
en- 使成為	sub- 下面
fore- 預先	inter- 在…之間

2. 複合動詞

二個名詞、動詞、形容詞或副詞等實詞共同形成的動詞為複合動詞，彼此之間可連接、分開或以連字號相連。複合動詞與組成字語意常無關連。

2.1 不及物複合動詞

■ Tom cannot ice-skate very well.
湯姆不太會溜冰。

■ I usually window-shop in Xinyi on holidays.
假日我常在信義區逛街。

■ I will go backpacking in Australia this summer.
今年夏天我要到澳洲自助旅行。

★常見的不及物複合動詞：

babysit　臨時保姆	roller skate　溜冰
backbite　背地罵人	spacewalk　太空漫步
daydream　白日夢	stargaze　想入非非
kowtow　磕頭	waterski　滑水

2.2 及物複合動詞

■ I test-drove the new car during its development.
新車研發期間我曾試開過。

■ He was hired to ghostwrite the general's autobiography.
我受雇為將軍的自傳代筆者。

■ We can download films for free at streaming video sites.
我們瀏覽影像網站時下載影片。

★常見的及物複合動詞：

blow-dry　用吹風機吹乾	ill-treat　惡待
court-material　軍事審判	proofread　校對
deep-freeze　冷凍	rubber-stamp　蓋橡皮圖章
field-test　現場試驗	tape-record　錄音

2.3 兼具及物與不及物性質的複合動詞

■ You had better double-check.
你最好再確認。

■ You have to double-check the data.
你必須再確認一下資料。

■ Most mothers prefer breast-feeding to bottle-feeding.
大多數母親偏向餵母乳,而不喜歡餵奶瓶。

■ The woman was breastfeeding her baby.
婦人在餵嬰孩母乳。

■ They will mass produce hybrid vehicles.
他們將大量生產混合動力車輛。

■ The company has decided to mass produce.
公司已決定大量生產。

★常見兼具及物與不及物性質的複合動詞

chain-smoke 菸一支一支地吸	short-circuit 短路
countdown 倒數	sight-read 即興演奏
hitchhike 搭便車	play-act 扮演
lip-read 讀唇	sweet-talk 奉承

3. 片語動詞

動詞搭配介副詞或介系詞共同形成片語動詞。就結構而言,片語動詞分為「動詞＋副詞」、「動詞＋介系詞」、「動詞＋介副詞＋介系詞」等類型;就語意而言,片語動詞有及物、不及物、連綴或授與等性質。

3.1 及物片語動詞

3.1.1 「動詞＋介副詞」結構:受詞為名詞片語時,置於動詞或介副詞右側,受詞為代名詞時,置於動詞右側。

■ Please pick the note up.
請將紙條撿起來。

■ The old man left behind a lot of inheritance.
老先生留下大筆遺產。

■ You had better nail down the conclusion soon.
你最好儘快下定結論。

■ Please turn it on.
請打開開關。

★常見「動詞＋介副詞」結構的片語動詞：

add up　合計	hold down　壓制
bring up　養育	put away　收拾
carry out　執行	scale down　縮減
drag off　拖離	talk over　討論
find out　發現	wash away　沖掉

3.1.2 「動詞＋介系詞」結構：受詞置於介系詞右側。

■ The director dealt with the case in person.
主管親自處理案件。

■ We are planning on our vacation to China.
我們在規畫到大陸度假。

■ Yesterday, I happened to run across Linda.
昨天我碰巧遇到琳達。

■ CEO stands for Chief Executive Officer.
CEO 表示執行長。

★常見「不及物動詞＋介系詞」結構的片語動詞

abide by　遵守	laugh at　嘲笑
burst into　突然	object to　反對
come across　巧遇	quarrel with　爭吵

depend on 依賴	think of 想起
guard against 守護	wait for 等待

3.1.3 「及物動詞＋受詞＋介系詞」結構，這種結構可分析為搭配受詞與受詞補語的不完全及物動詞。

(1) 受詞為慣用語詞

■ Don't take notice of the message from Leo.
不要在意里歐的訊息。

■ Linda finally quit to take care of her children.
為了照顧孩子，琳達最後辭去工作。

■ We cannot find fault with his presentation.
對他的說明我們無從挑剔。

■ We really should make good use of our money.
我們實在需要善用金錢。

■ The chief editor pays attention to details all the time.
主編一向注意細節。

(2) 受詞為任意指涉

■ The entrepreneur's son cannot tell right from wrong.
富二代不知明辨是非。

■ They have provided food for victims of disaster.
他們提供食物給災民。

■ I need to hire a lawyer to defend me against a lawsuit.
我需要請律師幫我辯護。

3.1.4 「動詞＋介副詞＋介系詞」結構

■ They have made up for my loss.
他們必須賠償我損失。

■ I can't put up with that smell any more.
我再也忍受不了那味道。

■ My brother came down with flu last week.
我弟弟上週染上流感。

■ I have been looking forward to seeing you again.
我一直期待再見到你。

★常見的「動詞＋介副詞＋介系詞」片語動詞：

average out to　平均	live up to　達到
break out in　突然出現	look down on　輕視
carry on with　繼續堅持	look in on　短暫拜訪
catch　keep up with　趕上	play up to　討好
come down on　下降	run out of　用盡
date back to　回朔	run up against　偶遇
do away with　廢除	stick up for　支持
face up to　面對事實	trace back to　追朔
get on with　相處融洽	walk out on　違反

3.2 不及物片語動詞，結構為：「動詞＋介副詞」，不搭配受詞。

■ The plane finally touched down safely.
飛機終於安全著陸。

■ The student often dozes off during class.
學生時常上課打瞌睡。

■ My partner asked me to calm down.
我的夥伴要我冷靜。

■ They decided to give in until the next day.
他們一直到隔天才放棄。

■ Mr. Lin stepped aside for a younger person to take over.
林先生讓位給一位年輕人來接手。

★常見的「動詞＋介副詞」片語動詞：

back up　支持	push ahead　繼續前進
cool off　冷靜下來	sleep in　很晚起床
fade away　消失	tumble down　倒塌
look back　回顧	walk out　罷工
meet up　不期而遇	wear off　磨損

3.3 連綴片語動詞：少數「動詞＋介副詞」結構的片語動詞具
有連綴性質，搭配補語。

■ After years of trials, the team ended up successful.
多年考驗之後，隊伍終於成功了。

◆ 5-2 動詞的分類：依動詞的性質

1. 本動詞

即主要動詞，具詞彙意義，又稱為詞彙動詞。本動詞表示主詞
的動作或狀態，左側常搭配助動詞，因此置於動詞組最右側。
句子至少存在一個本動詞

■ The team won first place in the game.
該隊伍贏得比賽第一名。

■ The secretary was checking email at that time.
那時候秘書在檢視電子郵件。

■ The freezer has been moved away from the kitchen.
冷藏庫已搬離開廚房。

2. 助動詞

伴隨或代替本動詞，以增添語意或語法功能的語詞為助動詞。
助動詞主要分為一般助動詞與情態助動詞二類。

2.1 一般助動詞：be, do, have 等與本動詞共現時為一般助動詞。一般助動詞只有語法功能，沒有詞彙意義，因此又稱為作用詞。

2.1.1 be：搭配現在分詞形成進行時態動詞組，搭配過去分詞形成被動語態動詞組，或前述動詞組的代詞。另外，助動詞 be 可搭配不定詞，形成特定語氣。

(1) 進行時態

■ Hank was listening to music online when the earthquake happened.
地震發生時，漢克正在收聽線上音樂。

■ Peter is growing tomatoes in his own backyard.
彼得在自家後院種番茄。

■ I will be travelling around Indonesia on my own.
我打算獨自到印尼各地旅遊。

(2) 被動語態

■ Sam was suddenly laid off last month.
山姆上個月突然遭到解職。

■ CCTV is selected as Building of The Year at Arch Daily.
央視被 Arch Daily 選為年度最佳建築。

說明 除了 be，become, get, grow, stand 也可搭配過去分詞，形成被動語態。

■ I became acquainted with my new neighbor in a short time.
我很快就熟悉我的新鄰居。

■ Amy quickly grew accustomed to her new routine.
艾咪很快就適應她的新作息。

■ My car got towed away today.
今天我的車子被拖吊。

■ The man stood convicted of sexual harassment.
男子被控性侵。

(3) 代詞

〔be 動詞組的代詞〕

■ Fred is an exchange student, but Leo isn't.

弗雷德是一名交換學生，但李奧不是。

〔be 動詞組的附加問句〕

■ Mr. Lin was the chair of the meeting, wasn't he?

林先生不是會議的主席嗎？

(4) 搭配不定詞片語

■ You're to come straight home.

= You must have tocome straight home.

你得直接回家。

■ You are not to say that again.

= You should not say that again.

不許你再那麼說。

■ You are to blame.

= You should be blamed.

你該受責備。

■ The soldier was not to return again.

= The soldier was destined not to return again.

士兵註定無法回來。

■ We are to get engaged next month.

= We are going to get enganged next month.

我們下個月要訂婚。

■ You are not to smoke in here.

= You can may not smoke in here.

你不可在這裡面抽菸。

2.1.2 do：插入現在或過去簡單式本動詞組，形成否定、疑問、加強語氣
句型或附加問句，或常動詞組的代詞。與一般助動詞 do 共現的
本動詞應是原形動詞。

(1) 形成否定

■ Dave didn't attend the funeral yesterday.
戴夫昨天沒有出席葬禮。

■ Don't do that.
別這麼做。

■ A vegetarian is a person who doesn't eat meat.
素食者是不吃肉的人。

(2) 形成疑問

■ Does your nephew speak French?
你的姪子說法文嗎？

■ Didn't the woman ask for help?
婦人未尋求幫助嗎？

■ Do I need to apply for a PR card？
我需要申請永久居留卡嗎？

No, you don't.
不，你不需要。

> 說明 "Must I apply for a PR card？" – "No, you needn't." 的句子較不普遍。

(3) 加強語氣

■ I did get 990 on the TOEIC exam.
多益考試我真的考到 990 分。

■ Health does seem to be more important than anything else.
健康確實比任何事都來得重要。

■ Do behave yourself on stage.
好好在舞台上表現。

(4) 附加問句

■ Judy didn't pass the final exam, did she?
茱蒂沒通過期末考試，對吧？

■ Susan works as a funeral director, doesn't she?
蘇珊在當禮儀師，不是嗎？

(5) 過去或現在簡單式動詞組代詞

■ I care about you. I really do. (I really care about you.)
我很關心你，我說真的。

■ Tate worked harder than you did. (you worked hard)
泰德工作比你認真。

2.1.3 have：搭配過去分詞形成完成時態動詞組，have / has / had 為限定動詞，過去分詞為本動詞，若包含 been，been 為助動詞。一般助動詞 have 也可當完成式動詞組的代詞。

(1) 完成時態

■ Kelly had set the table properly when I arrived.
當我抵達時，凱莉已擺放好餐具。

■ The injured has man been sent to the hospital.
受傷的男子已送往醫院。

(2) 完成式附加問句

■ You have never seen a hyena, have you?
你從沒看過鬣狗，是嗎？

■ Leo hasn't ever watched the pantomime, has he?
里歐沒看過那齣默劇，是嗎？

(3) 完成式動詞組的代詞

■ Have you ever been to Thailand?
你去過泰國嗎？

Yes, I have. (Yes, I have ever been to Thailand.)
是的，我去過。

■ The foreigner has eaten snails, but I haven't. (but I haven't eaten snails)
那名老外吃過蝸牛，但我沒吃過。

2.2 情態助動詞：表達作說者賦予本動詞所述內容主觀意念、
　　語氣或態度的助動詞，語意明確。就結構而言，情態助動
　　詞分為單詞與片語情態助動詞二類。

2.2.1 單詞情態助動詞：包括 can, could, dare, may, might, must, need, shall,
　　　　　　　　　　　should, will, would 等。單詞情態助動詞可搭配原形
　　　　　　　　　　　動詞、「be ＋現在分詞片語」、「have ＋過去分
　　　　　　　　　　　詞片語」等。

　(1) 單詞情態助動詞＋原形動詞

　　■ Will you come to the housewarming party tomorrow?
　　　你明天要來喬遷派對嗎？

　　　Yes, I will.
　　　是的，我會去。

　　　說明 簡答中的 will 表示強調。

　　■ You must stay behind tonight.
　　　你今晚必須留守。

　　★義務或責任的情態助動詞，由強而弱程度排列順序為：

　　　強 must → shall → should → can → may → could 弱

　　■ The hikers should take weather into consideration.
　　　健行者應考慮天氣。

　　■ There must be something wrong with my waist.
　　　我的腰一定怎麼了。

　　■ The woman must be the CEO's wife.
　　　那婦人一定是執行長的妻子。

　　■ The woman cannot be the CEO's wife.
　　　那婦人一定不是執行長的妻子。

　　　說明
　　　1. must not／mustn't 表示禁止，與推測語意無關。
　　　2. 表示可能或推測的情態助動詞，由高到低程度排列順序如下：
　　　高 must → will → would → should → may → might → could → can 低

■ The front door could not open itself.
前門無法自動開啟。

★表示能力的情態助動詞，由強到弱程度排列順序如下：

強 can → could → would be able to → should be able to → may/might beable to 弱

① shall 的用法：shall 用於第一人稱主詞，簡答應配合語意。

〔徵求意見〕

■ Shall we reserve a table for you?
我們幫您預留一桌，好嗎？

Yes, please.　No, thanks.
好的，麻煩了。　不用了，謝謝。

■ Shall I turn off the computer?
要我將電腦關機嗎？

Yes, please do.　No, you better not.
好的，請關機。　不用了，最好別關機。

■ Shall we take a break now?
我們現在休息一下好嗎？

We may as well.
＝ We may as well take a break now.
休息一下也好。

Yes, let's.　No, let's not!
好，休息一下。　不，不要休息。

〔請求許可〕

■ Shall I go for a walk?
我可以去散步嗎？

Yes, do it.　No, don't do it.
好的，你可以去。　不行，你不可以去。

〔詢問可能性〕

■ Shall we arrive at the awarding ceremony in time?
我們趕得上頒獎典禮嗎？

Yes, we will.

是的，我們一定可以。

② need／dare 的用法：

〔否定句或疑問句中兼具情態助動詞與一般動詞性質〕

■ Tom need not do that.（情態助動詞）

= Tom doesn't need to do that. （一般動詞）

湯姆不用做那件事。

■ Need Tom do that?（情態助動詞）

肯定回答：Yes, he must. 是的，他必須去。

否定回答：No, he needn't. 不，他不需要去。

說明 must not 表示禁止。

■ Does Tom need to do that?（一般動詞）

湯姆需要做那件事嗎？

Yes, he does.   No, he doesn't.

是的，他要 不，他不用。

■ Dare John say that?（情態助動詞）

=Does John dare to say that?（一般動詞）

約翰敢說嗎？

肯定回答：Yes, he dares.   Yes, he does. 是的，他敢。

否定回答：No, he dares not.   No, he doesn't. 不，他不敢。

〔肯定直述句僅具一般動詞性質〕

■ Leo needs to say no.   里歐必須說 no

Leo dares to say no.   里歐敢說 no

(2) 單詞情態助動詞＋ be V-ing

① could be V-ing

〔推測過去正在進行〕

■ Chad could be waiting at the meeting point when we arrive.

我打電話給查德時，他可能正在相約的地點等。

〔推測現在正在進行〕

■ Miss Lin could be talking on the cellphone now.
　林小姐可能正在講手機。

② may／might be V-ing 現在或未來可能的推測

■ Leo may　might be looking for his tablet.
　里歐可能正在找他的平板電腦。

■ I may　might be coming home next weekend.
　我可能下週末回家。

■ I might be studying abroad in Sydney for thesummer of 2014.
　我可能要出國到雪梨念 2014 年的夏季課程。

③ must be V-ing

〔推測現在正在進行〕

■ You must be kidding!
　你一定是在開玩笑吧！

■ It must be raining heavily outside.
　現在外面一定正在下雨。

■ Linda must be staying at home.
　琳達現在肯定待在家裡。

【比較】Linda must stay at home.
　　　　琳達必須待在家裡。

〔推測即將發生〕

■ It must be snowing tonight.
　今夜一定會下雪。

■ The guest must be arriving soon.
　客人一定很快到達。

④ should be V-ing 現在應該

■ You should be working on the task at hand.
　你應該做你手邊的工作。

■ He should be wearing a bullet-proof vest.
　他應該穿著防彈背心。

■ You shouldn't be playing video games now.
　你不該現在還在玩電動遊戲。

⑤ will be V-ing：未來某時正在。／預定即將發生。

■ We will be having fun all the way!
　我們會一直很開心的。

■ I will be taking an official visit to the city next Monday.
　下週一我將正式在那城市進行正式訪問。

(3) 單詞情態助動詞＋ have 過去分詞

① 推測動作發生可能：「must/can/could/may/might have ＋過去分詞」，可能性由大而小順序為：

大 must → can → could → may/might 小

(a) must have ＋過去分詞：依據客觀事實或邏輯推斷過去必然發生。
■ It must have rained last night.
　昨夜一定有下雨。

■ Michael Schumacher must have been hurt seriously when hitting that rock.
　撞擊石頭時，舒馬克一定身受重傷。

(b) may/might have ＋過去分詞：過去或現在的可能推測。
〔過去〕
■ Do you think Jack may　might have completed the project by now?
　你想傑克完成工作了嗎？

■ Linda may　might not have passed the test because she looks depressed.
　琳達可能考試沒過，因為她看起來蠻沮喪的。

〔現在〕

■ Bella's English may　might have improved by the time the test comes around.
貝拉的英文在考試前可能會進步。

■ Jennifer might have fallen in love with Andy.
珍妮佛好像愛上了安迪。

(c) could／can have ＋過去分詞：過去、現在、未來可能的推測，若為過去否定則可視為「must have ＋過去分詞」的否定式。

〔過去〕

■ It can't　couldn't have rained last night.
昨夜一定沒有下雨。

■ Leo could have overslept and got up too late.
里歐一定是睡過頭，太晚起床。

■ Youcannot have noticedthat side entrance.
你一定沒注意到側門。

■ Tom：Gina took a trip to Hong Kong last weekend.
湯姆：吉娜上週末去香港玩。

Bella：She cannot have done that. She attended the studyclub meetinglast Saturday night!
貝拉：她不可能去的。上週六晚上她有參加讀書會。

Tom：Oh, she must have lied about it.
湯姆：喔！她一定撒了謊。

說明 過去肯定推測多用「could/may/might/must have ＋過去分詞」，而不用「can have ＋過去分詞」。

【誤】She canhave gone to Hong Kong last weekend.

〔現在〕

■ The girl can't have eaten all eight pizzas by herself.
女孩不會一個人吃光八塊披薩。

〔未來〕

■ You can have walked on both feet tomorrow.
或許明天你就能用雙腳行走。

■ We have the best coffee that you can have made into your favorite drink.
我們提供台灣最醇的咖啡，你可以一嚐自己的最愛極品。

(d) should have ＋過去分詞：現在、未來可能的推測。

■ They should have arrived at the station by now.
他們現在應該到達機場了。

【語意】It is very likely that they have arrived at the airport by now.

■ The cargo ship should have arrived tomorrow.
運輸船明天可能會到。

② 過去該發生而未發生的動作：

(a) could have ＋過去分詞：過去能做而未做的動作。

■ Hank could have completed the work in less than the scheduled amount of hours.
漢克原本能在正常上班時間內完成工作的。

■ I could have gone to Cambridge University but I preferred UCLA.
我要去劍橋大學讀書，雖然我較喜歡 UCLA。

說明 「can have ＋過去分詞無此用法。

【誤】I can have gone to Cambridge University but I preferredUCLA.

(b) might have ＋過去分詞：過去應發生，卻未發生，或責難、批評的語氣，「may have ＋過去分詞」無此用法。

■ You might have reported me earlier.
你應該提早向我報告。

(c) need have ＋過去分詞：過去需要做而沒做。

■ You need tohave changed the front tires.
你本來就該換前輪的輪胎。

【比較】You needn't have changed the front tires.
你原本不用換前輪的輪胎。

(d) should have ＋過去分詞：原本該做而沒做。

■ The test report should have arrived yesterday, but it didn'tarrive.

= The test report ought to have arrived yesterday, but itdidn't arrive.

檢測報告昨天就該收到，但是卻沒有。

■ You should have made a reservation in advance.

= You ought to have made a reservation in advance.
你原本該事先預訂的。

說明

1. should 表示應當時，可代換為 ought to。
2. 比較：
■ You shouldn't have made a reservation in advance.

= You ought not to have made a reservation in advance.
你原本不該事先預訂的。

(e) would like to have ＋過去分詞：原本想要。
■ I would like to have attendedtheir wedding party.
我原本想去參加他們的婚禮。

(f) would have ＋過去分詞：過去假設語氣。
■ But for your assistance, we would have failed.
若非你的協助，我們就失敗了。

(g) 其他搭配：have ＋過去分詞的單詞情態助動詞。

(h) will have ＋過去分詞：未來某時已完成或仍持續。
■ They will have arrived at the destination site within twodays.
他們將於二天內抵達目的地。

■ By the end of this year, I will have taught for 20 years.
到今年年底前，我教書滿 20 年了。

③ must/could/may/might ＋ have been V-ing：對過去正在發生的動作的推測

- Sam didn't know where histablet was, but he thought Dave might have been using it before he went to bed.

  山姆不知道他的平板電腦在哪裡，但他想戴夫睡覺前可能一直在用。

- Leo wasn't home last night when I dropped by. He could have been studying at the library.

  我昨晚順道去里歐家時沒人在。他可能是在圖書館 K 書。

- A: Why didn't you answer my cellphone?

  你怎麼沒接我手機？

  B: Well, I must have been taking a shower, so I didn't hear it.

  我一定是在洗澡，沒聽到電話鈴聲。

2.2.2 片語情態助動詞：片語情態助動詞兼具動詞與情態助動詞性質，搭配原形動詞、「beV-ing」、「have 過去分詞」等動詞組。片語情態助動詞也常搭配單詞情態助動詞，形成語意豐富的動詞組。

(1) 片語情態助動詞非限定形式：一些片語情態助動詞具不定詞、動名詞或分詞等非限定形式。

① 不定詞

- It's a pity to have to cancel the activity.

  很可惜，不得不取消活動。

② 動名詞

- My boss has admitted having to lay off some staff.

  我老闆承認不得不解聘一些員工。

- The student denied being about to cheat during test.

  學生否認要在考試時作弊。

③ 分詞

- She walked down the pavement, not daring to look behind the man.

  她沿著人行道走去，不敢回頭看那名男子。

■ Having to compensate the loss, Fred sold his own apartment.
= Because he had to compensate the loss, Fred sold his own apartment.
由於必須賠償損失，弗雷德賣掉自己的公寓。

(2) 片語情態助動詞的時態：一些片語情態助動詞具時態變化。

① dare 當一般動詞時可搭配各種時態。

■ The girl dares (to) catch live cockroaches.
那女孩敢抓活的蟑螂。

■ Don't you dare to contradict me!
你不敢反駁我嗎？

■ The employee didn't dare to argue withher superior.
那名員工不敢與上級抗衡。

■ I will never dare to ride on hot-balloons again.
我再也不敢搭熱氣球了。

■ The dog has never dared to enter my house.
那隻狗從來不敢進到我屋子。

② 進行式的「have to」表示目前或過去某時必須。

■ The man is having to pawn his car to get the money.
男子現在得典當車子兌現。

■ Joe was having to force himself to calm down at that moment.
那時候喬還得強迫自己冷靜

■ We have been having to work on the project for a while.
這工作我們還得忙一陣子。

③ 現在完成式的「have to」表示截至目前的經驗或事實。

■ I have had to accept the conditions.
我不得不接受這些條件。

■ Leo has had to stay at home these two days.
這二天里歐不得不待在家裡。

■ If Hank had taken a leave, I should have had to take his place.
要是漢克請假，我就得替代他的職務。

④ 過去完成式的「have to」表示過去某時之前的必須。

■ That was something Dave had had to do the previous night.
那是戴夫前一夜不得不做的事。

■ Tina said she had had to resign before she started to find a new job.
緹娜說她開始找新工作之前不得先辭職。

⑤ 過去式的「be to 原形動詞」表示過去安排好的動作。

■ Jill was to take a leave of absence the next day.
吉兒第二天請假。

■ Fred said he was to go on a vacation next month.
弗雷德說他下個月要去度假。

⑥ 「was/were to have 過去分詞」表示過去原本打算。

■ Kelly was to have called a meeting this afternoon, but not many people were available.
凱莉今天下午本來打算要召開會議，但能到的人不多。

⑦ 過去式的「be about to」表示過去即將進行的動作。

■ The assistant said the presentation was about to start.
助理說介紹即將開始。

⑧ 過去式的「be going to」表示原本打算進行的動作。

■ I was going to call the police.
我本來打算報警。

⑨ 過去完成式的「be going to」表示過去某時原本打算進行的動作。

■ I had been going to adopt a dog when I visited the animal shelter.
我造訪動物收容所時原本打算領養一隻狗。

(3) 片語情態助動詞＋原形動詞

- Leo is bound to quit his job.
  里歐準備辭掉他的工作。

- Kate is about to leave Taipei for Singapore.
  ＝ Kateis going to leave Taipei for Singapore.
  凱特即將離開台北，前往新加坡。

- They seem to be able to solve the problem soon.
  他們似乎很快就能夠將問題解決。

- My family used to live in a fishing village.
  我的家人曾住在漁村。

- You had better change your mind.
  你最好改變心意。

- John used to stay up late because of insomnia.
  約翰以前常因失眠而晚睡。

說明 used to 表示過去習慣時，較 would 普遍。

(4) 片語情態助動詞＋ have 過去分詞

① 「would rather have 過去分詞」表示過去寧願。

- I would rather have attended a private high school.
  我寧可就讀私立高中。

- I would rather have completed the task myself.
  我寧願獨立完成工作。

② 「had better have 過去分詞」表示假設語氣。

- You had better have backed up your file.
  你要是有備份檔案就好了。

說明 had better 可搭配副詞 far。

③ 「ought to have 過去分詞」可表示對現在的推測。

■ The delegation ought to have arrived by now.

= The delegation should have arrived by now.

訪問團應該抵達了。

④ 「ought to have 過去分詞」可表示原本應該做，但不含否定語意。

■ They ought to have properly examined their vehicles before start up.

= They should have properly examined their vehicles before start up.

他們出發前應該徹底檢修車輛才對。

【比較】Leo started to quit smoking last week. His doctor said he ought to have done that.

里歐開始戒菸了。他的醫師說他早該戒掉菸癮。

⑤ 「be going to have 過去分詞」表示即將完成。

■ I am going to have made my bed before leaving the house.

離開屋子前我要整理好我的床。

(5) 片語情態助動詞＋ be V-ing

① 「had better be V-ing」表示最好立即進行。

■ I suppose you had better be taking a rest.

我想你該休息一下。

② 「have to be V-ing」 表示必須立即進行。

■ We will have to be staying at the hotel.

我們必須待在飯店。

③ 「ought to be V-ing」表示現在未做該做的動作。

■ John ought to be working now, but he isn't.

約翰應該開始工作，但他沒有。

(6) 情態助動詞 ＋ 片語情態助動詞

① 情態助動詞 ＋ have to

■ I suppose I may have to stop my car here.
我想我可能必須在這裡停車。

■ You should have to pay the bill before deadline.
你應該要在截止日前繳帳單。

■ I might have to get used to my new job as soon as possible.
我必須儘快適應我的新工作。

② 情態助動詞 ＋ be able to

■ You might be able to encourage Leo to sign up for the camp.
你或許可以鼓勵里歐報名參加營隊。

■ *"No man will be able to stand before you all the days of your life."* − (*Joshua 1:5*)
「*你平生的日子、必無一人能在你面前站立得住。*」《*約書亞記 1 章 5 節*》

③ 情態助動詞 ＋ be going to

■ Someone might be going to take my place soon.
應該很快就有人頂替我的位置。

(7) 片語情態助動詞 ＋ 片語情態助動詞

■ The professor used to be able to speak Greek.
＝ The professor could speak Greek.
教授以前會講希臘文。

> 說明 表示過去完成某一特定動作時，通常用「was／were able to」，若是否定語意，則用 couldn't, wasn't／weren't able to。

■ The injured child was able to walk soon after the operation.
受傷的孩子在手術後不久便能走路。

■ The man couldn't was not able to raise his hands before the operation.
男子手術前手舉不起來。

■ Young people ought to be able to buy their own house.
年輕人應該要能買自己的房子。

■ The employees are going to have to be able to use the latest version of Java.
員工將必須能夠使用最新版本的 Java。

3. 限定動詞

受主詞人稱與數目限制，黏接屈折詞素的動詞為限定動詞，又稱述語動詞。

■ Zoe does the laundry every day.
柔依每天洗衣服。

■ Bella lived in London few years ago.
貝拉四年前住在倫敦。

■ We will make a comeback next time.
我們下次會扳回一城。

■ Leo has watched the film a couple of times.
那部影片里歐看了二三次。

3.1 限定動詞的主要用法：

3.1.1 限定動詞構成限定子句，限定子句必須包含限定動詞。

■ The suspect denied committing the crime.
這名嫌疑犯否認犯罪。

■ My grandfather was to have a checkup last week.
我祖父上週原本打算去健檢。

■ A pigeon was caught in the net, hanging upside down, and struggling to get free.
一隻鴿子被網子勾到，倒掛著掙扎逃脫。

3.1.2 限定動詞之間應以連接詞連結。

■ Tom turned on the computer and started to download games.
湯姆打開電腦，開始下載遊戲。

■ My in-law arrived at the airport earlier but forgot his passport.
　我姊夫提早抵達機場，但忘了帶護照。

3.1.3 限定動詞可搭配助動詞。

■ Don't count your chickens before they hatch.
　不要打如意算盤。

■ Candidates must arrive at the meeting hall on time.
　候選人必須準時抵達會議廳。

3.2 非限定動詞：相對於限定動詞，不受主詞人稱與數目限制，無屈折詞素，具部分時態與語態特徵的動詞為非限定動詞，包括不定詞、動名詞與分詞。非限定動詞構成非限定子句，可扮演主詞、受詞、補語或修飾語詞。例如：

■ I went to the station to pick up my date.
　我去車站接我女朋友。

說明 不定詞修飾動詞片語，表示目的。

■ Eating roast meat is not good for your health.
　吃烤肉對健康不好。

說明 動名詞當主詞。

■ Anika stayed at the dorm reading a novel.
　艾妮卡待在宿舍看小說。

說明 現在分詞表示附帶動作。

■ I have received the same call, without a message left.
　我接到相同電話，沒留下任何訊息。

■ The dolphin stranded on the beach has been released to sea.
　海豚擱淺在沙灘上已被釋放回海裡。

說明 過去分詞表示被動語態。

3.2.1 非限定動詞的否定：否定式不定詞是在 to 或省略 to 的原形動詞前加副詞 not，否定式分詞是片語前加 not，否定式動名詞是片語前加形容詞 no。

- The principal asked children not to peek at the gift.
  園長要孩子們不要偷看禮物。

- The police made people not pass through the blockade line.
  警方要求人們不得越過封鎖線。

- Not fixing dinner, they ate out at a French restaurant.
  因為沒煮晚餐，他們到一家法式餐廳吃晚餐。

- No smoking in here. = There is no smoking in here.
  這裡面禁止吸菸。

4. 不定詞

「to 原形動詞」是不定詞基本形式，to 為不定詞標記，可省略。不定詞性質非常活潑，具多種詞性與修飾功用，是最常見的非限定動詞。

4.1 不定詞形式：不定詞標記 to 可省略，也可搭配其他語詞構成名詞或副詞片語。

4.1.1 to 原形動詞

- Those students volunteered to join the military.
  這些學生自願從軍。

- They are reluctant to quit their part-time job.
  他們不願意辭去兼職工作。

4.1.2 省略 to，不定詞搭配一些語詞時，to 應省略。

(1) 助動詞後面

- Ruby didn't practice gymnastics today.
  露比今天不練體操。

- You will work the night shift tonight.
  你今晚值夜班。

- You had better make an apology to your landlord.
  你最好跟你的房東道歉。

(2) 使役動詞的受詞補語

- ■ Let me think about it.
  讓我考慮一下。

- ■ Mr. Lin made us work overtime today.
  林先生要我們今天加班。

(3) 強調事實的感官動詞受詞補語

- ■ I noticed a cat nervously hide behind the fence.
  我注意到一隻貓緊張地躲在籬笆後面。

- ■ I observed a mouse move around the trap.
  我觀察到有一隻老鼠在陷阱周圍活動。

(4) believe, declare, imagine 等知覺動詞可搭配不定詞當受詞補語，若是「to be」結構，「to be」可省略。

- ■ They believed the hostage (to be) still alive.
  他們相信人質仍然活著。

- ■ The police believed the lady to have been kidnapped.
  警方相信那名女子已遭挾持。

- ■ Many people considered the event (to be) an overall success.
  許多人認為活動十分成功。

- ■ We considered the management to have made the final decision.
  我們認為管理階層已做最後決定。

- ■ Judy has just proved herself (to be) a valuable employee.
  裘蒂已證明自己是一位有價值的員工。

- ■ The manager thought them (to be) a potential rival.
  經理認為他們是潛在對手。

- ■ The boy felt himself (to be) innocent.
  男孩覺得自己很無辜。

- ■ We found the trainee (to be) very diligent.
  我們發現那名實習生非常勤奮。

(5) 口語中 help, come, go, cannot help but, 等語詞可搭配省略 to 的不定詞。

■ Doing yoga helpsstay in shape.
做瑜珈有助於保持身材。

■ My stepmother is to come visit me tomorrow.
我乾媽明天要來看我。

■ Go check it on the Internet.
上網去查看看。

■ We could not help but accept it as an alternative.
= We could not but accept it as an alternative.
= We could not help accepting it as an alternative.
= We had no choice but to accept it as an alternative.
我們不得不接受以此作為替代方案。

說明 cannot help 搭配動名詞片語，have no choice but 搭配含 to 的不定詞片語。

(6) 數個不定詞接連共現時，第一個 to 保留，其餘皆可省略。

■ Khelia wants to quit school and (to) find a job.
凱莉想休學，然後去找工作。

■ Would you like to use credit card or (to) pay in cash?
你要刷卡或付現？

說明 表示對比或強調時，to 不可省略。
【對比】

■ *"To be, or not to be: that is the question."- William Shakespeare*
「生存還是毀滅，這是一個值得考慮的問題。」- 莎士比亞

【強調】

■ The apartment is to be sold, not to be let.
公寓要出售，不要出租。

(7) 疑問語詞 why,「why not」搭配省略 to 的不定詞，表示評論或提供意見。

■ Why hesitate to make a difference?
為什麼對與眾不同感到猶豫？

【語意】You don't need to hesitate to make a difference.

■ Why not eat out for a change?
出去外面吃飯換換口味，怎樣？

【語意】Why don't we　you eat out for a change?

(8) 主詞為 what, all 引導的強調句或「thing ＋形容詞子句」時，不定詞結構的主詞補語多省略 to。

■ What we need to do now is (to) catch up with the progress as soon as possible.
我們現在要做的就是儘快趕上進度。

■ All Leo did yesterday was (to) prepare for his presentation in the room.
里歐昨天就只是關在房間準備他的發表。

■ The last thing you need to do is (to) connect your computer to the Internet.
最後你就是要將電腦連上網路。

4.2 不定詞的否定形式：否定不定詞通常在 to 前面加 not，也可在 to 後面加 never。

4.2.1 not to ＋原形動詞

■ Miss Lin asked me not to play with an ouija board again.
林老師要我別再玩碟仙。

■ My pet dog made me not feel alone.
我養的狗讓我不感到孤單。

4.2.2 to never 原形動詞

■ I've made the decision to never act as a mediator.
我決心不再扮演和事佬的角色。

■ The bachelor has decided to never fall in love again.
那名單身漢決定不再談戀愛。

4.3 不定詞的主詞形式：不定詞構成非限定子句，底層結構存在主詞，但表層結構可能省略，或以不同形式出現。

4.3.1 表層結構主詞缺項：

(1) 不定詞主詞為句子主詞。

■ The miners planned to go on a strike again.
礦工們計畫再次進行罷工。

說明 不定詞主詞是「the miners」，但結構上缺項。

■ To save money, you have to pinch pennies.
為了存錢，你必須精打細算。

■ To avoid infection,I applied the ointment to the wound.
為避免感染，我在傷口上抹藥膏。

說明
1. 修飾全句的不定詞其主詞應與句子主詞一致。
2. 修飾全句的不定詞與句子主詞不一致時，不定詞為垂懸不定詞，不符文法的錯誤結構，例如以下錯誤句子：
【誤】To save money, it's necessary for you to pinch pennies.
【誤】To avoid infection, the nurseapplied the ointment to the wound.
3. 科學論著或公告陳述中，一般可接受指涉作說者或閱聽者的垂懸不定詞主詞。

■ To check the medicine's effects, human subject research will be conducted soon.
為檢視藥物效果，即將進行人體試驗。

【語意】：To check the medicine's effects, we will conduct human subject research soon.

■ To protect the wax statue, it is necessary to prohibit visitors from touching them.
為保護蠟像，有必要禁止遊客觸摸。

【語意】：To protect the wax statue, we need to prohibit visitors from touching them.

(2) 不定詞主詞為任意指涉。

■ It's necessary to have a command of an extra language.
多會一種語言是必要的。

■ It's important to follow traffic regulations all the time.
時時遵守交通規則很重要。

(3) 不定詞當受詞補語時，不定詞前方的句子主詞或受詞為其語意上的主詞。

■ Jack wanted to sign up for the newsletter.
傑克想要註冊索取通訊資料。

說明 句子主詞 Jack 是不定詞的主詞。

■ The receptionist wanted the man to sit in the first row.
接待人員要那名男子坐到第一排。

■ Kelly urged her cousin to accompany her to the mall.
凱莉慫恿她表妹陪她去大賣場。

說明 句子受詞 the man, her cousin 是不定詞的主詞。

4.3.2 介系詞 for/of 的受詞：for 搭配描述事件的形容詞，of 搭配描述不定詞的主詞的形容詞。

■ It's not difficult for me to solve the rubik's cube in one minute.
要我在一分鐘之內解答魔術方塊不難。

■ It's urgent for your father to have an operation.
你父親要緊急開刀。

說明 for 的受詞「your father」是不定詞主詞，urgent 修飾不定詞所述的事件。

■ It is quite important for you to be viewed as a trust worthy person.
讓其他人將你視為一位可信託的人相當重要。

說明 搭配 for 介系詞片語的不定詞通常是主動語態。

■ It's cruel of the girl to treat her cat that way.
女孩真殘忍，竟然那樣對待自己的貓咪。

■ It's so kind of you to buy me breakfast.
你真好，幫我買早餐。

★ of 的受詞「you」是不定詞的主詞，so kind 修飾不定詞的主詞 you。

★ 常搭配 of 片語的形容詞：

brave　勇敢的	polite　客氣的
considerate　體諒人的	thoughtful　思慮周到的
generous　慷慨的	rude　魯莽的
horrid　可惡的	stupid　愚昧的
mean　自私的	wrong　錯誤的

4.4 不定詞的性質與功用：不定詞的性質非常活潑，具有多種詞性，扮演句中許多成分及修飾角色。

4.4.1 名詞

(1) 主詞

■ To forgive is divine.
寬恕是神聖的。

■ To see is to believe.
= Seeing is believing.
百聞不如一見。

■ It's too bad to hear aboutso many problems.
聽到這麼多問題真是糟糕。

說明 不定詞結構的主詞常移至補語右側。

(2) 主詞補語

① 表示主詞狀況的主詞補語：appear, be, look, prove, remain, seem 等連綴動詞可搭配不定詞當補語，說明主詞的狀況。

- The problem of releasing waste water remains to be solved.
  排放廢水問題有待解決。

- The consultant doesn't seem to accept the proposal.
  諮詢顧問似乎不接受提案。

- The street performer looks to be an artist from Ireland.
  街頭藝人看起來就像一名愛爾蘭藝術家。

- The sudden news proved to be a disappointment for investors.
  突來的消息證明令投資大眾失望。

- The van appears to have been poorly maintained.
  箱型車似乎一直沒什麼保養。

- Greece was to leave the Euro Zone.
  希臘原本打算退出歐元區。

- The purpose of the policy is to increase the level of GDP.
  政策目的是提升國民生產毛額。

- An interesting thing to do is to place an egg upright on its end.
  將雞蛋直立很好玩。

② 表示主詞動作的主詞補語：bother, happen, hesitate, long, trouble 等動詞具連綴性質，搭配不定詞時，表示主詞的動作。

- Don't bother to fix dinner for me.
  別麻煩為我準備晚餐了。

- Don't trouble yourself to offer me any food.
  不要再提供我食物了。

  說明 否定式的 bother, trouble 才能搭配不定詞。

- The mountain climbers happened to run across a little waterfall.
  登山客碰巧發現一處小瀑布。

■ Please don't hesitate to contact me anytime.
隨時和我連絡，不要猶豫。

(3) 及物動詞受詞：許多及物性質的動詞搭配不定詞當受詞，句子主詞為不定詞語意上的主詞。

■ The candidate failed to pass the oral test.
那名候選人口試沒過。

■ The team has managed to solve the main portion of the problem.
團隊已將問題的主要部份解決了。

■ The man was demanded to pay off the financial loan.
男子被要求清償借款。

■ Tom has decided to expand his business into China.
湯姆決定將業務擴展到大陸。

■ They will guarantee to maintain their prices during high season.
他們保證旺季價格不變。

① 可搭配不定詞當受詞的動詞：

afford 付得起	propose 建議
agree 同意	promise 承諾
beg 懇求	refuse 拒絕
consent 答應	resolve 決定
determine 決定	scorn 不屑
endure 忍受	swear 發誓
fear 害怕	threaten 威脅
intend 打算	undertake 答應
neglect 忽略	wish 期望
pretend 假裝	want 想要

② 有受詞補語：受詞功用的不定詞伴隨受詞補語時，不定詞常移至受詞補語右側，受詞位置以填補受詞 it 填補。

■ We think it our duty to reduce air pollution.

= We think it is our duty to reduce air pollution.

我們認為減低空氣污染是我們的責任。

■ I found it difficult to get along with my colleague, Gina.

= I found it was difficult to get along with my colleague, Gina.

我發現很難和我同事吉娜相處。

■ Nobody feels it comfortable to sit on such a chair.

= Nobody feels it is comfortable to sit on such a chair.

沒有人覺得坐在那張椅子上是舒服的。

■ Tom felt it so comfortable to get relief from the burden of his credit card debt.

湯姆脫離卡債束縛讓他感到十分暢快。

(4) 介系詞受詞：不定詞可當 about, besides, but, except, than 等介系詞的受詞。

■ The manager is about to go abroad on business.

經理就要出國洽公了。

■ Mom never asked me to do anything besides clean my room.

除了打掃自己房間，媽媽從不叫我做任何事。

■ The policeman had no choice but to shoot and kill the guy.

警察只好開槍擊斃那人。

■ I couldn't do anything except do the dishes.

除了洗碗，我什麼都不會。

■ The young girl knew better than to go to India alone.

那位年輕女孩明知道不可獨自前往印度。

(5) 受詞補語：不定詞可搭配受詞當受詞補語，受詞是不定詞語意的主詞。使役與感官動詞受詞補語的不定詞常省略 to。

■ I think it to be my fault.

我想那是我的錯。

■ This book enables learners to share their own stories.
這本書能讓學習者分享自己的故事。

■ My parents never allow me to stay out late.
我父母從不准我在外晚歸。

■ We convinced Wang, Chen-ming to remain in the MLB.
我們相信王建民會留在美國大聯盟。

■ Chemotherapy can cause cancer cells to become difficult to destroy.
化療可能導致癌細胞變得難以破壞。

★搭配不定詞當受詞補語的動詞：

advise　建議	remind　提醒
ask　要求	request　要求
command　命令	forbid　禁止
compel　迫使	force　強迫
encourage　鼓勵	persuade　說服
expect　期待	prefer　寧願
induce　誘使	recommend　建議
instruct　指示	tempt　誘使
leave　任憑	urge　催促
permit　允許	warn　警告

⑹ 同位語：不定詞可當一些名詞的同位語，提供與名詞相關的訊息。

■ Michael refused the invitation to play in India.
麥克拒絕在印度演出的邀請。

■ Voters approved the proposal to build a new theater.
選民贊成新建劇場的提案。

■ The government has made a decision to explode the building.
政府決定炸毀建築物。

★ 常搭配不定詞當同位語的名詞：

suggest　提議	idea　主意
determination　堅定	insistence　堅持
decision　決定	plan　計畫

4.4.2 形容詞：形容詞性質的不定詞後位修飾名詞，名詞為不定詞的受詞時，受詞省略，不定詞搭配主動語態。

■ There's no time to waste.

　沒有時間可浪費了。

■ There's plenty to choose from here.

　這裡有很多選擇。

■ Leo is looking for a suite to rent.

　里歐正在找尋出租套房。

■ They really need some water to drink.

　他們實在需要一些水喝。

■ I need a pen to write with.

　我需要一支筆寫字。

【比較】I need a pen to sign my name.

　　　 我需要一支筆簽名。

說明 不定詞的受詞和所修飾的名詞不一致時，不可省略。

4.4.3 副詞

(1) 修飾動詞：不定詞修飾動詞時，通常表示目的、結果、原因、條件。句子的主詞或受詞通常是不定詞語意上的主詞。另外，不定詞的語態與動作實際情況一致。

① 表示目的，不定詞可移至句首，to = in order to = so as to。

■ *I come to bury Caesar, not to praise him.*

　Julius Caesar by William Shakespeare: Act 3. Scene II

　我來是要埋葬凱薩，不是要稱頌他。《凱撒大帝：第三章第二幕》
　- 莎士比亞

■ The official declined the invitation to avoid arousing suspicion.

為了避嫌，官員婉拒邀請。

■ The guy came to confess his crime.

那人來投案。

■ The dog was sent to the animal hospital to be examined.

小狗被帶到動物醫院體檢。

■ Bill came to my office only to say good-bye to me.

比爾來我辦公室只為向我告別。

■ To increase the sales volume, they lowered the price.

= They lowered the price to increase the sales volume.

為了增加銷售量，他們降低價格。

■ In order to find the evidence, the police searched around the building.

為了找到證據，警方搜遍整個建築物。

② 表示結果

■ The team must practice a lot to win championship.

球隊一定苦練多時才會拿下冠軍。

■ Leo must have done much for the company to get promoted so soon.

里歐對公司一定多有貢獻才會這麼快就晉升。

說明 不定詞搭配 only，可表示未料到的結果，置於動詞組後面，說明較晚發生的動作令人意外。

■ I rushed to the train station, only to find the train had left.

= I rushed to the train station, and only found the train had left.

我趕到火車站，不料發現火車已開走了。

③ 表示原因

■ We rejoiced to see peace return to the tribe.

我們非常高興部落又回復和平。

④ 表示條件

■ To reach your sales goal, you can receive your base salary.
你要達到銷售目標才能領到基本底薪。

【比較】 To reach your sales goal, you will have to continue to work hard every day.
為了達到銷售目標，你必須繼續每天努力工作。

■ To take various sales strategies, you can reach—and surpass your sales goal.
運用各種銷售策略你才能達到，並且超越你的銷售目標。

(2) 修飾形容詞

① 不定詞受詞不是句子主詞或受詞時，不定詞受詞應保留。

〔原因/情緒〕

■ I'm glad to see you.
很高興見到你。

■ I'm sorry to hear that.
很遺憾聽到那事。

〔可能〕

■ Tina is likely to give up her plan.
緹娜可能會放棄她的計畫。

〔能力〕

■ The assistant is able to speak German.
助理會說德語。

② 不定詞受詞是句子主詞或受詞時，不定詞受詞省略，以主動語態代替被動語意。

■ Such an excellent salesperson is difficult to find.
如此優秀的業務員不好找。

■ The national park is worthy to visit during winter season.
冬季時，國家公園值得一遊。

■ They found the case not easy to deal with.
他們發現案子不易處理。

■ There are many questions impossible to answer with simple yes's or no's.
許多問題不可能以簡單的是或不是就能回答。

■ In this area, tap water is not fit to drink to be drunk.
這地區的自來水不宜生飲。

> 說明 修飾形容詞 fit 的不定詞可以主動或被動表示與句子主詞的語態關係。

★ 常搭配不定詞的形容詞：

ashamed　難為情的	glad　高興地
certain　確定	interesting　有趣的
determined　有決心的	ready　願意
hesitant　猶豫的	sure　確定
necessary　需要的	willing　情願的

(1) 修飾副詞

■ The hound can run fast enough to catch a speeding cyclist.
那隻獵犬跑得夠快，追得上一部狂飆的單車。

■ The interpreter spoke too fast to follow.
口譯員講太快，跟不上。

【語意】The interpreter spoke so fast that I couldn't follow him.

> 說明
> 1. 不定詞修飾副詞 enough/too，表示結果。
> 2. too 搭配 ready, likely, eager, willing 等形容詞時，「too」意同「very」，不定詞沒有否定意。

■ Fred is too ready to accept the job.
弗雷德很樂意接受這工作。

■ The trainee is too willing to take advice.
實習生很樂意接受建議。

3. too 前面搭配 all, but, only 等副詞時，不定詞片語也沒有否定意。

■ We're all／only／only too pleased to help out.

= We're very pleased to help out.

我們很高興能夠幫忙。

■ Hank can jump high enough to reach the roof of the cellar.

漢克跳得夠高，摸得到地窖屋頂。

★不定詞修飾副詞 enough，表示肯定結果。

(4) 修飾句子：修飾全句的不定詞為獨立不定詞，表達做說者對句子所
述的想法或評論。

■ To be honest, I don't accept his apology at all.

坦白說，我完全不接受他的道歉。

■ The March band's performance, to be brief, was excellent.

簡單來說，樂隊的演出真是太棒了。

■ The gymnastics contestant was really second to none, to be
fair.

平心而論，體操選手個個都是箇中好手。

■ Needless to say　add, smartphones have become a necessity.

不用多說，智慧型手機已成為一種必需品。

■ To top it off, my cellphone was out of power.

更糟的是，我的手機沒電。

★ 常見的獨立不定詞：

to be frank　坦白說 = to be frank with you = frankly speaking	to put it differently　換言之 = to put it simply
	to sum up　總而言之
to be exact　精確地說	to begin with　首先
to tell the truth　老實說	glad to say　說來很高興
to be sure　的確	not to mention　更不用說
to make matters worse 更糟的是	to do ＋人＋ justice 為…說句公道話

163

4.5 不定詞的語態：不定詞有主動與被動語態，主動語態不定詞有簡單式、進行式、完成式、完成進行式等，被動語態不定詞只有簡單式與完成式。

時態	主動語態	被動語態
簡單式	to ＋原形動詞	to be ＋過去分詞
進行式	to be ＋現在分詞	✕
完成式	to have ＋過去分詞	to have ＋過去分詞
完成進行式	to have been ＋現在分詞	✕

4.5.1 主動語態

(1) 簡單式：不定詞所示動作與主動詞同時發生，或尚未發生。

① 與主動詞同時發生

■ I'm sorry to bother you.
抱歉打擾你了。

■ I'm glad to see you again.
很高興再次見到你。

② 搭配意願或計畫語意的動詞時，不定詞表示尚未發生。

■ The victim chose to forgive the motorcyclist.
被害人選擇原諒機車騎士。

■ I decided to stay at the hostel for a while.
我決定在民宿待一陣子。

■ I am hoping to get a raise in the near future.
我希望很快就能加薪。

■ My nephew wishes to raise a dog of his own.
我姪子希望養一條自己的狗。

■ Judy promised to forward the email below.
茱蒂答應轉寄下列電子郵件。

■ The woman expected to lose some weight with this surgery.
婦人期待外科手術能讓她減輕一些重量。

(2) 進行式：強調不定詞所示動作與主動詞同時發生，或即將發生。

① 強調與主動詞同時發生

- When the director came, Leo pretended to be checking email.
  主管過來時，里歐假裝在看電子郵件。

- I am pleased to be working with my partner.
  我很高興能與我的夥伴共事。

② 即將發生

- The dog appears to be going crazy.
  那隻狗看起來快要抓狂。

- The suspension bridge seems to be falling down.
  吊橋似乎就要掉下去了。

(3) 完成式：表示不定詞所示動作較早發生的事實或想法。

① 較早發生的事實

- I'm sorry to have kept you waiting for a while.
  很抱歉讓你等了一會兒。

- I deeply regret not to have seen Mr. Lin again.
  對於未能再見到林先生一面，我深感遺憾。

② 較早發生的想法

- The girl seems to have been sick.
  這名女孩似乎生過病。

- Judy desired to have won the match.
  茱蒂希望贏得比賽。

- I hoped to have seen the author at the book fair.
  我原本希望能在書展見到作者。

- Oh, how I wished to have visited theBritish Museum.
  我好希望能夠造訪大英博物館。

■ They planned to have completed the task in two weeks.
他們原本計畫二週內完成工作。

> 說明 意願或計畫語意的動詞搭配完成式不定詞時，僅表示想法，不
> 確定是否完成。

(1) 完成進行式：表示不定詞所示動作持續至主動詞發生時或仍要繼續
進行。主動詞為 wish 時，則表示過去事實相反的假設。

① 持續至主動詞發生時或仍要繼續進行

■ Hank seems still to have been thinking over the proposal.
漢克好像還在考慮提案。

■ My boss admits to have been worrying about money.
我老闆承認他一直很擔心資金。

■ When Leo made his career choice many years ago, he could
not have hoped to have been doing anything better than that.
里歐多年前選擇職業時，從不曾盼望能有比那更好的差事。

② 過去事實相反：通常搭配主動詞 wish。

■ The long hours of work were unbearable since Jane quit a year
ago. Fred wished to have been working with her.
自從珍一年前辭職後，長時間工作下來真令人難以忍受。弗雷德一
直希望能與她一起工作。

4.5.2 被動語態

(1) 簡單式

〔受詞〕

■ My director likes to be flattered.
我的主管喜歡有人拍馬屁。

〔不定詞當受詞補語〕

■ The manager wanted the file to be forwarded to the client soon.
經理要求馬上傳檔案給客戶。

■ The members agreed for the proposal to be discussed at the next meeting.

會員同意下次會議討論該提案。

〔不定詞當名詞修飾語〕

■ The product launch to be held next week is very important.

下週要舉行的產品發表會非常重要。

(2) 完成式：表示不定詞所示動作較早發生

■ The engineer hoped to have been transferred overseas.

工程師原本希望外派到海外。

■ The British terrorist is believed to have been killed in Somalia.

一般相信該名英籍觀光客已在索馬尼亞遇害。

(3) 一些語詞或語境中，主動語態不定詞表示被動語意。

① 功用為修飾名詞，執行者為句子主詞或受事者為所修飾的名詞時，不定詞搭配主動語態。

■ Bill has a lot of homework to do.

比爾有很多功課要做。

說明 不定詞的主詞是句子主詞「Bill」，受詞是所修飾的名詞「homework」，省略。

■ The clerk offered me a magazine to read.

職員提供一本雜誌讓我翻閱。

說明 不定詞修飾主動詞的直接受詞「a magazine」，「a magazine」是不定詞的受詞，省略。

■ It was really a difficult task to work on.

那真是一件難以執行的工作。

說明 不定詞修飾名詞片語「a difficult task」，「a difficult task」是不定詞的受詞，省略。

② 主詞補語功用的 blame, find, let, seek 等不定詞。

- The naughty boy is to blame.
  調皮男孩該受責備。

- Plumbers are not hard to find.
  水電工不難找。

- Sometimes the fact is difficult to seek.
  有時候真相難以找尋。

- The apartment is to let.
  公寓要出租。

說明 強調被動的動作時，不定詞仍應搭配被動語態。

- The scooter is to be sold, not to be let.
  機車是要出售，而不是要出租。

- The villa is to be let for a minimum term of six months.
  別墅租約一期至少六個月。

- The man is to be blamed and punished for what he did
  男子對自己的所做所為遭受譴責與懲罰。

4.6 不定詞的特殊結構

4.6.1 搭配疑問語詞（why 除外），不定詞構成名詞片語，名詞性質。疑問語詞為不定詞片語的移出受詞或副詞，詞性與語意應與底層結構一致。

(1) 主詞：

- Which to choose depends on many factors.
  選擇哪一個要視許多因素而定。

- Where to go is an important part of planning a trip.
  要去哪裡是規劃旅行的重要部分。

(2) 主詞補語

- *"The problem is how to remain an artist once he grows up". – Pablo Picasso*
  「問題是如何讓一名藝術家長大後還是藝術家。」- 畢卡索

(3) 受詞：

〔及物動詞受詞〕

■ Knowing what to do in case of fire is quite important.

= Knowing what we should do in case of fire is quite important.

知道發生火災的應變措施相當重要。

〔授與動詞受詞〕

■ Could anyone tell me where to park my car?

= Could anyone tell me where I can park my car?

有人可以告訴我該在哪裡停車嗎？

〔介系詞受詞〕

■ Linda can make an intelligent decision about whether to get married or not.

= Linda can make an intelligent decision about whether she should get married or not.

琳達對於是否結婚的做出智慧決定。

(4) 口語中，「疑問語詞＋不定詞」結構可獨立存在，可視為疑問句的縮減。

■ Where to go?

= Where are we to go?

= Where shall we go?

我們要去哪裡？

■ How to say the word in Chinese?

= How do you say the word in Chinese?

這字中文怎麼說？

4.6.2 搭配複合連接詞 as if，為 as if 子句的縮減。

■ The guest cleared her throat as if to say something.

= The guest cleared her throat as if she wanted to say something.

來賓清了一下喉嚨，好像想說些什麼似的。

■ My director nodded his head simply as if to agree with me.
= My director nodded his head simply as if he agreed with me.
我主管點點頭，好像是表示同意。

4.6.3 分離不定詞：to 與原形動詞之間插入副詞、相關連接詞或插入語，
　　　　to 與原形動詞形成遠距關係，這種結構的不定詞為分
　　　　離不定詞。

(1) to ＋副詞組＋原形動詞：

■ You need to really understand the importance of friendship.
你需要真正了解友誼的重要。

■ You don't have to long wait for the final result.
最後結果你不必等候太久。

■ It's essential to completely realize the peaceful use of nuclear energy.
It's essential to realize the peaceful use of nuclear energy
（底層結構）
completely.
徹底了解核能的和平用途非常重要。

說明 修飾動詞的副詞組移至原形動詞前面，強調副詞組。

(2) to ＋相關連接詞＋原形動詞：

■ Many species managed to both survive and grow in extreme climates.
許多物種在極端氣候下不僅存活下來，還能成長。

■ My mom wanted me not to either use the cellphone or surf the Internet.
我母親不要我不是在玩手機就是上網。

■ To neither quit nor get fired, the apprentice is making all the effort.
不想放棄也不想遭解雇，學徒盡了全力。

(3) to ＋插入語＋原形動詞：

■ Farmers attempted to, if necessary, trap rock monkeys that frequented their house.
如果有必要，農民需誘捕時常侵入他們家的獼猴。

4.6.4 不定詞獨立結構：不定詞主詞與句子主詞不一致時，不定詞為獨立結構，副詞性質，說明主要子句的附加狀況。不定詞獨立結構也可搭配介系詞 with／without，表示主要子句的原因或條件。

(1) 不定詞獨立結構

① 說明附加狀況

■ Many people are in the park, some to play chess, and some to folk dance.

= Many people are in the park. Some are playing chess, and some are folk dancing.

許多人在公園裡，有些人下棋，有些人跳土風舞。

■ We'll just make an oral agreement now, the contract to be signed as quickly as possible.

= We'll just make an oral agreement now, and the contract will be signed as quickly as possible.

我們先達成口頭協定，合約會儘快簽訂。

② 感嘆句：不定詞獨立結構可當感嘆句。

(a)「To think that ＋子句！」，表示對過去事件或狀況的負面情緒。

■ To think that I used to have an affair for a year!
我不願回想我曾經有一年的婚外情！

■ To think that my boss could be so shameful!
真沒想到我的老闆這麼無恥！

■ To think that the student should die a sudden death!
真沒想到那名學生竟會突然死亡！

(b)句子的述語動詞縮減為不定詞，to 可省略。

■ What! My ex-girlfriend calling me!

=What! My ex-girlfriend to call me!

什麼！我前女友打電話給我！

What! My ex-girlfriend called me!
（底層結構）

■ Absolute power to make people corrupt absolutely!

絕對的權力使人絕對的腐化！

Absolute power makes people corrupt absolutely!
（底層結構）

(c) 句子述語動詞縮減為不定詞，主詞省略，但可從引導的呼格或語境中得知。

■ Oh, to stuff a cat into a small jar!

噢，竟然將貓塞進一個小罐子！

■ You fool, to forget to fill up your car!

你這傻瓜，竟然忘記幫車子加滿油！

(d) Oh 引導的不定詞結構感嘆句表示假設的願望，主詞為第一人稱。

■ Oh to win the lottery!

唉，若能中頭彩該多好！

【語意】 I wish I won the lottery.

■ Oh to be a college student again!

= I wish I were a college student again.

唉，若能重回大學時代那該多好！

(2) with／without 不定詞獨立結構

① 原因

■ My computer is shutting down, with the antivirus software beingoverdue.

= My computer is shutting down because the antivirus software being overdue.

因為防毒軟體過期，我的電腦當機了。

■ Without money to buy a car, Dave rides a motorcycle every day.

= Because Dave doesn't have money to buy a car, he rides a motorcycle every day.

因為沒錢買汽車，戴夫每天騎機車。

② 條件

■ Without Mr. Lin to help out, you would have gotten into trouble.

= If Mr. Lin had not helped out, you would have gotten into trouble.

若非林先生相助，你會惹上麻煩。

■ With someone to call the police, the man would not have died.

= If someone had called the police, the man would not have died.

假如有人報警，男人也不會喪命。

③ 關係代名詞＋不定詞：形容詞子句主詞明確時，結構可縮減為「關係代名詞＋不定詞」，將限定動詞降為非限定動詞。

■ It is not the tool which to be used for that.

它不是那麼用的工具。

It is not the tool which is used for that.
（形容詞子句）

■ I finally found the one with whom to share my life.

我終於找到與我分享生活的人。

I finally found the one with whom can sharemy life.
（形容詞子句）

■ Cambridge is a great place in which to study.

劍橋是個讓人讀書的好地方。

Cambridge is a great place in which people study.
（形容詞子句）

5. 動名詞

兼具名詞與動詞特徵的非限定動詞，名詞性質方面，動名詞具有複數形，可搭配一些限定詞，還可搭配 of 片語，形成句子概念的片語；動詞性質方面，動名詞具有時態、語態形式，也有必要成分的共現限制。

5.1 動名詞的形式：

5.1.1 限定詞＋ V-ing：動名詞為名詞性質，動名詞可搭配限定詞或複數形式。

(1) 零限定詞＋ V-ing

- Seeing is believing. 　　眼見為憑。
- Teaching is learning. 　　教學相長。

(2) 限定詞＋ V-ing

- the rising of prices 　　　　　　　　　價格上漲
- the releasing of the film 　　　　　　發行影片
- a building in the re-planning district 　重畫區中的一棟建築物
- a painting in a gallery 　　　　　　　美術館裡的一幅畫
- I'm sorry for my being late.
  很抱歉我遲到了。

- That may affect my winning the game.
  那會影響到我贏得比賽。

- Mrs. Lin went downtown to do some shopping.
  林太太到市中心買些東西。

- Fred completed three reports in one sitting.
  弗雷德一口氣完成三份報告。

- There is no eating or drinking in classrooms.
  = It's not allowed to eat or drink in classrooms.
  = No eating or drinking in classrooms.
  教室內不准吃東西或喝飲料。

- There is no swimming across the huge lake.
  = It is impossible　forbidden to swim across the huge lake.
  游泳橫渡大湖是不可能的。

  說明 「There is no ＋動名詞」表示禁止或不可能。

(3) 一些動名詞以複數形式呈現

- The findings will be posted online.
  調查結果會公布在網路。

- The maid throws the sweepings away every day.
  女僕每天都會丟垃圾。

■ Don't leave your personal belongings on the bus.
不要將個人物品留在巴士。

■ The woman is applying for a savings account.
女子在申請儲蓄帳戶。

■ The man supported the family on his little earnings.
男子依靠微薄收入養家。

■ With his unbearable failings, Bella broke up with her boyfriend.
由於難以忍受的缺點，貝拉和男朋友分手了。

5.1.2 「the／所有詞動名詞 of 名詞」：動名詞可搭配「of ＋介系詞片語」，說明動名詞的主詞或受詞，形成句子概念的動名詞片語。

(1) 動名詞＋主詞

■ the spreading of flu
= Flu spreads.
流感散佈

■ the calling of the saints
= The saints called.
聖徒的呼聲

(2) 動名詞與受詞

■ the using of the instrument
= The instrument is used.
使用儀器

■ the killing of ten Israeli soldiers
= Ten Israeli soldiers were killed.
十名以色列士兵被殺。

■ the many readings of the manuscript
= reading the manuscript many times
= The manuscript has been read many times.
多次閱讀手稿

■ Chinese workers' building of the transcontinental railroad.
= Chinese workers built the transcontinental railroad.
中國工人建造洲際鐵路

5.2 動名詞的否定式：動名詞的否定式通常搭配 no, not, never 等否定詞。

■ There's no parking on campus.
校園禁止停車。

■ Did you mind my not coming to the meetup yesterday?
你介意我昨天聚餐沒來嗎？

■ The old man regretted having never returned his hometown.
老先生懊悔從未回去家鄉。

5.3 動名詞的主詞：動名詞為句子概念的片語，包含主詞與動詞部分，結構上，動名詞主詞常省略，但不難從語意上判斷主詞的指涉對象。

5.3.1 表層結構未省略主詞：動名詞的所有詞通常就是其動作執行者，也就是主詞。

■ I'm sorry for my interrupting you.
很抱歉打擾你。

■ Mrs. Lin was worried about her husband's losing his job.
林太太擔心她先生失業。

■ May the blessing of God be upon you.
願神的祝福降臨於你。

說明 excuse, forgive, mind, pardon 等動詞常搭配主詞共現的動名詞。

■ Please forgive my neglecting you.
我怠慢你了，請原諒。

■ Pardon my talking back.
原諒我頂嘴。

5.3.2 表層結構省略主詞：動名詞未搭配所有詞時，主詞應依語意而判定。

■ Smoking is strictly prohibited in a public place.
公共場所嚴禁吸菸。

Smoking ＝ everyone smoking　　　　泛指一般人

■ Reading is important for a variety of reasons.
因著各種原因，閱讀很重要。

Reading ＝ everyone reading　　　　泛指一般人

■ Laboring too much is not good for our health.
過勞對我們的健康有害。

Laboring ＝ you or me laboring　　　說話者與聽話者

■ There is no dissuading my boss when he gets an idea.
我老闆打定主意後要勸阻是不可能的。

5.4 動名詞的功用：

5.4.1 主詞：

(1) 動名詞置於主詞位置

■ Cooking is interesting.
烹飪很有趣。

■ Talking mends no holes.
空談無益。

■ Smoking is bad for health.
吸菸有害健康。

■ Running through the red light is dangerous.
闖紅燈很危險。

(2) 動名詞移位

① 虛主詞 it 填補主詞位置：動名詞結構龐大時，常移至補語右側，主詞位置以虛主詞 it 填補。

■ It was pleasant and comfortable staying in this hostel.
待在這家民宿令人愉快舒適。

■ It's no use crying over spilt milk.

= It's no use to cry over spilt milk.

覆水難收。

說明 口語中，動名詞可代換為不定詞。

② 引介字 there 填補主詞位置

■ There's no knowing what will happen next.

不知道再來會怎樣。

5.4.2 受詞

(1) 主動語意的及物動詞受詞：動名詞主詞通常是前面的指涉對象或或
句子主詞

■ Would you mind my me using the computer here?

你介意我在這裡使用電腦嗎？

■ My grandfather practices doing Tai Chi every day.

我祖父每天練太極拳。

■ When I eat sashimi, I cannot help throwing up.

我吃生魚片時，我會忍不住吐出來。

■ They decided to put off holding a public hearing until a later
date.

他們決定延後舉行公聽會。

■ The child is feeling like eating something else.

孩子正想吃點別的。

■ They left off arguing the matter with each other.

他們不為那件事爭吵了。

★可只搭配動名詞當受詞的動詞：

admit　承認	involve　包括
advise　建議	mention　提及
anticipate　期待	miss　錯過

avoid　避免	postpone　put off　延期
delay　延遲	recall　回想
deny　否認	repent　後悔
enjoy　喜愛	resist　忍住
escape　逃離	risk　冒險
finish　完成	suggest　建議
keep　繼續	tolerate　容忍
imagine　設想	quit　give up　放棄
include　包括	understand　理解

★一些搭配動名詞當受詞的片語動詞：

burst out　突然發出	give up　quit　放棄
cannot stand　受不了	have done　結束
come near　幾乎	insist on　堅持

(2) 被動語意的受詞：deserve, need, require, want 及否定式的 bear 搭配主
　　動式動名詞受詞表示被動語意。

■ You really deserve scolding.

　　= You really deserve to be scolded.

　　你真該罵。

■ The vending machine required repairing.

　　= The vending machine required to be repaired.

　　販賣機需要修理。

■ The Galaxy Gear needs recharging every day.

　　= The Galaxy Gear needs to be recharged every day.

　　三星的 Galaxy Gear 需要每天充電。

■ The carpet wants cleaning.

= The carpet wants to be cleaned.

地毯需要清潔。

■ I cannot bear laughing anymore.

我再也受不了被嘲笑。

說明 形容詞 worth 搭配主動式動名詞，表示被動語態，可代換為 worthy 搭配被動式不定詞或動名詞。

■ The film is worth watching.

= The film is worthy to be watched.

= The film is worthy being watched.

這部影片值得一看。

(3) 可搭配不定詞與動名詞當受詞，但語意不同。

① forget, regret, remember, stop 等動詞搭配不定詞表示即將要做的事，搭配動名詞表示做過的事。

■ I forgot to attach the sound file to previous message.

上一封訊息我忘記附加聲音檔進去。

■ I forgot attaching the sound file to previous message.

我忘記上一封訊息有附加聲音檔了。

■ I regret to say that you did not gain admission to Beijing University.

很遺憾通知你，你未能錄取北京大學。

■ I regretted dropping out of high school.

我很後悔高中沒讀完。

■ Please remember to recharge your card.

記得要儲值你的卡片。

■ I remember recharging my card with NT400.

我記得我有儲值 400 元。

■ I stopped to kick back and rest for a while.

我停下來休息放鬆一下。

■ It has stopped raining.
雨停了。

② mean 搭配不定詞表示打算、有意，搭配動名詞表示意味著。

■ I didn't mean to lie to you.
我不是有意欺騙你。

■ What do you mean to deal with the case?
你打算怎麼處理這案子？

■ Rising inflation means decreasing purchasing power.
通膨上升意味著購買力下降。

③ try 搭配不定詞表示設法、盡力，搭配動名詞表示試驗。

■ They are trying to get through the situation.
他們一直設法度過難關。

■ Have you tried changing your diet to clear your skin?
你試過改變飲食來使皮膚潔淨嗎？

④ go on 搭配不定詞表示完成某事之後繼續進行另一件事，搭配動名詞表示持續進行一件事。

■ After two meetings in a row, John will go on to attend another one.
連續二場會議之後，約翰還要繼續參加另一場會議。

■ In spite of rain, workers went on paving asphalt.
儘管下雨，工人持續鋪柏油。

⑤ dread 搭配不定詞表示特指的行為，搭配動名詞表示一般的行為。

■ My son dreads to see the dentist next week.
我兒子下星期要去看牙醫，他嚇呆了。

■ My son dreads going to the dentist.
我兒子害怕去看牙醫。

■ Many senior employees dread being laid off.
許多資深員工怕被解雇。

(4) 動名詞移至受詞補語右側，受詞位置以填補受詞 it 填補。

■ I find it troublesome using the new version of Windows.
我發現使用新版 Windows 很麻煩。

■ Hank considered it necessary rebooting his computer system.
漢克認為他的電腦有必要重灌。

5.4.3 介系詞受詞

(1) 主動語意

■ Amy insisted on going into another shoe store.
艾咪堅持要到另一家鞋店。

■ The old man is pretty good at doing calligraphy.
老先生書法寫得很好。

■ I prefer taking the MRT to driving my own car.
我寧願搭捷運也不要自己開車。

■ What's the purpose of me signing my name here?
我在這裡簽名的目的是什麼？

說明 介系詞受詞的動名詞可搭配人稱代名詞受格當主詞。

■ I am looking forward to seeing you again.
期待再次與你會面。

■ The engineer is getting used to living in the countryside.
工程師漸漸習慣住在鄉下。

■ When it comes to performing hip-hop, no one can hold a candle to John.
一提到街舞，無人能與約翰一較高下。

■ Despite there being a typhoon, the competition will still be held as scheduled.
即使有颱風，比賽仍將按賽程進行。

★存在句「there be」具有動名詞形式，可當介系詞受詞

★介系詞 to 結尾的語詞應搭配動名詞，例如：

片語介系詞	片語動詞
as to　至於	amount to　等於
close to　接近於	descent to　墮落到
in addition to　除 ... 以外	get to　即將進行
according to　依據	object to　反對
in reply to　回覆	pay attention to　注意
owing to　due to　由於	see to　負責
with a view to　為了	take to　開始
with regard to　關於	come near to　幾乎
with reference to　關於	feel equal to　勝任
with an effect to 造成 .. 效果	testify to　證明

(2) 被動語意：否定式的 beyond, pass 搭配主動語態動名詞表示被動語意。

■ It is really beyond comparing with anything else.
它實在無法與任何其他事物相比。

■ The machine has been past using.
機器已無法使用。

5.4.4 省略介系詞的動名詞受詞：

(1)「have difficulty／fun／trouble／a good time／a bad time in ＋動名詞」結構中，「in」通常省略。

■ The boy has difficulty writing his own name.
男孩寫自己名字有困難。

■ My family had great times spending holidays together abroad.
我和家人一起出國度假，我們玩得很開心。

■ They had a lot of fun playing bridge together.
他們一起打橋牌，玩得很開心。

【比較】It's fun to play bridge with my friends.
和我朋友打橋牌很好玩。

(2) spend 搭配介系詞片語時，介系詞受詞若是動名詞，介系詞可省略。

■ I spent some time (on) working on the ranch today.
我今天花了一些時間在農場工作。

■ The tourist spent a lot of money buying gold and other goodies in Hong Kong.
觀光客在香港花大把鈔票買黃金及其他精品。

(3) 表示戶外活動的「go on ＋動名詞片語」中，on 通常省略。

go shopping　去購物	go picnicking　去野餐
go swimming　去游泳	go hiking　去健行
go mountain climbing　去爬山	go roller-skating　去溜冰

說明 「go on a vacation／go on a picnic」片語中的 on 不可省略。

5.4.5 主詞補語

■ One of my hobbies is collecting antiques.
我的其中一項嗜好是收集古董。

■ The old man's job is catch elves at nighttime.
老先生的工作是夜裡抓鰻苗。

5.4.6 受詞補語

■ We call this lobbying illegally.
我們稱這為關說。

■ Some people call it mind mapping.
一些人稱它為心智圖。

5.4.7 形容詞補語

■ Kelly has been busy designing her own website.
凱莉一直忙著設計自己的網站。

> 說明 「busy with ＋名詞/動名詞」結構中，搭配動名詞時，with 可
> 省略。

5.4.8 名詞同位語

■ The project, building another website, is urgent.
架設另一網站的工作很急迫。

■ Your goal, selling 100 cars within ten days, is unreachable.
你無法達到十天內賣一百部汽車的目標。

■ This is my grandmother's recreation, watching soap operas.
這是我祖母的娛樂─看連續劇。

5.4.9 形成複合名詞：動名詞可與名詞共同形成複合名詞。

(1) 動名詞表示名詞的功用：動名詞表示名詞功用時，動名詞置於名詞
左側，詞重音落在動名詞。

■ camping area
= area for camping　露營區

■ compensating expense
= expense for compensation　賠償金

■ hunting bow
= bow for hunting　打獵弓

■ operating table
= table for operating　手術台

■ recharging station
= station for recharging　充電站

■ drinking water
= water for drinking　飲用水

■ spending money
= money for spending　零用錢

■ vending machine

　= machine for vending　販賣機

(2) 名詞表示動名詞的受事者：名詞表示動名詞的受事者時，動名詞置
　　於名詞右側，詞重音落在動名詞。

■ back-packing

　= going with a pack on the back　自助旅行

■ brainstorming

　= storm the brainwith ideas　腦力激盪

■ fact-finding

　= finding the facts　徵信

■ fault-finding

　= finding faults　挑剔

■ peace-making

　= making peace　調解

■ sightseeing

　= seeing the sights　觀光

■ stamp-collecting

　= collecting stamps　集郵

■ story-telling

　= telling stories　說故事

(3) 名詞修飾動名詞：名詞為副詞功用，說明動名詞的時間、地方、方
　　式等訊息。

① 時間

■ day-dreaming

　= dreaming in the day　白日夢

■ night-watching

　= watching in the night　夜間巡視

② 地方

■ church-going

= going to church　去教堂

■ water-skiing

= skiing in the water　滑水

■ street fighting

= fighting in the street　街頭鬥毆

■ sun-bathing

= bathing in the sun　日光浴

③ 方式

■ figure skating

= skating with figures　花式溜冰

■ handwriting

= writing by hand　手寫

■ mercury poisoning

= poisoned with mercury　鉛中毒

■ formation flying

= flying in formation　編隊飛行

★一些片語動詞常形成動名詞結構，介副詞可能移至動詞左側。

cutting-down　縮減	out-loading　卸除
filling-in　填入	speeding-up　加速
heating-up　加熱	taking-off　起飛
making-up　製作	undertaking　任務

5.5 動名詞的時態與語態：動名詞有主動與被動語態，各有簡單式與完成式。

時態	主動語態	被動語態
簡單式	V-ing	being 過去分詞
完成式	having 過去分詞	having been 過去分詞

5.5.1 主動語態簡單式：

(1) 動名詞與主要動詞同時發生

■ Please stop making so much noise.
請停止製造這麼多的噪音。

■ My cousin enjoys playingthe Ukulele.
我表妹喜愛彈奏烏克麗麗。

■ My parents like playing mahjong in their free time.
我父母喜歡在空閒時打麻將。

■ They can participate in the event without beinga member.
他們不是會員也能參加活動。

(2) 動名詞與主要動詞非同時發生

① 動名詞較早發生

■ The student admitted falsifying test scores.
該名學生承認竄改測驗成績。

■ Bella remembered forwarding the attachment to the client.
貝拉記得她已將附件傳給客戶。

② 動名詞較晚發生

■ How about meetingat DNA Cafeteria for lunch?
在 DNA 餐廳見面吃中餐好嗎？

■ Excuse me for not going to the entrance with you.
抱歉，我就不送你們到出口。

■ Linda proposed going on a vacation to California this summer.
琳達提議今年夏天到加州度假。

5.5.2 主動語態完成式：強調動名詞較早發生。

(1) 以完成式表示較早發生

■ Mr. Lin has denied having had an affair with his assistant.
林先生否認與助理外遇。

■ Peter mentioned having had an operation on his leg two years ago.
彼得提到他的腿二年前開過刀。

■ You are allowed to participate in the activity without having signed up in advance.
如果沒有事先報名，你就不能參加活動。

(2) 簡單式與完成式都可表示較早發生：有些動詞述及動態動名詞時，簡單式與完成式都可表示較早發生。

■ My roommate admitted stealing ／ having stolen my identity.
我的室友承認盜用我的帳號。

■ I remembered meeting ／ having met that man a couple of times.
我記得見過那男子一二次。

■ I have deeply regretted lending ／ having lent money to Charles.
我很後悔借錢給查爾斯。

■ The terrorist organization acknowledged hijacking ／ having hijacked the plane.
恐怖組織承認挾持飛機。

■ I seem to recall sending ／ having sent a complaint in about one week ago.
我似乎想起大約一週前投訴過。

說明 動名詞為靜態動詞時，不以完成式表示較早發生。
■ No one admitted having dual nationalities.
沒有人承認有雙重國籍。

5.5.3 被動語態簡單式：句子主詞是動名詞所示動詞的受詞時，動名詞搭配被動語態簡單式。

(1) 動名詞與主要動詞同時發生

- The pedestrian narrowly escaped being hit by the bicycle.
  那名行人差一點就被單車撞到。

- Residents managed to prevent the pond from being polluted.
  居民設法讓池塘不受汙染。

(2) 動名詞較主動詞早發生

- The man got into the control area without being permitted.
  男子未經許可擅闖管制區。

- I almost forgot being asked to turn off my cellphone during visit.
  我幾乎忘了有人要我參觀中關掉手機。

(3) 動名詞與主動詞發生時間無關

- My dog enjoyed being massaged on the back.
  我的小狗喜歡背部按摩

5.5.4 被動語態完成式：表示動名詞較主要動詞早發生，多可代換為簡單式。

- Kate remembered having been reminded of that earlier.
  = Kate remembered reminding of that earlier.
  凱特記得稍早有人提醒他那件事。

- No packages are delivered without having been checked strictly.
  = No packages are delivered without checking strictly.
  每一份包裹須經嚴密檢查後才能寄出。

- The brochure appears to have been printed without having been proofread.
  = The brochure appears to have been printed without proofreading.
  小冊子看起來好像沒有校稿就印了。

6. 分詞：

分詞是動詞性質的名詞修飾語，分為現在分詞與過去分詞。另外，分詞片語包括其組成動詞的必要或非要成分，例如受詞、補語或修飾語。

- The girl playing the cello comes from Austria.
  拉大提琴的女孩來自奧地利。

- Jack wrote an email to his parents, sending them his best wishes.
  傑克寫一封電子郵件向他的父母問候。

- Cherry wine is especially for women, tasting a little light.
  櫻桃酒特別對女性來說，味道嚐起來有點淡。

- Sam received a note from Anita, written in Japanese.
  山姆收到艾妮塔用日文寫的紙條。

6.1 分詞片語的功用：分詞可扮演形容詞、副詞、名詞等角色。現在分詞搭配 be 形成進行式，過去分詞搭配 be 形成被動語態，搭配 have 形成完成式。

6.1.1 主詞補語：簡單式分詞當主詞補語，表示與主要動詞同時發生，或是附帶動作。

- The news sounds encouraging.
  這消息聽起來令人鼓舞。

- The man stood leaning against the fence.
  男子靠著圍籬站立。

- The young man was found hiding in a boat in the backyard.
  有人發現年輕男子躲在後院的一艘船上。

- The given prize has come unpacked.
  贈送的獎品已經打開了。

- Cory went unemployed for most all of 2013.
  柯尼 2013 年一整年幾乎都沒工作。

說明 come, go 可搭配否定過去分詞當主詞補語。

6.1.2 受詞補語：分詞除可當受詞補語，還可置於完全及物動詞的受詞右側，扮演補語角色。過去分詞當受詞補語多表示完成。

(1) 不完全及物動詞的受詞補語

- I heard someone knocking at the window.
  我聽見有人敲打窗戶。

- I'm sorry to have kept you waiting.
  抱歉，讓您久等了。

- I noticed a snake moving with a rat in its mouth.
  我注意到一條蛇爬著，口中咬著一隻老鼠。

- The show left me feeling depressed and disappointed.
  表演讓我感到又沮喪又失望。

(2) 完全及物動詞的受詞補語

- Mr. Lin caught the student cheating during test.
  = Mr. Lin caught the student who cheated during test.
  林老師抓到那名學生考試作弊。

- The policeman arrested the man wanted for theft.
  = The policeman arrested the man who was wanted for theft.
  警察逮到因竊盜而遭通緝的男子。

- The couple adopted a child born in a foreign country.
  = The couple adopted a child who was born in a foreign country.
  那對夫婦領養一名在外國出生的嬰兒。

6.1.3 名詞修飾語

- Many teenagers are crazy about the exciting film.
  許多青少年對那部刺激的影片為之瘋狂。

- Le Coq Sportif is a French company producing sports equipment.
  = Le Coq Sportif is a French company which produced sports equipment.
  公雞是一家生產運動器材的法國公司。

■ Cosima Wagner is a musician known to the world.
華格納是世界知名的音樂家。

■ The email dated May 5ᵗʰ has been deleted.
日期為五月五日的電子郵件已刪除。

■ The assistant was looking for the email deleted.
助理在找刪除的郵件。

說明 單詞過去分詞可後位修飾名詞或代名詞,單詞現在分詞無此用法。

6.1.4 代名詞修飾語

■ I've never heard of anyone passing the test in their eighties.
我從沒聽過有人八十多歲時通過測試。

■ There's nothing interesting about my cousin.
我表弟沒什麼趣聞。

■ Those waiting outdoors are desperate to get in.
等候在外的那些人使勁地要進來。

說明 修飾代名詞的分詞片語置於代名詞右側。

■ She is among those nominated for 2015 Emmy Awards.
她是 2015 年艾美獎入圍者之一。

6.1.5 扮演副詞:

(1) 分詞構成分詞構句,說明時間、原因、條件、讓步或附加狀況。

■ When seated in a wheelchair, the patient can still have full use of his arms.
病患坐在輪椅時,他還能充分運用雙臂。

■ There being a typhoon warning, the concert was put off until next week.
= Because there was a typhoon warning, the concert was put off until next week.
因為有颱風警報,音樂會延至下星期。

■ Weather permitting, we will go fly a kite on the riverbank.

= If the weather permits, we will go fly a kite on the riverbank.

天氣若是允許，我們將去河堤放風箏。

■ Although not knowing the details, the lawyer promised to deal with the case.

雖然沒聽到細節，律師還是答應處理案件。

■ The assistant went to the office, reporting the incident to the officer in charge. (附加狀況)

= The assistant went to the office and reported the incident to the officer in charge.

助理去辦公室，將事件報告給負責的官員。

(2) 後位修飾 come／go

〔方式〕

■ A hare came hopping to my house.

一隻野兔跳著來到我家。

■ The kangaroo went jumping to the pond.

袋鼠跳著去池子。

■ Children went running to the playground.

孩子們跑著去遊戲場。

■ Some people came walking in the square.

一些人走來廣場。

〔目地〕

■ Some people came to walk in the square.

一些人來廣場散步。

■ The police went patrolling around the community.

= The police went to patrol around the community.

警方去社區周圍巡邏。

6.1.6 扮演名詞：分詞與 the 共同形成名詞片語，表示具分詞性質的群體
或個體，例如：

the drowning 溺水的人	the accused 被告
the dying 垂死的人	the disabled 殘障人士
the living 活著的人	the wounded 傷者

說明 英美人士多不以此結構表示個體，他們表示具分詞性質的個體時，多搭配指涉的名詞，例如：

■ The wounded man has been sent to the hospital.
受傷的男子已被送往醫院。

■ The accused person must not be subjected to outside influence.
被告必須不受任何外界影響。

6.1.7 現在分詞形成進行式

■ The monk was chanting the Scriptures.
和尚在誦經。

■ They are burning ghost money.
婦人在燒紙錢。

6.1.8 過去分詞形成完成式

■ The suspect has confessed crime.
嫌犯已認罪。

■ They have been in love with each other for years.
他們已相戀多年。

■ The coon had escaped the trap when the hunter arrived.
獵人抵達時，浣熊已逃離陷阱。

6.1.9 過去分詞形成被動語態

■ The buggy has been towed away.
運輸車已被拖走。

■ A stone coffin was placed in the hall.
石棺安置於大廳。

6.1.10 分詞形成複合形容詞：分詞與名詞、形容詞或副詞等實詞共同形成複合形容詞

(1) 名詞＋現在分詞

■ The vice president is an awe-inspiring executive.
副總裁是一名令人敬畏的主管。

■ Jenny is really a heart-breaking girl.
珍妮現在是名心碎的女孩。

■ I'm looking into buying an ocean-going yacht.
我正考慮買一艘遠洋遊艇。

■ For a quiet village, it was an earth-shaking incident.
對一處平靜的村莊來說，那是一件驚天動地的大事。

(2) 名詞＋過去分詞

■ We serve up fresh and healthy homemade cuisine.
我們供應新鮮又健康的手工佳餚。

■ We have over ten large state-owned enterprises as clients.
超過十家國營企業都是我們的客戶。

■ My fiancé is an American-born Chinese.
我的未婚夫是一名華裔美國人。

★常見的「名詞＋過去分詞」複合形容詞：

air-conditioned	有空調設備的	power-driven	電力發動的
breast-fed	吃母奶的	special-made	特製的
duty-bound	義不容辭的	water-cooled	水冷式的
hand-picked	精選的	wind-blown	風吹的

(3) 形容詞＋現在分詞

■ Let's relax with some nice-sounding music.
讓我們來點好聽的音樂放鬆一下。

第五章 動詞

■ Sandy was very odd-looking in her costume.
珊蒂的服裝非常怪異。

■ A high-ranking official is under investigation for bribery.
一名高階官員正因賄賂而遭到調查。

■ I'm an easy-going person who gets along well with everyone.
我是個隨和的人，跟大家都很好相處。

★常見的「形容詞＋現在分詞」複合形容詞：

good-looking 好看的	high-sounding 誇張的
high-flying 雄心大志的	sweet-smelling 好聞的

⑷ 形容詞＋過去分詞

■ My roommate usually wear ready-made clothes.
我室友經常穿現成衣服。

■ The woman is breastfeeding her newborn baby.
婦人哺育母乳給她的新生兒。

■ My boss just ordered a high-priced sports car.
我老闆剛訂了一部高價跑車。

■ A remote-controlled helicopter killed a young man in
Brooklyn.
一部遙控直升機奪走住在布魯克林一名年輕人的性命。

★常見的「形容詞＋過去分詞」複合形容詞：

high-born 出身高貴的	low-pitched 低調的
low-born 出身低微的	strong-voiced 聲音高亢的

⑸ 副詞＋現在分詞

■ Diabetes is such a long-suffering disease.
糖尿病是種慢性疾病。

■ The middle-aged man is a hard-working laborer.
這名中年男子是位辛勤的勞工。

■ These pictures will leave an everlasting memory in your mind.
這些相片將在我心裡留下永恆的回憶。

■ It is never comfortable to wear close-fitting clothes in hot weather.
天氣熱時穿著緊身衣物一定很不舒服。

★常見的「副詞＋現在分詞」複合形容詞：

far-reaching　深遠的	never-ending　不斷的
far-seeing　有先見的	never-setting　永不落下

⑹ 副詞＋過去分詞

■ My daughter is very well-behaved.
我女兒很有規矩。

■ The model student must be a well-educated child.
模範生一定是位有教養的孩子。

■ Tom is working in a low-paid job full time.
湯姆現在做著低薪的全職工作。

■ I need an article on the above-mentioned subject.
我需要一篇有關上述主題的文章。

★常見的「副詞＋過去分詞」複合形容詞：

long-lived　長住	free-spoken　直率的
short-lived　短暫居住	smooth-spoken　口齒伶俐的

6.2 分詞的時態與語態：現在分詞有簡單式、完成式、被動語態，過去分詞只有簡單式。

現在分詞	主動語態	被動語態
簡單式	V-ing	being 過去分詞
完成式	having 過去分詞	having been 過去分詞

過去分詞	主動語態	被動語態
簡單式	過去分詞	

6.2.1 主動語態簡單式現在分詞

■ Turning to the left, you will find the pub.

When you turn to the left, you will find the pub.
（副詞子句）

向左轉，你會找到那家夜店。

■ The participant smiled, with tears glistening in her eyes.

The participant smiled and tears glistened in her eyes.
（限定動詞）

參加者面帶微笑，眼角泛著淚光。

■ Mrs. Lin entered into the office, making a call to her husband.

She entered into the office and made a call to her husband.
（限定動詞）

林太太進入辦公室，然後打電話給她先生。

6.2.2 主動語態完成式現在分詞：強調較早發生

■ The course having finished, the instructor gave the trainees an achievement test.

As the course had finished, the instructor gave the trainees an
（副詞子句）
achievement test.

課程結束，指導員給受訓學員做成就測驗。

■ Having resigned, Mr. Lin occupies himself by working on his book.

After he has resigned, Mr. Lin occupies himself by working on
（副詞子句）
his book.

退休之後，林先生致力於創作自己的書。

■ Having finished the work, Dave went out for dinner.

After Dave had finished the work, he went out for dinner.
（副詞子句）

戴夫完成工作後外出吃晚餐。

■ Having been told several times, Leo finally understood it.

After Leo had been told several times, Leo finally understood it.
（副詞子句）

里歐聽了幾次終於了解。

6.2.3 被動語態簡單式現在分詞：表示同時發生

■ The machine being assembled is imported from Germany.

組裝用的機械自德國進口。

■ Being repaired, my iPod is at the repair center now.

= Because my iPod is being repaired, it is at the repair center now.

我的 iPod 目前正在維修中心進行維修。

6.2.4 被動語態完成式現在分詞：強調較早發生

■ Having been invited to the feast, Dave arrived at the hotel, dressed up.

Since he had been invited to the feast, Dave arrived at the
（副詞子句）

hotel, dressed up.

戴夫受邀參加宴會，盛裝抵達飯店。

■ Having been warned not to wander too far from the hotel, the tourists stayed at the hotel all night.

Since they had been warned not to wander too far from the
（副詞子句）

hotel, the tourists stayed at the hotel all night.

稍早有人警示不要離開飯店活動，因此觀光客整晚待在飯店。

6.2.5 主動語態簡單式過去分詞：

■ There are still many left behind.

還有許多落後的地方。

■ Stranded on the beach for a while, the dolphin seemed almost dead.

Because the dolphin was stranded on the beach for a while, the
（副詞子句）
dolphin seemed almost dead.

因為海豚陷在海灘有一段時間，海豚似乎快死了。

◆ 5-3 動詞的分類：依動詞的搭配成分

　　動詞就其語意完整需求，有完全與及物二種性質，需要補語的是不完全性質，不需補語的是完全性質；需要受詞的是及物性質，不需受詞的是不及物性質。

　　完全及物動詞不需補語，需要受詞

　　完全不及物動詞不需補語，不需受詞

　　不完全及物動詞不需補語，需要受詞

　　不完全不及物動詞不需補語，不需受詞

　　另外，授與動詞需二個受詞，為雙及物動詞。值得一提的是，動詞幾乎是一字多義，因此，一個動詞會依不同語意而有不同的性質，衍生不同的搭配成分，這是動詞的一種次分類現象。

1. 完全不及物動詞

僅搭配主詞，不搭配受詞或補語，語意即完整的動詞為完全不及物動詞。

■ Tell me what happened.
告訴我發生什麼事。

■ The oil price is rising.
油價上漲。

■ The baby is sleeping.
嬰兒在睡覺。

■ All the passengers died.
乘客都身亡。

■ The rainbow has vanished.
彩虹消失了。

■ I think such vehicle doesn't exist.
我不認為會有這樣的車子。

★常見不搭配補語的完全不及物動詞：常見的感嘆詞

ache 痛	kneel 跪
arise 發生	occur 發生
arrive 抵達	pause 暫停
bleed 流血	persist 堅持
blush 呈現紅色	prosper 興盛
cease 停止	roar 吼叫
collapse 倒塌	scream 尖叫
cough 咳嗽	shine 照耀
cry 哭	shiver 顫抖
decay 衰退	sigh 嘆氣
depart 分離	slip 滑動
dine 用餐	smile 微笑
disappear 消失	sneeze 打噴嚏
doze 打瞌睡	surrender 撤銷
expire 屆滿	swim 游泳
faint 模糊的	vary 變化
fall 掉落	vibrate 振動
falter 蹣跚	wait 等候
hesitate 猶豫	weep 哭泣
itch 癢	yawn 打哈欠

1.1 說明表現或行為的完全不及物動詞常伴隨狀態或程度的副詞。

■ You shouldn't act that way.
你不該那樣表現。

■ Mr. Lin's business is doing well.
林先生的生意經營得很好。

■ Participants should behave properly.
參加者應當行為合宜。

■ The player performed worse than expected.
選手表現較預期差。

1.2 說明位置或移動的完全不及物動詞常伴隨空間相關的副詞,以使訊息明確。

■ My instructor comes from Canada.
我的老師來自加拿大。

■ The manager has gone to Japan.
經理已去日本了。

■ The helicopter is flying to Green Island.
直升機飛向綠島。

■ Fred was walking along the riverbank.
弗雷德沿著河堤散步。

■ Black-faced spoonbills have flown north.
黑面琵鷺已南飛。

■ The shuttle bus runs between several points in the city.
接駁車行駛市區幾個點。

■ A lamp hung above the dinner table.
一盞燈掛在餐桌上頭。

■ The backpacker usually stays at a cheap hostel.
背包客經常投宿在廉價民宿。

■ The retired man is living in a fishing village.
退休男子住在漁村。

■ Jeal remained in the dormitory yesterday.
吉爾昨天待在宿舍裡。

■ A temple stands on the hilltop.
一座廟宇位在山丘上。

■ The Great Lakes lie between the United States and Canada.
五大湖區位於美加交界。

說明 lie/sit/stand 等表示「位於」時常搭配現在簡單式。

1.3 完全不及物動詞可搭配形容詞，說明主詞動作時的狀態，可視為主詞補語。

1.3.1 搭配名詞

■ The firefighter died a hero.
消防隊員英勇地犧牲。

■ The scholar is born a genius.
學者一出生就是天才。

■ The millionaire died a beggar.
富翁死時是個乞丐。

1.3.2 搭配形容詞

■ The window blew open.
窗子被風吹開了。

■ The movie star married young.
電影明星英年早逝。

■ The patient lay awake all night.
病患整夜躺著睡不著。

■ The woman broke free from the cellar.
女子從地窖逃逸。

■ You should have played fair in the game.
你原本該在比賽中公平行事的。

1.3.3 搭配過去分詞

■ The incident passed unnoticed.

事件已是過往雲煙。

■ The guy came into the hall unobserved.

那人進入大廳，沒引起注意。

2. 不完全不及物動詞

除了主詞，還需補語語意才完整的動詞為不完全不及物動詞。
不完全不及物動詞搭配動詞描述對象的主題主詞，聯繫主詞與
補語，因此又稱連綴動詞。

2.1 不完全不及物動詞的語意

2.1.1 表示現狀或特徵

■ I'm feeling better now.

現在我覺得好多了。

■ Everything will go well tomorrow.

明天凡事都會順利。

■ The main road will run parallel to the riverbank.

幹道將與河堤並行。

(1) appear, seem 的補語結構：appear, seem 除搭配形容詞、不定詞，還可
搭配 like 介系詞片語、as if / as though 子句。

① 形容詞片語

■ Your boss appears displeased with you.

你老闆一副對你不滿意的樣子。

■ Mr. Suzuki seemed satisfied with Tom's answer.

鈴木先生對湯姆的回答似乎很滿意。

② 不定詞片語

■ He appeared to be on his high horse at the meeting.

開會時他顯得趾高氣揚。

■ She seems to have been to Jiuzhaigou Valley ScenicArea.
她似乎去過九寨溝。

③ like ＋介系詞片語，like 可搭配名詞片語或子句。

(a) like ＋名詞片語
■ It seems like their relationship is over.
他們的戀情似乎完了。

■ The chariot and horses appeared like multicolored sparkling.
馬車和馬匹像五彩繽紛的燦爛煙火。

(b) like ＋名詞子句
■ The dropouts appeared like they don't care.
中輟生一副不在乎的樣子。

■ It seemed like no one wanted to work overtime.
似乎沒人要加班。

(c) 名詞子句
■ It seems as if they are no longer in love.
他們似乎不再相愛了。

■ The lady appeared as though she were haunted by a ghost.
女子一副被鬼附身的樣子。

(2) stand/lie 的不完全不及物用法：stand/lie 具不完全不及物性質，意思是「處於…狀態」，搭配形容詞或過去分詞當補語。

① stand/lie ＋形容詞
■ The vagrant lay asleep on the bench.
流浪漢躺在凳子上睡著了。

■ Due to heavy rain, the tank stood full today.
由於今天大雨導致水槽滿了。

② stand/lie ＋過去分詞
■ The driver stood blamed for being careless.
駕駛人因粗心而遭責備。

■ The barn has stood deserted for few years.
穀倉已廢棄多年。

(3) be 動詞的補語結構：be 動詞是最常見的不完全不及物動詞，補語結構也最多。

① 名詞片語

■ My uncle is a computer technician.
我叔叔是電腦技術員。

■ My niece used to be a choir member.
我姪女曾經是合唱團員。

② 代名詞

■ It's me, Anita.
是我，艾妮塔。

③ 動名詞片語

■ My main interest is traveling.
我的興趣是旅遊。

■ One of my hobbies is collecting movie posters.
我其中一項嗜好是收集電影海報。

④ 不定詞片語

■ You are to be blamed for it.
你該受責備。

■ My dream is to study medicine at university.
我的夢想是在大學念醫學。

⑤ 現在分詞

■ The film is inspiring.
影片很激勵人。

■ The comic book is very interesting.
漫畫書很有趣。

⑥ 過去分詞

■ Many tourists were confused aboutthe situation.
許多觀光客對狀況感到困惑。

■ Mr. Chen was pleased with his son's progress.
陳先生對自己兒子的進步很滿意。

⑦ 形容詞片語

■ The stray dog is still alive.
流浪狗還活著。

■ My parents are fond ofexotic food.
我父母喜愛異國食物。

⑧ 副詞片語

■ Happiness is allaround.
幸福來了。

■ The manager is not in now.
現在經理不在。

⑨ 介系詞片語

■ The woman is between jobs.
女子待業中。

■ The proposal is under discussion.
提案正討論中。

⑩ 名詞子句

■ This house is where I am living now.
這是我目前住的房子。

■ This is the way they dealt with the chaotic circumstances.
他們就是這樣處理混亂狀況的。

■ It is because I don't trust you at all.
那是因為我一點也不信任你。

2.1.2 表示主詞狀態的改變：不完全不及物動詞表示狀態改變時，補語結構為名詞、形容詞、不定詞、過去分詞或介系詞片語。

(1) 名詞

■ He will make a capable executive.
他會是一位能幹的主管。

■ The child will turn into a teenager soon.
孩子很快就會變成青少年。

■ The drug dealer finally became an anti-drug volunteer.
最後毒販成為反毒志工。

(2) 形容詞

■ The pork has gone bad.
豬肉壞掉了。

■ She fell asleep while watching the film.
她看影片時睡著了。

■ The chief's dream will come true one day.
總舖師的夢想有一天將實現。

(3) 不定詞

■ It has proved to be impracticable.
已證實那是不可行。

■ The vice captain's got to realize the real reason.
副機長已了解真正原因。

(4) 過去分詞

■ The court yard has become deserted.
庭院已荒廢。

■ The event finally went unnoticed.
後來沒人再注意那次事件。

⑸ 介系詞片語

■ That style has grown out of fashion.
那款式已退流行。

說明 不完全不及物性質的片語動詞常表示狀態的改變，搭配介系詞 into/to，例如：

■ Tadpoles change into frogs.
蝌蚪變成青蛙。

■ The area is developing into a business district.
這地區要開發成商業區。

■ The match might end up in a draw.
比賽可能會平手。

■ The man ended up with no friends whatsoever.
男子落得沒有朋友。

■ The square is turning into a meeting place for street performers.
廣場要成為街頭藝人聚集地。

■ This research evolved into an important conceptual framework.
研究結果產生一個重要的概念框架。

2.1.3 表示狀態的持續：continue, keep, remain, stay 等動詞具不完全不及物性質，表示持續處於某種狀態。

⑴ continue 的用法：continute 的補語結構可以是名詞、形容詞、不定詞或動名詞。

■ Aunt Amy continued the tale.
愛咪阿姨繼續講故事。

■ The weather continued to be cloudy.
持續陰天的天氣。

■ Tom continued to wait for the client at the meeting point.
湯姆持續在會面點等客戶。

■ They continued playing mahjong after dinner.
晚餐後，他們繼續打麻將。

說明 「go on」搭配動名詞表示持續，或中斷後繼續進行，搭配不
定詞表示繼續進行。

■ The mechanic usually goes on working all night without a rest.
技術員經常工作一整夜，都沒休息。（持續不中斷）

■ He put down his book and went on telling the story.
他放下書，然後繼續講故事。（中斷後持續）

■ Go on to do your homework after you have done the dishes.
洗完碗後繼續做功課。（中斷後持續）

(2) keep 的用法：keep 可搭配現在分詞、過去分詞或介系詞片語當補語。

■ The stray dog kept barking for a while.
流浪狗吠了一會兒。

■ The stray dog has been kept locked in the cage for few days.
流浪狗被關在籠子裡好幾天了。

■ Leo is keeping in contact with his brothers.
里歐和他兄弟一直保持聯絡。

(3) remain 的用法：remain 表示保持時，補語結構可以是名詞、形容詞或名詞子句。

■ The two parties remain in an argument.
雙方一直爭執中。

■ The suspect remained silent during the investigation.
調查期間嫌犯一直保持緘默。

■ The problem remained that he tended not to tell the truth.
問題他還是堅不吐實。

(4) stay 的用法：stay 表示保持時，搭配形容詞當補語。

■ Try to stay calm during an earthquake.
地震時儘量保持冷靜。

說明
1. rest 搭配 easy, assured 時，表示保持。
■ I will never rest easy about this case.
我對這案子始終無法寬心。

■ You may rest assured that we will take your benefits into consideration.
我們會將你的利益考慮進去，你可以放心。

2. go 搭配過去分詞，也可表示保持。
■ The freelancer's contribution went unnoticed.
自由作家的投稿未受青睞。

2.1.4 表示動作的狀態：feel, look, smell, sound, taste, wear 等動詞與主詞之間為被動關係，補語所述狀態不是主詞主動產生，而是被動接受的狀況。

■ The smartphone looks very thin and stylish.
這款智慧型手機看起來相當輕薄時尚。

■ She looks to be in a bad mood.
她看來心情很不好。

■ The model looks like a jellyfish.
那名模特兒看起來像水母。

■ It looks like that the coach is not satisfied with the team's performance.
看起來教練對球隊表現不滿意。

■ It looks as if it's going to rain.
看起來要下雨了。

說明 look 可搭配形容詞、不定詞、like 片語或 as if/as though 子句，
like 搭配名詞片語或子句。

■ The blanket feels a little heavier.
毯子感覺有點重。

■ The cloth feels like card stock.
布料摸起來像厚紙。

■ The girl felt like she was going to faint.
女孩感覺快昏倒了。

說明

1.「feel like」另有「想要」的意思,搭配動名詞片語。
■ My sister actually felt like going shopping today.
事實上我妹妹今天想要去逛街。

2. touch,觸摸,無不完全不及物性質,不可搭配形容詞或 like 片語。
■ The dish smells inviting.
這道菜很棒。

■ The food smells like stinky tofu.
食物聞起來像臭豆腐。

■ The chicken-fried steak tastes delicious.
炸雞排很好吃。

■ The baby food tasted like a sponge.
嬰兒食物嚐起來像海綿。

■ The veal tastes like it had been on the stove too long.
小牛肉嚐起來像是烤太久。

■ The corners of the mat have broken off.
墊子的角落磨破了。

3. 完全及物動詞

語意上須伴隨受詞的動詞為完全及物動詞,反身動詞與同源動詞同屬完全及物動詞,受詞結構包括名詞、代名詞、不定詞、動名詞、名詞子句等語詞。

3.1 反身動詞:結構上搭配反身代名詞當受詞的動詞為反身動詞,其中反身代名詞為動詞的執行者。

■ The section chief excused himself from the meeting.
科長會議缺席。

■ I have accustomed myself to working night-shift.
我習慣上夜班了。

■ She availed herself of the opportunity to make a comeback.
她抓住機會反敗為勝。

■ The boy behaved himself well.
男孩表現很好。

■ The chef busied himself in the kitchen.
主廚在廚房裡忙。

■ The accountant prides herself on her good memory.
會計為自己的好記憶感到驕傲。

說明 有些完全及物動詞的主詞指涉人時才搭配反身代名詞受詞，例
　　　如：

■ Bella applied herself to taking care of her children.
貝拉專心照顧孩子。

■ We enjoyed ourselves during the trip to Kenting.
墾丁旅遊期間我們玩得很開心。

3.2 同源動詞：一些完全不及物動詞搭配副詞功能的同源受詞
組，以提供動詞進一步訊息，這種動詞為同源動詞。同源
受詞組常搭配 a/an、所有詞或修飾語。

■ The clerk smiled a sweet smile.
店員甜美地笑著。

■ The soldier died a glorious death.
士兵光榮戰死。

■ I have walked a long walk to freedom.
我走一大段路才走到自由。

■ Leo and his partner danced a light dance.
里歐和舞伴跳一支輕快舞曲。

■ I dreamed a horrible dream last night.
我昨夜做一個可怕的夢。

■ We will have to fight a violent fight.
我們即將面臨激烈戰鬥。

■ The man laughed a hysterical laugh.
男子歇斯底里地大笑。

■ The old couple is living a simple life.
老夫婦過著簡單的生活。

■ My brother ran a long race today.
我弟弟今天跑了一段很長的路。

■ My instructor shouted a loud shout.
我的老師大叫一聲。

■ The homeless man sighed a deep sigh.
流浪漢長嘆一聲。

■ The child slept a sound sleep.
孩子睡得很沉。

■ The patient breathed his last breath at dawn.
這位病患在黎明時往生。

說明 受詞指涉明確或易於聯想時，可省略或形成隱匿受詞，使完全及物動詞具不及物性質。

■ The class started at 2 P.M.
下午二點開始上課。

■ School began on August 30th.
八月三十日開學。

■ Please stop singing (songs) now.
現在請勿唱歌。

■ No eating (food) in the car.
車廂內禁止飲食。

■ You go first, and I will follow (you).
你先請，我隨後就到。

■ The pilot drank (wine) a lot last night.
機長昨晚酗酒。

■ The captain has quit smoking (cigarettes) for years.
警長已戒菸多年了。

3.3 受詞結構：

3.3.1 名詞片語

■ She fixed a big dinner for the guests.
她預備一頓豐盛的晚餐招待賓客

■ Sam ordered a bunch of roses for Amy.
山姆訂一束玫瑰送給艾咪。

3.3.2 代名詞

■ Trust yourself, and you will make it.
相信我，你會成功的。

■ God helps those who help themselves.
天助自助者。

3.3.3 不定詞

■ My boss offered to tide me over.
我老闆願意幫助我度過難關。

■ Leo decided to apply for the position.
里歐決定申請那份工作。

3.3.4 動名詞

■ The butcher has quit drinking for years.
屠夫已戒酒多年了。

■ I have been regretting leaving the company.
我一直懊悔辭職。

3.3.5 名詞子句

■ I am hoping that Tate would come back safe and sound.
我一直希望泰德能夠平安歸來。

■ I was wondering if you were available after the conference.
不知道你會議之後有沒有空。

4. 授與動詞

語意上搭配二個或三個受詞的動詞為授與動詞，又稱雙及物動詞。直接受詞為動詞的受事者，間接受詞通常是直接受詞的目標或受益者。結構上，間接受詞可搭配相關語意的介系詞，形成介系詞片語。值得一提的是，名詞片語與介系詞片語結構的間接受詞語意常常不同。

■ We wish you a merry Christmas.
祝你聖誕快樂。

■ They quoted me a price higher than Sears.
他們給我的報價較希爾斯來得高。

■ The principal awarded me the first prize.
校長頒首獎給我。

■ The driver has granted me compensation forthe damage.
駕駛人答應我賠償損壞。

■ I have forwarded the file to the client.
我將檔案傳給客戶了。

■ Tom bet me a steak that the team would lose.
湯姆跟我賭一客牛排，那支隊伍會輸。

4.1 授與動詞與介系詞的搭配：

4.1.1 to，受詞表示直接受詞的方向或目標

■ Mrs. Lin leased her suite to me.
林太太將她的套房租給我。

■ The bank loaned one million dollars to the factory.
銀行貸給工廠一百萬元。

■ I rented an apartment out to a single-parent family.
我把公寓租給一個單親家庭。

■ You had better send the parcel to the client by air.
你寄包裹給客戶最好用航空郵件。

■ Bob sold his digital camera to his senior schoolmate.
包柏將他的數位相機賣給學長。

■ Hank owed some money to his landlord.
漢克欠他的房東一些錢。

■ The company advanced Peter some money for marriage expenses.
公司預支一些錢給彼得作為結婚費用。

★常與介系詞 to 搭配的授與動詞：

deal 給予	pay 支付
feed 餵食	play 表演
hand 交給	read 讀
leave 遺留	serve 提供
lend 借給	show 顯示
mail 寄出	sing 唱歌
offer 提供	take 拿
pass 傳	tell 告訴

4.1.2 for，受詞表示直接受詞的受益者

■ My mom bought me a pair of sneakers.
我媽媽幫我買一雙運動鞋。

■ The hostess prepared a special dinner for the children.
女主人為孩子們預備一頓特別的晚餐。

■ The couple paid a sum of money for their children's education.
這對夫婦為孩子教育費付出大筆金錢。

■ I have paid money for the vendor.
我已付錢給攤販。

【比較】for 介系詞也可表示目的，例如：

■ Leo spared some of his income for his brother.
里歐將一些收入分給他弟弟。

■ I will cash the check for you.
我要將支票兌現給你。

說明 該句另一語意是「我要幫你去兌現支票」。

★常與介系詞 for 搭配的授與動詞：

book　預定	make　製造
build　建造	mix　混合
cut　切割	order　訂貨
design　設計	paint　繪畫
fetch　去拿回	pour　傾倒
find　找到	reserve　保留
fix　修理	secure　保護
get　給	set　放置
keep　保存	win　贏得

4.1.3 from，受詞表示直接受詞的來源

■ Brian borrowed an encyclopedia from the library.
布萊恩從圖書館借了一本百科全書。

4.2 授與動詞的被動語態：授與動詞搭配直接受詞語間接受詞，一般情況下，二者都可以當被動句主詞，但語意必須符合邏輯。

■ I was brought a package bythe guard.

The guard brought me a package.
（主動句）

A package was brought to me by the guard.
（被動句）

警衛帶一個包裹給我。

My roommate sold me his used computer for ＄20.
（主動句）

My roommate's used computer was sold to me for ＄20 by him.
（被動句）

我室友將他的二手電腦賣我 20 美元。

【誤】I was sold my roommate's used computer for ＄20 by him.

說明 邏輯上，我不會被賣。

■ My teacher chose a reference book for me.
（主動句）

A reference book was chosen for me by my teacher.
（被動句）

我的老師幫我選一本參考書。

【誤】I was chosen a reference book by my teacher.

■ My friend cooked me abowl of beef noodles.
（主動句）

A bowl of beef noodles were cooked for me by my friend.
（被動句）

我朋友幫我煮一碗牛肉麵。

5. 不完全及物動詞

不完全及物動詞搭配受詞與受詞補語，受詞補語說明受詞狀況，知覺與使役動詞都是不完全及物動詞。

5.1 知覺動詞：又稱感官動詞，主詞是感受知覺的經驗者，受詞是提供主詞知覺感應的動作產生者，受詞補語說明與受詞有關的事件，也是主詞感應的內容。原形動詞結構的受詞補語強調動作已完成，現在分詞片語強調動作持續，過去分詞片語表示被動語態。另外，副詞語詞也可當受詞補語，說明補語的狀況。

■ I observed a Chihuahuajumpover the fence.
我留意到一隻吉娃娃跳過圍欄。

■ The assistant smelled the fish burning.
助理聞到魚燒焦了。

■ Children listened to Mrs. Lin tell the fairy tale.
孩子們聽林太太講童話故事。

■ I was hearing the reporter talking on channel 55.
我在 55 頻道聽記者們談話。

■ I was looking at the patient walking in slow motion.
我注意看著病患緩步行走。

說明 感官動詞可搭配進行式。

■ The security guard perceived a stranger entering the factory.
警衛查覺到一位陌生人進到廠區。

5.1.1 知覺動詞的受詞補語結構：

(1) 主詞為主動狀態

① 受詞補語為主動狀態：受詞補語為受詞的主動動作時，以原形動詞強調事實，現在分詞強調過程。

■ I felt the ground shaking just now.
我剛剛感到地面在搖動。

■ I saw a mouse eating cheese under the table.
我看見一隻老鼠在桌底下吃起司。

② 受詞補語為被動狀態：受詞補語為受詞的被動動作時，結構為過去分詞。

■ I noticed a woman injured in the accident.
我注意到有一名婦人在意外中受傷。

(2) 主詞為被動狀態

① 受詞補語為主動狀態：受詞補語以不定詞強調事實，現在分詞強調過程。

■ A rat was noted to die under the cupboard.
我注意到一隻老鼠死在櫥櫃底下。

■ The lady was watched dancing in the snow.
有人看女子在雪中起舞。

② 受詞補語為被動狀態：受詞補語結構為過去分詞。

■ The carpet was discovered damaged seriously.
   有人發現地毯嚴重損害。

■ A Formosan pig was found caught in the trap by the hunter.
   獵人發現陷阱捕捉到一隻山豬。

説明 感官動詞可搭配進行式。

5.2 使役動詞：驅使受事者進行某一動作或處於某一狀態的動詞為使役動詞，通常表示命令、迫使、建議、指示、勸導等語意。受詞是使役動作的受事者，也是受詞補語的執行者或事件主詞。

5.2.1 受詞補語的結構：使役動詞的受詞補語結構常因字而異，包括原形動詞、不定詞、形容詞、副詞或介系詞片語等。

(1) 原形動詞

〔have〕

■ The man had his wolf dogs hut up.
   男子要他的狼犬閉嘴。

■ Your comment has made me out of mind.
   你的評論讓我抓狂。

〔make〕

■ My dad made me turn off the computer.
   我父親要我關上電腦。

説明 make 可搭配原形動詞、名詞、形容詞或介系詞片語當受詞補語。

■ The earthquake has made the village a ruin.
   地震已讓村莊變成廢墟。

■ The news made the mother depressed.
   新聞讓那名母親十分沮喪。

〔get〕

■ Someone got me wait in here.

= My friends got me to wait in here.

有人要我在這裡面等。

說明 get 可搭配原形動詞或不定詞當受詞補語。

〔help〕

■ My executive helped me solve some problems.

= My executive helped me to solve some problems.

= My executive helped me with some problems.

我主管幫我解決一些問題。

說明 help 可搭配原形動詞、不定詞或 with 介系詞片語當受詞補語。

(2) 不定詞

■ Linda dared her boss to quit smoking.

琳達要他老闆戒菸。

■ The negotiator persuaded the hijacker to surrender.

談判人員說服劫機者投降。

(3) 形容詞片語

■ Those nature conservationists set the animal free.

自然保育人士將動物放走。

(4) 副詞片語

■ Don't let me down.

不要讓我喪氣。

(5) 介系詞片語

■ It may put you on the downside.

那可能會讓你居下風。

★常見搭配不定詞當受詞補語的使役動詞：

aid　協助	induce　導致
advise　勸告	inspire　鼓舞
assist　協助	instruct　指導
bribe　賄賂	invite　邀請
cause　引起	lead　引導
command　命令	oblige　強迫
compel　強迫	order　命令
constrain　強迫	press　強迫
convince　使信服	push　迫使
direct　指示	recommend　建議
drive　驅使	start　開始
enable　使能夠	teach　教導
encourage　鼓勵	tell　告訴
force　強迫	tempt　誘惑
impel　強制	train　訓練
incline　使傾向於	urge　催促

5.2.2 使役動詞的被動語態：受詞補語應改為不定詞結構，但仍需維持受詞補語的語態。

■ We will make the article revised soon.

我們很快將文章修改完。

The article will be made to be revised by us soon.
（被動語態）

■ Children got the lantern hung up at the door.

孩子們將燈籠掛在門口。

The lantern was got to be hung up at the door by children.
（被動語態）

5.3 表示意念或認知的動詞：常搭配不定詞當受詞補語

■ I took the dog to become a guide dog.
我以為那隻狗是導盲犬。

■ I know my roommate to be available.
我知道我室友正處於感情空窗期。

■ They imagined the lecturer to be a scholar.
他們將演講者想像成學者。

■ We assumed the skater to win the championship.
我們猜測那名溜冰選手會奪冠。

■ The woman still felt her husband to be with her.
婦人仍感覺她丈夫與她同在。

■ The trainee denied it to be his fault at first.
學習生一開始否認那是他的錯。

■ The director confessed it to be a mistake.
導演承認那是一項錯誤。

■ The candidate challenged him to debate the issue.
候選人挑戰他並針對議題展開辯論。

說明 challenge 也可搭配 to 介系詞片語。

■ The man challenged him to a fight.
男子挑戰和他打一架。

■ The principal has forbidden faculty members to smoke on campus.
校長禁止教職員在校園吸菸。

★其他搭配不定詞當受詞補語的動詞：

acknowledge　感謝	guess　猜測
admit　承認	hold　握著
allow　允許	intend　打算

ask 詢問	judge 審判
bear 承受	like 喜歡
beg 乞討	love 愛
believe 相信	mean 意指
conceive 想像	permit 許可
consider 考慮	prefer 寧可
count 計算	presume 擅自
deem 視作	request 要求
desire 渴望	suppose 以為
esteem 尊重	suspect 懷疑
expect 預料	think 思索
fancy 猜想	want 想要
find 發現	wish 但願

5.4 表示命名、提名或宣稱的動詞：多以名詞或 as 介系詞片語當受詞補語。

■ The couple named their baby Bella.
夫婦將他們的小孩命名為「貝拉」。

■ They proclaimed Mr. Szuki CEO.
他們宣布鈴木先生為執行長。

■ The man professed himself an atheist.
男子聲稱自己是無神論者。

■ They entitled their company Wonderland.
他們將公司命名為「Wonderland」。

■ We nominated Roberto Baroni as chairperson.
我們提名羅伯特‧巴羅尼為主席。

■ Americans elected Barack Hussein Obama as their President.
美國人推選歐巴馬作為他們的總統。

★搭配名詞或 as 介系詞片語當受詞補語的動詞：

appoint　指定	pronounce　宣布
call　稱呼	style　命名
choose　選擇	term　稱呼⋯為

5.5 表示保持或改變受事者位置或狀態的動詞：主詞為起因者，受詞為受影響者，受詞補語為影響結果，結構通常是形容詞、副詞或介系詞片語。

5.5.1 受詞補語表示保持受詞狀態

■ The man wears his hair long.
男子蓄長髮。

■ Please leave the window closed.
麻煩讓窗戶關著就好。

5.5.2 受詞補語表示受詞位置改變，結構通常是副詞或介系詞片語。

■ The ranger drove the stray dogs away.
巡守員將流浪狗趕走。

■ They moved the bookshelf out.
他們將書櫃搬出去。

■ Miss Lin took John to the Health Center.
林小姐帶約翰去健康中心。

■ Don't put your cell-phone on the desk.
別將你的手機放在桌上。

5.5.3 受詞補語表示受詞狀態改變，結構通常是副詞或 into 形成的介系詞片語。

■ Wipe your face dry.
把你的臉擦乾。

■ The boy dyed his hair blonde.
男孩將頭髮染成金色。

■ The vase was broken into pieces.
有人將花瓶打破成碎片。

■ The vendor cut the watermelon into halves.
攤商將西瓜剖成兩半。

■ The assistant translated the article into Spanish.
助理將文章譯成西班牙文。

★常見搭配起因者主詞的不完全及物動詞：

bake　烘培	paint　畫
beat　打擊	render　翻譯
boil　煮沸	stain　著色
burn　燒	transform　變形
drink　喝	turn　轉變

5.5.4 不完成及物動詞的被動語態：名詞結構的受詞補語不能作為被動語態的句子主詞。

■ The president designated Mr. Lin chair of the committee.
總裁任命林先生為委員會主席。

Mr. Lin was designated chair of the committee by the president.
（被動語態）

【誤】Chair of the committee was designated as Mr. Lin by the president.

■ The advocators declared the accused a political prisoner.
擁護者宣稱被告是政治犯。

The accused was declared a political prisoner by the advocator.
（被動語態）

■ The commission has made the community a better place.
委員會使社區成為一個較佳的地方。

The community has been made into a better place by the
（被動語態）
commission.

5.5.5 完全及物動詞的受詞可搭配補語：一些完全及物動詞的受詞搭配修飾語詞，以提供受詞訊息，此修飾語詞可視為受詞補語。

- The Lin family bought the apartment cheap.

  林氏夫婦這間公寓買得便宜。

- The investor sold the house at half of the price.

  投資客攔腰出脫房子。

　　針對某一時間的動作或狀態所做的描述為時態，包括時式與態貌二因素，時式包括過去、現在、未來等時式，態貌包括簡單、進行、完成、完成進行等，因此，英文有十二時態：

	過去	現在	未來
簡單	過去簡單	現在簡單	未來簡單
進行	過去進行	現在進行	未來進行
完成	過去完成	現在完成	未來完成
完成進行	過去完成進行	現在完成進行	未來完成進行

以「Tom　watch TV」為例，各時態如下：

過去簡單式：Tom watched TV ten minutes ago.

過去進行式：Tom was watching TV at that time.

過去完成式：Tom had watched TV for two hours when I got home.

過去完成進行式：Tom had been watching TV before he called me.

現在簡單式：Tom watches TV after dinner every evening.

現在進行式：Tom is watching TV now.

現在完成式：Tom has watched TV for two hours.

現在完成進行式：Tom has been watching TV for two hours since he came home.

未來簡單式：Tom will watch TV after he finishes his homework.

未來進行式：Tom will be watching TV when I finish my homework.

未來完成式：Tom will have watched TV for two hours when he goes to bed.

未來完成進行式：Tom will have been watching TV for two hours by the time you come.

説明 許多人認為英文無未來時態，因為未來動作或狀態乃以情態助動詞搭配原形動詞或現在簡單式、現在進行式表示，例如：

■ Could you come to the garden party tomorrow?
你明天方便來參加園遊會嗎？

■ Mr. Suzuki will take over my position next quarter.
鈴木先生從下一季將接掌我的職務。

■ It is a pity that they have to leave the camp tomorrow.
他們明天必須離開營隊，真是可惜。

■ Tomorrow is Thursday.
明天是星期四。

■ Mr. Lin is going to marry his assistant.
林先生即將與他的助理結婚。

■ The chief editor is leaving for Beijing in two days.
兩天後，主編要前往北京。

◆ 6-1 各時態的使用時機

1. 過去簡單式

1.1 過去為真的動作或狀態。

■ The civil engineer graduated from UCLA.
土木工程師畢業自加州大學洛杉磯分校。

■ Tomoko's grandmother loved her very much.
智子的祖母非常愛她。

■ Hip-Hop started in New York City in 1970s.
街舞於 1970 年代起源於紐約。

■ The late principal was devoted to special education.
前任校長致力於特殊教育。

■ I didn't notice what Yoshiko just wrote on the paper.
我沒注意到芳子剛剛在紙上寫什麼。

■ Mika printed out the file, turned off the computer and left the office.
美嘉將檔案列印出來，關閉電腦，然後下班。

> 說明 主要子句與補語子句的動作未強調因果或先後順序時，補語子句可以過去簡單式表示較早發生的動作。

1.2 過去習慣或經常發生的動作。

■ Victoria used to be addicted to Facebook games.
維多莉亞曾經沉迷於臉書的遊戲。

■ My husband went to a bar every Friday night before marriage.
我先生婚前每周五晚上都去酒吧。

■ Almost every weekend, Mr. Takei would visit his in-laws in Ilan.
幾乎每周末，武井先生都會去看望在宜蘭的岳家。

1.3 since 子句多搭配過去簡單式，現在完成式或過去完成式的主要子句可搭配過去簡單式 since 子句。

■ There have been a lot of changes since I last visited the village.
自從我上次造訪村落之後，這裡已有很多改變。

■ I had not heard from my brother for years since he went abroad.
我弟弟出國以來已有多年沒有聽到他的音信。

1.4 hope, think, want, wonder 常以過去簡單式表示婉轉語氣。

■ I hoped you could help out.
希望你能幫個忙。

■ I thought you could stay for dinner with my family.
我想你能留下來與我的家人一起用晚餐。

■ I wondered if you would come to chat over tea with us.
不知道你會不會來和我們泡茶聊天。

2. 過去進行式

2.1 過去某一時間正在進行。

- Kyoko was surfing the Internet at 10 pm.
  京子早上十點時正在上網。

- They were doing Tai Chi in the park at six this morning.
  他們今天早上六點在公園打太極拳。

- Miss Takeda was speaking when the guest entered the meeting room.
  來賓進到會議室時，武田小姐正在發言。

2.2 過去某一時段一直進行。

- It was raining all day yesterday.
  昨天一整天都在下雨。

- All the chief executive officers were discussing the proposal this morning.
  今天早上所有的一級主管都在討論提案。

2.3 過去同時發生的動作，強調過去二動作同時發生，對比語氣，主要子句與副詞子句搭配過去進行式，以連接詞 while 連接。

- While her daughter was sleeping, Rowling was writing at a café.
  女兒睡覺時，羅琳在咖啡廳寫作。

- While Miwa was reading the magazine, Chie was playing online games.
  美和看雜誌時，千惠在玩線上遊戲。

2.4 過去已發生的動作。

- Andre Sorlie deleted the file that he was checking.
  = Andre Sorlie deleted the file that he had checked.
  安德烈‧索力刪掉他剛剛在看的檔案。

■ The boy who was talking on the cellphone has left.

= The boy who had talked on the cellphone has left.

剛剛在講手機的男孩離開了。

2.5 過去說明即將發生的動作。

■ They told me that they were arriving in ten minutes.

他們告訴我十分鐘內抵達。

■ Ayako said that she was visiting the client next Friday.

= Ayako said that she will be visiting the client next Friday.

= Ayako said that she was visiting the client last Friday.

綾子說她下周五會去拜訪客戶。

2.6 一些瞬間動作可以過去進行式表示過去即將發生。

■ Ryoko told me that she was riding a bike to the remote village.

良子告訴我說她要騎單車去那個偏遠鄉鎮。

■ I wanted to know whether Naoko was flying to Seattle or not the next day.

我想知道真子隔天要不要搭飛機到西雅圖。

2.7 hope, think, want, wonder 以過去進行式表示婉轉語氣。

■ I was hoping you could give me a lift to the station.

我希望你能送我到車站。

■ I was wondering if you had a table for eight people.

不知道你們有沒有八人桌。

■ I was thinking it might be fun to go for a ride tonight.

我想今晚去騎單車可能會很有趣。

3. 過去完成式

3.1 以過去某時為觀點，描述完成的動作或存在的狀態，動詞組為「had +過去分詞」結構。

■ I met a woman who had been to Antarctica twice.

我遇見一名去過南極二次的女子。

■ Masami had got the materials ready before the meeting.
會議前雅美就將資料預備好了。

■ It was the first time that the trainee talked to me that way.
那是實習生第一次那樣跟我說話。

■ The editor didn't leave the office until she had completed all the work.
編輯直到完成所有工作之後才下班。

■ Nicole had studied Chinese for two years when she came to Taipei.
妮可來台北前已讀了二年中文。

說明

1. 比較：The guest left before the workshop had been over. 過去完成式動作較晚發生。
2. 連接詞明確表示動作先後順序時，先發生的動作可以過去簡單式表示。

■ Yumiko did the laundry after she ate／had taken a bath.
由美子泡完澡後洗衣服。

■ I got to know the truth until Kaoru told／had told me the whole story.
直到小薰告訴我事件始末，我才知道真相。

■ Maiko fell／had fallen asleep before her roommate came back.
麻衣子的室友回來前她已睡著了。

■ I read the book that I borrowed／had borrowed from my instructor.
我讀了向老師借的書。

3.2 描述過去一直持續的狀態，常搭配 for, since 語詞。

■ Boris said he had been depressed since he broke up with Takiko.
波利斯說他和多喜子分手後一直很沮喪。

■ Mizuho told me that she had been worried about money for a long while.
瑞穗說她長久以來一直在擔心錢。

4. 過去完成進行式

4.1 直至過去某時已完成，可能仍進行的動作，動詞組為「had been ＋現在分詞」結構。

■ I had been working in the factory for ten years by the time my son was born.
我兒子出生時，我已在工廠工作十年了。

■ Mariko had been playing violin for two hours before her instructor came.
麻里的老師來之前她拉了二小時的小提琴。

4.2 直至過去某時重覆發生的動作。

■ The maid had been cleaning the carpet before he put it away.
幫傭收拾地毯前都會清洗一下。

■ The mechanic said he had been trying to take apart the machine.
技術員說他一直試著要拆解機器。

5. 現在簡單式

5.1 目前為真的狀態。

■ I am depressed and disappointed now.
我現在沮喪又失望。

■ Samba is one of Brazil's most popular types of music.
森巴是巴西最受歡迎的音樂之一。

■ Bats are the only mammals that are able to fly.
蝙蝠是唯一會飛的哺乳類動物。

■ Giant Arctic jellyfish have tentacles that can reach over 36 meters in length.
北極大水母有伸長 36 公尺的觸角。

5.2 目前仍存在的習慣或狀態。

■ Kaori doesn't usually go drinking on a Friday night.
香織不常在週五夜晚去小酌。

■ My grandfather goes to the temple on the first day every month in Lunar Calendar.
我祖父每月農曆初一都會去廟裡拜拜。

5.3 永遠為真的事實。

■ Light travels faster than sound.
光行速度較聲音快。

■ The moon doesn't shine on its own.
月亮不會自行發光。

■ The sun rises in the east and sets in the west.
太陽在東邊升起，西邊落下。

■ Mr. Itou said the moon moves around the Earth.
伊藤老師說月亮繞著地球轉。

■ Mr. Asada told me that the average housefly only lives for two or three weeks.
淺田老師告訴我說一般的家蠅壽命只有兩、三個星期。

> 說明 主要子句雖是過去式，但述及恆久或目前為真的客觀事實或習慣時，間接引句仍用現在簡單式。

5.4 格言或諺語多以現在簡單式呈現，也常出現過去簡單式。

■ Haste makes waste.
欲速則不達。

■ Charity begins at home.
慈善始於家人。

■ A leopard cannot change his spots.
本性難移。

■ A bad shearer never had a good sickle.
劣工尤器。

■ The course of true love never did run smooth.
好事多磨。

■ God made the country and man made the town.
上帝造鄉村，人造鎮。

5.5 正式的宣告。

■ I declare the conference open.
本席宣布會議開始。

■ I announce you husband and wife.
＝ I pronounce you husband and wife.
＝ I will announce the winner after the votes are counted.
我宣布你們成為夫妻。

■ I will fine you NT＄500 for not wearing a helmet.
你未戴安全帽，開罰五百元。

5.6 一些動詞以現在簡單式表示剛剛完成。

■ I forget when Yuriko began to work here.
我忘了百合子什麼時候開始在這裡工作的。

■ I guess Dave is regretful for what he has done.
我猜戴夫一定對自己做過的事懊悔不已。

■ Moe says you are looking for a pet dog to raise.
小萌說妳想找一隻狗來養。

■ I hear Chika felling love with a Tao guy in Orchid Island.
我聽說千香和一名蘭嶼達悟男孩相戀。

5.7 敘述作品情節

■ In the drama, Youko plays a fashionable doctor.
這部戲中，洋子扮演一名時髦的醫生。

■ In Act 1, Hamlet meets the ghost for the first time in this scene.
第一幕，哈姆雷特在這場景第一次遇見鬼魅。

6. 現在進行式

6.1 說話時正在進行的動作。

■ Yuki is singing a love song on the guitar.
小雪正用吉他自彈自唱一首情歌。

■ The dentist is removing the boy's tooth decay.
牙醫要幫男孩補蛀牙。

6.2 目前正在進行的事情，但說話時不一定在進行。

■ My uncle is growing burdocks in southern Taiwan.
我叔叔在南台灣種植牛蒡。

■ The filmmaker is writing a script for a documentary.
製片人正在寫紀錄片腳本。

6.3 暫時狀態或強調特質，連綴動詞搭配現在進行式。

■ You are really being a genius.
你真是個天才。

■ The little girl is being sulky today.
小女孩今天有點生氣。

■ I do not think Akina is being reasonable here.
我想明菜失去理性了。

6.4 剛剛發生的動作。

■ Are you kidding me?
你在跟我開玩笑嗎？

■ I think you're lying to me.
我想你是在騙我。

■ What are you talking about?
你剛剛說什麼？

6.5 連綴動詞搭配現在進行式時，表示逐漸或持續地變化，通常搭配比較語詞。

■ The economic situation is getting worse by the moment.
經濟情勢每下愈況。

■ In Taipei, the house prices are becoming higher and higher.
在台北的房價愈來愈高。

6.6 持續動詞常以現在進行式表示暫時狀態。

■ Eiko is working part time in a cupcake shop.
英子在一家杯子蛋糕店打工。

■ The diplomat's family is staying in a seaside villa.
外交官的家人暫住在一處海濱別墅。

7. 現在完成式

7.1 以現在為觀點，描述已持續一段時間的動作或狀態，可能要繼續。

■ The backpacker has stayed in the hostel for two weeks.
背包客在民宿待兩天了。

■ The researchers have already completed the market survey.
研究人員已完成市場調查。

■ An American guy has eaten nothing but raw meat for five years.
一位美國人有五年時間只吃生肉。

■ The section chief has worked in the company since he graduated from college.
科長大學畢業後就一直在公司工作。

7.2 截至目前的經驗

■ The foreigner has always missed his hometown.
那名外國人一直想家。

■ I haven't talked to my new neighbor since he moved to the community.
我的新鄰居搬進社區後，我從未和他講過話。

7.3 未來時間或條件子句的時態，表示未來時間的 when/if 副詞子句可依語意搭配簡單式、進行式、完成式、未來式等。

7.3.1 現在簡單式

■ Vania will wait till her fiancé comes.
汎尼亞要等到她的未婚夫來。

7.3.2 現在完成式

■ Do not leave class unless you have completed your data analysis.
除非完成資料分析，不然不能下課。

7.3.3 現在進行式

■ If you are still working, you will have to sign this document.
如果你還在工作，你就必須簽署這份文件。

7.3.4 未來式

■ If the store will be open at 10 pm, Jelena will go there for some shopping after work.
如果晚上十點商店還開著，珍蓮娜下班後會去買些東西。

說明

1. if 條件子句強調所述為未來狀況時，搭配未來式。
2. 時間/條件子句搭配未來式的情況：
① before 副詞子句述及不可能實現的內容。
■ The world will come to an end before Mark will go bungee jumping.
馬克要高空彈跳前就會世界末日。

② if 條件子句述及未來的結果。
■ We should adjust the production structure if it will increase productivity.
如果要增加生產力，我們就應調整生產架構。

■ You should make an apology to Steve if it will improve your relationship.
若要改善你們彼此的關係的話，你該向史帝夫道歉。

③ if 條件子句表示意願。
■ If you won't support me, I will face the situation alone.
如果你不支持我，我將獨自面對情勢。

■ If you will make a concession, you will benefit in the future.
你若讓步，將來對你有好處。

8. 現在完成進行式

8.1 描述過去某時進行到現在的動作，可能持續，或剛結束。

■ The little panda has been sleeping for four hours.
圓仔睡了四個鐘頭。

■ Yakov has been working on the construction site all day long.
亞可夫一整天都在工地工作。

■ Mr. Yuri has been living alone in the village since he resigned.
尤里先生退休後就一直在村子獨居。

8.2 截至目前一直重覆發生的動作。

■ Some candidates have been visiting temples these days.
這幾天候選人不斷造訪各廟宇。

■ Justine has been losing his temper unnecessarily with her family members.
賈斯汀一直對家人無端發脾氣。

9. 表示未來動作或狀態的句型

9.1 未來簡單式

9.1.1 單純表示未來的狀況。

■ There will be at hunder shower today.
今天會有大雷雨。

■ You will have to practice Yoga every morning.
你每天早上都要練瑜珈。

■ The Japanese whaling fleet will depart from Japan in five days.
日本捕鯨船隊五天後就要出航。

9.1.2 現在開始進行。

■ The real negotiations will start now.
真正的談判將要開始。

■ From now on, we will have close cooperation with you.
從現在開始，我們將終止與你的合作。

9.1.3 未來的希望或想法。

■ I hope Sotnikova will make a comeback.
我希望索尼科娃能夠反敗為勝。

■ I think they will release the hawk soon.
我想他們很快就會野放老鷹。

■ I guess Olga will waive her right to appeal the case.
我猜歐爾加會放棄上訴的權力。

■ I'm afraid the stray dog will die
我怕流浪狗活不了。

9.2 未來進行式

9.2.1 未來某一時間或階段正在進行的動作。

■ I will be doing my report at 11 tonight.
今晚 11 點我會做我的報告。

■ They will be developing the new website within the next couple of months.
往後幾個月內，他們都會做新的網站。

9.2.2 計畫或臆測即將發生的動作。

■ I will be seeing Ms. Shekhovtseva soon.
我很快就能見到謝荷塞娃女士。

■ It will be raining in the mountain soon.
山區很快就會下雨。

■ We will be making a new plan in the meeting.
我們在會議中會規畫新的計畫。

■ The shuttle bus will be leaving in five minutes.
接駁專車五分鐘後開出。

■ The wounded will be walking on both feet in two weeks.
傷者二週後就能用雙腳走路。

9.2.3 推測當下正在發生的動作。

■ Be quiet! My grandmother will be taking a nap.
安靜！我祖母可能正在小憩。

■ Sonia is not here. She will be teaching in the classroom.
索尼亞不在這裡。她應該在教室上課。

9.2.4 婉轉表達詢問或命令。

■ You will be working overtime tonight.
你今晚要加班。

■ Where will you be seeing my chihuahua?
你是在哪裡看見我的吉娃娃？

■ Will you be coming over to have lunch together?
要一起過來吃晚餐嗎？

9.3 未來完成式

9.3.1 持續至未來某時的動作或狀態，可能繼續，常搭配時間語詞。

■ When they beat the Dragons, they will have won ten games in a row.
他們擊敗紅襪隊的話，他們就十連勝。

■ The Turkish chef will have worked in the restaurant for two years on Christmas this year.
直到今年聖誕節，土耳其主廚就在餐廳工作滿兩年了。

> 說明 未來某時之前將完成的動作，常搭配「by/by the time/before+時間語詞。

■ The cubs will have been killed by the time their mother comes back.
幼獸在牠們母親回來之前就會被殺害。

■ By the end of this year, Kisa will have fulfilled all degree requirements.
今年底之前，奇莎將修完所有學位必修課程。

9.4 未來完成進行式

9.4.1 描述一直持續至未來某時的動作，常搭配時間語詞。

■ By next June, Tanya will have been living in Taipei for three years.
到明年六月，坦雅就在台北住三年了。

■ By 12 a.m., they will have been playing mahjong for ten hours without a pause.
到凌晨 12 點，他們就毫無停歇地打了十個鐘頭的麻將。

■ If it doesn't stop snowing this weekend, it will have been snowing for two weeks without a break.
要是這週末雪還下不停，這場雪將會持續再下 2 個禮拜。

説明 日常語料中，「by/by the time/before ＋時間語詞」不限於搭配未來完成式。

■ I hope by the end of this month, I will have a job again.
我希望這個月底前我能再度找到工作。

■ By next Valentine's Day, I may not remain a single anymore.
明年情人節前我可能就不再是單身了。

9.5 其他表示未來狀態或動作的句型。

9.5.1 即將發生

（1）現在進行式

■ The ferry is leaving in ten minutes.
渡船十分鐘後開出。

■ The plane is taking off in ten minutes.
飛機將於五分鐘後起飛。

■ The tourist is staying at the farm till next Monday.
觀光客將在農場待到下週一。

■ Maurice Sklar is playing the violin during the ceremony.
典禮中摩立斯將演奏小提琴。

■ The CEO is flying to the headquarters of HP tomorrow.
明天執行長要飛到惠普總部。

■ Is the coach having breakfast with us tomorrow morning?
明天教練要和我們一起吃早餐嗎？

（2）am/is/are about to ＋ V，不搭配時間副詞組

■ The debate is about to get started.
辯論會即將開始。

■ The photographic exhibition in the port is about to end.
在港口的攝影展就要結束了。

9.5.2 計畫或預定的動作，可搭配時間副詞組。

(1) 現在簡單式：表示移動、停留、開始、結束等動詞可以現在簡單式表示計畫或預定的未來動作。

■ The visiting scholar arrives this Friday.
訪問學者將於本週五抵達。

■ My summer vacation ends on August 29th.
暑假在八月二十九日結束。

■ Christmas break begins on Sunday, December 23rd.
聖誕假期自十二月二十三日開始。

(2) am／is／are ＋ to V

■ They are to make the novel into a film next summer.
明年夏天他們要將小說拍成電影。

■ We are to attend the funeral the day after tomorrow.
我們後天要出席喪禮。

(3) am／is／are due to ＋ V

■ They are due to have a child in January next year.
他們明年一月要有自己的寶寶。

■ The pope is due to make his final public appearance tomorrow.
明天是教宗最後一場的公開露面。

(4) am／is／are going to ＋ V：表示打算的意念，即將進行或長時間之後，搭配時間副詞組。

■ What are you going to do when you quit school?
你休學後打算做什麼？

■ Isaac is going to be a sailor when he grows up.
以薩長大要當一名水手。

■ The gardener is going to mow the lawn tomorrow morning.
園丁明天一早上藥除草。

語態

　　說明名詞與動詞，尤其是主詞與述語動詞之間主動或被動的語意關聯稱為語態。

◆ 7-1 語態的種類

1. 主動語態：

主詞為動詞所示動作的執行者，句子為主動語態，著重主詞。

■ The vendor cut the watermelon in half.
攤販將西瓜切成兩半。

★常搭配主動語態的動詞：

agree　同意	like　喜歡
belong　屬於	try　嘗試
desire　意欲	watch　觀看
laugh　嘲笑	wish　希望

2. 被動語態：

主詞為動詞所示動作的受事者，句子為被動語態，著重動作本身或其受事者。

■ The watermelon was cut in half by the vendor.
西瓜被攤販切成兩半。

★常搭配被動語態的動詞：

accuse　控訴	delight　使歡喜
arrest　逮捕	determine　決定
bother　打擾	entitle　使…具資格
concern　關心	devote　貢獻
compose　組成	qualify　准予

1. 被動式動詞的時態結構：

被動語態限定動詞組結構是「be ＋過去分詞，be 動詞為限定動詞，表現時態、人稱與數目的變化，但搭配助動詞時，be 動詞為助動詞性質。另外，被動語態罕以未來進行或完成進行式呈現。

> 說明
>
> 1. 被動語態祈使句應搭配 let。
>
> ■ Check the ventilation.
>
> 　　檢查一下通風設備。
>
> **被動**：Let the ventilation be checked.
>
> ■ Don't remove the piston.
>
> 　　不要拆掉活塞。
>
> **被動**：Don't let the piston be removed.
>
> 2. let 無被動語態句型，通常以「be allowed to」代替。
>
> ■ No one is allowed to leave now.
>
> 　　現在誰都不准離開。

1.1 過去簡單式：was/were ＋過去分詞

■ The tool was used by the carpenter.
工具是供木工使用。

■ The nails were driven through the wooden table.
有人將鐵釘穿過木桌。

■ Google was founded by Larry Page and Sergey Brin.
Google 是賴利 ・ 佩吉及謝爾蓋 ・ 布林創立的。

■ Yakov was accused of committing the murder of the tourist.
亞科夫被控謀殺觀光客。

1.2 過去進行式：was/were ＋ being ＋過去分詞，being 是助動詞

■ The machine was being depreciated at ＄1,000 annually.
機器每年折舊 1000 美元。

■ The new systems were being developed during that time.
那期間一直在研發新系統。

1.3 過去完成式：had been ＋過去分詞，been 是助動詞

■ The industrial area had been developed by the end of 2000.
工業區在 2000 年之前就已開發。

■ The problem had been solved before the CEO came to the factory.
問題在執行長來工廠之前就解決了。

1.4 現在簡單式：am/is/are ＋過去分詞

■ The policeman says I am fined for driving without a license.
我因無照駕駛而被罰。

■ English is used in the workshop.
研討會使用英文。

■ Ticket vending machines are located to the right of the escalator.
售票機在手扶梯右邊。

1.5 現在進行式：am/is/are being ＋過去分詞，being 是助動詞

■ I think I am being scammed.
我想我一直遭到詐騙。

■ The telephone is being tapped by the government.
電話一直遭到政府監聽。

■ Live animals are being sold by sidewalk vendors.
路邊攤販都在販售活體動物。

1.6 現在完成式：have/has ＋過去分詞

■ The schedules have been finalized.
行程表都已拍板定案。

■ Some employees have been laid off already.
一些員工已遭解雇。

■ The patient has been transferred to a psychiatric hospital.
病患已轉到精神病院。

1.7 未來簡單式：will be＋過去分詞，be 是助動詞

■ The mail will be forwarded to my executive assistant.
郵件將轉寄給我的主管。

■ The current model of copy machine will be eliminated soon.
這部影印機很快就要淘汰。

1.8 未來完成式：will have been＋過去分詞，been 是助動詞

■ The proposal will have been confirmed by Christmas break.
聖誕假期前企劃就會確認。

■ The consolidation will have been achieved by the end of this year.
今年底之前併購案會完成。

2. 搭配助動詞的被動式動詞結構：
被動式動詞組可搭配情態助動詞，左側的 be/have 應改為原形。

■ The vehicle must have been towed away.
這部車子必須拖走。

■ Investigation into the scandal should be completed as soon as possible.
醜聞案的調查應該儘速完成。

■ The accused ought to have been sentenced to death.
被告應該處死。

■ Extra influenza vaccines have to be destroyed at the end of the flu season.
多餘的流感疫苗在疫情結束後必須銷毀。

3. 被動式動詞組的否定形式

3.1 不含 have 或情態助動詞時，be 動詞右側加入 not。

■ The pregnant woman was not sent to jail.
孕婦未送進監獄。

■ Users are not allowed to log on at this moment.
目前使用者不得登入。

3.2 含 have 或情態助動詞時，have 或情態助動詞右側加入 not，或配合情態助動詞否定形式。

■ The lock had better not be changed.
鎖最好不要更換。

■ My purchase has not been completed yet.
我還沒完成採購。

■ The California firefighter will not be charged.
那名加州消防隊員不會遭到起訴。

■ Reservation may not be cancelled for any reason.
不得以任何理由取消預定。

■ The patient doesn't have to be moved to another hospital.
病患不必移至另一家醫院。

◆ 7-3 被動語態的適用時機

1. 動作執行者（主詞）的考量

1.1 不須述及動作執行者或未知對象

■ Rice is grown in Asia and Australia.
亞洲及澳洲種植稻米。

■ The statue was erected in New York Harbor.
雕像豎立於紐約港。

■ Toxins will be released into your bloodstream.
毒素會排到你的血液。

1.2 刻意不提動作執行者，以使語氣婉轉

- Cellphones need to be turned off or set on vibrate.
  手機要關機或轉震動。

- Personal belongings should be permanently labeled.
  個人物品要一直貼著標籤。

2. 動作受事者（受詞）的考量

- Taxis are not allowed to pick up passengers at this exit.
  計程車不許在這出口載客。

- The elderly and disabled are advised to take the elevator.
  建議老人及殘障人士搭電梯。

- Children under the age of 6 should be accompanied by adults.
  六歲以下孩童應由大人陪伴。

3. 文體用法的考量

3.1 習慣用法

- Well done !
  做得好！

- Easier said than done.
  說得容易，做得難。

- Shakespeare was born in 1564.
  莎士比亞出生於 1564 年。

3.2 句構簡潔

〔對等子句〕

- The lady met many children and was asked for her candies.
  = The lady met many children and they asked her for her candies.
  女子遇見許多孩子，他們都要糖果吃。

〔對等子句〕

■ Katarina is a leader who respects others and is respected by others.

= Katarina is a leader who respects others and she is respected by others.

卡特蓮娜是一名尊重他人，也受人尊重的領導人。

3.3 媒體或科技文體

■ Vice President Shot!

副總統遭槍擊！

■ Glucose can be transformed into energy.

葡萄糖能轉換成能量。

◆ 7-4 被動語態的主詞限制

結構上，及物動詞的受詞移位至被動語態主詞，但基於動詞性質、語意邏輯、格位相容、主詞指涉等限制，不是任何受詞皆可扮演被動句主詞角色。

1. 動詞性質限制：

一些及物動詞沒有或罕用被動語態形式，因此，受事者不可扮演被動句主詞。

■ Mandy resembles her grandmother.

曼蒂長得像她祖母。

■ India used to belong to Great Britain.

印度曾經隸屬於英國。

■ Only a couple of passengers survived the air-crash.

只有兩、三位乘客自空難中生還。

■ 99.9% of air consists of only four compounds.

= 99.9% of air is composed of only four compounds.

99.9% 的空氣僅由四種成分所構成。

★其他沒有或罕用被動語態的及物動詞：

benefit　有益	lack　缺少
contain　包含	last　度過
cost　花費	let　允許
fail　失敗	like　喜歡
flee　逃離	own　擁有
have　擁有	suit　適合

說明 受詞為一些特定結構時，主動句不能改寫為被動句：

〔限定詞指涉主詞〕
■ The copperhead snake bit its own tail.
　　響尾蛇咬自己的尾巴。

〔反身代名詞〕
■ Children enjoyed themselves in the playroom.
　　孩子們在遊戲試玩得很開心。

〔相互代名詞〕
■ They do not trust each other.
　　他們彼此不信任。

〔不定代名詞 it〕
■ Believe it or not!
　　信不信由你。

〔不定詞〕
■ Vadim likes to play Tetris.
　　瓦第姆喜愛玩俄羅斯方塊遊戲。

〔動名詞〕
■ Marina practices playing the cello every day.
　　瑪麗娜每天練習拉大提琴。

2. 語意邏輯限制：

授與動詞搭配直接受詞與間接受詞，但邏輯上無法成為授與動詞受事者的名詞不可扮演被動語態主詞。

■ Sacha bought Nika a glass of pearl milk tea.
莎嘉幫妮卡買一杯珍珠奶茶。

= A glass of pearl milk tea was bought for Nika by Sacha.

【誤】Nika was bought a glass of pearl milk tea by Sacha.

說明 邏輯上，Nika 不會被買，除非述及人口販賣的事實，例如：

■ The boy was bought by a captain for ＄2,000.
船長以 2,000 美元買走男孩。

■ Joseph was bought by a captain named Potiphar.
約瑟被一位名叫波提法的頭子買去。

■ Yeva sold her used camera to Kisa.
耶娃將她的二手相機賣給奇莎。

= A used camera was sold to Kisa by Yeva.

【誤】Kisa was sold a used camera by Yeva.

說明 邏輯上，Kisa 不會被賣，除非述及人口販賣，例如：

■ Joseph was sold into slavery to serve the rulers of Egypt when he was 17.
約瑟十七歲時被賣給埃及統治者。

■ The boy was sold into slavery at the age of seven.
男孩七歲時被交易成為奴隸。

3. 格位相容限制：

限定動詞與介系詞賦予後方名詞受格格位，因此，這些位置的名詞不可移至主詞位置。過去分詞不可賦予後方名詞受格格位，因此，該名詞可移至主詞位置。

被動語態底層結構中，受格性質的名詞不可前移成為句子主詞。

句型一：主詞＋ be ＋過去分詞＋名詞（無格位）

■ Someone awarded Galina a prize.

　有人頒獎給佳莉娜。

　--- was awarded <u>Galina a prize</u> (by someone)
　（底層結構）　　　　無格位

　= Galina was awarded a prize.

　= A prize was awarded to Galina.

句型二：主詞＋ be ＋過去分詞名詞＋ for/to ＋名詞（無格位受格）

■ They offered some food for the children.

　他們提供一些食物給孩童。

　--- was offered <u>some food</u> for the children (by them)
　（底層結構）　　無格位受格

　= Some food was offered for the children by them.

　= They offered the children some food.

　--- were offered <u>the children</u> some food
　（底層結構）　　　　無格位

　= The children were offered some food by them.

4. 主詞指涉限制：

主動語態句子中，they/people 等不定指主詞，搭配「believe/say/think ＋受詞子句」時，若代換為被動語態，主詞以 it 填補。

■ They say the woman has been divorced three times.

　據說女子已離婚三次。

　= It is said that the woman has been divorced three times.

■ It is expected that students will be responsible for their own learning.

　大家都期待學生能為自己的學習負責。

■ People believe the human brain is sensitive to electromagnetic radiation from cell phone exposure.

　=It is believed the human brain is sensitive to electromagnetic radiation from cell phone exposure.

　一般相信人腦會因手機接觸所產生的電磁波而受損。

■ It is considered that the government should raise the minimum wage standard.

一般認為政府應該調高最低工資標準。

■ It is alleged that the driver was driving at 120 miles an hour.

據聲稱，駕駛人飆到時速 120 英哩。

■ It is reported that the temperature will decline sharply tonight.

據報導，今晚氣溫會急速下降。

◆ 7-5 主動句型的被動語態

除了「be ＋過去分詞」表示被動語態之外，一些主動句型搭配被動語意的補語，形成被動語態。

1. 主詞補語

1.1 連綴動詞與主詞之間是被動關係。一些連綴動詞是主事者（某人）施予其主詞（受事者）的動作，這時，主詞與連綴動詞之間是被動關係。

■ The organic coffee tastes great. （咖啡被人品嚐）

■ The incident sounds a little melodramatic. （事件被人聽見）

■ The experiment proved (to be) successful. （實驗被人證實）

■ The essential oil smells natural and delicious. （香油被人聞）

1.2 become／get／grow／stand ＋過去分詞：說明狀態的變化。

■ I can't stand bombarded by brainless news.

我受不了腦殘式新聞的轟炸。

■ Many people grew surprised at the news.

許多人對消息感到訝異。

■ Singh got caught in the rain on the way home.

辛格回家途中遇到大雨。

■ I get dressed, eat breakfast and then leave the house.

我穿衣服、吃早餐，然後出門。

■ I got to become acquainted with a photographer during the trip.

我在旅遊期間認識一名攝影師。

1.3 need/require ＋動名詞，主詞是動名詞的受詞，動名詞可代換為被動式不定詞。

■ The wall needs painting.

= The wall needs to be painted.

= We need to paint the wall.

牆壁需要粉刷。

■ The oil required testing.

= The oil required to be tested.

= We require testing the oil.

油品需要檢驗。

説明 現代英語用法中，want 較少直接搭配動名詞。

〔罕用〕

■ The lawn wants mowing.

■ The lawn wants to be mowed.

〔常用〕

■ The lawn wants for mowing.

草地需要除一下。

1.4 blame/find ＋不定詞片語表示被動語意。

■ Verma is to blame for what happened.

= Verma should be blamed for what happened.

樊馬該為所發生的事受到責備。

■ The clue is easy to find.

= It's easy to find the clue.

= The clue is found easily.

線索容易尋獲。

説明 當代英語用法中，我們多以 rent 或 lease 表示出租，let 較少用。

■ The apartment is to be rented/leased.

公寓要出租。

〔罕用〕

■ The apartment is to let.

2. 不及物動詞：

一些不及物動詞與主詞之間為被動關係，主詞指涉對象不拘，
也不出現於表層結構。

2.1 進行式

■ Our task is finishing.

= Our task is being finished.

我們的工作完成了。

■ The flyers are printing.

= The flyers are being printed.

傳單正在印。

■ The pizza is baking.

= The pizza is being baked.

披薩正在烤。

■ The African drums are beating.

= The African drums are being beat.

有人正在打非洲鼓。

■ My used camera is selling online.

= My used camera is being sold online.

我的二手相機正在線上求售。

2.2 簡單式

■ The tour bus stopped at a little caf in the hills.

= The driver stopped the tour bus at a little caf in the hills.

觀光巴士停在山丘上的一處小咖啡店。

■ Most areas in the industrial zone are flooded.

工業區裡大部分區域淹水。

■ The side door opened.

= Someone opened the side door.

側門開著。

■ The window blew shut.

風把窗戶給吹開了。

【比較】The window won't open.

窗戶打不開。

2.3 否定式

■ The film won't play.

= The film won't be played.

電影不上映了。

■ The tool box won't open.

= The tool box cannot be opened.

工具箱打不開。

■ The wheelchair doesn't move.

= We cannot move the wheelchair.

輪椅動不了。

■ The bottom drawer won't lock.

= The bottom drawer won't be locked.

底部抽屜無法上鎖。

2.4 搭配副詞語詞

■ Dry wood burns easily.

乾木材容易燃燒。

■ This brand of wine sells well.

這牌子的酒賣得很好。

■ The marker writes very well.

馬克筆非常好寫。

■ The tablecloth doesn't wash easily.

桌巾不好洗。

■ This type of grass doesn't trim easily.

這類型的草不易修剪。

★其他能以主動式表示被動語意的動詞：

break 破裂	hang 掛
build 建造	operate 運作
develop 研發	read 閱讀
drop 掉落	shake 搖動
frighten 驚嚇	run 經營
fry 煎	turn 轉

◆ 7-6 被動句型的主動語態

一些被動句型不具被動語意，可視為主動式慣用片語。

■ The train is bound for Chicago.
火車開往芝加哥。

■ My boss is engaged in his business.
我老闆忙於業務。

■ United Nations Headquarters is located in New York City.
聯合國總部位於紐約市。

■ Krishnan was dedicated to educational reform and improvements.
克瑞希南致力於教育改革與提升。

★其他常見的主動語態被動句型：

be absorbed in 專注於	be opposed to 反對
be concerned about 關心	be told = hear 聽說
be inclined to 傾向於	be accustomed to 習慣於
be supposed to 認為	be well-known for 以…聞名

語氣

語氣表示作說者表達事情時的態度，分為直說、祈使、假設等三種。

◆ 8-1 直說語氣

直接表達敘述或疑問的語氣為直說語氣，肯定句、否定定、疑問句、感嘆句等都是直說語氣。

1. 直述句

■ African cats do not eat plants.
非洲貓不吃植物。

■ The octopus catches most of its prey by stealth.
章魚獵食大多都靠奇襲抓來的。

■ Water is composed of both hydrogen and oxygen.
水是由氫和氧組成的。

■ Almost half of the teenagers in the world have never eaten a steak.
世界上半數的青少年幾乎從未吃過牛排。

2. 疑問句

2.1 Yes-No 問句

2.1.1 be 動詞為首

■ Are killer whales endangered?
殺人鯨瀕臨絕跡嗎？

■ Was there a real King Arthur?
真的有亞瑟王嗎？

2.1.2 一般助動詞為首

■ Did you stay up late last night?
你昨晚熬夜嗎？

■ Are you going to Andre Rieu's concert next month?
　你要去下個月的安德烈里歐音樂會嗎？

■ Have you ever been to Stratford-Upon-Avon, William Shakespeare's hometown?
　你去過史特拉福，莎士比亞的故居嗎？

2.1.3 情態助動詞為首

■ Will the world come to an end in 2050?
　世界終結於 2050 年嗎？

■ Could you please show me your room card?
　麻煩讓我看一下房間卡？

■ Did you used to smoke?
　你以前抽過香菸嗎？

> 說明 將「used to」視為獨立動詞組時，搭配 did 形成問句。若將「used to」視為一般動詞組或助動詞時，則有不同的問句形式。

〔一般動詞組〕
■ **Did you use to smoke?**
〔助動詞組〕
■ **You used to smoke?**

2.2 Wh- 問句

■ Who's in charge here?
　這裡誰負責？

■ What did you feed your iguana?
　你餵什麼給你的綠鬣蜥吃？

■ Why not give them a surprise visit?
　何不給他們來個驚喜的一訪？

■ Where was the large flying squirrel found?
　大飛鼠在哪裡發現的？

■ When will we visit the Maori tribe in New Zealand?
　我們什麼時候要造訪紐西蘭毛利部落？

■ How come you came home earlier from school today?
你今天怎麼提早下課回家？

2.3 附加問句

■ You have been to Israel before, haven't you?
你以前去過以色列，不是嗎？

■ You forgot to turn off the air conditioner, didn't you?
你忘了關冷氣，對吧？

■ Let's go out for dinner, shall we?
我們出去吃晚餐，好嗎？

■ Please restart your system first, will you?
麻煩先重新啟動系統，好嗎？

2.4 間接問句

■ Do you know whose heating pad this is?
你知道這是誰的暖暖包嗎？

■ I cannot feel where the keys are.
我摸不到鑰匙在哪裡。

■ I don't know when we will see each other again.
不知我們哪時候才能再見到彼此？

■ I'm wondering what time I should check out tomorrow.
不知道我明天幾點退房？

■ Please show me how I can remove my phone number from search engines.
麻煩告訴我要怎樣從搜尋引擎除去我的手機號碼？

3. 感嘆句

■ What a cute raccoon!　　　　　　　好可愛的浣熊！
= What a cute raccoon it is!
= It is such a cute raccoon!

■ How luxurious a hostel! 　　　好豪華的民宿！

　= How luxurious a hostel it is!

　= It is such a luxurious a hostel!

說明 感嘆句是主詞補語的倒裝句型。

1.1 感嘆詞：表達情緒或意願的語詞為感嘆詞。感嘆詞與句子結構無關，但語意上卻是息息相關。感嘆詞可由名詞、動詞、形容詞或副詞等實詞功能轉變而產生。

1.1.1 常見的感嘆詞

Gosh 啊；糟了	Yuk 呸！啐！討厭！
Hey 嗨；喂	Sh 噓！別作聲！
Ooh 哦！	Wow 哇！噢！
Ouch 哎喲！	Uh-huh 嗯嗯！

1.1.2 源於名詞的感嘆詞

Congratulations! 恭喜！	Nonsense! 胡說！廢話！
Danger! 危險！	Shame! 羞愧！
Fire! 失火！	Shit! 呸！放屁！
Horrors! 恐怖！	Silence! 安靜！別作聲！

1.1.3 源於動詞的感嘆詞

Come! 來吧！	Help! 救人阿！
Listen! 注意聽！	Hush! 噓；別作聲
Look! 看！	Stop! 停下來！
Come on! 少來！	Welcome! 歡迎！

1.1.4 源於形容詞的感嘆詞

Fine!　好！	Stranger!　奇怪！
Great!　很棒！	Ridiculous!　荒唐！

1.1.5 源於副詞的感嘆詞

Well　喲，啊，嗯	Really　真的；是嗎；真是的
There　你瞧；好啦；喂	Indeed　真是；哦，不見得吧

1.1.6 片語結構的感嘆詞

Bless me!　哎呀！我的天啊！	Look out!　小心！
Damn me!　我太吃驚了！	My goodness!　我的天哪！
Dear me!　哦，我的天啊！	So long!　再見！
Hurry up!　快一點！	Well done!　幹得好，太棒啦！

◆ 8-2 祈使語氣

表達命令、禁止、勸告、請求、建議、邀請的語氣為祈使語氣。

〔命令〕

■ Turn off the smartphone now. It's time to go to bed.
　馬上關掉手機，睡覺時間到了。

〔禁止〕

■ Don't touch the statue.
　請勿觸碰雕像。

〔勸告〕

■ Be careful when shopping online.
　上網購物時要當心。

〔請求〕

■ Please lend me your flashlight.
　請借我你的手電筒。

〔建議〕
- Help yourself to the handmade cookies.
  請自行取用手工餅乾。

〔邀請〕
- Come join us for a drink.
  和我們去喝一杯。

1. 祈使句的語氣：

1.1 否定式：「Don't／Never／Let's not／Don't let ＋原形動詞…」形成否定式祈使句。

- Don't be afraid.
  不要怕。

- Don't use the flash on your camera.
  請勿使用相機上的閃光燈。

- Don't park here!　這裡請勿停車。
  ＝ No parking.

說明 「No ＋動名詞／名詞」表示禁止語意的祈使句，例如：
- No entrance.　　禁止進入。
- No admittance.　禁止入場。

- Please don't stand so close to me.
  不要站的離我這麼近。

- Never give up.
  絕對不要放棄。

- Let's not stay here.
  我們不要待在這裡。

- Don't let the file be deleted upon closing.
  不要讓檔案給刪掉了。

說明 受詞為第三人稱的被動式祈使句否定句型為「don't let..」。

1.2 強調：祈使句搭配助動詞 do 可表示強調。

■ Do be quiet in here.
在這裡面務必要安靜。

■ Do turn off your cell phone.
務必要關掉手機。

1.3 婉轉：祈使句表示婉轉時，句首可搭配 kindly，或句首與句尾搭配副詞 please。

■ Please be seated.
請坐下。

■ Dear all, kindly check your e-mail.
各位，麻煩收一下電子郵件。

■ Kindly, don't hesitate to contact me.
不用客氣，儘管跟我聯絡。

2. 祈使句的語態：

祈使句可表示被動語態，受詞為第二人稱時，原形動詞直接加過去分詞；受詞為第一、人稱時，受詞後接「be +過去分詞」。

■ Let it be done now.
現在就動手。

■ Let the civet cat be kept in the cage.
把果子狸關在籠子裡。

■ Don't get bit by snakes while hiking in the mountains.
去山區健行時不要被蛇咬到。

3. 祈使句主詞的保留：

祈使句主詞為第二或第三人稱已知的主詞，通常省略，表示強調或區分時，可保留。

■ Nino, don't go hunting in a restricted hunting area.
尼諾，不要去禁獵區打獵。

■ You shut up!
你閉嘴。

■ You come to my office right now.
你馬上到我辦公室。

■ Tessa and Primo come to the front.
提莎和普莉摩到前面來。

■ Everybody put down your pen.
各位，放下你們的筆。

■ Someone go answer the door.
有人要去應門。

■ Nobody move.
都不許動。

4. 祈使語氣的語詞：

除了原形動詞之外，其他一些語詞也可表示祈使語氣。

■ Patience !　　　要有耐心！
= Be patient.

■ Fresh paint !　　油漆未乾。
= The paint is not dry.

■ Careful !　　　　小心！
= Be careful!

■ Quickly!　　　　趕快！

■ At ease !　　　　放輕鬆！
= Stand at ease.

■ Hats off !　　　　帽子脫下來。
= Take off your hat !

■ Hands up !　　　手舉起來！
= Put your hands above your head.

■ Down in front !　　坐到前面來。
= You sit down in front.

5. 祈使句的子句加接：

祈使句搭配未來式 and ／ or 對等子句，表示結果，這時祈使句可視為條件句。

■ Work hard, and you will pass the test.

= If you work hard, you will pass the test.

努力，你就能通過測驗。

■ Hurry up, or you will miss the bus.

= If you don't hurry up, you will miss the bus.

趕快，否則你會錯過公車。

◆ 8-3 假設語氣

1. 假設語氣的形式：

就動詞結構而言，假設語氣的動詞組有假設過去式、假設過去完成式、假設未來式、假設未來完成式等四種形式，分別表示不同時間或可能性的假設狀況。

1.1 假設過去式：表示現在事實相反，或意願、勸告的假設語氣，搭配現在結果或過去結果的子句。

1.1.1 現在條件 - 現在結果：結果子句動詞結構為「過去式動詞/ could / might / should / would ＋原形動詞」。

■ If I were you, I would not choose that hotel again.

如果我是你，我不會再去那家民宿。

■ If it were raining, the hikers would get wet.

如果現在下著雨，健行的人會淋濕。

> 說明 條件子句可搭配進行式以表示正在進行。

■ If I had enough money, I could take over the restaurant.

如果我的資金充裕，我會頂下那家複合餐廳。

■ I wouldn't get into the pool even if I could swim.

即使我會游泳，我也不會進去池子。

說明 「even if」的意思是即使，適用各種條件句型，強調假設語氣。

■ Even if we reach an agreement, I will not sign any contract.
即使我們達成協議，我也不會簽任何合約。

■ Even if we had made a reservation earlier, it wouldn't have been cheaper.
即使我們提早預訂，價格也不會較便宜。

1.1.2 現在條件 - 過去結果：結果子句動詞結構為「過去式動詞/ could / might / should / would ＋ have ＋過去分詞」。

■ If I were you, I would have gone to karaoke with them last night.
如果我是你，我昨晚會跟他們去唱卡拉 OK。

■ If I were you, I would have called the police that time without hesitation .
如果我是你，我那時候會毫無猶豫地報警。

說明

1. 過去條件若是真實，未來結果以未來式表示。

■ If you missed the first shuttle bus, you won't get to the station by 7.
如果你錯過第一班接駁車，你就無法七點以前抵達車站。

2. 未來條件若是可能，條件子句用現在式，結果子句用未來式。

■ If you miss the first shuttle bus, you will not get to the station by 10.
如果你錯過第一班接駁車，你就無法十點以前抵達車站。

1.1.3 would rather 句型：表示意願或勸告。美式英語中多用 had rather，而「would sooner/would rather」意思一樣，但較不常用。

(1) 表示對現在或未來的意念。

① would rather ＋原形動詞…than ＋原形動詞，寧願…而不要。

句型：would rather ＋原形動詞…than ＋原形動詞

＝ would ＋原形動詞…rather than ＋原形動詞

倒裝：rather than ＋原形動詞 , would ＋原形動詞

■ I would rather choose to buy a domestic car.

＝ I prefer to choose to buy a domestic car.
我寧願選擇買國產車。

■ I would rather not to make an order online.
我寧願不在線上訂貨。

■ They would rather die than surrender.
　= They would die rather than surrender.
他們寧死不投降。

【倒裝】Rather than surrender, they would die.

■ Bansi would rather stay at home than go shopping with you.
　= Bansi would stay at home rather than go shopping with you.
　= Bansi prefers to stay at home rather than go shopping with you.
　= Bansi prefers staying at home to going shopping with you.

【倒裝】Rather than go shopping with you, Bansi would stay at home.
班西寧可待在家裡，也不跟你去逛街。

■ I would rather fail than cheat during the test.
　= I would fail rather than cheat during the test.
　= I prefer to fail rather than cheat during the test.
　= I prefer failing to cheating during the test.
我寧願被當，也不要考試作弊。

【倒裝】Rather than cheat during the test, I would fail.

■ Henry would rather that his girlfriend worked in the same department as he does．
亨利希望他的女朋友和他在一個部門工作。

② would rather ＋過去式句子

■ When would you rather I arrived at the destination?
　= When would you prefer me to arrive at the destination?
你要我什麼時候到目的地？

■ I would rather you didn't chew betel nuts in here.
　= I would prefer you not to chew betel nuts in here.
　= I would prefer it that you didn't chew betel nuts in here.
我寧可你不在這裡面嚼檳榔。

■ I would sooner that boy didn't lie to me.

= I would like that boy not to lie to me.

寧願那男孩沒對我說謊。

(1) 表示過去未實現的意念

① would rather + have 過去分詞…過去分詞：，寧願…而不要，句子主詞與「have + 過去分詞」的動作產生者一致。

■ I would rather have visited you last week, but I didn't.

我上星期本來要去看你，後來沒去。

■ I would rather have gone to the library than stayed at the dorm yesterday.

我昨天寧願去圖書館，也不要待在宿舍。

② would rather ＋過去完成式子句，主要子句與補語子句主詞不一致。

■ I would rather the client had not cancelled the contract.

= I would prefer that the client had not cancelled the contract.

真希望客戶沒有取消訂單。

■ I would rather the incident had never happened.

= I wish the incident had never happened.

= I would prefer it if the incident had never happened.

事情都沒發生就好了。

■ What would you rather I had talked about at that time?

= What would you have preferred me to talk about at that time?

你是要我那時候談什麼？

說明 「had better/best」動詞組所述內容尚未成真，屬於假設語氣。

■ We had better not touch that snake.

我們最好不要碰那條蛇。

■ You had best come back to the dormitory before midnight.

你最好半夜之前回到宿舍。

1.2 假設過去完成式：過去事實相反的假設，結果子句依過去或現在時間搭配不同的動詞結構。

1.2.1 過去條件 - 過去結果

句型：had ＋過去分詞

could/might/should/would ＋ have ＋ 過去分詞

■ If I had attended the meeting, I would have opposed the proposal.

我若出席會議，我會反對提案。

【事實】I didn't attend the meeting, so I didn't oppose the proposal.

■ If I had not adopted the Labrador Retriever, it would have been killed by the animal shelter.

我若不領養這隻拉不拉多犬，牠會遭到安樂死。

【事實】I adopted the Labrador Retriever, so it wasn't killed by the animal shelter.

■ If you had applied for the position earlier, then you might have been accepted.

你若早點申請這職位，你或許會錄取。

【事實】You didn't apply for the position earlier, so you were not accepted.

■ If you had been staying in the inn overnight, you would have felt how horrible it was.

你若待在飯店過夜，你就能感受有多恐怖。

【事實】You didn't stay in the inn overnight, so you didn't feel how horrible it was.

1.2.2 過去條件 - 現在結果

句型：had ＋過去分詞

could/might/should/would ＋原形動詞

■ If I had parked my car on the red line, it would be towed away by now.

我若將車子停在紅線，現在就被拖吊了。

【事實】I didn't park my car on the red line, so it has not been towed away by now.

■ If you had bought that stock, you would have lost a lot of money by now.

你若買那檔股票，你現在就虧大了。

【事實】 You didn't buy that stock, so you didn't lose a lot of money by now.

■ If you had rejected financial support, you would not be accused of bribery now.

你若拒絕金援，你現在就不會遭到賄賂的指控了。

【事實】 You didn't reject financial support; you are accused of bribery now.

1.2.3 對過去行為表示懊悔或婉惜，常搭配 wish／if only 句型。

(1) 假設過去完成式：

■ I wish I had tested the oil thoroughly last year.

= If only I had tested the oil thoroughly last year.

= I'm sorry that I didn't test the oil thoroughly last year.

去年我若徹底檢查油品就好了。

■ I wish I had been to the costume party last Friday, but I didn't.

= I wish I could have been to the costume party last Friday.

= I wish it had been possible for me to go to the costume party last Friday, but it wasn't.

= If only I could have been to the costume party last Friday. I'm sure it was a great occasion.

= I'm sorry that I couldn't go to the costume party last Friday.

我上週五要是有去參加化裝舞會就好了。

■ Adam Martin really wishes he hadn't drunk so much last night.

= Adam Martin regrets drinking so much last night.

馬丁懊悔昨夜實在喝太多了。

1.3 假設未來式：針對未來的假設依實現可能性分為「were to ＋原形動詞」、「should ＋原形動詞」、「過去式動詞／ were」等三種句型。值得注意的是，從邏輯而言，未來的假 設尚未驗證，因此不存在未來事實相反的假設。

1.3.1 were to ＋原形動詞：

(1) 未來不可能實現：

句型：were to ＋原形動詞

　　　 could / might / should / would ＋ 原形動詞

　　　 were to be ＋現在分詞直說句型

- ■ If a pig were to fly, I would change / change my mind.
  豬要是能飛，我就改變心意。

- ■ Even if a tsunami were to happen, the nuclear facilities in this country are fortified.
  即使發生海嘯，這國家的核能設施防護沒問題。

(2) 現在事實相反：

- ■ If I were to come down with H1N1 now, I would stay at home all day.

【事實】I do not come down with H1N1 now, so I won't stay at home all day.
  我現在若是感染了 H1N1，我會整天待在家裡。

- ■ If it were raining now, the July heat would not be so unbearable.

【事實】It is not raining now, so the July heat is still so unbearable.
  若是現在下雨，七月熱氣就不會那麼難耐。

(3) 過去事實相反，搭配過去完成式。

- ■ If I were not working part time, I would have quit school.

【事實】I worked part time, so I didn't quit school.
  我若沒去打工，我就會休學。

- ■ If I were not transferred to Tokyo, I would not have gotten to know my wife.

【事實】I was transferred to Tokyo, so I got to know my wife there.
  我若沒外調東京，我就不會與我太太相識。

- ■ If there were a tornado touchdown, I would likely have known about it from Twitter.
  若是有龍捲風侵襲，我可能是從推特得知的。

1.3.2 should ＋原形動詞：未來實現可能性小，強調不經意發生，意思是「萬一」。另外，主要子句可搭配祈使句型、「will ＋原形動詞」、「should/would ＋原形動詞」等動詞結構。

■ If you should not arrive on time, please let me know soon.
萬一你無法準時抵達，請儘快告知。

■ If we should be off due to typhoon tomorrow, we will go to enjoy karaoke together.
萬一明天放颱風假，我們就一起去唱卡拉 OK。

■ If there should be rain tonight, the campfire would be cancelled.
萬一今晚下雨，營火晚會就要取消了。

説明 述及主詞意願時，條件子句搭配 would。

■ If Okosa would sell his old Mercedes-Benz, I would buy it right away.
歐克薩若是要賣掉他的老賓士，我會立刻買下。

【事實】Okosa isn't willing to sell his old Mercedes-Benz, so I won't buy it.
歐克薩無意賣掉他的老賓士，因此我無法立刻買下。

■ If Reggie should make an apology, we would forgive him.
瑞及若是要道歉，我們會原諒他。

【事實】Reggie isn't willing to make an apology, so we are not willing to forgive him.

1.3.3 過去式動詞/were：表示未來實現的可能性大。

■ If I were invited to the luncheon, I would show up.
要是我受邀午宴，我會出席。

■ If you forgot your password, just insert the USB drive and you can reset your password.
若是你忘記密碼，你就放入隨身碟，這樣你就能重設密碼。

1.3.4 對現在的期待或懊悔,搭配 wish/if only 句型。

- I wish I stayed at that hotel. Then I could meet the Korean actress.

  = If only I stayed at that hotel. Then I could meet the Korean actress.

  = I'm sorry that I don't stay at that hotel, so I can't meet the Korean actress.

  我要是投宿在那家飯店,我就會遇到那位韓星。

- Matt wishes he were taller.

  = If only Matt were taller.

  = Matt is sorry that he is not tall.

  馬帝希望自己長高一點。

說明

1. wish/if only 句型搭配假設語氣未來式,同樣表示對現在的期待或懊悔。

- I wish I could do magic.

  = I'm sorry I can't do magic.

  要是我會變魔術就好了。

- Excellent! I wish I could do a calculation in my head like you.

  = I'm sorry that I can't do a calculation in my head like you.

  好厲害!要是我的心算也能像你這樣就好了。

2. 假設未來式的 wish/if only 句型可表示未來的期待。

- I wish it would be a sunny day tomorrow.

  但願明天天氣晴朗。

- I wish more people would visit my website.

  但願更多人到我的網站。

3. 「wish…would…」句型常表示抱怨或要求。

- I wish they wouldn't stay in here.

  我不待在這裡面就好了。

1.4 假設未來完成式:動詞組結構「should + have + 過去分詞」,表示主觀意念或對事實的情緒反應。

■ How should we have dealt with the situation in that case?
我們該如何處理目前的狀況在這件案子中？

■ I sometimes wonder if I should have left my hometown.
有時候我會想我該不該離開家鄉。

■ The student on duty should have cleaned the blackboard.
值日生該清理黑板。

■ It's strange that it should have been so hot on a winter day.
　= It's strange that it (should) be so hot on a winter day.
　= It's strange that it is so hot on a winter day.
在冬天這樣的日子不該這麼熱的。

> 說明　「It's strange that…」句型強調對所述事實的訝異、懊悔或期待
> 的情緒，that 子句可搭配「should have ＋ 過去分詞」、「should
> ＋ 原形動詞（美式英語省略 should）」、直說語氣等。

2. 假設語氣的結構：

除了假設語氣副詞子句之外，其他語詞也可表示不存在的事物、
未實現的狀況或非真的敘述，這些都是假設語氣的表現。

2.1 名詞

■ An immortal person would feel no pain at all.
不死的人不會有任何疼痛感覺。

■ A special penguin could fly to Antarctic to find its birthplace.
一種特殊的企鵝會飛到南極找尋他們的出生地。

2.2 不定詞

■ It would be a great pity not to help and encourage that poor
child.
　= It would be a great pity if we didn't help and encourage that
poor child.
要是不協助並鼓勵那位貧童，那就太遺憾了。

■ To listen to you, I would believe you to be a person of wisdom.

= If I listened to you, I would believe you to be a person of wisdom.

要是聽你說話，我就會相信你是位智慧人。

2.3 分詞片語

■ The same crime, committed in Malaysia, would result in caning as a punishment.

= The same crime, if it should be committed in Malaysia, would result in caning as a punishment.

相同的犯罪要是在馬來西亞就會被處鞭刑。

■ Separated from its master, the dog would suffer from separation anxiety.

= If the dog were separated from its master, it would suffer from separation anxiety.

若是和主人分開，小狗會有分離焦慮的症狀。

■ Weather permitting, the campaign will be held as scheduled.

若是天氣允許，活動會如期舉行。

2.4 形容詞片語

■ The bitter sugar cane would taste strange.

苦的甘蔗嚐起來會很奇怪。

■ Any zebra stronger than a lion would attack and kill it.

任何較獅子強壯的斑馬都會擊殺牠。

■ We need proper amount of food every day. Too much, and we will gain weight. Too little, and we will lose weight.

我們每天需要適量的食物。太多，體重會增加；太少，體重會減少。

2.5 介系詞片語：but for, in case, in the absence of, without 等介系詞片語呈現假設語氣。

2.5.1 but for：若非，意思是 without，加接片語，可代換為條件句「if it weren't for」或「if it hadn't been for」，表示現在或過去的結果。

■ But for your help, we would have been in big trouble.

要不是你的幫忙，我們麻煩就大了。

= Without your help, we would have been in big trouble.

= If it hadn't been for your help, we would have been in big trouble.

■ But for Manny, the team wouldn't know what to do now.

要不是曼尼，球隊現在會不知所措。

= Without Manny, the team wouldn't know what to do now.

= If it weren't for Manny, the team wouldn't know what to do now.

【比較】With thick fur, polar bears can exist in the very cold Arctic climate.

因為有厚重皮毛，北極熊能生存在極冷的北極氣候下。

■ In the absence of proper training, your dog would be hard to control.

要是沒有適當訓練，你的狗會難以馴服。

2.5.2 in case：引導表示原因的片語或子句，子句常搭配 should。

■ In case of blackout, an emergency exit sign will turn on by itself.

= If there should be blackout, an emergency exit sign will turn on by itself.

萬一停電，緊急逃生信號會自動開啟。

■ I'll stop to take a nap in case I get tired.

萬一我累了，我會停下來休息。

= I'll stop to take a nap because I may get tired.

【比較】I'll stop to take a nap if I get tired.

= I'll stop to take a nap when I get tired.

如果我累了，我就會停下來休息。

2.6 連接詞：but, except that, only (that), or else 等連接詞引導的子句表示主要子句的條件時，主要子句應搭配假設語氣。

■ But that I saw it, I wouldn't have believed such a sight.

若不是親眼目睹，我也不會相信那樣的景象。

■ I would attend the marathon except that I am in poor health condition.

要不是我健康狀況不佳，我會參加馬拉松活動。

■ I would have quit my current job, only(that)my director encouraged me to keep going.

〔直述語氣〕

要不是我主管鼓勵我繼續往前，我可能放棄目前的工作。

■ We had to take immediate action, or else we would lose the contract.

我們必須立即行動，否則會丟掉合約。

3. 子句的假設語氣：

除了條件副詞子句，其他子句也可表現假設語氣。

3.1 名詞子句

3.1.1 主詞：補語為表示意願、要求、命令、建議等語詞時，子句的真主詞可搭配假設語氣。

■ It's advisable that the proposal (should) be rejected.

建議駁回該提案。

■ It's imperative that the patient (should) be taken to the isolation ward.

病患應送往隔離病房。

■ It's recommended that we (should) organize a special committee.

建議我們規劃一個特別任務小組。

■ Is it probable that the contractor (should) have changed his mind?

承包商可能改變想法嗎？

説明

1. 美式英語中 should 通常省略。

2. impossible, likely 通常搭配 would，而不是 should。

■ It's impossible that Khelia(would) have done such a stupid thing.

凱莉亞不可能做這樣的事情。

■ It's not likely that they (would) become reconciled now.
現在他們可能和解了。

★其他可搭配假設語氣的主詞子句的形容詞：

appropriate 適當的	essential 重要的
crucial 關鍵的	necessary 必須的
desirable 理想的	proper 適當的

3.1.2 受詞：表示意願、建議、要求、命令、情緒等語意的動詞，受詞子句可搭配假設語氣。

■ Lisa desires that she (should) become a flight attendant.
麗莎想要成為一名空姐。

■ Prof. Lin requested that the report (should) be submitted this week.
林教授要求這週交報告。

■ Dr. Chen suggested that I (should) be taking exercise.
陳醫生建議我要運動。

■ The dietician proposed that Chloë should eat more vegetables.
營養師建議克萊爾多吃蔬菜。

■ Sam resolved that he would marry no one but Nesbitt.
山姆執意非內比斯不娶。

★其他可搭配假設語氣受詞子句的動詞：

advice 建議	insist 堅持
arrange 安排	intend 企圖
ask 要求	order 命令
command 命令	prefer 偏好
demand 要求	require 要求

情態助動詞 may 表示祝福時，搭配的名詞子句搭配假設語氣未來式，should 省略。

- ■ May you be blessed.　　　願你蒙福！
  = I hope you are blessed.
  = It is hoped that you are blessed.

- ■ May you succeed!　祝你成功！
  = I hope you succeed.
  = It is hoped that you succeed.

3.1.3 主詞補語：主詞為表示意願、建議、判決等語意的名詞時，補詞子句可搭配假設語氣。

- ■ Their desire is that the negotiation (should) be continued.
  他們希望能夠繼續協商。

- ■ My suggestion is that we (should)reduce the price by 10%.
  我建議我們降價一成。

- ■ The final sentence is that the robber (should) be in jail for the rest of his life.
  最後判決是搶匪終生監禁。

- ■ Méav's idea is that the child (should) be transferred to the emergency room.
  梅夫的想法是將孩子送到急診室。

3.2 形容詞子句：形容詞子句所述尚未成真時，搭配假設語氣。

3.2.1 限定句型：It is high time that…：「該…的時候了」表示意念尚未成真，形容詞子句應搭配假設現在式或未來式（should 可省略），補語連詞 that 及強調詞 high 可省略。

- ■ It's high time that Hayley should go to bed.
  海莉該去睡覺囉！
  = It's time Hayley go to bed.
  = It's time Hayley went to bed.

- ■ It's high time that you should leave the house.
  你該出門了。
  = It's time you leave the house.
  = It's time you left the house.

3.2.2 非限定句型：即一般的形容詞子句。

- It's never easy to find an employee who would be able to use Latin.

  要找到能夠使用拉丁文的員工很難

- Any one who would join the military should be in good health condition.

  任何要從軍的人要有良好的健康狀況。

3.3 讓步副詞子句：假設語氣可用於從屬連接詞或 wh-ever 語詞 引導的讓步副詞子句。

3.3.1 從屬連接詞引導的副詞子句

- Though he be a leading cadre, Mr. Westenis quite humble.

  雖然身為領導幹部，威斯騰拉先生相當謙遜。

- Even if it were raining, my neighbor would still walk his dog.

  即使下著雨，我鄰居還是在遛狗。

3.3.2 wh-ever 語詞引導的副詞子句

(1) 複合關係代名詞

- Come what may, we would be on your side.

  不論發生什麼事，我都支持你。

  = Whatever happens, we would be on your side.

- Whatever the witness might say, the investigators would verify it.

  不論目擊者說什麼，調查員都會查證。

(2) 複合關係副詞

- Wherever the snake might hide, the snake-catcher could find it.

  不論蛇躲到哪裡，抓蛇的人都找得到。

- However risky it might be, I would make the investment.

  不論會是怎樣的風險，我都會投資下去。

3.4 目的副詞子句：假設語氣可用於目的副詞子句，強調目的尚未達成。

3.4.1 肯定目的

■ MacLane is practicing hard that/so that/in order that he might pass the test.

麥克萊恩一直努力練習，就為了能夠通過測試。

3.4.2 否定目的

■ The technician turned off the machine lest it (should) be overheated.

技術員關掉機器，以免過熱。

■ The transfer student is working hard at her studies for fear (that) she should fail.

轉學生一直努力用功，以免被當。

3.5 方式副詞子句：假設語氣用於方式副詞子句，表示非真的意念。

■ Boone talked as though he had been to Huis Ten Bosch.

布甫說起話來宛如自己去過豪斯登堡。

■ Some owners treat their dog as if it were their own child.

一些飼主對待他們的狗宛如家人。

3.6 同位語子句：建議、期望、命令或邀請等語意的名詞，因所述內容尚未成真，同位語子句可搭配未來式假設語氣，should 可省略。但真實語料中，非假設語氣的同位語子句更是常見。

■ There was a suggestion that the regular meeting (should) be held on Monday.

建議例會於週一舉行。

■ The commander gave the order that the army (should) make an attack at dawn.

指揮官下令部隊拂曉出擊。

■ Kelly sent me an e-mail with the request that I should give him the desired information.

凱莉寄一封電子郵件給我，要求我提供他要的資料。

■ I agree with their insistence that children should not use smartphones for more than 30 minutes a day.

我同意他們對孩童使用智慧型手機一天不超過 30 分鐘的堅持。

4. 條件句構的省略

4.1 省略 if：假設語氣條件子句的連接詞 if 可省略，were 及助動詞移至主詞左側。

■ If it were a Friday night, I would go out with Claire.

如果是星期五晚上，我就會和克萊爾出去。

【省略】Were it a Friday night, I would go out with Claire.

■ If there should be a problem, just give me a call without hesitation.

【省略】Should there be a problem, just give me a call without hesitation.

有問題的話，儘管打電話給我。

■ If we had made a final decision earlier, we would have obtained the contract.

【省略】Had we made a final decision earlier, we would have obtained the contract.

我們若早點做最後決定，我們就獲得合約了。

4.2 只保留 if 及補語：一些慣用語詞中，條件子句的 if 及主詞通常省略。

■ If in doubt, get it checked out.

若有存疑，就過來看看。

■ I'd like a seat by the window, if possible.

可能的話，我要坐窗邊座位。

■ If necessary, contact me at any time.

有需要的話，隨時和我聯繫。

■ It might rain in the mountains this weekend. If so, we will not go mountain climbing.

週末山區可能下雨，若是這樣，我們就不去爬山。

> 說明 已知上下文時，「if so」、「if not」可視為條件句的縮減。

4.3 只保留受詞或補語：傳達條件訊息

■ With full effort, Caroline wouldn't have failed.

如果盡力以赴，卡羅不會失敗。

If Caroline had made full effort, she wouldn't have failed.
（底層結構）

■ An experienced technician, Chad wouldn't make such a mistake.

If he were an experienced technician, Chad wouldn't make
（底層結構）
such a mistake.

如果是有經驗的技術員，查德就不會犯這樣的錯誤。

4.4 省略條件子句：「條件 - 結果」順序的掉尾句中，表示結果的主要子句置於句子右側，傳達句子的訊息焦點。因此，句子左側的條件子句省略後，言談重點完全在結果子句。

4.4.1 主要子句為直述句

■ That would be fine with me.

那我可以。

If the meeting were from 10 to 11 a.m., that would be fine with me.
（底層結構）

如果會議是在上午 11 點至 12 點之間，那我可以。

■ They would have lost the game.

他們可能輸掉比賽。

But for your instruction, they would have lost the game.
（底層結構）

要不是你的指導，他們可能輸掉比賽。

■ You might go out for dinner with us.

你或許可以和我們外出吃晚餐。

If you were not in a hurry, we might go out for dinner together.
（底層結構）

你若不趕，或許可以和我們外出吃晚餐。

4.4.2 主要子句為疑問句：禮貌而婉轉地表達請求或詢問。

■ Would you lend me some money?

可以借我一些錢嗎？

If it were convenient for you, would you lend me some money?
（底層結構）

你如果方便，可以借我一些錢嗎？

■ Could you have misunderstood the customer's explanation?

你可能對顧客的說明有誤解？

4.5 省略結果子句：相對於省略條件子句的掉尾句，條件子句置於句子右側，承載訊息焦點，因此，句子左側的結果子句省略後，言談重點在條件子句。

■ If I were still young !

要是我還年輕的話！

■ I would climb Mt. Everest if I were still young.

要是我還年輕的話，我會去爬艾佛倫斯山！

■ If I lost the final !

要是我輸了決賽！

■ What should I do if I lost the final?

要是我輸了決賽，我該怎麼辦？

■ If Michael denied it?

要是麥可否認！

■ What would happen if Michael denied it?

要是麥可否認，那會怎樣？

■ Well, if I had not parked my car at the entrance!

嗯，要是我沒將車子停在入口就沒事了！

説明 否定式的 if 子句可表示驚訝或沮喪的情緒。

■ Suppose/supposing you won the lottery?
　要是你中頭彩呢？

■ Suppose/supposing you won the lottery, what would you do?
　要是你中頭彩，你會怎樣呢？

■ Suppose/supposing you can't reach your sales goal?
　要是你達不到銷售目標呢？

■ What if your proposal is not accepted to the committee?
　要是委員會不接受你的提案呢？

> 說明 「suppose/supposing, what if…」與 if 同意思，主要用於日常口語，不伴隨主要子句。

4.6 省略「I wish」主要子句，僅呈現述部內容，凸顯訊息焦點。

■ God bless you！　神祝福你！
　＝ I wish God (should) bless you!
　＝ Bless you!

> 說明 名詞子句主詞也可省略。

■ Heaven preserve you!　　願上天保護你！
　＝ I wish Heaven (should) preserve you!

形容詞

◆ 9-1 形容詞的特徵

形容詞為名詞修飾語，名詞有程度差異，因此可搭配程度副詞；名詞之間可比較，因此有比較級；名詞可以具有多種特徵，因此可以多個形容詞同時修飾一個名詞。

1. 搭配程度副詞

■ fast asleep
熟睡

■ wide awake
清醒

■ a very severe cyclonic storm
非常強烈的龍捲風

■ an extremely dangerous opponent
極度危險的對手

2. 構成比較級與最高級

■ The density of oil is more than that of water.
油的濃度大於水。

■ The Australian Sea Snake is much more poisonous than the cobras.
澳洲水蛇毒性較眼鏡蛇強得多。

■ The world's most dangerous scorpion is the Death Stalker.
以色列的殺人蠍是世界上最危險的蠍子。

■ The Brazilian Wandering Spider is considered the most poisonous spider in the world.
一般認為巴西漫遊蜘蛛是世界上毒性最強的蜘蛛。

★無比較級的形容詞：表示物質、形態、社會、科學、空間、時間的形容詞不具比較級。

物質	形態	社會	科學	空間	時間
carbonic copper gold iron oxygen silver wooden woolen	cubic plane round solid liquid gaseous atomic nuclear	cultural economic financial military political religious social	artistic biological chemical historical medical phonetic physical	back middle front left right east west south north bottom local	daily weekly monthly yearly annual periodic regular

3. 可接連共現

形容詞可接連共同修飾名詞，數量不拘，可依音節數依序排列。

■ fast and furious
　生動活潑的

■ The businessman is rich and famous.
　那名商人春風得意。

■ Charlotte is a skillful, capable and efficient secretary.
　夏綠蒂是一名工作技能佳、能力好又有效率的秘書。

■ My Mr. Right should be rich, gentle, handsome, sincere, and humorous.
　我的白馬王子要具備富有、英俊、誠懇又幽默。

說明 非並列的前位修飾形容詞之間通常不需 and 連接。

■ ninety-nine pink roses　　　　　99 朵粉紅色玫瑰
■ an old stubborn man　　　　　　一名老頑固
■ an elegant American all-you-can-eat restaurant
　一家優雅的美式吃到飽餐廳

★不同種類形容詞的排列詞序如下：

限定詞	性質	年齡	長度	顏色	國籍	名詞	中心詞
a an the this those my your many some the same	an the this those my your many some the same	old young	long short	red beige purple tan golden, silver	American Japanese French Spanish Italian German	wool syntax	×

◆ 9-2 形容詞的構詞

1. 單詞形容詞：

未黏接綴詞或其他單詞的形容詞為單詞形容詞。單詞形容詞常與其他實詞，甚至虛詞同形，可視為同形異義字。

形容詞	名詞	動詞	副詞	介系詞
average	average	average		
calm	calm	calm		
dark	dark			
equal	equal	equal		
fast	fast	fast	fast	
right	right	right	right	
past	past		past	past

2. 派生形容詞

2.1 黏接字首綴詞的形容詞

- anti + government = antigovernment　　反政府
- over + head = overhead　　上頭的
- under + sea = undersea　　海底的

2.2 黏接字尾綴詞的形容詞

- care + ful = careful 　　　　　　小心的
- move + able = movable 　　　　　可移動的
- depend + ent = dependent 　　　依賴的

3. 複合形容詞：

複合形容詞重音落於最右側語詞。

3.1 名詞＋形容詞

fat-free　不含脂肪的	snow-white　雪白的
red-hot　火紅的	tax-free　免稅的
skin-deep　膚淺的	water-proof　防水的
user-friendly　使用方便的	world-famous　舉世聞名的

3.2 形容詞 + 名詞

full-time　全職的	high-quality　高品質的
part-time　兼職的	low-level　低水準的

3.3 名詞 + 名詞

- name-brand 　　　　名牌的

3.4 形容詞＋形容詞

bitter-sweet　又苦又甜的	self-confident　自信的
dark-blue　深藍色	wide-open　寬大的
icy-cold　冰冷的	light-gray　淺灰色

3.5 名詞＋介系詞

child-like　天真的	lady-like　優雅的

3.6 數詞＋名詞

a **ten-speed** bicycle　十段變速單車

a **five-year** plan　五年計畫

3.7 數詞＋名詞 ＋形容詞

a **five-month-old** dog　五個月大的狗

a **three-feet-wide** box　三尺寬的箱子

3.8 名詞＋現在分詞

a **peace-loving** people　喜愛和平的民族

an **animal-loving** family　喜愛動物的家庭

a **heart-warming** story　溫馨的故事

a **heart-breaking** moment　心碎的時刻

3.9 形容詞/副詞＋現在分詞

a **sweet-smelling** rose　芬芳的玫瑰

an **odd-looking** hat　模樣怪異的帽子

a **fast-growing** development　快速成長的發展

a **slowly-moving** train　行駛緩慢的火車

3.10 名詞＋過去分詞

a **hand-made** cake　手工蛋糕

a **man-caused** accident　人為意外

3.11 現在分詞＋形容詞

soaking-wet clothes　溼透的衣服

the biting-cold wind　冽寒風

3.12 形容詞/副詞＋過去分詞

brown-dyed hair　染成棕色的頭髮

a ready-made pizza　現成的披薩

a well-known writer　知名作家

the above-mentioned statement　上述說明

3.13 數詞＋名詞＋ ed

a one-eyed snake　單眼蛇

a two-headed monster　雙頭怪物

a two-seated sofa　雙人座沙發

a one-wheeled bike　獨輪單車

3.14 名詞＋名詞＋ ed

a heart-shaped box　新型盒子

a chicken-hearted guy　膽小的人

a V-necked sweater　V 型領毛衣

3.15 形容詞＋名詞＋ ed

a middle-aged man　中年男子

a sweet-tempered guy　性情溫和的人

a long-sleeved T-shirt　長袖 T 恤

3.16 過去分詞＋介副詞

a **grown-up** son	長大成人的兒子
a **broken-down** car	故障車輛
a **blacked-out** area	停電地區
a **cut-off** road	中斷的道路

3.17 形容詞平行結構：and, but, or 連接形容詞而構成的平行結構也是複合形容詞。

rich and famous	春風得意的
slow but sure	緩慢而穩當
both young and old	老少
not only good but also cheap	物美價廉

■ Heaven's vengeance is slow but sure.
法網恢恢，疏而不漏。

◆ 9-3 形容詞功用的語詞

1. 名詞：

一些名詞搭配另一名詞，構成複合名詞，前面名詞可視為形容詞。

summer vacation　暑假	stock market　股市
information desk　服務台	soccer player　足球選手
water sports　水上運動	raincoat　雨衣
concept car　概念車	ticket stub　票根

2. 分詞：

現在與過去分詞皆具形容詞性質，表示名詞的主動或被動狀態。

2.1 單詞分詞：

2.1.1 搭配名詞時，前位修飾

現在分詞	過去分詞
a boring presentation 乏味的說明	boiled water 滾燙的水
surprising news 令人驚訝的消息	a broken heart 破碎的心
a tiring journey 疲憊的旅途	an aged patient 年邁的病患
neighboring communities 鄰近社區	a naked woman 裸體的婦人

2.2 搭配代名詞時，後位修飾

■ All those remaining must be released.
所有剩餘的都必須放走。

■ Almost everyone invited attended the party.
受邀幾乎的都出席了派對。

■ The one nominated has to be approved by the committee.
被提名者必須經過委員會同意。

説明 fallen leaves = leaves which are falling 落葉，不表示被動。

2.3 分詞片語：分詞片語具形容詞性質，後位修飾名詞或代名詞，可視為形容詞子句的縮減。

■ The hunter was looking for the cub hiding in the bush.
= The hunter was looking for the cub that which hid in the bush.
獵人在找尋躲在樹叢裡的幼獸。

■ The animal caught in the trap is an endangered species.

= The animal that   which was caught in the trap is an endangered species.

被陷阱抓住的是瀕臨絕種的動物。

3. 不定詞

■ The staff members have many projects to work on now.

職員現在有許多工作要做。

■ The Formosan Reeve's Muntjac was the first animal to come into the trap.

山羌是第一隻落入陷阱的動物。

4. 動名詞：

動名詞搭配名詞構成複合名詞時，動名詞可視為形容詞，說明名詞的功用，詞重音落在動名詞。

dining room　餐廳	vending machine　販賣機
sleeping car　臥車廂	walking stick　拐杖
swimming pool　游泳池	reading corner　閱讀區

5. 介系詞片語：

介系詞片語具有形容詞性質，後位修飾名詞。

■ The police have found a clue of great value.

警方找到一個很有價值的線索。

■ The snake with two heads and without a tail is the rarest of the rare.

兩個頭，沒有尾巴的蛇是稀有中的稀有。

6. 副詞：

away 是副詞，但可置於名詞前面，限定形容詞性質。

■ The team rarely won when they played an away game.

那支隊伍客場比賽時很少贏。

7. 形容詞子句：

形容詞子句為子句結構的形容詞，後位修飾名詞。

- The olive oil that Julia purchased online contains Copper Chlorophyll.

  茱莉亞網購的橄欖油含銅葉綠素。

- The man who produced oil bad for health was sentenced to 20 years in prison.

  生產有害健康的油的男子被判刑 20 年。

◆ 9-4 形容詞的語意分類

1. 隱性／顯性形容詞：

表示外觀、狀態或年齡的形容詞有隱性與顯性之分。隱性形容詞用於慣用而不須強調的語境，例如詢問的狀況時都用隱性形容詞。顯性形容詞常是隱性形容詞的相反詞，用於特殊而須強調的情況。

1.1 隱性形容詞／顯性形容詞

- how old　　／　young
- how long　　／　short
- how tall　　／　short
- how many　 ／　few
- how much　 ／　little

2. 動態／靜態形容詞：

形容詞有動態與靜態之分，動態形容詞表示可任意開始、結束或持續、一時的狀況，因此常搭配祈使句或進行式。靜態形容詞則無動態形容詞的性質。

2.1 動態形容詞

- Be careful when driving.

  開車時要小心。（可任意開始或結束的狀態）

■ The interviewee is being polite when talking to the interviewers.
應試者和口試官談話時很有禮貌。

說明 動態形容詞搭配進行式多表示一時的狀態。

2.2 靜態形容詞：無法立即改變的狀態

■ The engineer is tall and handsome.
工程師又高又帥。

3. 形容詞的相反詞

3.1 互補相反詞：一詞為另一詞的否定時，彼此為互補相反詞。

■ The kitty is awake, not asleep.
小貓醒著，不在睡覺。

■ The sparrow is still alive, not dead.
燕子還活著，沒有死掉。

■ The accountant was present, not absent.
會計有出席，沒有缺席。

3.2 程度相反詞：相對互補相反詞，具有程度差別而無絕對量度的形容詞之間的相反詞為程度相反詞，例如靜態形容詞與其相反詞之間為程度相反詞。

■ The compass is big, not small.
指南針是大的，不是小的。

■ The beef soup felt hot, not cold.
牛肉湯感覺起來是燙的，不是冷的。

■ The bullet train is fast, not slow.
子彈列車很快，不慢。

■ The story has a happy ending, not a sad one.
故事結局是快樂的，不是悲傷的。

- The car is going at a high speed, not at a low one.
  汽車高速行駛，不是慢速。

- The husky dog looks old, not young at all.
  哈士奇看起來蠻老的，一點也不年輕。

◆ 9-5 形容詞的位置

1. 前位修飾：

形容詞置於所修飾的名詞前面，限定用法。

- Hyenas are a social animal.
  豺狼是群居動物。

- The Venus Flytrap is a carnivorous plant.
  捕蠅草是肉食性植物。

- The US and Canada are the largest chocolate consumers in the world.
  美國和加拿大是世界最大的巧克力消費者。

2. 後位修飾：

形容詞置於所修飾的名詞後面，述語用法。

- The dog is feeling defensive now.
  現在狗狗感覺是在防衛。

- The twin sisters look very much alike.
  雙胞胎姊妹看起來很像。

- My 10-month-old daughter is falling sick very often.
  我十個月大的女兒很常生病。

- The Japanese maple leaves have turned crimson.
  日本楓樹已變成深紅色。

2.1 一些形容詞只有述語用法。

- The little panda has fallen asleep.
  圓仔已睡著。

■ The Chinese Moccasin is still alive.
百步蛇還活著。

■ I was kept awake all night by the noise.
噪音把我吵得整夜難眠。

■ Molly is afraid that she might lose her job.
莫莉擔心可能會失去工作。

說明 a- 字首的形容詞只有後位修飾的述語用法。

■ I'm glad to see you all.
很高興見到你們各位。

■ My family members are all well.
我的家人都安康。

■ My uncle is fond of photography.
我叔叔喜歡攝影。

■ The interpreter is able to speak many different languages.
口譯員會說許多不同語言。

2.2 搭配不定詞或介系詞片語的形容詞應後位修飾名詞

■ We need an employee able to speak French.
我們需要一名會講法文的員工。

■ Jingdezhen is a town famous for its porcelain industry.
景德鎮是一個以瓷器工業聞名的小鎮。

■ Charles M. Russell was an artist skillful in sculpture.
Charles M. Russell 是一名雕刻技術精湛的藝術家。

2.3 複合不定代名詞僅搭配後位修飾形容詞

■ There's nothing worth keeping.
沒有值得留存的東西。

■ Is there anyone willing to help out?
有人願意幫忙嗎？

■ We need someone familiar with Microsoft Excel.
我們需要熟悉 Excel 作業系統的人？

■ I heard something different from what you had told me.
我聽見一些事，可是和你告訴我的不一樣。

2.4 度量衡名詞搭配後位修飾形容詞

■ The area is ten feet square.
面積是十平方英尺。

■ The boy is 10 years old and 150 centimeters tall.
男孩是 10 歲大，150 公分高。

■ This safe is two meters wide and one-hundred inches high.
保險箱是二公尺寬，一百英吋高

■ The ditch is two kilometers long, two feet deep and one foot broad.
水溝是二公里長，二尺深，一尺寬。

2.5 一些職業或頭銜搭配後位修飾的形容詞

attorney general	檢察總長	devil incarnate	魔鬼的化身
secretary general	秘書長	poet laureate	桂冠詩人
heir apparent	法定繼承人	president-elect	總統當選人
court martial	軍事法庭	sergeant major	士官長

2.6 述語與限定用法語意不同的形容詞：一些形容詞兼具述語與限定用法，但語意不同。

■ The late president was late for the press conference.
前任校長記者會遲到。

2.7 enough 可前位或後位修飾名詞，後位修飾時可置於名詞右側。

■ There's still enough time left.

  = There's still time enough.

  = The time is still enough.

時間還夠。

◆ 9-6 形容詞的功用

1. 句中角色：

形容詞為名詞修飾語，可扮演主詞補語或受詞補語。

1.1 主詞補語

■ I'm good and ready now.

  = I'm completely ready.

我現在完全準備好了。

■ It's nice and comfortable in here.

  = It's very comfortable in here.

在這裡面非常舒服。

■ Here's the fact, pure and simple.

  = Here's the fact, and nothing else.

這就是事實。

■ All the milkfish went bad.

所有的虱目魚都臭掉了。

■ The fence was painted white.

圍籬漆成白色。

■ O'Bryant's dream has come true now.

歐布萊恩的夢想已成真。

■ The stray dog was found dead in the ditch.

有人發現流浪狗死在水溝。

■ The sausage meat tasted nice but a little too greasy.

香腸嚐起來很棒，但有點太油膩。

說明 一些形容詞片語置於句子外側，提供主詞訊息，可視為副詞子
句的縮減。

■ *"Hungry and thirsty, their soul fainted in them."* --（*Psalms 107:5-*）

「又飢又渴，靈魂發昏。」《詩篇 107:5》

■ Curious, the little panda wandered around the new room.

= Being curious, the little panda wandered around the new room.

= Because she was curious, the little panda wandered around the new room.

出於好奇，圓仔在新房舍走來走去。

■ Unable to deal with the crisis, the Prime Minister stepped down from office.

= Being unable to deal with the crisis, the Prime Minister stepped down from office.

= Because he was unable to deal with the crisis, the Prime Minister stepped down from office.

缺乏危機處理能力，行政院長下台。

1.2 受詞補語

■ We thought the trainee reliable.
我們認為實習生可信賴。

■ The patient's illness is growing worse.
患者的病情逐漸加劇。

■ The worker dyed the material dark-blue.
工人將原料染成深藍色。

■ Please get everything ready in advance.
請事先將每件事預備好。

■ You should keep your room neat and clean.
你要保持自己房間整潔。

■ You had better drink the beer cold.
= You had better drink the beer when it is cold.
你最好趁著啤酒冰的時候喝下去。

【補充】Do you drink the beer cold or room temperature?
你喝的啤酒要冰的或不冰的？

2. 語詞搭配

2.1 搭配 the：一些形容詞與 the 構成名詞片語，表示具有該形容詞性質的人、事物或概念。

2.1.1 個人或群體：多表示人的身心特徵。

(1) 個人

■ Joney is the youngest in his family.
強尼是他家年紀最小的。

■ Allen is the tallest on the basketball school team.
艾倫是籃球校隊個子最高的。

(2) 群體

■ The blind are not able to see.
盲人看不見。

■ Maybe the living should respect the dead.
或許活人應當尊受亡者。

■ *"Always the innocent are the first victims, so it has been for ages past, so it is now."* -J.K. Rowling-
「*無辜者總是最先受害的人，以前如此，現在也是如此*」。*-J.K. 羅琳 -*

★其他表示個體或群體的名詞片語：

the deaf　耳聾的人	the poor　窮人
the dumb　啞巴	the unfortunate　不幸的人
the old　老年人	the young　年輕人

2.1.2 整體國民：「the ＋國家名稱形容詞」表示該國整體國民。

■ The Chinese live on rice.
中國人以米為生。

■ The French are not crazy about Americans.
法國人對美國人不會趨之若鶩。

■ The Japanese prefer to use their last names.
日本人偏好使用他們的姓。

■ The Irish might be close genetic relatives of the people of northern Spain.
愛爾蘭人可能是北西班牙人的近親。

2.1.3 事物：the 搭配評論事物的形容詞，表示該類事物。

■ Aida is trying to make the impossible possible.
相田小姐一直要將不可能變為可能。

■ The unknown are not always the mystical nor the unusual.
未知不盡然就是神祕或是獨特。

2.1.4 抽象概念：the 搭配抽象狀況的形容詞，表示抽象概念。

■ The True, the Good, the Beautiful.
真・善・美。

★一些形容詞可當介系詞受詞，形成慣用的介系詞片語。

at all 完全	in general 一般地
at large 逍遙法外	in brief 簡短地說
at least 至少	in common 共同
at most 最多	in public 公開地
at present 目前	in private 私下地
for certain sure 確定	in particular 尤其
from bad to worse 每下愈況	in vain 無效地

2.2 搭配動詞：一些形容詞平行結構修飾動詞，左側形容詞說明程度，右側形容詞描述狀況。

■ Aoki kicked the ball good and hard.
= Aoki kicked the ball very hard.
青木使盡力氣踢球。

■ The construction is going nice and smooth.

= The construction is going very smoothly.

工程進行非常順利。

◆ 9-7 形容詞的補語

形容詞有結構與語意二種補語。少數形容詞不可獨立存在，需與特定語詞共現，這些語詞為形容詞的結構補語。另一方面，一些形容詞雖可獨立存在，但需搭配一些修飾語詞，語意才完整，這些語詞為形容詞的語意補語。

1. 結構補語

■ Furuya is fond of Celtic music.

古屋先生喜歡聽凱爾特音樂。

說明 of 介系詞片語是形容詞 fond 的補語，必要成分。

■ The biography is worth reading over and over again.

這本傳記值得一讀再讀。

說明 動名詞是 worth 的補語。

2. 語意補語：

形容詞的語意補語有不定詞、介系詞片語、補語子句等。

2.1 不定詞

■ My puppy is afraid to walk up the stairs.

我的小狗很怕走上樓梯。

■ The new model is due to launch tomorrow.

新款明天上市。

■ The history teacher is able to read Greek well.

歷史老師很會念希臘文。

■ We are bound to win the knock-out competition.

我們即將贏得淘汰賽。

2.2 介系詞片語

■ Everybody was surprised at the message.
每個人對訊息都很驚訝。

■ The town is famous for its historic castle and cathedral.
這小鎮以歷史性的城堡及教堂聞名。

■ We are anxious about the result of the professor's surgery.
我們對教授手術結果感到憂心。

■ The resort is popular with skiers from around the world.
渡假勝地很受來自世界各地滑水人士的歡迎。

■ Not every student is aware of the importance of English.
不是每位學生都明白英文的重要。

【比較】Not every student is aware that English is important.

說明 介系詞片語強調名詞，that 補語子句強調事件。

2.3 補語子句：表示情緒或意念的形容詞常搭配補語子句，說明形容詞的原因。引導補語子句的補語連詞常省略

■ I'm delighted that you got a high score on the IELTS.
我很高興你的雅思檢定考試得高分。

■ I'm sure that the guide dog has arrived at the destination by now.
我相信現在導盲犬已抵達目的地。

■ We have determined that you are eligible to receive a tax refund of NT10,000.
我們決議你能收到台幣 10,000 元的退稅。

★其他搭配補語子句的形容詞：

afraid 害怕的	disappointed 失望的
amazed 驚訝的	glad 高興的
angry 生氣的	pleased 滿意的

annoyed　困擾的	proud　驕傲的
ashamed　羞恥的	sorry　抱歉的
astonished　震驚的	surprised　驚訝的
certain　確定的	upset　不安的
conscious　有知覺的	worried　擔憂的

◆ 9-8 形容詞的比較

　　形容詞有原級、比較級、最高級等三個比較等級，每個等級有肯定與否定類型，等級之間又可相互代換。

1. 原級：

結構為「as＋原級形容詞＋as」，形容詞前的 as 是副詞，後面的是連接詞，引導子句，但述語動詞可省略，這時候 as 可視為介系詞。

1.1 肯定原級

1.1.1 不同主詞：語意不混淆的狀況下，as 子句的述語動詞可省略。

■ A snow leopard's tail is nearly as long as the rest of its body!
雪豹的尾巴幾乎和身體其他部分一樣長。

■ The water at the beach is every bit as clear as the Caribbean.
海灘的水和加勒比海一樣清澈。

■ The smartphone is almost twice as expensive as that one.
這支智慧型手機幾乎是那支的二倍價錢。

■ The first tunnel is only one third as long as the second one.
第一座隧道的長度只有第二座的三分之一。

■ Vitamins may not be as helpful as we'd hoped.
維他命可能不如我們期望的那麼有幫助。

■ The African grayparrot might be just as smart as you think it would be.
非洲灰鸚鵡可能如你想的一樣聰明。

1.1.2 相同主詞：as 子句的述語動詞也可省略。

■ The businesswoman is just as wise as kind.
女企業家明智又仁慈。

■ The temperature is as cold today as yesterday.
今天氣溫和昨天一樣冷。

■ The resort is exactly as beautiful as in the photos!
渡假勝地真如照片一樣美麗。

■ They have consumed twice as much gas as last quarter.
他們消耗掉的天然氣是上一季的二倍。

1.2 否定原級：結構為「not as/so ＋原級形容詞 ＋ as」，但 as 較常用。否定原級句型可搭配否定語意的代名詞或副詞。

■ The construction cost is not as much as estimated.
營造成本不如估價的那麼高。

■ Neither of the tribes is as strong as ever.
這兩支部落都不如以前強盛。

■ None are so deaf as those who won't hear.
沒有人耳聾到完全聽不見。

■ No hotels in the city are so nice as that one.
這城市裡沒有飯店和那一家一樣棒。

■ Nowhere else in the island is there a hostel as elegant as that one.
島上沒有其他民宿像那家一樣別緻。

2. 比較級

2.1 「比較級 + than」，肯定比較級，表示程度優於，可搭配程度、倍數或差距等語詞。就句法而言，相等的組成成分才能比較。

2.1.1 主詞與主詞比較：

■ Blood is thicker than water.
血濃於水。

■ China is much bigger than Serbia.
中國較塞爾維亞大得多。

■ Guangzhou is farther from Shianghai than Nanking is.
比起上海，廣州離南京來得遠。

■ Haneda is already at least half a head taller than his father.
羽田已經比他父親至少高出半個頭。

■ Hino is taller than me by 10 centimeters.
日野比我高十公分。

■ It's better to be safe than sorry.
= It's better to be safe than to be sorry.
安全勝過遺憾。

2.1.2 受詞與受詞比較：

■ Some people like dogs decidedly better than cats.
有些人喜愛狗的程度遠超過貓。

■ My company prefers to work overtime rather than hire temporary workers.
我的公司寧可加班，而不願雇請臨時員工。

2.1.3 補詞與補詞比較：

■ Harada is more diligent than intelligent.
與其說有田先生聰明，不如說他勤奮。

■ Teaching is more of an art than a technique.
與其說教學是一種技術，不如說是一項藝術。

■ Annual vaccinations may do your dog more harm than good.
= Annual vaccinations may do your dog more harm than it may do good.
你的愛犬每年預防注射可能害處大於益處。

2.1.4 動詞與動詞比較：

■ A good reputation is sooner lost than won.
好名聲失去要比獲得還得快。

■ I would rather stay at home than go to the cinema.
我寧願在家，也不要去看電影。

2.1.5 副詞與副詞比較：

■ Better late than never.
= It's better to do it late than to never do it.
亡羊補牢，為時不晚。

■ It was hot yesterday, but it's even hotter today.
昨天很熱，但比今天熱得多。

2.1.6 介系詞與介系詞比較：

■ It takes much less time to travel by THSR than by bus.
搭高鐵所花的時間較巴士少很多。

■ Noodles made by hand taste better than those by machine.
手工製的麵比機器製的麵好吃。

2.1.7 子句與子句比較：

■ The athlete performed even better than we had expected.
運動員表現遠超出我們的期待。

■ The American speaks Chinese a little better than you speak English.
那名美國人講中文比起你講英文要好一些。

2.2 the ＋比較級：相對於二者比較，「the ＋比較級」表示比較範圍或前提背景下的比較。

2.2.1 比較範圍：搭配介系詞片語以表示比較範圍，可移至句首。主詞為限定，搭配定冠詞 the。

■ Chris is the better of the two athletes.
克里斯是二名運動員中較優秀的。

■ The cow is the younger of the two.
獅子犬是二者中較年輕的。

■ Of the two children, Tina looks more like a Japanese girl.
二名孩子中，緹娜比較像日本女孩。

2.2.2 none the worse／less：並未更…，雙重否定。

- A good tale is none the worse for being told twice.
  好故事百聽不厭。

- It took so much of my time to labor for my project, but I am none the worse for the experience.
  我花很多時間在我的工作上拼命，但也沒有比較有經驗。

- Peter's dog looks strange, but he loves her none the less.
  彼得不會因他的狗長相奇怪而不愛牠。

> 說明 「less ＋原級形容詞」表示程度不如，否定比較級。

2.3 無比較形式的比較級：一些形容詞具比較級語意，不須比較句型即表示比較。

- Actually, Hirayama is senior to the principal.
  事實上，平山先生比校長年輕。

- Kusano is junior to his roommate.
  草野小姐比他的室友年輕。

- This proposal seems to be superior to that one.
  這份企劃案似乎優於那一份。

- This approach is inferior to that one.
  這個方式不比那方式來得好。

3. 最高級：

三者或三者以上比較時，程度最高或最低者以形容詞最高級表示，限定用法，常搭配 the，且須伴隨比較範圍的語詞，結構有介系詞片語、形容詞、不定詞片語、分詞片語或子句等。

3.1 比較範圍的語詞結構

3.1.1 介系詞片語

- It is the heaviest pig on record.
  那是紀錄上最重的豬。

■ Ms. TsaiAh-shin was the first female doctor in Taiwan.
蔡阿信女士是台灣第一位女醫師。

■ Hoshino is the least experienced among the competitors.
星野是競爭者中最沒經驗的。

■ The River Amazon is the second longest river in the world.
亞馬遜河是世界第二長河流。

說明 序數詞可修飾最高級形容詞。

■ It is by far the best solution to the problem we're working on.
那是解決我們正在處理的問題的最好方案。

■ "Beyond Beauty - Taiwan From Above" is one of the best documentaries in recent years.
「看見台灣」是這幾年最佳紀錄片之一。

3.1.2 形容詞

■ It should be the most practical proposal imaginable.
可以想像這將是最實在的建議。

■ It is estimated to be the world's oldest parrot alive.
據估算，牠是活著的鸚鵡中最老的一隻。

■ Targeted therapy might be the most efficient therapy available.
標靶療法可能是現行最有效的療法。

3.1.3 不定詞

■ It is the very best location to watch the fireworks.
那是觀賞煙火最棒的位置。

■ Typhoon Chebi was the strongest to hit the Philippines in ten years.
奇比颱風是十年來侵襲菲律賓最強烈的颱風。

■ Ikegami is the first salesperson to reach the sales target this month.
池上先生是本月首位達成銷售目標的銷售員。

3.1.4 分詞片語

■ He's the greatest vocal artist living.
他是現存最偉大的聲樂家。

■ It is the greatest musical ever played.
這齣是史上演過的最偉大音樂劇。

3.1.5 形容詞子句

■ It is the most serious accident that we have ever experienced in the Philippines.
這是我們在菲律賓經歷過最嚴重的意外事件。

■ Gao Xingjian was the first Chinese writer that won the Nobel Prize in Literature.
高行健是第一位獲得諾貝爾文學獎的中國作家。

3.2 最高級語詞的省略

3.2.1 省略 the：最高級語詞當主詞補語，且未與其他人或事物比較時，可省略 the。

■ My brother is best in math.
我弟弟的數學最棒。

■ This is the location where the pond is deepest.
這裡是池子最深的位置。

3.2.2 省略名詞：指涉對象明確時，最高級形容詞修飾的名詞可省略。

■ Igarashi is the most generous (friend) of all my friends.
我的所有朋友中，五十嵐是最大方的。

■ Last night, I reviewed from the first chapter to the last (chapter).
昨天晚上，我從第一章複習到最後一章。

■ The Sahara is the largest (desert) of all the deserts on the African continent.
非洲大陸所有沙漠中，撒哈拉沙漠面積最大。

3.2.3 省略比較範圍：指涉對象明確時，比較範圍也可省略。

- The chief technician is the most experienced employee (in the company).
  主任技術員是經驗最豐富的員工。

- Could you please show me the nearest post office (in the neighborhood)?
  麻煩告訴我這一帶最近的郵局，好嗎？

4. 無最高級形式的最高級表示法：

4.1 最高級語意的語詞：一些形容詞具最高級語意，不搭配最高級句型即可表示最高級。

- Reading is my favorite hobby.
  閱讀是我最喜愛的嗜好。

- As a gymnast, Chen Fei is second to none.
  身為體操選手，陳飛是所向無敵。

- Kyle and Kelly are perfect for each other.
  凱爾和凱莉是天作之合。

- About 6 in 10 workers only earn the minimum wage or less.
  大約六成的工人只賺取最低工資，甚至更少。

- The Pope is the supreme leader of the Roman Catholic Church.
  教宗是羅馬天主教會的最高領袖。

- In the Bible, the Song of Songs is also called the Song of Solomon.
  聖經中，歌中之歌也稱為所羅門之歌。

★其他最高級語意的形容詞：

maximum　最多的	paramount　首要的
minimal　最少的	prime　主要的
optimal　最好的	superlative　最高級的

4.2 原級句型：否定主詞或比較對象含 any 時，原級句型表示最高級語意。

■ No other warriors were as brave as Charles.
查爾斯是最勇敢的戰士。

■ No tomb is as wonderful as Taj Mahal in India.
印度泰姬馬哈陵是最奇妙的墓穴。

■ Lin Chi-ling looks as elegant as any model.
林志玲是最高雅的模特兒。

■ Nelson Mandela is as brilliant a politician as ever lived.
曼德拉是世上最卓越的政治家。

4.3 比較級句型：否定主詞或含 any other 的比較對象時，比較級句型表示最高級語意。

■ Elephants are bigger than any other animal on land.
　= Elephants are bigger than all the other animals on land.
大象是陸地最大的動物。

說明 比較範圍包含主詞時，應以 other 排除主詞。

■ There's nothing more valuable than freedom.
沒有比自由更有價值的東西。

■ Nobody can sell more cars all over the world than Joe Girard.
喬吉拉德是全世界賣出最多汽車的人。

◆ 9-9 倍數的表示法

1. 倍數詞 as 形容詞原級 as 名詞

■ Gina's essay is three times as long as that one.
　= Gina's essay triples that one in length.
吉娜的論文字數是那一篇的三倍。

■ The house is four times as large as my apartment.

= The house quadruples my apartment in size.

這棟房子的價錢是我的公寓四倍。

■ Tom's heavy motorcycle costs twice as much as my car.

= Tom's heavy motorcycle doubles my car in cost.

湯姆的重機價錢是我的汽車二倍。

> 說明 「two times」通常搭配比較級,而不搭配形容詞原級倍數句型。
>
> 【誤】Tom's heavy motorcycle costs two times as much as my car.

2. 倍數詞形容詞比較級 than 名詞

■ The article is three times longer than that one.

這篇文章篇幅是那篇的三倍。

■ The population of this country is five times more than that country.

這國家的人口是那國家的五倍。

■ The team scored three times against the challenger in the match.

該隊比賽分數是挑戰隊的三倍。

> 說明 「倍數+ as +形容詞原級+ as」(幾倍大),與「倍數形容詞
> +比較級」(多出倍數減一)語意相同,但是以中文來說,前
> 者會解釋為「是…的幾倍」,而後者解釋為「多出幾倍」,二
> 者語意相異。「倍數形容詞+比較級」中譯時應倍數減一。

■ The house is three times as big as that one.

中譯:這房子面積是那房子的三倍大。

= The house is three times bigger than that one.

中譯:這房子面積比那房子多出二倍。

【誤譯】:這房子面積比那房子多出三倍。

3. 倍數詞比較內容(比較對象)

■ The moon is just one quarter the size of Earth.

月球只有地球的四分之一大。

■ The commissioner's office is double the size of mine.

　= The commissioner's office is twice as big as mine.

　局長辦公室是我的兩倍大。

■ Amy's smartphone costs four times what mine does.

　= Amy's smartphone costs quadruple the price which my smartphone costs.

　艾咪的智慧型手機費用是我的四倍。

■ The manager's income is triple what it was five years ago.

　= The manager's income is triple what his income was five years ago.

　經理的收入是五年前的三倍。

■ The wrestler is twice the man he used to be.

　摔角選手比以前強一倍。

■ I have done half the things you required me to do.

　你要求我做的事，我已做一半了。

4. 表示倍數的動詞：

double, triple, quadruple 等動詞可直接表示主詞的倍數變化。

■ The technology product output has doubled.

　科技產品出口增加一倍。

■ The oil price has tripled.

　油價漲了二倍。

■ The company's revenue will quadruple next quarter.

　下一季公司營收將增加三倍。

副詞是修飾語詞，修飾名詞、動詞、形容詞、副詞或句子，提供時間、空間、原因、結果、條件、程度、方式、狀態等訊息。

◆ 10-1 副詞的功用

副詞的功用主要是修飾語詞，少數情況中能扮演主詞、補語或介系詞受詞角色。

1. 修飾語詞

1.1 修飾名詞或代名詞

1.1.1 前位修飾

■ Even an adult can't lift the big pumpkin.
即使成人也無法舉起大南瓜。

■ Nearly half of UK teenagers today use a smartphone.
時至今日將近一半的英國青少年使用智慧型手機。

■ *"Only those who dare to fail greatly can ever achieve greatly."- Robert F. Kennedy*
「只有敢嚴重挫敗的人才能成就大業。」-- 約翰 · 甘迺迪

1.1.2 後位修飾

■ See the remarks below for more information.
若要獲得更多資訊，請看以下資訊。

■ I saw an owl in the yard the night before.
前天晚上我在院子看見一隻貓頭鷹。

■ The rodents in the mountain sare entertaining creatures.
山區的齧齒動物是有趣的動物。

1.2 修飾數詞

■ The baby squirrel has lived for fully two months.
松鼠出生滿二個月。

■ The Tibetan Mastiff costs over 2 million dollars.
西藏獒犬值二百多萬元。

■ A rat can breed within approximately 60 days from birth.
田鼠出生後大約六十天就可繁殖。

1.3 修飾動詞

■ The St. Bernard ran swiftly after a wild hare.
聖伯納犬快速追趕一隻野兔。

■ Mosquitoes make noise by rapidly moving their wings.
蚊子藉由快速拍動翅膀發出聲音。

■ The cheetah can run very fast, reaching a top speed of 120 km h.
獵豹跑得很快，時速達 120 公里。

1.4 修飾不定詞

■ Hummingbirds are able to fly backwards.
蜂鳥能夠向後飛行。

■ Mrs. Danielson decided to work voluntarily with no pay.
丹尼爾森太太決定從事志工服務。

■ Excited fans are waiting to welcome the victorious team warmly.
興奮的粉絲正熱情等待迎接勝利隊伍。

1.5 修飾動名詞

■ Sleeping too much makes me more tired.
睡太久讓我更加疲倦。

■ I usually go shopping leisurely with no purpose.
我經常毫無目的地悠閒逛街。

■ The accountant spent a lot of time checking accounts accurately.
會計花很多時間確認帳目無誤。

1.6 修飾分詞

■ I heard some dogs barking fiercely last night.
昨夜我聽見一些狗在狂吠。

■ The serval was waiting patiently to attack its prey.
藪貓耐心等待襲擊獵物。

■ The staff was apparently wounded due to an explosion.
由於爆炸，工作人員顯然受傷了。

■ The program doesn't make much sense if analyzed systematically.
若是系統化分析，這計畫就沒意義了。

1.7 修飾形容詞

■ My grandfather is very fond of classical music.
我祖父很喜歡古典音樂。

■ The rock monkey is too young to take care of itself.
獼猴太小了，無法照顧自己。

■ Glaciers exist in extremely cold regions, including Rocky Mountains.
冰河存在於極度寒冷的地區，包括洛磯山脈。

■ The mountain climber rescued was dead tired.
獲救的登山客累死了。

■ The tablecloth is light blue, not bright red.
桌巾是淺藍色，不是鮮紅色。

★一些形容詞與另一形容詞構成形容詞片語，前面的形容詞為副詞性質。

★常搭配主動語態的動詞，其他例子如下：

dark gray　暗灰色	jolly good　非常好
bitter cold　嚴寒刺骨的	wide open　大開的

1.8 修飾副詞

■ My Formosan dog has to be alone very often.
我的台灣土狗常常要獨處。

■ The elevator has been operating so smoothly.
電梯運作一向十分平順。

1.9 修飾介系詞片語

■ My cousin got pregnant soon after the marriage.
我表妹結婚後就馬上懷孕。

■ The arrow went right through the center of the apple.
箭從蘋果正中心穿過。

■ Many Palestinian refugees died just because of famine.
許多巴勒斯坦難民死亡原因只是飢餓。

1.10 修飾句子

■ Luckily, the zebra wasn't seriously hurt.
幸運地，斑馬未受重傷。

■ Basically, "CSI" is a hit television series in Taiwan.
基本上，「刑案現場」在台灣是一部深受好評的電視連續劇。

■ Ironically, my dentist treated me with sugar and spun cotton candy!
反諷的是，我的牙醫師請我吃棉花糖。

■ Undoubtedly, the blue whale is the largest mammal in the sea.
無疑地，藍鯨是海裡最大的動物。

2. 語詞成分

2.1 主詞

■ Twice is enough.
兩次夠了。

■ Now is the time to make a comeback.
現在是反敗為勝的時刻。

2.2 主詞補語

■ Anybody home?
　有人在家嗎？

■ Are you still up?
　你還醒著嗎？

■ The shop manager is out.
　店經理出去了。

■ The chief engineer is not in.
　主任工程師不在。

2.3 受詞補語

■ Let me in.
　讓我進來。

■ I've not noticed my Schnauzer out.
　我一直沒注意到我的雪納瑞出去了。

2.4 介系詞受詞

■ Income from abroad should be taxable.
　境外所得應該課稅。

■ The baby panda will be teething before long.
　圓仔不久就要長牙了。

■ I have been working on my assignments since then.
　那時起我就一直在做我的作業。

■ All my posts from January 2014 till now were accidently deleted.
　我從 2014 年 1 月到現在的所有貼文都被刪。

★其他搭配副詞的介系詞片語：

at once 立刻	from downstairs upstairs 從樓下 樓上

by now 到現在	from here　there 從這裡 那裡
for once 僅這一次	from now on 從現在起
from behind 從後面	in here 這裡面

2.5 代詞

■ World War II ended in 1945, and a post-World War II baby boom started soon after then.

第二次世界大戰結束於 1945 年，戰後嬰兒潮隨即出現。

■ There are Jersey Barriers on the right side. So, be careful when driving there at night.

右側有護欄，因此夜間開車經過那裡時要小心。

■ A：Jordan's big luxurious house might be too expensive to sell.

喬登的豪宅可能太貴，賣不出去。

B：I suppose so.

我也這樣認為。

說明

1. so 是上一句的代詞。
2. I think so. 語意與「I suppose so.」相同，語氣較強。

◆ 10-2 副詞的形式

1. 單詞副詞：

單詞副詞為獨立詞素結構，大多與形容詞或介系詞同形。

1.1 與形容詞同形：

■ You would have to be extra cautious.

你必須格外小心。

■ Daniel usually turns the stereo right up to the maximum level.

丹尼爾經常將音響轉得很大聲。

■ The soldier lay on his back, with his eyes closed tight.
士兵仰躺著，雙眼緊閉。

■ The disaster area is accessible only by helicopter.
只有直升機可到達災區。

■ The mayor-elect bowed low to the assembled crowd.
市長當選人向聚集群眾低頭鞠躬。

★其他形容詞同形的單詞副詞：

alike　相像地	first　首先
alone　獨自地	further　更遠地
awful　十分	half　部分地
back　向後地	long　長久地
even　甚至	next　接下去
far　遠	slow　慢慢地
fast　禁食	straight　直地
fine　細緻地	well　很好地

說明

1. 有些形容詞同形的副詞可接字尾綴詞「-ly」，形成另一副詞，二者語意常不一致。

■ The hawk is flying high above in the sky.
老鷹在高空飛翔。

■ The author spoke highly of her hometown during the presentation.
作者在演說中讚揚她的故鄉。

■ The receptionist arrived late to the station by a few minutes.
接待人員慢了幾分鐘抵達車站。

■ My mind has been occupied lately with thoughts of my family.
最近我的心思都懸念著我的家人。

■ The team has been working hard for a long time.
團隊努力很長一段時間了。

■ We can hardly complete the project without your help.
沒有你的援助，我們幾乎無法完成工作。

■ You guessed wrong!
你猜錯了。

■ The newspaper delivery person has been wrongly convicted as being a sexual offender.
送報生曾被誤指為性侵犯。警長已戒菸多年了。

★其他副詞／副詞 -ly 的詞組：

cheap／cheaply	full／fully
clear／clearly	large／largely
close／closely	loud／loudly
dead／deadly	low／lowly
dear／dearly	near／nearly
deep／deeply	quick／quickly
direct／directly	right／rightly
easy／easily	sharp／sharply
fair／fairly	short／shortly
fine／finely	slow／slowly
firm／firmly	sound／soundly
free／freely	tight／tightly
right／rightly	wide／widely

1.2 有些形容詞同形的副詞，語意與形容詞無關。

■ Seismic waves travel pretty fast.
地震波傳送非常快速。

■ The parrot is standing still on one leg.
鸚鵡能單腳站立。

■ They just stayed at the hostel for another night.
他們在民宿多待一晚。

1.3 與介系詞同形：與介系詞同形的副詞為介副詞，通常是介系詞的衍生語意。動詞與介副詞構成片語動詞。

■ I cannot put up with my husband's temper any more.
我再也無法忍受我丈夫的脾氣。

■ My niece went abroad for further study two years ago.
我姪女兩年前出國進修。

■ I came down with the flu just two days before the final.
我在期末考前患了流感。

■ The government put off holding the election until two months later.
政府將選舉延至兩個月後。

■ I borrowed some money from my colleague to tide me over till payday.
我向同事借一些錢週轉直到發薪日。

★其他常見的介副詞：

about　關於	besides　此外
above　在上面	beyond　在更遠處
across　橫過	in　在裡頭
around　到處	near　接近
behind　在背後	opposite　在對面
below　在較低位置	out　到外面
beneath　向下	past　經過

說明

1. 限定詞中的序數詞句副詞性質，可視為單詞副詞。

■ First, you need to stop bleeding immediately.
首先，你必須立刻止血。

■ Second, you need to research your customers.
第二，你必須研究你客戶。

2. 有些單詞副詞修飾句子，表達作說者對句子內容的意念或觀點，又稱為句子副詞。

■ Please help yourself to some cake.
= If you please, help yourself to some cake.
請隨意取用一些蛋糕。

■ Luckily for me, my parents aren't really strict.
我真幸運，我父母不是很嚴格。

■ You should be responsible for all the consequences, anyhow.
不管怎樣，你該為所有後果負責。

■ The head coach was obviously satisfied with the result of the match.
明顯地，總教練滿意比賽結果。

2. 派生副詞：

名詞或形容詞黏接字首或字尾綴詞而構成的副詞為派生副詞。

2.1 a- ＋名詞/形容詞：

■ An oil tanker ran aground in the fog.
一艘油輪在霧中擱淺。

■ The restaurant was set afire by a neighborhood bully.
餐廳遭到附近的惡霸縱火。

■ After the accountant realized the money was missing, there was a mystery afoot at the company.
會計知道錢不見之後，公司裡就流傳著一個秘密。

■ Becky looked straight ahead to avoid eye contact with the boy.
為避免與男孩眼神交會，貝琪直視前方。

■ The wounded fell asleep soon after taking her medication.
傷患服藥後睡著了。

★其他常見 a- 字首構成的副詞：

abed　在床上	abroad　國外地
aloud　大聲地	aside　在旁邊
ashore　岸上	away　離開

2.2 形容詞＋ ly

■ Hopefully, the project will be completed as scheduled.
希望工作能如期完成。

■ Obviously, the candidate's comment has sparked a heated debate again.
候選人的留言顯然又激起熱烈討論。

■ You are sincerely requested to be present at the year-end party.
敬請您蒞臨尾牙宴。

■ My manager was texting while driving. Consequently, he got into a car accident.
我經理開車時傳訊息，結果發生車禍。

★其他常見「形容詞＋ ly」構成的副詞：

pparently　明顯地	truly　真實地
fully　完全地	generally　一般地
personally　個人上	politically　政治上
theoretically　理論上	publicly　公開地

2.3 名詞＋ ly

■ Only one student failed the course twice, namely Fujita.
這科目只有一名學生被當兩次，就是藤田。

■ The project failed partly because of a lack of relevant information.
因為缺乏相關資訊，部分工作不成功。

■ The general manager will convene a performance review meeting quarterly.
總經理將召開每季績效檢討會議。

★其他常見「名詞＋ly」構成的副詞：

hourly 小時地	purposely 故意地
monthly 每月地	weekly 每週地

2.4 現在分詞＋ly

■ The Japanese grill house is surprisingly cheap and good.
日式燒烤店出人意料地便宜又好吃。

■ The single mother has been astonishingly persistent recently.
最近的單親媽媽一直都是堅毅驚人。

■ It's becoming increasingly evident that the crisis will be over soon.
危機即將結束的證據愈趨明顯。

■ Interestingly enough, the guinea pig enjoys playing with the kitten.
真有趣，天竺鼠喜歡和小雞玩在一起。

2.5 過去分詞＋ly

■ Hart's stepfather died quite unexpectedly several years ago.
哈特的繼父數年前意外身亡。

■ Supposedly, economic recovery in that area is gaining strength.
想必那地區的經濟復甦力道逐漸增強。

■ President Obama has repeatedly urged Congress to pass the bill soon.
歐巴馬總統一再催促國會儘快通過法案。

■ Undoubtedly, the village fellows will feel very disappointed about it.
無疑地，鄉親會非常失望。

★其他常見「過去分詞＋ly」構成的副詞：

admittedly	明白地	excitedly	興奮地
contentedly	滿意地	heatedly	激烈地
delightedly	歡喜地	hurriedly	匆忙地
distractedly	分神地	wickedly	惡意地

2.6 複合形容詞＋ly：大多是含 heart, hand 的複合形容詞＋ly。

■ Some children tend to avoid schoolwork or work half-heartedly.

一些孩童會逃避學業或敷衍塘塞。

■ Several of my senior schoolmates used to treat me high-handedly.

我的幾位學長曾對我非常粗暴。

■ They enjoyed a lighthearted journey through Scotland this summer.

他們今年夏天輕鬆玩遍蘇格蘭。

2.7 名詞或介系詞＋ward／way／wise

■ Turn the key clockwise, not counterclockwise.

鑰匙要順時鐘方向轉動，而不是逆時鐘方向。

■ The crabs walk sideways because their legs bend.

螃蟹的腿彎曲，所以側著走路。

■ Does the side door open inwards or outwards?

側門往內或往外開？

■ I took a step backwards to allow the lady to pass.

我後退一步讓女士通過。

■ The hikers had got only halfway when it started to rain.

下雨時健行的人只到半途。

■ The patient's health deteriorated rapidly, and he died shortly afterwards.
病患健康狀況急轉直下，之後旋即過世。

■ The national debt will leap upwards in case the interest rate on government bonds rises.
如果政府公債利率上升，國債將往上飆升。

3. 複合副詞：

數個單詞構成的副詞為**複合副詞**，常用的複合副詞多是二個單詞所構成。

■ Somehow, Itou always manages to overcome each crisis.
伊藤都會設法克服危機。

■ I hereby acknowledge receipt of your letter of 10 May.
特此告知貴方五月十日的來函收悉。

■ September's bright full moon will be rising overhead tonight.
九月的明亮滿月今晚會高掛上空。

■ We assumed beforehand that the candidate would lose the election.
我們預測候選人會敗選。

■ Nearly 100 residents stayed overnight at a Red Cross emergency shelter.
大約 100 位居民在紅十字緊急庇護所過夜。

■ Cicada bugs are set to emerge after 17 years in hibernation underground.
蟬在地底下冬眠 17 年後開始出現。

★其他常見的複合副詞：

overtime	加班	however	無論如何
sometime	某時	meantime	同時
sometimes	有時候	otherwise	否則

| therefore　因此 | somewhere　某處 |
| overseas　海外地 | wherever　無論在哪裡 |

4. 副詞片語：

片語結構的副詞是以副詞為中心詞的副詞片語。另外，副詞功用的名詞、不定詞、介系詞等片語都是副詞片語。

■ The girl has never had a very closely connected family.
女孩沒有關係密切的家人。

■ I remembered my dream so vividly when I awoke from my nap.
我從小憩中醒來時，我的夢還記得很清楚。

4.1 副詞功用的語詞

4.1.1 名詞片語

■ The lioness is two years old.
母獅兩歲大。

■ A bomb exploded just meters away.
炸彈在幾英尺遠爆炸。

■ The hippo just had a baby last week.
上星期河馬才產下一隻小河馬。

■ No doubt, we will visit the resort again.
無疑地，我們將再次造訪該度假勝地。

■ World Zombie Day falls on October 12 this year.
今年世界殭屍日在十月十二日。

■ The athlete consumes around 1250 calories every day.
運動員每天攝取大約 1250 卡路里。

■ The old nun died a peaceful death yesterday morning.
老先生於昨天早上安詳去世。

4.1.2 不定詞

■ My godfather has to work at two jobs to make ends meet.
為應付需要，我義父必須做二份工作。

■ The painter combined yellow and blue paint to make the green hills.

為畫出綠色山丘，畫家將黃色及藍色顏料混合。

■ To tell the truth, it's possible to complete the task before the deadline.

坦白說，工作還是可能在截止日前完成。

4.1.3 介系詞片語

■ Around the world, there exist a variety of zombie events.

殭屍事件世界各地都有。

■ As a matter of fact, the argument has nothing to do with me.

事實上，爭論與我無關。

■ With no hesitation, the pedestrian called the police for help.

毫無猶豫地，路人打電話向警方求助。

■ Pennsylvania has one of the biggest zombie walks in the world.

賓州有世界最大的殭屍走路活動。

■ Children dressed up and went "trick-or-treating" from door to door.

孩子們盛裝打扮，然後挨家挨戶玩「不給糖就搗蛋」的遊戲。

5. 副詞子句：

副詞子句為子句結構的副詞，修飾子句。

■ Even though they may be scary, zombies remain very entertaining.

儘管可能會引起驚慌，殭屍還是非常有趣。

■ The young guy did not appreciate the importance of health until he got seriously ill.

一直到重病倒下，這年輕人才知道健康的重要。

6. 分詞構句：

分詞構句是分詞結構的副詞子句，修飾子句。

■ Miss Lee sat by the window doing translation.
李小姐坐在窗邊翻譯。

■ When seen from the distance, the island looks like a rock.
從遠處看，島嶼看起來像一顆岩石。

■ Japanese people are not allowed to eat while walking along the streets.
日本人走在街上是不准吃東西的。

7. 獨立結構

獨立結構為「with＋主詞語詞」，and 引導的對等子句的縮減，主詞與主要子句主詞不同，功用為說明主要子句的附帶狀況。

■ The girl sat on the dental chair, with her mouth closed tight.
＝ The girl sat on the dental chair, and her mouth was closed tight.
女孩坐在牙醫診療椅上，嘴巴閉得緊緊的。

■ The cormorant came back to the boat, with several fish in its throat.
＝ The cormorant came back to the boat, and several fish were in its throat.
鸕鶿回到船上，喉嚨裡塞著幾條魚。

◆ 10-3 副詞的分類

1. 按語意分類

1.1 時間副詞：說明狀況或動作發生的時間訊息的副詞為時間副詞。

1.1.1 形式

(1) 單詞副詞

■ The otter is caught in the cage now.
水獺被關在籠子裡。

■ The catering chef was fixing dinner then.
當時外燴主廚正在料理晚餐。

■ The assailant escaped immediately after the incident.
事件後襲擊者立刻逃脫。

(2) 副詞片語

■ The cook is frying up some chicken right now.
廚師正在煎一些雞肉。

■ A policeman shot the gunman dead right away.
一名警察立即射殺槍手。

■ My roommate just came back not long ago from a night out with friends.
不久前我室友才和朋友出去回來。

(3) 副詞子句

■ The wanted criminal was fastened by a shackle soon after he was arrested.
通緝犯遭到逮捕後馬上被戴上手銬。

■ The seal dove into the water as soon as it noticed a polar bear approaching fast.
海豹一注意到北極熊快速接近就馬上潛入水中。

1.1.2 時間副詞功用的語詞

(1) 名詞片語

■ The murderer was hanged for his crime this morning.
殺人犯今天早上為所犯罪行遭到絞刑。

■ The next day, the army invaded and destroyed everything in sight.
第二天，軍隊入侵，看得見的都摧毀殆盡。

(2) 介系詞片語

■ The mountain climbers reached the peak at last.
登山客終於攻上山頂。

■ The police reached the crime scene without delay.
警方毫無延遲地抵達刑案現場。

■ For Susie, there was no reason to sit at home on a Friday night.
對蘇西來說，週五夜晚沒有理由待在家裡。

1.2 地方副詞：說明狀況或動作發生的位置或方向的副詞為地方副詞。

1.2.1 形式

(1) 單詞副詞

■ Here we are!
我們到了！

■ Is there anybody home?
有人在家嗎？

■ I've been there several times.
我去過那裡幾次。

說明 and 連接的單詞副詞平行結構，表示回復的狀況。

■ Swallows are flying to and from above the field.
燕子在田上方飛來飛去。

■ Children were jumping up and down on the floor.
孩子們在地板上跳來跳去。

■ The assistant has been in and out during the meeting.
會議期間助理一直進進出出。

■ A killer whale is swimming backward and forward off the coast.
殺人鯨在海岸附近來回地游。

(2) 不定地方副詞：anywhere, everywhere, nowhere, somewhere 為不定地方副詞，表示不確定的地點或位置。

■ Flattery will get you nowhere.
諂媚使你無所獲。

■ I can't find my beagle anywhere.
我哪裡都找不到我的米格魯。

■ There are moths everywhere in the room!
  = There are moths here and there in the room!
  房裡到處都是飛蛾。

■ Should we try for a loan at the bank or somewhere else?
  = Should we try for a loan at the bank or elsewhere?
  我們要在這家銀行或其他銀行貸款嗎？

說明 不定地方副詞可搭配 else，表示其他地方。

■ I must have left my cell phone somewhere inside the caf .
  我一定是將我的手機丟在咖啡店裡的什麼地方。

(3) 副詞片語：多由單詞副詞搭配位置介副詞構成，介副詞可視為副詞修飾語。

■ Mars is still far away from the Earth.
  火星離地球很遠。

■ Sky lanterns are flying high up in the sky.
  天燈往上飛向高空。

■ The fish hawk can dive deep down to catch fish.
  魚鷹能夠潛到水中深處抓魚。

■ The tadpole has a tail to help it swim far and near.
  蝌蚪有尾巴幫助它們游來游去。

(4) 副詞子句

■ Where there is a will, there is a way.
  有志者事竟成。

■ We can go anywhere we wish now.
  現在我們想去哪裡，就能去哪裡。

■ Everywhere the president went, he was under risk of having shoes thrown at him.
  總統去的每一地方都有被丟鞋的風險。

1.2.2 具地方副詞功用的語詞

(1) 介副詞：與介系詞同形的副詞為介副詞，位置或方向的介副詞可視為地方副詞。

■ May I come in?
（介副詞）

我可以進來嗎？

■ I was sitting in the lounge.
（介系詞）

我就坐在交誼廳。

■ I'm just looking around.
（介副詞）

我只是四處看看。

■ I was looking around the lobby.
（介系詞）

我看看大廳四周。

■ The ship took many tons of cargo aboard.
（介副詞）

船上載很多貨物。

■ The man standing opposite the actress is a security guard.
（介副詞）

站在對面的男子是一名女演員。

■ A security guard stood opposite to the actress.
（介系詞）

一名警衛站在女星對面。

(2) 介系詞片語

■ Go stand in the corner.
去站在角落。

■ It's hot and humid in here.
這裡面又熱又悶。

■ There is a cat beneath the coffee table.
茶几底下有一隻貓。

■ The summer sun is slowly setting under the horizon.
夏日太陽正緩慢下到地平線。

1.2.3 位置

(1) 名詞片語之後

■ The refrigerator upstairs needs to be moved away.
樓上的冰箱需要搬走。

■ These are spacers between the shelf above and the rack below.
上面的櫃子和底下的架子之間有隔間。

(2) 動詞片語之後

■ English spread worldwide in the 20th century.
英語在二十世紀傳遍全世界。

■ I wish I could travel all over the world one day.
但願有一天我能環遊世界。

■ The victims could only stay outdoors overnight.
災民只能在戶外過夜。

■ Black faced spoon bills fly south to spend their winter.
黑面琵鷺向南飛去過冬。

(3) 句首：

一些地方副詞移至句首，表示強調，主詞與動詞詞序倒裝。

■ Off flew the swallow.
麻雀飛走了。

■ Away ran the shoplifter!
扒手跑走了！

■ Up out of the water jumped the dolphin.
海豚往上跳出水面。

■ Down are falling the Bombax Ceiba leaves.
木棉花樹葉往下掉落。

■ Ahead will we face a number of challenges.
我們面對許多樹立在前的挑戰。

1.3 否定副詞：表示否定語意的副詞為否定副詞。

■ I am not hungry at all.
　＝ I am not the least bit hungry.
　＝ I am not hungry in the least.
我一點也不餓。

■ I will never more rely on you.
我絕不再信任你。

■ Such a sea creature has never before been seen.
這類海洋生物從未見過。

■ The copy machine performs none too efficiently.
影印機的效率一點也不好。

■ The auditor never so much as said hello to the teacher.
旁聽生都不會向老師打招呼。

■ The film is none the worse for its low-budget production.
影片沒有因為製作預算低而質感較差。

1.3.1 否定副詞的強調用法：強調否定副詞時，否定副詞可移至句首，主詞與動詞詞序倒裝。

■ Never have I seen such a long eel.
我從未看過這麼長的鰻魚。

■ Not until the midnight did it stop snowing.
直到半夜雪才停。

■ By no means will you become wealthy overnight.
你絕不會一夜致富。

■ On no occasion did the government seek an apology from the parliament.
政府絕不會要求議會道歉。

1.3.2 部分否定：not, all, always, both, every 等共同出現時，可表示部分否定。

■ Not all the birds are transient.

不是所有的鳥都是候鳥。

■ *"Great men are not always wise."*-（*Job 32:9*）

「尊貴的的人不是都兼具智慧」。《約伯記 32:9》

■ Not every kind of fish is perfect for grilling.

不是每一種魚烤起來都很美味。

■ My parents are not both Albanian.

= Either one of my parents is Albanian.

我的父母中只有一位是阿爾巴尼亞籍。

= My parents are not Albanian.

我的父母都不是阿爾巴尼亞籍。

1.3.3 雙重否定：not, never 搭配否定詞，形成肯定語意的加強語氣。

■ That is not a small amount of money.

這不是一筆小錢。

■ My boss is not an inconsiderate smoker.

我老闆抽菸時會顧及別人感覺。

■ It's never too late to learn.

學到老，活到老。

■ Mr. Kharla・mova is not a careless driver.

卡拉摩瓦先生不是一位粗心的駕駛。

■ My niece never comes to my home without a reason.

我姪女來我家都有理由。

★相對於否定副詞，肯定副詞表示肯定語意。

assuredly 確實地	surely 確定地
absolutely 絕對地	undoubtedly 無疑地
certainly 一定	beyond a doubt 無疑地

definitely 確定地	beyond question 毫無疑問地
positively 肯定地	without question 毫無疑問地

1.4 程度副詞：說明動詞、形容詞或副詞的程度的副詞為程度副詞。

1.4.1 充分程度副詞

■ You're absolutely wrong about that incident.
那件事你完全錯了。

■ The military base has been utterly destroyed.
軍事基地已徹底摧毀。

■ The machine has been thoroughly examined.
機器已徹底檢查。

■ These references are not sufficiently precise.
這些參考資料不夠準確。

■ The coach seemed pretty pleased with his team's performance.
教練似乎相當滿意團隊的表現。

■ I don't like the meal much.
= I don't much like the meal.
我沒有很喜歡這種食物。

★ much 表示非常時，僅修飾動詞。

★ 其他表示充分語意的程度副詞

awfully 非常地	incredibly 不可思議地
considerably 相當地	profoundly 高度地
deeply 深入地	quite 相當地
enormously 龐大地	rather 相當
extraordinarily 特別地	significantly 顯著地
extremely 極度地	terribly 極度地

fairly　非常地	tolerably　可忍受地
fantastically　極度地	tremendously　非常地

1.4.2 限制程度副詞

■ Ella is merely a trainee.
雅拉只是一名實習生。

■ You can but give another try.
你只能再試一下。

■ Yulia was simply playing a joke on the child.
尤莉亞只是在和孩子開玩笑。

■ The girl committed such a crime just for revenge.
女孩犯下這樣的罪只是要報復。

■ The manager was somewhat disappointed with the performance.
經理對業績表現有些失望。

1.4.3 否定程度副詞

■ Uranus can scarcely be seen without a telescope.
沒有望遠鏡看不到天王星。

■ We can hardly find a Formosan Clouded Leopard in the mountains in Taiwan.
我們在台灣山區幾乎看不到台灣雲豹。

1.4.4「那麼的」程度副詞

■ It isn't all that hot here.
這裡沒有那麼熱。

■ Don't walk this far down!
要往前走那麼遠！

■ I have a simple diet and eat only that much.
我的飲食簡單，就只吃這麼多。

■ There has been so much spam on my computer since the software was installed.

安裝這軟體後我電腦立刻有這麼多垃圾信件。

1.4.5 修飾比較級的程度副詞

■ The tumor is even larger than a fist.

腫瘤比一個拳頭還大。

■ The device is none the more functional for its high price.

機器並不會因價錢高而有較多的功能。

■ The Windows 7 Beta 1 runs much faster than Lite Vista.

Windows 7 Beta 1 跑得比 Vista 快得多。

1.4.6 修飾比較級與最高級的程度副詞

■ Microsoft Excel is the very most indispensable product.

微軟 Excell 作業系統是最不可或缺的產品。

■ "The snake spa" is by far and away the most unique massage in the world.

「蛇 spa」是世界上最獨特的按摩。

■ The farm is by far the most perfect place for a vacation with friends or family!

這農場是與親朋好友一同度假的絕佳場所。

1.5 情態副詞：描述狀態、方式、心情或態度的副詞，通常是「形容詞＋ly」所構成。

1.5.1 位置

(1) be 動詞或助動詞之後

■ Many members were fiercely opposed to the proposal.

許多會員強力反對提案。

■ The food manufacturer was wrongly accused by authorities concerned.

有關當局對該食品廠的指控有誤。

■ The management should have properly dealt with the issues.

管理階層原本該妥善處理這些議題。

■ The journalist will directly complain to the Federal
Communications Commission.
記者直接向聯邦通訊委員會投訴。

⑵ 不及物動詞之後，少見於不及物動詞之前。

■ My uncle has been working very hard.
我岳父一直都很努力工作。

■ My stepfather died accidently last year.
我繼父去年意外身亡。

■ The man stared thoughtfully at the picture.
男子若有所思地凝望著那幅畫。

⑶ 動詞片語（動詞＋必要成分）之前或之後。

■ The baby miraculously survived the accident.
嬰兒在意外中奇蹟似地生還。

■ The woman treated her badger hound very nicely.
婦人對她的臘腸狗非常好。

■ The plaintiff reluctantly signed the recognizance.
原告不願簽切結書。

■ The entrepreneur generously donated money to the orphanage.
企業家慷慨捐款給孤兒院。

■ The government will develop the area into a business district
gradually.
政府將逐漸開發該區域成為商業區。

■ The committee formally nominated Mr. Bruno to be
ambassador to that country.
委員會正式提名布魯諾先生擔任那國家的大使。

⑷ 句首，表示加強語氣

■ Luckily, I found my missing American Curl soon after.
很幸運，我一下子就找到我走失的捲耳貓。

■ Obviously, it was a self-defense deal.
很明顯，那是自我防衛的行為。

■ Suddenly, the rock monkey took away the hiker's fruit in his hand.
突然間，獼猴搶走登山者手上的水果。

★情態副詞可代換為介系詞片語：情態副詞可代換為含同字源的介系詞片語。

actually　事實上 = in actuality	hastily　急迫地 = in haste
angrily　氣憤地 = with anger	hurriedly　匆忙地 = in a hurry
carefully　小心地 = with care	proudly　驕傲地 = with pride
confidently　有信心地 = with confidence	really　事實上 = in reality
easily　輕易地 = with ease	secretly　祕密地 = in secret
fluently　流利地 = with fluency	suddenly　突然地 = all of a sudden
fairly　非常地	tolerably　可忍受地
fantastically　極度地	tremendously　非常地

1.6 頻率副詞：說明動作發生次數或頻率的副詞為頻率副詞，包括相關語意的片語或子句。

1.6.1 形式

(1) 單詞

■ My Siamese usually pees on the carpet.
我的暹邏貓經常尿在地毯上。

■ Judy doesn't go visit her biological parents much.
茱蒂不常看望她的親生父母。

(2) 副詞片語

■ The clerk made the same mistake again and again.
職員一再犯同樣的錯誤。

■ The president only comes to the factory now and again.
總裁偶爾才會來工廠。

(3) 副詞子句：whenever／every time 引導的子句表示動作的頻率。

■ Kawana burst into tears whenever she heard the song.
川奈每次聽到這首歌都不禁流淚。

■ Every time Miss Kita drinks milk, she gets diarrhea that will last for a couple of days.
每次木田小姐喝牛奶，她都會拉個兩三天。

(4) 具頻率副詞功用的語詞

① 名詞片語

■ You should take the medication every four hours.
你要每四個小時吃一次藥。

■ My roommate does his laundry every other second day.
我的室友每兩天洗一次衣服。

■ The performance review meeting is held once a quarter.
業績檢討會議每一季開一次會。

■ Your Turkish Angora stared up in the corner all the time.
你的土耳其安哥拉貓一直在角落凝視。

② 介系詞片語

■ Your love will last for all time.
你的愛永遠長存。

■ Chimps will eat meat from time to time.
黑猩猩偶爾會吃肉。

■ King Cobras will on occasion eat small animals.
眼鏡蛇王偶爾會吃小動物。

說明 from time to time

= at times = once in a while

= every now and then。

■ The manager comes to the franchise stores on alternate day.
經理每隔一天就去一次特約商店。

1.6.2 位置

(1) 動詞組前

■ My son hardly ever eats junk food.
我兒子幾乎不曾吃過垃圾食物。

■ The couple continually argued until they got the point across.
這對夫婦一直爭執到彼此終於有交集。

■ Mike regularly goes jogging along a lonely road in the late afternoon.
麥克習慣傍晚時沿著一條寂靜的道路慢跑。

■ The paparazzi generally use a pinhole camera to take a sneaky snapshot.
狗仔經常使用針孔相機偷拍。

(2) 動詞組之後

■ Birds need to eat continually for at least 12 hours a day.
鳥類一天需要持續進食至少十二小時。

■ The pregnant woman vomits in the morning very often.
孕婦很常晨吐。

■ The soldier has come back to his hometown once and for all.
士兵就只回過家鄉一次 。

■ I'll love you forever forever and a day for ever and ever forevermore.
我永遠愛妳。

(3) be 動詞或助動詞之後，強調 be 動詞時，頻率副詞可置於前面。

■ *"Reality is frequently inaccurate."- Douglas Adams*
「真實常是不正確的」。-- 道格拉斯・亞當斯

■ It is normally very cold this time of the year.
= It normally is very cold this time of the year.
一年的這時候通常會很冷。

■ We will eternally cherish priceless memories of this period of time.
我們永遠珍惜這段期間的寶貴回憶。

■ The fortune teller doesn't always tell fortunes precisely.
算命師不是每次都算得準。

■ Deer don't usually eat herbs or plants that have a strong fragrance.
鹿通常不吃味道太重的草或植物。

(4) 句首

① 表示強調：

■ Repeatedly, the rock monkey provoked the wolfhound.
獼猴一再地激怒狼狗。

■ Sometimes, the office worker fixes meals, and sometimes eats out with friends.
有時那位上班族自己煮飯，有時候和朋友上館子。

■ Once in a while, I go have a drink with friends in a Japanese-style bar.
偶爾，我會和朋友去居酒屋小酌。

② 否定頻率副詞置於句首表示強調，句子為倒裝句型。

■ Rarely does my Akita eat raw meat.
我的柴犬幾乎沒吃過生肉。

■ Never will I venture into the jungle without a guide.
沒有嚮導，我絕不會冒險進到叢林裡。

■ Seldom did the manager come to work later than scheduled.
經理很少上班遲到。

③ 祈使語氣：always, never 可搭配祈使句，表示勸戒或禁止。

- ■ Always be joyful. 時常喜樂。
- ■ Never stop praying. 不停止禱告。

1.7 讓步副詞

1.7.1 單詞

■ The weather was awful, but they carried on with the search though regardless.

= The weather was awful, yet they carried on with the search.

天氣惡劣，但他們還是去做研究。

1.7.2 副詞片語

■ It is raining, but even so we have to mow the lawn.

= It is raining, but that being the case, we have to mow the lawn.

外面在下雨，但我們還是要去除草。

> 說明 even so ＝ even now ＝ even then ＝ still ＝ anyway ＝ nevertheless

■ You don't have to stay, but I wish you would all the same.

= You don't have to stay, but I wish you would nevertheless notwithstanding.

你不必留下來，但我還是希望你能留。

1.7.3 副詞子句

■ Be that as it may, I will still demand an apology from you.

儘管如此，我還是要求你道歉。

> 說明 "Be that as it may" 可代換為 "despite that, nevertheless"。

1.7.4 讓步副詞功用的介系詞片語

■ The flights were delayed and the hotel was awful, but for all that, I still had a nice trip.

= The flights were delayed and the hotel was awful, but in spite of that, I still had a nice trip.

班機誤點，飯店很差，儘管這樣，我還是玩得很愉快。

1.8 因果副詞：表示動作或狀態的條件或原因的副詞為因果副詞，多置於動詞之前或句首、句尾。

- The salesperson reached the sales goal, and he thus received the bonus.

  銷售員達到銷售目標，因此獲得獎金。

  說明 thus = therefore = hence = consequently = accordingly

- But for the discount, I would not buy such an expensive item.

  = Without the discount, I would not buy such an expensive item.

  要不是打折，我不會買這麼貴的物品。

- There would be little hope to survive under the circumstances.

  在那情況下，存活希望很小。

- In that case, we'd better cut our losses and call it a day.

  那樣的話，我們最好砍掉損失，就此退場。

- In that event, you should call the Emergency Service Hotline at once.

  那樣的話，你應該立即撥打緊急服務專線。

- As a result of the accident, my colleague couldn't get out of the bed for few days.

  由於意外事件，我同事有好幾天無法下床。

1.9 強調副詞：強調句子或詞組的副詞為強調副詞，多置於強調語詞前。

1.9.1 一般強調

- The film is truly awkward.

  影片真的很爛。

- The undertaker is mainly to blame.

  主要是承辦人該受責備。

- A friend in need is a friend indeed.

  患難見真情。

■ The challenger will surely be the winner.
挑戰者一定會獲勝。

■ It is by no means to make everyone pleased.
不可能讓每個人都滿意。

■ You have to submit the documents on schedule by all means.
你必須準時繳交文件。

1.9.2 強調確定語意

■ Actually, I don't agree with the accountant's statement 100%.
事實上，我完全不同意會計的講法。

■ I'll tell you precisely how to maintain the tap water cleaner.
我要清楚告訴你如何保養淨水器。

■ No one can tell me exactly when the world will come to an end.
什麼時候世界末日，沒人說得準。

1.9.3 強調限定語意

■ The test is merely for fun.
測驗只是好玩罷了。

■ Your parents alone can support you.
只有你父母能支援你。

■ Nancy came here solely to say goodbye to me before she left.
南西來這裡只是要跟我行前道別罷了。

1.9.4 強調否定語意

■ My dog isn't interested in the toy at all.
我的小狗對玩具一點興趣都沒有。

■ I disagree fundamentally with what you're saying.
基本上我不同意你所說的。

■ We need to adopt radically different approaches to information exchange.
我們需要採取完全不同的情資交換方式。

2. 按語法功能分類

2.1 疑問副詞

2.1.1 how

(1) 詢問方法、狀況或程度。

■ How do jellyfish move through the water?
水母是怎麼在水裡活動的？（詢問方法）

■ How did you do on your TOEIC test last Sunday?
你上週六多益考得怎樣？（詢問狀況）

■ How fast can a polar bear run?
北極熊能跑多快？（詢問程度）

■ How long is the longest bridge in the world?
世界上最長的橋樑有多長？（詢問程度）

■ How soon will the next version of Windows be released?
新版視窗多久要出？（詢問程度）

說明 how 常搭配隱性形容詞或副詞，形成語意豐富的疑問語詞。

how deep　多深	how old　多老
how much　多少	how large　多大
how often　多久	how far　多遠

(2) 徵求意見

■ How would you like your steak cooked?
你的牛排要幾分熟？

■ How did you enjoy Andre Rieu's concert last night?
昨晚安德烈・里歐的音樂會怎樣？

■ How about a pitcher of beer?
來一大罐啤酒，好嗎？

(3) how come：搭配直述句，詢問原因，帶有責備語氣。

■ How come you took pictures of the dish with your smartphone?

= How did it come that you took pictures of the dish with your smartphone?

你怎麼用智慧型手機拍食物呢？

■ How come your phone bill suddenly went sky high?

= How did it come that your phone bill suddenly went sky high?

你的電話費怎麼突然飆高？

2.1.2 when：詢問時間

(1) 副詞用法

■ When did Mozart pass away?

莫札特什麼時候過世的？

■ When will the annual conference be held?

年會什麼時候舉行？

■ When have you submitted a request for are fund?

你什麼時候要求退款的？

說明 when 可搭配完成式。

■ When is the ferry due to arrive in Bordeaux in French local time?

渡輪當地時間什麼時候抵達法國波爾多港？

(2) 名詞用法：when 有代名詞性質，搭配介系詞，形成語意更為豐富的疑問語詞。

■ Since when has your poodle been missing?

你的貴賓狗從什麼時候走丟的？

■ By when will we have to pay the initial deposit?

我們什麼時候之前要付開戶存款？

■ From when till when was the Civil War in US fought?
　美國南北戰爭是從何時開始到結束？

2.1.3 where：詢問地方

(1) 副詞用法

■ Where have you been these days?
　這幾天你去了哪裡？

■ Where do green sea turtles lay their eggs?
　綠蠵龜在哪裡下蛋？

(2) 名詞用法：where 搭配介系詞 from, to 時，代名詞性質，形成疑問語詞。

■ From where shall we start?
　我們從哪裡出發？

■ Where does the new director come from?
　新主任哪裡人？（詢問籍貫或國籍）

【比較】Where did the new director come from?
　　　新主任從哪裡調過來的？（詢問空間的移動）

■ Let's go for a ride?
　咱們去兜兜風？

■ Where to?
　去哪裡？（Let's go for a ride to where.）

2.1.4 why：詢問原因

(1) Why ＋疑問句：詢問原因或目的。

■ Why did you leave your last job?
　你為什麼離開前一份工作？（原因）

■ Why do rattlesnakes vibrate their tails?
　響尾蛇為什麼要搖尾巴？（目的）

(2) Why not ＋原形動詞：徵求意見

■ Why not go out for afternoon tea?

= Why don't we go out for afternoon tea?

何不出去喝個下午茶？

■ Why not go for a walk around the block with your Maltese?

= Why don't you go for a walk around the block with your Maltese?

何不帶你的瑪爾濟斯到街區周圍走走？

■ A: Let's go play a game of tennis.

咱們去打一場網球。

B: Why not?

好啊！

(3) Why ＋原形動詞？：why 搭配原形動詞，表示不贊同，意思是何必。

■ Why decline the invitation?

何必拒絕邀請呢？

■ Why risk being fined for speeding?

何必冒超速被罰的風險呢？

■ Why care about such a trivial matter?

何必在意這樣的芝麻小事呢？

■ Why (be) so fault-finding?

何必這麼挑剔？

2.2 關係副詞：兼具副詞與連接詞功用的語詞為關係副詞。關係副詞引導形容詞子句，為形容詞子句中的副詞語詞，代替包含先行詞所涉名詞的介系詞片語。關係副詞依結構有單詞與複合二類型，when, where, why, that, the 等為單詞關係副詞，whenever, wherever, however 等為複合關係副詞。

2.2.1 單詞關係副詞

(1) when：詢問時間

【限定用法】

■ There was a time when French was the language of the world.

= There was a time during which French was the language of the world.

法語曾經是世界語言。

■ There are occasions when one must yield.

= There are occasions on which one must yield.

任何人都有低頭的時候。

■ That was the year when the Republic of China was founded.

= That was the year in which the Republic of China was founded.

中華民國是在那一年創立的。

補述用法：補述用法的關係副詞 when 引導對等子句，補充前面子句訊息，可代換為「and then…」。

■ The hawk is due to be released next month, when it will be able to fly again.

= The hawk is due to be released next month, and then it will be able to fly again.

下個月老鷹重獲飛行能力時我們要將牠野放。

(2) where：where 指涉空間位置，先行詞為 place 時，where 可省略。另外，where 也可指涉情境、狀況等。

【限定用法】

■ The police found the place where the killer may have been staying.

= The police found the place at which the killer may have been staying.

= The police found where the killer may have been staying.

警方找到兇手可能窩藏的地方。

■ We erected a memorial at the spot where the brave man's body was found.

= We erected a memorial at the spot at which the brave man's body was found.

我們在尋獲英勇男子屍體的地方豎立紀念碑。

■ The wounded is in a condition where CPR is urgently required.

= The wounded is in a condition in which CPR is urgently required.

傷者的狀況需要緊急施行心肺復甦術。

■ It has come to the stage where we have to make a decision.

= It has come to the stage at which we have to make a decision.

我們得做決定的時候到了。

> 補述用法：關係副詞 where 也有補述用法，可代換為「and there…」。

■ Welcome to our boutique hotel within the resort, where you can check in in private.

= Welcome to our boutique hotel within the resort, and there you can check in in private.

歡迎光臨精品渡假飯店，在這裡你能享有登記入住的隱私。

(3) that：時間、reason、the way 等先行詞，關係副詞可以 that 代替。

■ I am waiting for the time when　that we can get together again.（that 不可省略）

期待我們再相聚的時刻。

■ I wonder the reason（why　that）my son is slow with arithmetic.（why　that 可省略）

不知道我兒子為什麼算術比較緩慢。

■ The student could not accept the way（that）her parents treated her.（that 可省略）

那名學生無法接受父母的對待方式。

(4) the：the 搭配比較語詞，構成條件子句，置於句前。主要子句置於句後，由連接詞 "the" 引導比較語詞，形成與條件子句平行的結構。

【名詞】

■ The more money you have, the more things you think you need.

= If you have more money, you think you need more things.

你的錢愈多，你需要的東西愈多。

■ In an organic lawn, the more grass there is, the less weeds there are!

= In an organic lawn, if there is more grass, there will be less weeds!

在有機草場上，草愈多，雜草就愈少。

【形容詞】

■ The older we grow, the more forgetful we become.

我們年紀愈大，就變得更健忘。

■ The happier we are, the more friendships we develop.

我們愈快樂，就能發展更多的友誼。

■ The bigger the area of the house or the closer to the city center, the higher the house price is.

房子愈大，或愈靠近市中心，房價愈高。

【副詞】

■ The faster a kangaroo hops, the less energy it consumes.

= If a kangaroo hops faster, it will consume less energy.

袋鼠跳得愈快，消耗的熱量就愈少。

■ The deeper a diver descends, the more pressure is exerted on his body.

= If a diver descends deeper, there will be more pressure exerted on his body.

潛水夫下降得愈深，身體承受的壓力就愈大。

2.2.2 複合關係副詞：「關係副詞＋ ever」構成複合關係副詞，引導副詞子句，表示讓步或加強語氣。複合關係副詞有 whenever, wherever, however 等。

(1) whenever：每當

■ I will drop by whenever I am in town.

= I will drop by no matter when I am in town.

= I will drop by regardless of when I am in town.

= I will drop by at any time I am in town.

每當我在城裡，我都會順道拜訪。

(2) wherever：無論在哪裡

■ The guide dog gets to go wherever its owner goes.

= The guide dog gets to go no matter where its owner goes.

= The guide dog gets to go regardless of where its owner goes.

主人去到哪裡，導盲犬就到哪裡。

(3) however：無論如何，可搭配形容詞或副詞以共同構成語意豐富的語詞。however 引導的子句可省略與主要子句重複的語詞。

■ However you look at it, it's really a tough problem to solve.

= No matter how you look at it, it's really a tough problem to solve.

無論你怎麼看，這真是難以解決的問題。

■ However much Jeffrey earns, his wife will never be satisfied.

無論傑佛瑞賺多少錢，他太太都不會滿意。

■ However cold the weather is, Ibrahim goes snorkeling every weekend.

無論天氣多冷，伊布拉欣每週末都會去浮潛。

■ However hard the clerk tried, he could not control his emotions.

無論那名店員怎麼努力，他都無法克制自己的情緒。

■ Deal with the case however you can.

處理這件案子不管你會不會。

■ You can arrange the furniture however you prefer.

你可以佈置這些家具只要你喜歡。

2.3 連接副詞：具有承接句子語意功用的副詞或介系詞片語為連接副詞。連接副詞不具連接詞的語法功能，連接副詞引導的子句與主要子句共同形成複句時，仍須搭配分號或對等連接詞 and/but。未與主要子句共同形成複句時，連接副詞與子句之間應以逗號相隔。

■ Gina worked overtime tonight; therefore, she didn't go shopping with us.

= Gina worked overtime tonight, and therefore she didn't go shopping with us.

= Gina worked overtime tonight. Therefore, she didn't go shopping with us.

吉娜今晚加班，因此她沒跟我們去逛街。

■ You'd better hurry up; otherwise, you'll be late for the meeting.

= You'd better hurry up, or otherwise you'll be late for the meeting.

= You'd better hurry up. Otherwise, you'll be late for the meeting.

你最好趕快，否則開會就遲到了。

說明

1. consequently, hence, thus, in consequence, as a result 等連接副詞引導結果子句。

■ Jack was fined a sum of money; furthermore, his driver's license was suspended.

= Jack was fined a sum of money, and furthermore his driver's license was suspended.

= Jack was fined a sum of money. Furthermore, his driver's license was suspended.

傑克被罰一筆錢，而且他的駕照也被吊銷。

2. also, moreover, in addition 等連接副詞引導表示累積語意的子句。

■ Issac is entitled to apply for the position; unfortunately, he didn't.

= Issac is entitled to apply for the position, but unfortunately, he didn't.

= Issac is entitled to apply for the position. Unfortunately, he didn't.

伊薩克夠資格申請這職務，然而他沒有。

★ nevertheless, nonetheless, instead, still, on the contrary 等連接副詞引導表示相反語意的子句。

★ 其他語意的連接副詞：

indeed　確實	similarly　相似地
then　然後	likewise　同樣地

◆ 10-4 副詞的比較

一些情態副詞與少數頻率副詞可形成比較級或最高級。

- My brother is driving more carefully than before.
  我哥哥開車比以前更加小心。

- Cheetahs are able to run faster than the leopard.
  獵豹能夠跑比美洲豹快。

- A sperm whale can dive much deeper than a killer whale.
  抹香鯨潛水深度遠超過殺人鯨。

- Power failure may occur more often than currently estimated.
  停電次數可能多於目前的評估。

- They are 50 most frequently used kanji characters in Japanese newspapers.
  目前日本報紙有五十個最常用的日本漢字。

- The name skylight is still in use in England, but less commonly than before.
  天窗在英國仍舊使用著，一般來說卻比之前少很多。

◆ 10-5 副詞的排列順序

1. 數個副詞同時修飾一個句子時，若無特別強調，通常按方式、地方、頻率、時間等順序排列。

- Today, the lawmaker went hurriedly back to his electoral district twice.
  今天，立委二次趕回自己的選區。

- At times, my grandfather gets up at five for a morning swim.
  有時候，我祖父五點起來晨泳。

2. 若有數個地方或時間副詞，則分別按小範圍至大範圍排列。

■ The wounded was sent to a hospital in a small town in the mountains.

傷者被送到山區一個小鎮上的醫院。

■ Prince William's wife, Kate, gave birth to a boy at 4:24 p.m., July 23, 2013.

威廉王子的妻子凱特於 2013 年 7 月 23 日下午 4:24 產下一名男嬰。

3. 程度副詞置於修飾副詞前面，但 enough 置於修飾副詞後面。

■ Many people think this battery of batteries dies rather too fast.

許多人認為這款電池太快就沒電了。

■ My Pug barked loudly enough to distract me from my work.

我的巴哥吠得好大聲，我沒辦法專心工作。

第11章 介系詞

　　置於名詞性質的語詞或代名詞前面，連接其他語詞的單詞或片語為介系詞。

◆ 11-1 介系詞的結構

1. 單詞介系詞

　　一個單詞構成的介系詞為單詞介系詞，例如 at, for, under 等。
單詞介系詞常兼具其他詞性，辨識與用法上易產生混淆，例如：

介系詞	off	but	down	concerning	for	for
連接詞		but		concerning	for	for
副詞	off	but	down	concerning		
介副詞	off		down			
分詞				concerning		
名詞		but	down			
形容詞	off		down			
動詞	off		down			

1.1 off

■ The salesperson offered to take a 15% <u>off</u> the original price.
（介系詞）

銷售員願意按原價打 85 折。

■ Hank has paid <u>off</u> his school loan.
（介副詞）

漢克已清償他的學貸。

■ Yesterday was my day <u>off</u>.
（形容詞）

昨天我休假。

1.2 down

■ The temple is located half-way <u>down</u> the hill.
（介系詞）

廟宇位於半山腰。

■ The oil price has gone <u>down</u>.
（副詞）

油價已下跌。

■ My Yorkshire Terrier has been feeling a bit <u>down</u> recently.
（形容詞）

我的約克夏最近情緒有些低落。

■ My boss has his ups and <u>downs</u>.
（名詞）

我老闆大起大落。

■ The defender <u>downed</u> his opponent in the last round.
（動詞）

衛冕者在最後一回合扳倒對手。

1.3 considering

■ <u>Considering</u> the weather conditions, we had better cancel the
（介系詞）
campaign.

考慮到天氣狀況，我們最好取消活動。

■ <u>Concerning</u> Linda is only a trainee, she is performing very well.
（連接詞）

考慮到琳達只是一名實習生，他的表現一直都很好。

1.4 following

■ There will be a banquet <u>following</u> the award ceremony.
（介系詞）

頒獎典禮後有一場宴會。

■ The suspect is under criminal detention based on the <u>following</u>
（形容詞）
reasons.

嫌犯基於以下理由遭到羈押。

2. 片語介系詞

介系詞搭配一個或數個單詞所構成的介系詞為片語介系詞，介系詞大多置於片語介系詞右側。

■ Due to declining birth rate, many schools will have to close.
由於少子化，許多學校必須關閉。

■ But for your assistance, I couldn't have gotten over the hardship.
若非你的協助，我無法克服難關。

■ On top of the base salary, you will get commission from any sale.
除了底薪，你還能從每一筆交易獲得佣金。

■ The worker quit drinking for the sake of his health.
為了健康的緣故，該名工人戒酒了。

■ In the event of the president's death, his son will take over his business.
倘若總裁往生，他兒子將接手他的事業。

■ The restaurant has become more popular among customers by virtue of its constant innovation.
由於創新，餐廳愈加受到顧客的歡迎。

2.1 片語介系詞的組成

1.2.1 名詞＋介系詞

■ Thanks to your advice, I avoided the risk of default.
幸好有你的建議，我才避開違約的風險。

1.2.2 分詞＋介系詞

■ Depending on the agreement, we can choose an installment planof up to 12 months.
依照協議，我們可選擇 12 個月的分期付款。

■ According to reliable sources, the country will develop nuclear weapons.
根據可靠消息來源，該國將發展核武。

■ Owing to the heavy traffic, the delegation arrived at the city hall late.

由於交通壅擠，代表團延遲抵達市政府。

1.2.3 形容詞＋介系詞

■ Due to the severe storm, the gallery will be closed at 3 pm today.

由於暴風雪，美術館今天下午三點關閉。

■ Contrary to popular belief, pandas are a meat-eating animal.

不同於一般認知，貓熊是肉食性動物。

■ Irrespective of the potential risk, Mr. Lin decided to expand his investment scope.

不顧潛在風險，林先生決定擴大投資規模。

■ You have to submit your application form at least one week prior to the deadline.

你必須至少截止日期前一週繳交申請表格。

■ Regardless of the low salary, Mr. Lin has accepted the position of adjunct professor.

儘管薪水微薄，林先生接下兼任教授的職位。

■ You should proofread the draft preparatory to sending it to the editor.

寄稿件給編輯之前應該要校正。

■ The baby came near to screaming when she saw the big dog.

嬰兒看到大狗時幾乎失控大叫。

■ The two parties' opinions are opposite of each other.

兩造意見對立。

說明

1. 「opposite of」表示不同的或反對，「opposite to」表示位置關係。

2. 形容詞 opposite 表示相反的。

■ The boy hurried away in the opposite direction.

　男孩朝相反方向匆匆離去。

1.2.4 副詞＋介系詞

■ Instead of bones, sharks have a skeleton made from cartilage.
不是骨頭，鯊魚有軟骨構成的骨架。

■ We had a lot of fun together with along with some foreign students.
我們和一些外籍學生玩得很愉快。

■ Up until two years ago, the company was losing money.
一直到兩年前，公司都一直在虧錢。

說明 up until ＝ until ＝ up to

■ Apart from the security guard, we all went to the year end party.
除了守衛，我們都去尾牙宴。

說明 apart from、aside from 用法相同，兼具包含及排除的此外，表示可代換為 except for, in addition to, other than, with the exception of 等，表示排除的此外時與 but 同意思。

■ Nine out of ten employees have been laid off.
十個人之中有九個員工被遣散。

■ The task force completed the task ahead of time.
專案小組提前完成工作。

■ The final game between the two teams went down to the wire.
兩隊間的決賽難分軒輊。

■ These are the advantages of private businesses over against state-owned businesses.
相對於國營事業，這些是私人企業的優勢。

1.2.5 介系詞＋介系詞

■ There are maple trees in between the lanes.
巷子內有棵楓樹。

■ We will select from among these applicants.
我們要從這些申請人中挑選。

■ The visitors stayed in the lounge till after the meeting.
訪客在大廳一直待到會議結束。

1.2.6 連接詞＋介系詞

■ They enjoyed their vacation except for the expense.
除了費用之外，他們的假期很愉快。

■ As to hiring more employees, the board of directors hasn't reached a decision.
關於雇用更多員工，董事會還沒達成決議。

■ Myjob application was rejected at the first stage of the recruitment process because of my age.
由於年紀關係，我的工作申請在應徵第一階段就被拒絕。

1.2.7 連接詞＋動詞

■ As concerns the matter, I think nobody should be to blame.
關於那件事，我想沒人該受責備。

■ The executive knew nothing as regards the incident.
主管對事件一無所知。

> 說明 as regards, in regard to, with regards to, regarding, about, concerning 都有關於的意思，in regard to 較常用於口語，with regards to 則用於書信結尾敬辭，例如：

■ With my best regards to your family
謹代我向您的家人致意。

1.2.8 介系詞＋名詞＋介系詞

■ The legal guardian should sign the document on behalf of the child.
法定監護人應該代表孩子簽屬文件。

■ The flight went to London Heathrow by way of Singapore.
班機經由新加坡飛往倫敦希斯路機場。

■ Teachers carry out teaching in accordance of their own beliefs.
教師依據個人理念實施教學。

■ The lounge has emergency lighting equipment in case of blackout.

交誼廳有緊急照明設備，以防停電。

■ In spite of economic recession, the sale of e-commerce increased by 10%.

儘管經濟蕭條，商務銷售額有高達一成的增幅。

■ In terms of intellectual property law, the author might be accused of plagiarism.

以智慧財產權來看，作者可能會被控抄襲。

★其他「介系詞＋名詞＋介系詞」結構的片語介系詞：

by means of　藉著…方法	on guard against　防止
for want of　需要	in front of　在…前面
in addition to　此外	in back of　在…後面
in favor of　支持	in　with guard to　防衛

1.2.9 介系詞＋名詞片語＋介系詞

■ I applied for a visa for the purpose of sightseeing.

我以觀光目的申請護照。

■ The man was sent to jail as a result of drunk driving.

男子因為酒駕而被送進監獄。

■ The firefighter rescued the child from the fire at the cost of his own life.

消防隊員犧牲自己生命將孩子救出火場。

■ Neither should be overemphasized at the expense of the other.

二者不可偏廢。

■ The workers fulfilled the mission assigned to them at the risk of losingtheir lives.

工人們冒自己生命危險完成交付任務。

■ The old woman is in the charge of a foreign nursing worker.

老婦人由一名外籍看護照顧。

說明 其他「介系詞＋名詞片語＋介系詞」結構的片語介系詞：

■ in the front of　　在…前面
■ in the back of　　在…後面
■ in the middle of　在…中間

◆ 11-2 介系詞片語的功用

　　介系詞片語具有名詞、形容詞、副詞，甚至名詞性質，扮演句子必要成分與修飾功用。

1. 名詞

1.1 主詞：時間或空間訊息的介系詞片語可扮演主詞。

■ From here to the construction site is a little far.
從這裡到工地有點遠。

■ From 8 to 10 a.m. would be fine with everyone.
早上八點到十點大家都可以。

1.2 間接受詞：授與動詞的間接受詞置於介系詞受詞位置時，間接受詞可重新分析為介系詞片語。

■ Tom bought a bunch of roses for his fiancée.
（間接受詞）

湯姆買一束玫瑰送給他的未婚妻。

■ I borrowed some money from my colleague.
（間接受詞）

我向我同事借了一些錢。

■ Jack sold his used computer to his junior schoolmate.
（間接受詞）

傑克將他的二手電腦賣給學妹。

1.3 介系詞受詞：時間或空間訊息的介系詞片語可扮演介系詞受詞。

■ The farmer walked around behind the barn just now.
農夫剛剛在穀倉後面走來走去。

■ There has been no further contact with Mr. Lin since after the meeting.

會議過後一直沒有進一步和林先生聯繫。

1.4 主詞補語

■ It is of no use crying over spilt milk.

覆水難收。

■ The stick insect looks like a twig.

竹節蟲看起來像樹枝。

■ The surgeon was in a hurry to the hospital.

外科醫師趕到醫院。

■ The company seems to be on the edge of bankruptcy.

公司似乎瀕臨破產邊緣。

1.5 受詞補語：as, to, into 等常引導受詞補語功用的介系詞片語。

■ They recommended Mr. Lin as secretary-general.

他們推薦林先生擔任總幹事。

■ The president nominated three members to the special committee.

總裁推薦三名成員進到特別委員會。

■ The Internet has turned the world into a global village.

網際網路已使世界變成一個地球村。

■ The government will develop the area into a new town by land reclamation.

政府將藉由都更將這地區發展成新市鎮。

1.6 名詞同位語

■ I am going to take a trip to Paris during Christmas break.

我打算聖誕假期到巴黎旅行。

■ The journey between the two cities will take more than five hours' drive.

兩城市之間的路途最少要五小時車程。

2. 形容詞：

介系詞片語後位修飾名詞，可視為形容詞子句的縮減。

■ Birds of a feather flock together.
物以類聚。

■ A bird in the hand is worth two in the bush.
一鳥在手勝過二鳥在林。

■ The boy on the bus gave his seat to a pregnant woman.
= The boy who was on the bus gave his seat to an elderly woman.
公車上的男孩讓位給一名孕婦坐。

■ The information on this website is not guaranteed to be correct.
= The information which is on this website is not guaranteed to be correct.
這網站上的資料不保證正確。

說明 形容詞功用的介系詞片語不可移至句首。
【誤】On the website, the information is not guaranteed to be correct.

3. 副詞：

副詞性質的介系詞片語可修飾動詞、形容詞、副詞等片語或全句。

3.1 修飾動詞

■ The investigator rushed to the criminal scene ten minutes ago.
十分鐘前調查員趕去刑案現場。

■ Don't place your briefcase on the sofa.
不要將你的公事包放在沙發上。

■ Remember to put your umbrella in the umbrella stand.
記得將雨傘放進傘座。

說明 表示受詞位置移動的介系詞片語可視為受詞補語，動詞的必要成分。

■ The janitor unpacked the parcel with care.
管理員小心地解開包裹。

■ The new staff delivered his presentation with confidence.
新職員很有自信地發表說明。

■ The experienced technician passed the advanced skill test with ease.
經驗豐富的技術員輕鬆通過高級技術檢測。

說明 修飾動詞的介系詞片語可移至句首，形成倒裝句型。

■ With pride, the contest winner stepped onto the stage to receive his award.
充滿驕傲地，競賽獲勝者步向頒獎舞台。

■ Under the rock, I found a cobra skin.
在岩石下面，我發現一張眼鏡蛇的皮。

3.2 修飾形容詞，扮演形容詞補語角色

■ I was tired to death.
我累死了。

■ Let's get ready for the project.
我們為這工作好好預備。

■ The girl seems to be fond of dark colors.
女孩似乎喜歡暗色。

說明 「of 介系詞片語」是形容詞 fond 的必要成分，不可省略。

3.3 修飾副詞，扮演副詞補語角色

■ Wealthy people always think differently from others.
有錢人想的總是和別人不一樣。

■ In the experiment, carbolic acid reacts similarly with aqueous bromine.
實驗中，碳酸的反應和液態溴相似。

3.4 修飾句子

■ In conclusion, the proposal will be rejected as a result of thereview.
總之，提案在審查期間就會被駁回。

■ In fact, the financial minister didn't get involved in the scandal.
事實上，財政部長未涉入醜聞。

説明 in fact ＝ in actuality ＝ in reality ＝ as a matter of fact

■ In a word, the situation is still under control.
總之，情勢仍在掌控中。

説明 in a word ＝ in brief ＝ in short ＝ in sum

■ By the way, it's the instructor who paid the bill for you.
順道一提，是老師幫你付錢的。

★常見修飾句子的介系詞片語：

n other word　換句話說	for example　例如
in addition　此外	on the other hand　另一方面

◆ 11-3 介系詞片語的修飾語

　　介系詞片語常搭配一些程度、狀態或度量衡的語詞，使介系詞片語語意更為具體。

1. 限定詞

■ all over the world
全世界

■ There is a bar extending more than halfway across the river.
有家酒吧要擴展將座落於河流中央。

2. 名詞片語

■ quite a long while after the interview
訪談後很久一段時間

■ The bridge stretches a mile across the river.
橋樑跨越河流綿延一英里。

3. 副詞

■ All the attendees left the office soon after the meeting.
會議一結束，與會者都離開辦公室。

■ Walk straight down the street.
沿著街道直走。

■ Out of sight and very much out of mind.
眼不見，情就疏。

■ The situation is completely under control.
狀況已完全掌握。

◆ 11-4 介系詞的省略

一些語意明確的狀況下，介系詞常省略。

1. 「of 形容詞名詞」結構的介系詞片語當補語時，介系詞 of 可省略。

■ The tablecloth is (of) dark brown.
桌巾是深褐色的。

■ My smartphone is (of) a bright color.
我的智慧型手機是亮色系的。

■ The two models are (of) the same size.
這兩款式尺寸相同。

■ These shade trees are (of) different heights.
這些行道樹高度不一。

2. 副詞功用，且表示度量衡或狀態的介系詞片語中的介系詞可省略。

■ See you (on) Monday.
星期一見。

■ The fight has lasted (for) few days.
戰鬥已持續多日了。

■ The coach arrived at the gym (at) about 10 p.m.
教練大約晚上十點到體育館。

■ It is the hotel I stayed (at) during my last trip to the town.
這是我上次到鎮上旅行時投宿的飯店。

■ The backpacker walked (for) five miles.
背包客走了五英哩。

■ (At) What time will we take off?
我們什麼時候起飛？

■ You cannot treat your dog (in) that way.
你不能那樣對待你的狗？

3. 動名詞前面的介系詞可省略：一些「介系詞＋動名詞」結構中的介系詞可省略。

3.1 動詞＋介系詞＋動名詞

■ The clerk busied herself (in) re-arranging the files.
店員忙著重新整理檔案。

■ The man used to employ himself (in) programming.
男子以前從事程式設計。

■ You should lose no time (in) reporting a stolen credit card.
你應該把握時間將信用卡掛失。

■ The villagers were occupied (in) burying the dead elephant.
村民忙著埋葬死去的大象。

■ The salesperson spent a lot of time (on) visiting clients.
銷售員花很多時間拜訪客戶。

■ Leo has no business (in) criticizing my performances.
里歐無權批評我的表現。

■ The farmer has more trouble　difficulties (in) selling his fruits.
農夫的水果愈來愈難賣。

3.2 形容詞＋介系詞＋動名詞

■ The children were busy (in　with) decorating the playroom.
孩子們忙著裝飾遊戲室。

■ My family is engaged (in) planning our winter trip.
我的家人正在規劃冬季旅行。

■ It depends (on) how you regard responsibilities.
要看你怎麼看待責任。

> 說明 搭配名詞片語時，介系詞 on 不可省略。

■ It depends on the weather.
視天氣而定。

◆ 11-5 介系詞與受詞的遠距關系

介系詞及受詞應相鄰共現，但在一些句型中，二者形成遠距關係。

1. 不定詞修飾語

■ There is a bench for patients to sit on.
= On for patients to sit the bench.
有一張供病患坐的凳子。

■ Jack is considerate to work with.
= With to work Jack
和傑克共事時他很貼心。

2. 疑問句型

■ Where are you from?
   = You are from where?
   你是哪裡人？

■ Which model are you looking for?
   = You are looking for which model?
   你在找哪一款式？

■ Which room did you ask for?
   = You asked for which room?
   你要的是哪一個房間？

3. 被動句

■ Will the competition be called off?
   比賽要取消嗎？

■ We called off the competition.
   我們放棄了比賽。

4. 形容詞子句：

介系詞受詞移至形容詞子句首時，介系詞與其受詞形成遠距關係。

■ The woman whom I met with is my executive.
   我遇見的那位女士是我的主管。

■ There are many issues which we are interested in.
   有許多議題是我們有興趣的。

5. worth 的動名詞補語

■ The idea is worth thinking about.
   這主意值得考慮。

■ There must be something worth caring about.
   一定有什麼值得關心的。

◆ 11-6 介系詞獨立構句

　　介系詞 with　without 引導獨立構句，說明句子原因、條件或附加狀況，形成介系詞獨立構句，搭配名詞 代名詞 現在分詞 過去分詞 不定詞 形容詞 副詞 介系詞片語等語詞。另外，介系詞獨立構句與主要子句的主句不一致。

1. with / without 主詞＋名詞片語

■ The pilot died from an air crash, with his son yet a toddler.

= The pilot died from an air crash, and his son was only a toddler.

飛行員死於空難，他兒子才剛開始學走路。

■ The mother rhino was killed, with its cub the age of three months.

= The mother rhino was killed, and its cub was at the age of three months.

母犀牛被殺時，幼獸才三歲。

2. with / without 主詞＋形容詞片語

■ Don't talk to others with your mouth full.

= Don't talk to others if your mouth is full of food.

不要滿口食物還要跟別人說話。

■ The alligator remained still with its mouth open wide.

= The alligator remained still, and its mouth was open wide.

鱷魚靜止不動，嘴巴大大地張開。

3. with / without 主詞＋副詞片語

■ An ape lay on the rock, with some leaves around.

= An ape lay on the rock, and there were some leaves around.

一隻人猿躺在石頭上，四周有一些樹葉。

■ The giraffe was drinking water, with its head down.

= The giraffe was drinking water, and its head was down.

長頸鹿喝著水，頭往下低。

4. with / without 主詞＋介系詞片語

- A leopard climbed up to the tree, with a warthog in its mouth.

  = A leopard climbed up to the tree, and it held a warthog in its mouth.

  獵豹爬到樹上，嘴巴咬著一隻疣豬。

- The monkey passed through the court, with its baby on the back.

  = The monkey passed through the court, and it carried its baby on the back.

  那隻猴子通過庭院，帶著小猴子在背上。

5. with / without 主詞＋不定詞

- With nothing to do, the workers killed time playing mahjong.

  = Because there was nothing to do, the workers killed time playing mahjong.

  無事可做，工人們打麻將消磨時間。

- Without you to make a donation, the charity activity would be cancelled.

  = If you didn't make a donation, the charity activity would be cancelled.

  若沒有你捐獻，慈善活動會取消。

6. with / without 主詞＋分詞片語

6.1 現在分詞

- The female fox went hunting, with its cubs staying at the den.

  = The female fox went hunting and its cubs stayed at the den.

  狐狸母親出去打獵，幼獸留在獸穴。

6.2 過去分詞

- The zebras crossed the river, with several drowned in it.

  = The zebras crossed the river, yet several got drowned in it.

  整群斑馬過河，其中幾隻溺斃在河裡。

■ The suspect was brought in, with his hands handcuffed behind his back.

= The suspect was brought in and his hands handcuffed behind his back.

嫌犯被帶上來，雙手被銬在背後。

◆ 11-7 介系詞片語的語意傾向

介系詞的語意主導介系詞片語的語意傾向，因此，對於介系詞片語語意理解應從介系詞的語意著手。

1. at 表示「正在…」或「處於…狀態」，通常是主動語意。

■ You can come by to pick me up at your convenience.
你可以在你方便時過來接我。

■ The unpopular law put the people at odds with the lawmakers.
不受歡迎的法條造成人民與立法者意見不一。

■ The dentist was busy at work, drilling the cavities for a patient.
牙醫師正忙著工作，他在病患的蛀牙處鑽孔。

■ The witness was not at liberty to discuss the case with the reporters.
目擊者與記者談論案情時顯得不自在。

■ The airplane was on the runway at rest, awaiting the next passengers to embark.
飛機在跑道上靜止不動，等待下一批乘客登機。

■ Many Japanese businessmen spend time away at pleasure as well as for business.
許多日本商人隨時出門從事商務活動。

■ The sales team was away for the week at leisure, so they were unavailable for business.
那一週行銷團隊外出，因此無法與他們洽商。

■ Jeff decided to stay home rather than take the job overseas in order to be at peace every day.
為了每天得以安適

2. by 表示憑藉或方式。

■ Dexterity comes by experience.
熟練來自經驗。

■ The attorney was in great demand, and only accepted visitors by appointment.
律師業務繁忙，只接待預約的訪客。

■ The antique automobile was sold by the widow by auction.
丈夫已過世的婦人將骨董給拍賣掉了。

■ The famous artist was only available for hire by contract, but his services were expensive.
必須簽約才聘請得到那名知名藝術家，他的服務費非常昂貴。

■ The simple wooden toys were more expensive than other toys, because they were made by hand.
簡易木製玩具較其他玩具昂貴，因為它們是手工製作的。

■ The boy met his uncle by accident   chance while he was waiting for his flight.
男孩在等候班機時意外遇見他的叔叔。

■ The student sang the song so many times that he knew all of the words by heart.
那首歌學生唱好多遍了，所有歌詞都記得很熟。

3. on 表示「處於…狀況」。

■ The trading volume is on the decline.
成交量下跌。

■ The rate of unemployment is still on the increase.
失業率持續增加中。

■ The clerk priced the items before she put them on display.
貨品展售前店員先行標價。

■ The car rental company offers limousines for hire for set rental rates.
租車公司提供加長型轎車套裝出租服務。

■ The unsold inventory of calculators was placed on sale for a steep discount.
計算機的庫存在削價廉售。

■ The teachers went on strike, because they did not receive a raise in the last five years.
老師進行罷工,因為他們在過去五年來都沒有調薪。

■ The security guard on duty noticed a person entering the lobby that he didn't recognize.
值班警衛注意到一位他認不得的人進入大廳。

■ The number of Taiwanese applicants searching for jobs in China is on the rise.
台灣到大陸求職的人數一直在增加。

4. out of 表示「脫離…狀態」。

■ The textbook has gone out of print.
那本教科書已絕版了。

■ The copy machine was out of order, but is functional now.
影印機剛剛故障,但現在又恢復功能。

■ The disabled man has been out of employment for a couple of years.
殘障男子失業兩三年了。

■ Patricia sought fresh grapes during her shopping trip, but they were out of season.
派崔西亞購物時想買新鮮葡萄,但都沒有當季的。

■ The heavy workload given to Gary by his boss was out of proportion to his salary.
蓋瑞的老闆派給他的繁重工作負荷與他的薪資不符。

■ Steve received a notice that the computer he ordered was out of stock and wouldn't be available until July.

有人通知史蒂芬說他訂的電腦缺貨，要到七月才有貨。

■ Bringing June to the trade show was out of the question, because she lacked sales experience.

不可能帶珍參加商展，因為她缺乏行銷經驗。

5. under 表示「正在…中」，通常是被動語意。

■ The escalator is under repair now.

手扶梯正在維修中。

■ The proposal is currently under discussion in the committee.

提案仍在委員會討論中。

■ The authorities placed the financial services company under investigation after customer complaints.

客訴之後，有關當局對該金融公司展開調查。

■ The new terminal of the airport was still under construction, so there were delays in the flights.

機場新航站仍在施工中，因此航班常有延誤。

■ The applicant was young, but the company took his educational achievements under consideration.

應徵者年紀輕輕的，但公司考量他的教育成就。

第12章 連接詞

連接單詞、片語或子句，說明詞組間邏輯關係的語詞為連接詞。就語法功能而言，連接詞有對等與從屬連接詞二類；就組成結構而言，連接詞有單詞與片語二種形式。

◆ 12-1 對等連接詞

連接文法功能相同的單詞、片語或子句的連接詞。

1. 單詞對等連接詞

1.1 and：表示「和、加、連續、而且、然後、卻」等語意。

〔並存〕

■ Snakes and lizards are reptiles.
　蛇和蜥蜴都是爬蟲類。

〔順序〕

■ The proposal has been approved and will be forwarded to the foundation.
　提案已核准，即將傳給基金會。

■ The secretary turned on the computer, checked email, and tackled the usual tasks.
　秘書打開電腦，檢查電子郵件，然後處理一般事務。

> 說明 數個詞組依序並列時，and 出現於最後一個詞組前面，也可以省略。

■ *"I came, I saw, I conquered." -- Julius Caesar -*
　「我來之，我見之，我克之。」-- 凱撒 -

〔卻〕

■ Canciani promised to pay me money back, and he didn't.
　康伽尼答應還我錢的，但是沒有還。

390

〔因果〕

■ I fell from the ladder, and broke my leg.
我從梯子摔下來，腳給摔斷了。

〔加〕

■ Three and four makes seven.
三加四等於七。

〔持續〕

■ The girl just laughed and laughed and laughed at the boy.
女孩對那位男孩笑了又笑。

1.2 but：表示反意或讓步，搭配 never 時，表示「一…就」，搭配 not 時，表示「不是…而是」。

〔但是〕

■ A majority ofteenagers are good at reading, but poor at writing.
大多數青少年擅於閱讀，但寫作能力不佳。

■ I'm sorry, but you need to proofread it carefully.
不好意思，但是你需要仔細校對一下。

〔讓步〕

■ It's true the test is difficult, but the model student got a perfect paper.
測驗真的很難，可模範生考滿分。

1.3 or：主要表示選擇，但會隨著不同語境而有不同語意。

〔或者〕

■ Should I buy a Sony Xperia Z, hTC Butterfly S or LG G2?
我要買索尼、HTC 或 LG 呢？

〔無論，讓步〕

■ Rain or shine, we'll go to play cricket as usual.
無論雨晴，我們都照常去打板球。

〔否則〕

■ Activate the international roaming service, or your cell phone will be useless.

打開國際漫遊，否則你的手機會沒辦法用。

〔還是，疑問句〕

■ Are you for or against homosexuality?

你同意或反對同性戀？

〔也不，否定句〕

■ My father never smokes or chews beetle nuts.

我父親未曾抽菸或嚼檳榔。

2. 準單詞對等連接詞

nor, neither, so, yet 等兼具限定詞或副詞性質，結構為單詞的連接詞為準單詞對等連接詞，除連接語詞受限制外，都可搭配 and。另外，準單詞對等連接詞大多連接子句，引導的子句可倒裝。

2.1 nor：可代換為「and…not either」，意思是「也不」，搭配否定語詞，搭配子句時為倒裝句型。

■ Neither a janitor nor a security guard was in the building.

管理員或警衛都沒在大樓內。

■ Wolves are not in the cat family, and nor are meerkats.

= Wolves are not in the cat family, and meerkats are not, either.

狼不是貓科動物，狐獴也不是。

2.2 neither：也不，不搭配其他否定詞。

■ Neither the engineer nor the technicians could solve the problem.

工程師及技術員都無法解決這問題。

■ My partner has not completed the sales report, neither nor have I.

= My partner has not completed the sales report, and I have not, either.
（副詞）

我的夥伴還沒完成銷售報告，我也還沒。

■ Neither document has been filed.
（限定詞）

這二份文件都沒有歸檔。

2.3 so：也，可代換為「and⋯too」，兼具程度副詞性質。

■ Elephants are a social animal, and so are hyenas.

= Elephants are a social animal, and hyenas are, too.

大象是群居動物，豺狼也是。

■ So pretty a doll!
（副詞）

好漂亮的娃娃！

2.4 yet：但是 (but)

■ The little elephant couldn't swim, yet but it got into the water.

小象不會游泳，但還是進到水裡面。

■ The budget has not been approved yet.
（副詞）

預算還沒通過。

■ Have you delivered the parcel yet?

包裹你寄了嗎？

說明 連接詞 only 也有「但是、不過」的意思。

■ I'd offer to help out, only I'm really busy just now.

我很想幫忙，只是現在真的很忙。

■ You may use my motorcycle, only don't carry anyone else.

你可以用我的車子，只是不要載其他人。

3. 準片語對等連接詞

兼具介系詞或副詞性質，為片語結構的對等連接詞為準片語對
等連接詞，動詞單複數由前面名詞決定。

3.1 as well as：

■ Whales as well as seals are mammals.

鯨魚與海豹都是哺乳類動物。

■ The freelancer writes as well as publishes her own books.

自由作家自己寫書及出版。

The freelancer writes, as well as publishes, her own books.
（副詞）

3.2 as much as

■ Frogs, as much as toads, are amphibians.

青蛙和蟾蜍是兩棲動物。

3.3 along with

■ The blind man is taking his guide dog along with him all the
time.

那位盲胞隨時帶著導盲犬和他在一起。

■ Would you like something to eat along with fried rice?
（介系詞）

你要點什麼配著炒飯一起吃？

■ Along with tobacco, alcohol is taxed in my country.

除了菸，酒在我的國家也要課稅。

3.4 together with

■ The rescuers, together with volunteers, were working in the
disaster area.

救難隊員及志工正在災區工作。

3.5 other than

■ Do something other than play games on your smartphone.

= Do something instead of playing games on your smartphone.

不要再玩手機遊戲了，做點別的吧。

3.6 rather than：可代換為「and not」，連接名詞、代詞、形容詞、介系詞片語、動名詞、分句、不定式、動詞以形成平行結構。

3.6.1 名詞 rather than 名詞

■ Dahana is a philanthropist rather than an entrepreneur.

= Dahana is a philanthropist and not an entrepreneur.

與其說達哈拿是一位企業家，不如說它是慈善家。

■ The horn of a rhinoceros is made from compacted hair rather than bone.

= The horn of a rhinoceros is made from compacted hair and not bone.

犀牛角是由緊實的毛髮所形成的而不是骨骼。

3.6.2 代名詞 rather than 代名詞

■ You rather than Homer are going to write the sales report.

是你要寫銷售報告而不是荷馬。

> 說明 rather than 構成名詞或代名詞平行結構時，中心詞為前面語詞，動詞數目應與其一致。

3.6.3 動詞 rather than 動詞

■ I called the client rather than sent an email to him.

我打電話給客戶，而不是傳電子郵件給他。

3.6.4 不定詞 rather than 不定詞

■ Today, I would prefer to eat out rather than cook at home.

今天，我想上館子，而不要在家開伙。

■ Rather than become a cheap worker, Frank decided to be a freelancer.

不想成為廉價勞工，佛蘭克決定做一名自由作家。

> 說明 rather than 構成不定詞平行結構時，右側不定詞標記 to 通常省略。

3.6.5 動名詞 rather than 動名詞

■ Dori enjoys dancing rather than singing.

多莉喜愛跳舞，不喜歡唱歌。

3.6.6 形容詞 rather than 形容詞

■ The smartphone Gita bought is functional rather than expensive.

吉塔買的智慧型手機與其說是昂貴不如說是功能齊全。

3.6.7 介系詞 rather than 介系詞

■ Carrie had lunch with her classmate rather than with her instructor.

凱莉是和她同學一起吃午餐，而不是和她老師。

3.6.8 子句 rather than 子句

■ Caron is allergic to seafood rather than the fish is not fresh enough.

凱隆對海產過敏，而不是魚不夠新鮮。

■ Gina failed because the test was too difficult rather than because she was not well-prepared for it.

吉娜不及格是因為試題太難，而不是因為她沒有好好預備。

說明 有人將「not to say, let alone」也視為準片語對等連接詞。

■ The proposal is acceptable, not to say perfect.

這份企劃雖不算完美，但還能接受。

■ Richard cannot afford basic living expenses, let alone amusements.

李察連基本生活開銷都付不起，娛樂就不用說了。

4. 關聯對等連接詞

二組語詞接連出現的對等連接詞，連接語法功能相同的單詞、片語或子句，但詞類與結構可以不同。關聯對等連接詞連接名詞組時，動詞數目與後者一致。

4.1 both…and：不連接子句，且只連接二詞組。

■ As for giraffes, both males and females have horns.
關於長頸鹿，公的和母的都有角。

■ An amphibian can live both in water and on land.
兩棲動物能住在水裡及陸地。

4.2 either…or：either 是副詞，強調 or 語意，連接子句或詞組。

■ Many subspecies of the tiger are either endangered or extinct already.
許多老虎亞種不是瀕臨絕種，就是以絕跡。

■ The editor is either proud, overconfident or inexperienced.
編輯不是自滿、過於自信，不然就是沒經驗。

■ Either you tell the truth now, or I will report you to the police.
你不是現在說實話，就是我向警方舉發你。

4.3 neither…nor：neither 強調 nor 的語意，連接的語詞數量不限，都是否定語意，因此不搭配其他否定詞。另外，「neither…nor」不可連接子句結構。

■ The man has neither a smartphone nor a Tablet PC.
= The man doesn't have a smartphone or a Tablet PC.
男子沒有智慧型手機，也沒有平板電腦。

■ The applicant can use neither English, Japanese nor Spanish.
= The applicant cannot use English, Japanese or Spanish.
申請人不會使用英語、日語或西班牙語。

4.4 not only…but also：不但…而且…，also 可省略，語氣較「both…and」強烈，連接句子時，否定副詞「not only」移至句首形成倒裝。

■ Simon was not only permitted to attend the college but was awarded a full scholarship.

倒裝：Not only was Simon permitted to attend the college but he was also awarded a full scholarship.
西蒙不僅錄取該所大學，還獲得全額獎學金。

■ People in China not only eat tortoise jelly but they kill tortoises for food.

倒裝： Not only do people in China eat tortoise jelly but they kill tortoises for food.

中國人不僅吃龜苓膏，他們也殺烏龜當作食物。

◆ 12-2 從屬連接詞

引導名詞子句、形容詞子句、副詞子句、補語子句或同位語子句等從屬子句的連接詞為從屬連接詞。

1. 引導名詞子句：

引導名詞子句的從屬連接詞又稱為補語連詞，分為引導 that 子句與間接問句二類。

1.1 that： that 無語意，that 名詞子句可扮演主詞、受詞、補語等角色。

1.1.1 主詞： 位於主詞位置的名詞子句，that 不可省略。因為主詞子句結構龐大，常移至句子右側，主詞空缺以虛主詞 it 填補，此時 that 可省略。

■ That the professor would run for the election was never a surprise.

倒裝： It was never a surprise (that) the professor would run for the election.

教授出來競選一點也不意外。

■ That the high-tech company was acquired surprised everyone.

倒裝： It surprised everyone that the high-tech company was acquired.

那家高科技公司遭收購令大家驚訝。

■ It seems that the consulting company agrees with us on this point.

= The consulting company seems to agree with us on this point.

顧問公司在這一點上似乎認同我們。

說明 that 名詞子句的述語動詞為 seem 時，只能以倒裝句型呈現。

1.1.2 受詞

(1) 及物動詞受詞：補語連詞 that 可省略，但搭配表示建議或意願語意的動詞，或 and／but 連接的右側名詞子句時，that 不可省略。

■ *"I believe that we learn by practice."* - *Martha Graham* -
「我相信我們都是從練習中學習。」—瑪莎·葛蘭姆

■ I suggested that we take an X-ray of the patient's chest.
我建議我們幫病人照一張胸部 X 光。

■ Lopez promised (that) he would attend graduate school and obtain a master's degree.
羅培茲答應去唸研究所，然後取得碩士學位。

■ I agree that the information above is correct and that we can make a promotion plan now.
我贊同上述資料正確，我們現在可以擬訂促銷計畫。

(2) 不完全及物動詞受詞：that 名詞子句扮演不完全及物動詞受詞時，因子句結構龐大，移至受詞補語右側，受詞空缺以 it 填補，此時 that 不可省略。

■ We all think it is a pity that the president didn't show up at the farewell party.
我們都認為總裁未出席歡送茶會真是可惜。

■ I found it incredible that my Doberman Pinscher had been sitting beside me all the time
我的杜賓犬一直坐在我旁邊，真是不可思議。

1.1.3 主詞補語：非正式用法中，主詞補語功用的 that 子句補語連詞 that 可省略。

■ The fact is (that) the college student has had an abortion.
事實是該名大學生曾經墮胎。

■ We all know(that) you have to work harder to reach your sales volume objectives.
你要做的只是更努力達到銷售量目標。

1.2　間接問句

1.2.1 if, whether 引導的間接問句：間接問句為詢問或懷疑語意時，受詞子句搭配 if, whether。

(1) 主詞：主詞功用的名詞子句不搭配 if。

■ Whether you could give me some advice is another matter.

你是否能提供一些建議是另一回事。

(2) 受詞

〔及物動詞受詞〕

■ I doubt if　whether we could complete the project as scheduled or not.

我懷疑我們是否能夠如期完成工作。

【比較】I don't doubt that we could complete the project as scheduled.

> 說明　否定式 doubt 不具懷疑語氣，不搭配 if／whether 間接問句。

■ You must decide if　whether or not you will attend the negotiation.

你必須決定是否要參加協調會。

〔介系詞受詞〕

■ We had an argument about if　whether or not the wrestling match was real or just acting.

我們爭論搏鬥是真的，還只是表演罷了。

(3) 主詞補語：主詞補語功用的名詞子句不搭配 if。

■ The question is whether or not the enterprise is ready for a different way to work.

問題是該企業是否預備以一種不同方式運作。

1.2.2 疑問詞引導的間接問句：

(1) 疑問代名詞

〔who〕

■ Please check who was on duty at the restaurant.

查查看誰在餐廳值班

■ The electoral commission would announce who was nominated.
選委會宣布誰被提名。

〔whom〕

■ I don't care whom you invite.
我不介意你邀請誰。

■ Do you know whom you should contact for help?
你知道你該找誰求助嗎？

〔whose〕

■ I don't know whose idea is this.
不知道這是誰的主意。

■ I don't know whose smartphone this is.
我不知道這是誰的智慧型手機。

■ I just don't know whose side the new member's on.
我不知道新會員支持誰。

說明 whose 兼具限定詞性質，搭配名詞組以形成疑問語詞。

〔what〕

■ You should keep the focus on what you can do for this organization.
你應當持續專注於對組織的貢獻。

■ I don't know what kind of quality control your company has.
我不知道你們公司有什麼品管措施。

說明 what 兼具限定詞性質，搭配名詞組以形成疑問語詞。

〔which〕

■ *"One day you will ask me which is more important?" - Kahlil Gibran -*
「有一天你會問我哪一個比較重要？」- 紀伯倫 哈利勒 -

■ The Fed will announce which banks will be allowed to raise their dividends.
美國聯邦儲備理事會將宣布那些銀行得以調高他們的利息。

■ The principal will announce which ten students have been awarded this prize.
校長將公布有哪 10 位學生可以獲得獎學金。

說明 which 兼具限定詞性質，搭配名詞組形成疑問語詞。

(2) 疑問副詞

〔how〕

■ Could you please tell me how long the ticket is valid?
麻煩告訴我這張車票有效期間是多久？

■ I'm not sure how much it will cost to go there by ship.
我不確定坐船去那裡要多少錢。

〔when〕

■ I am not clear when I can pick up my ticket.
我不清楚什麼時候能拿到票。

■ Let me know when we have to head for the destination.
讓我知道我們什麼時候前往目的地。

〔where〕

■ I am looking for where the boarding gate for this flight is.
我在找這班飛機的登機門在哪裡。

■ The special assistant is searching for where the files are saved.
特助正在找尋檔案儲存的地方。

〔why〕

■ I am confused at why you refused to reconcile with the victim.
我很納悶你為什麼不和被害人和解。

■ I don't understand why you don't lodge a claim against the seller.
我不了解你為什麼不向賣方求償。

1.3 複合關係代名詞：兼具先行詞與關係代名詞的語詞為複合關係代名詞，包括 what, whatever, whichever, whoever, whomever, whosever 等。複合關係代名詞引導的是名詞子句，不是名詞子句。另外，what, whatever, whichever 兼具限定詞性質，搭配名詞組。

主格	所有格	受格
whoever	whosever	whomever
whichever	×	whichever
what	×	whatever
whatever	×	whatever

1.3.1 what：what ＝ all, something, things, the thing, some things ＋關係代名詞 that

■ I think what you claim is reasonable.

＝ I think the thing that you claim is reasonable.

我認為你的主張有道理。

■ We appreciate what you have done for our region.

＝ We appreciate all that you have done for our region.

我們感激您為我們地區所做的一切。

■ Something that influenced my decision to pursue a degree is my background.

＝ What influenced my decision to pursue a degree is my background.

影響我追求學位的決定是我的背景。

■ I don't remember what extension number I used just now.

我不記得我剛才使用的分機號碼。

1.3.2 whatever

■ I will choose whatever is recommended to me.

＝ I will choose anything that is recommended to me.

任何推薦給我的，我都要。

■ It is time to put away whatever you are working on.

= It is time to put away anything that you are working on.

所有你在進行的，都要放棄。

■ Whatever excuse the troublemaker uses will not be acceptable.

無論肇事者的理由是什麼都不被接受。

說明 whatever 兼具代名詞性質。

■ I don't really want to be an engineer, technician, mechanic, or whatever.

我真的不想成為工程師、技術員、技工，或諸如此類的工作。

1.3.3 whichever

■ You can pick whichever is most appealing to you.

= You can pick anything that is most appealing to you.

只要是最吸引你的，你就能挑。

■ I will choose whichever brand I prefer.

只要我喜歡的牌子，我都會選。

1.3.4 whoever

■ Whoever will take this job must be specialized in programming.

= Anyone who will take this job must be specialized in programming.

任何擔任這工作的人都必須擅長程式設計。

■ The mountain bike will be give to whoever wins the first prize.

= The mountain bike will be give to anyone who wins the first prize.

誰贏得首獎，登山車就頒給誰。

1.3.5 whomever

■ We will choose whomever we think will be the better leader for our association.

我們認為誰是學會最佳領導人，我們就選誰。

■ Give your heart and your love, to whomever you love. (Lyrics to 'Don't Worry Bout Me' by Marty Robbins)

把你的心，你的愛獻給任何你愛的人。

1.3.6 whosever

■ Remember to return the book to whosever name is on it.

= Remember to return the book to anyone whose name is on it.

記得誰的名字在上面，就把書還給誰。

2. 引導形容詞子句的從屬連接詞

2.1 關係代名詞：兼具連接詞與代名詞功能的語詞為關係代名詞。關係代名詞填補形容詞子句中的主詞、受詞、所有詞等缺項，並連結形容詞子句與主要子句。關係代名詞有格位之分，也有指涉對象與使用時機的限制。

2.1.1 主格：主格關係代名詞不可省略，形容詞子句不可縮減為分詞或介系詞片語

(1) that：先行詞為人或事物時，關係代名詞選用 that。

■ The man that caught a duckbill yesterday is a biologist.

昨天捉到鴨嘴獸的男子是一名生物學家。

■ This is an issue that ~~which~~ needs thoughtful consideration.

這是一個需要慎重考量的議題。

(2) which：先行詞為事或物時，關係代名詞選用 which。另外，先行詞不是指涉人的補述子句也選用 which。

■ It should be a case of aforce which is beyond our control.

那應該是不可抗拒的狀況。

■ They will provide compensation for damage which has caused material loss.

他們將提供造成原料損失的損害賠償。

■ Whales which are found in southern and northern hemispheres never meet each other.

在南半球與北半球發現的鯨魚從未相遇。

■ The athlete is very confident, which can be easily seen.

= The athlete is very confident, as can be easily seen.

= The athlete is very confident, and that can be easily seen.

運動員信心滿滿,這是常見的。

(3) who:先行詞為人時,無論補述或限定用法,關係代名詞選用 who。

【限定用法】

■ Do you know the girl who is taking selfies there?

你認識在那裡自拍的女孩嗎?

【補述用法】

■ The couple's only son, who died in a car accident, was very filial to them.

這對夫婦死於車禍的獨生子對他們非常孝順。

2.1.2 受格:填補形容詞子句受詞空缺的關係代名詞應具受格性質。受格關係代名詞前面未出現介系詞時可省略。受格關係代名詞通常可以主格關係代名詞代換。

■ The police have found the location which the suspect hid explosives in.

= The police have found the location <u>in which</u> the suspect hid explosives.　　　　　　　　　　介系詞移至關係代名詞前

= The police have found the location the suspect hid explosives in. (關係代名詞省略)

= The police have found the location <u>where</u> the suspect hid explosives.　　　　　　　　介系詞+關係代名詞=關係副詞

警方已找到嫌犯藏匿爆裂物的地點。

2.1.3 所有格:先行詞為形容詞子句中的所有詞時,關係代名詞選用所有格關係代名詞 whose。whose 語詞可代換為「名詞 of which」,也可搭配介系詞。

■ The telephone is being used by someone whose cell phone is broken.

= The telephone is being used by someone the cell phone of whose was broken.

有個手機故障的人正在用電話。

■ My instructor, in whose car I will take the test, taught me a lot about driving.
我的指導員教我很多駕駛技巧，我要用他的車子應考。

2.2 準關係代名詞：形容詞子句的先行詞搭配一些特定語詞時，常以 as, than 等連接詞引導，這時 as, than 為準關係代名詞。

2.2.2 as 的用法

(1) 先行詞含 as, so, such, the same 等語詞。

■ Don't visit such websites as are not worth visiting.
不要去不值得瀏覽的這樣的網站。

■ I hope you would like the same smartphone as I bought.
希望你喜歡的智慧型手機和我買的一樣。

(2) 先行詞為主要子句。

■ The woman was from Vietnam, as I know from her accent.
婦人來自越南，我從她的口音得知的。

■ My executive directed me to perform the task, as was her duty.
我的主管指導我執行工作，那是她的責任。

(3) 補述用法中，as 填補形容詞子句的主詞、受詞或補語缺項，或以主要子句為先行詞。

【主詞缺項】

■ My opinions are as follows.
我的意見如下。

■ As mentioned above, the question is not difficult at all.
依上述所提，這問題一點也不困難。

■ I have to work overtime this weekend, as is often the case.
= I have to work overtime this weekend, which is often the case.
= As is often the case, I have to work overtime this weekend.
我周末要加班，這是常有的事。

說明 as 引導的補述子句移至句前時，不可以 which 代換。

【受詞缺項】

■ A few days ago, as we all know, the local government shut down.

幾天前我們大家都知道，地方政府關閉了。

【補語缺項】

■ The man sounds like a political figure, as he is.

= The man sounds like a political figure, which he is.

男子聽起來像個政治人物，而他就是個政治人物。

説明 指涉身分或品格時，選用關係代名詞 which。

2.2.3 先行詞或主要子句含否定語詞時，選用準關係代名詞 but，意思是「that/who…not」。

■ There is nothing but helps us move on.

= There is nothing that doesn't help us move on.

凡事都能幫助我們往前。

■ There is no rule but has some exceptions.

= There is no rule that doesn't have any exceptions.

有規則就有例外。

■ There is scarcely a man but has his weakness.

= There is scarcely a man who doesn't have his weakness.

幾乎沒有人是沒有缺點的。

2.2.4 than：先行詞含比較語詞時，形容詞子句以準關係代名詞 than 引導，填補句中主詞或受詞缺項。

(1) 主詞缺項

■ The part timer has saved more money than was expected.

工讀生存的錢超過預期。

(2) 受詞缺項

■ My son never asks for more money than he really needs.

我兒子不會要求過多的零用錢。

■ The hurricane caused less damage than we had expected.
颶風造成的損失比我們預期輕微。

【比較】The lecturer arrived at the hall earlier than what was scheduled.
演講者比預定時間還早抵達演講廳。

2.3 關係副詞：when, where, why, that 等為關係副詞，兼具連接從屬子句與主要子句與填補子句中介系詞片語的功用。關係副詞引導的形容詞子句無主詞或受詞缺項。

2.3.1 when：限定用法中，when 可代換為 that；補述用法中，when 子句可代換為「and then⋯」對等子句。

■ This is the very hour when the mall is most crowded with shoppers.

= This is the very hour during which the mall is most crowded with shoppers.

= This is the very hour that the mall is most crowded with shoppers.
現在正是賣場擠滿購物人潮的時候。

■ The general manager resigned on Monday, when it was also his sixtieth birthday.

= The general manager resigned on Monday, and then it was also his sixtieth birthday.
總經理週一請辭，剛好也是他的六十歲生日。

2.3.2 where：限定用法中，where 可代換為 that，先行詞為 the place 時，where 可省略。補述用法中，where 子句可代換為「and there⋯」對等子句。

■ This is the place where I got to know my fianc e.

= This is the place in which I got to know my fiancée.

= This is the place that I got to know my fiancée.

= This is the place I got to know my fiancée.
這裡是我認識我未婚妻的地方。

■I stayed at a green hostel, where I met a famous architect.

= I stayed at a green hostel, and there I met a famous architect.

我住在一家綠建築民宿，在那裡我遇見一位知名建築師。

2.3.3 why：先行詞只有 reason，可代換為 for which、that，或省略。另外，why 沒有補述用法。

■The reason why the manager was laid off sounds incredible.

= The reason for which the manager was laid off sounds incredible.

= The reason that the manager was laid off sounds incredible.

= The reason the manager was laid off sounds incredible.

經理遭解雇的原因很不可思議。

2.3.4 that：先行詞 the way 可搭配關係副詞 that/in which。

■This is the way that the officer dealt with the situation.

= This is the way in which the officer dealt with the situation.

= This is the way the officer dealt with the situation.

官員就是這樣處理狀況的。

說明 how 不是關係副詞，不與 the way 共同出現。

3. 引導副詞子句的從屬連接詞：

引導副詞子句的從屬連接詞依照副詞子句語意分為時間、地方、條件、原因、目的、結果、比較、讓步、方式、限制、比例等。

3.1 時間：時間副詞子句提供時間訊息，不同的連接詞表示不同的子句時間關係。

3.1.1 副詞子句於主要子句進行時發生

■Even when a snake has its eyes closed, it can still see through its eyelids.

蛇即使閉上眼睛，它也能透過眼瞼看物體。

■Tiger cubs usually leave their mother when they are around two years of age.

幼虎經常在兩歲時離開母親。

3.1.2 副詞子句與主要子句同時發生

- Dave usually listens to music as he studies.
  戴夫經常在讀書時聽音樂。

- When Fred worked as a trainee, he would stay at the factory overnight.
  弗雷德當實習生時,他常待在工廠過夜。

> 說明 表示持續一段時間的副詞子句可搭配 when, while, as 等連接詞,表示與主要子句同時發生的副詞子句只能搭配 as。

3.1.3 副詞子句較主要子句早發生

- When the woman heard the news, she burst into tears.
  女子聽到消息時,她不禁落淚。

- After Hank watched the documentary, he went out for a walk.
  漢克看完紀錄片後,他外出散步。

- Where have you been since I last saw you?
  自從上次見到你以後你都去了哪裡?

3.1.4 副詞子句較主要子句晚發生

- Look before you leap.
  三思而後行。

- It was dawn before the female hyena returned to the den.
  天黑前母豺狼便回到獸穴。

- The leopard had stayed in the grass long before it attacked its prey.
  美洲豹襲擊獵物前已在草地守候多時。

【比較】 I had not waited long before the shuttle bus came.
我沒等多久專車就來了。

> 說明 before long 表示不久以後,等同於 soon。

- I am hoping to see you again before long.
  我希望不久之後能再見到你。

3.1.5 副詞子句表示主要子句開始時間

- Dave didn't quit his job until he found a new one.

  戴夫一直到新工作有著落後才辭職。

- The students didn't leave the classroom before the police arrived.

  學生直到警方抵達後才離開教室。

3.1.6 副詞子句表示主要子句結束時間

- The elephants stood guard until the Thomson's gazelles escaped.

  象群站立警戒到湯姆森瞪羚逃離。

3.1.7 副詞子句表示主要子句發生期間

- It is two years since the Mongol student came to Taipei.

  蒙古學生來台北已兩年了。

3.1.8 主要子句於副詞子句瞬間之後發生

- The antelope escaped as soon as it noticed a leopard heading rapidly in its direction.

  羚羊一發現美洲豹朝牠的方向奔馳而來變逃離了。

  > 說明 as soon as, directly, immediately, instantly, the instant/moment/minute/second 等連接語詞表示「一…就…」

3.1.9 主要子句於副詞子句瞬間之前發生

- No sooner had the salmon jumped out of the water than it was bitten by a bear.

  鮭魚一跳出水面便被熊咬住了。

- Every time I listened to the song, I had teary eyes.

  每當我聽見那首歌，我就熱淚盈眶。

- You're welcome to visit my family any time it's convenient for you.

  不管你哪時候有空，都歡迎到我家來坐坐。

- As often as I tried to call Judy, the line was engaged.

  每當我要打給裘蒂時，電話都在忙線中。

★ when, whenever, no matter when 等都可表示每當。

★其他引導時間副詞子句的連接詞：

單詞	片語
directly 一……就	any time 在任何時候
once 一旦	by the time 到 ... 的時候
immediately 即刻	as soon as 一經……
instantly 一……（就）	the moment 一……（就）
since 自從…以來	the instant 立即
while 一會兒	the minute 一 ... 就
	the second 瞬間

3.2 地方：地方副詞子句提供主要子句場所訊息，連接詞有 where, wherever。

■ The loyal dog is remaining where it is now.
忠心的狗一直都在那裡。

■ The cub goes wherever its mother goes.
= The cub goes no matter where its mother goes.
剛出生的幼獸總會一直跟著媽媽。

■ The concerts are packed out wherever the orchestra performs.
= The concerts are packed out no matter where the orchestra performs.
每次交響樂團演出，音樂會就會爆滿。

3.3 條件：陳述句子條件因素的子句為條件子句，通常不搭配未來式。另外，if 子句可搭配直說或假設語氣。

3.3.1 if

■ If you want to take a selfie in public, don't get caught!
你若要公開自拍的話，不要被發現。

■ If it were to rain tonight, we would quit night riding.
今晚若是下雨，我們就不去夜騎。

413

3.3.2 only if：引導條件子句，直述語氣，表示嚴格限制的條件，置於句首時，主要子句搭配倒裝句型。

■ You can get high scores only if you take more practice tests.
只要你多做練習，你會拿高分的。

■ Only if it rains heavily will the delta flood.
只要下大雨，三角洲就氾濫。

■ Only if you love rock music is the concert worth attending tonight.
只要你喜愛搖滾樂，今晚的音樂會就值得一去。

3.3.3 if only：表示事實相反的願望，引導假設語氣的子句，不搭配主要子句，意思是「要是…該多好」。

■ If only I studied harder, I could have gotten better result.
要是我更努力唸書得到好成績該有多好！

■ If only it would stop raining.
雨要是停了該多好！

■ If only I could work in that company.
我要是能在那家公司工作該多好！

■ If only I had done that the past two years ago.
要是我兩年前有那麼做就好了！

3.3.4 only that：要不是，搭配直述語氣。

■ I should have attended the meeting only that I got sick.
要不是我生病，不然是我該出席會議的。

3.3.5 unless：除非

■ They will go hiking in the mountains unless it rains tomorrow.
= Unless it rains tomorrow, they will go hiking in the mountains.
= They will go hiking in the mountains if it doesn't rain tomorrow.
他們會去爬山，除非明天下雨。

3.3.6 as long as 只要

■ You can leave as long as you complete your work.
你只要完成你的工作就可以離開。

3.3.7 in case：假如

■ I will sign the contract in case we reach an agreement.
= I will sign the contract on condition that we reach an agreement.
我們若達成協議就簽約。

3.3.8 provided/providing (that), assuming (that), supposing (that) 都表示假如，「provided that」比較正式。

■ Supposing the CEO is detained, what shall we do?
如果執行長遭到羈押，我們該怎麼辦？

■ It never rains but pours.
= It never rains but that   except that pours.
= It never rains without pouring.
不下則已，一下就是傾盆大雨。

> 說明 but 是 but that 的縮減，可代換為「except that」或「without ＋介系詞片語」。

★ 其他引導條件副詞子句的連接詞：

單詞	片語	片語
when where	according as so that in the event (that)	assuming (that) on the supposition that, on with the understanding (that) with the provision that

3.4 原因：說明句子原因的從屬子句為原因副詞子句，常見連接詞有 as, because, for, since 等，用法各有不同。

3.4.1 because：because 引導的子句強調理由或原因，語氣最明確，最適宜 why 的答句。

■ The manager was absent from the meeting because he caught a bad cold.

經理重感冒，因此會議中缺席。

說明 because 可代換為「for the reason (that)。」

■ Sean didn't call you only for the reason (that) his cellphone was out of power.

尚恩沒打電話給你，因為他的手機沒電。

3.4.2 for：引導的子句表示明顯的原因或理由，置於主要子句右側，常以逗號相隔。

■ It must have rained last night, for the ground is wet this morning.

昨晚一定下過雨，因為今天早上地面是濕的。

說明 本句中的 for 不可代換為 because。

3.4.3 since：since 引導的子句表示已知或明顯的原因，強調結果，語氣較 because 弱。

■ Since he was out on business, the manager was absent from the meeting.

= Now that he was out on business, the manager was absent from the meeting.

既然經理外出洽公，他就不出席會議了。

說明 considering (that), seeing that, in that 等語意與 since 相近，表示既然、鑒於。

■ Seeing that Syntax is a compulsory course, you cannot drop it.

既然句法學是必修科目，你不能當掉。

■ Considering (that) prices are rising faster than wages, people try not to save money.

既然物價上漲速度比工資還快，人們也就無法存錢了。

3.4.4 as：引導的子句表示附帶說明或已知的原因，強調結果，語氣較 since 弱。as 原因子句可置於主要子句左側或右側。

■ As you are exhausted, you had better stop to take a rest.
既然累了，你就停下來休息吧。

■ I want to stop to take a rest, as I am feeling a little tired.
我要停下來休息，因為我累了。

3.4.5 but that

■ *"It's not that I loved Caesar less, but that I loved Rome more."* -- *Caesar -*

「不是我不喜歡凱撒，而是我更喜歡羅馬。」 -- 凱撒

說明

1. 本句底層結構為 "It is not that I loved Caesar less, but that I loved Rome more."，為形成平行結構，句首「It is」省略。

2. it is that 可代換為「it is because」，因此本句語意為否定一個原因，同時肯定另一個原因。

■ It is not because I loved Caesar less, but becauseI loved Rome more.

★其他引導原因副詞子句的連接詞：

by the means that 依據	in respect that 有鑑於
for that 為了…	in as much as 由於

3.5 目的：表示為了或以便的副詞子句為目的副詞子句，有肯定與否定目的二種，連接語詞以 that 為中心詞。

3.5.1 肯定目的

■ A tadpole is a froglet with a tail and lungs so (that) it can breathe through lungs.

= A tadpole is a froglet with a tail and lungs so as to breathe through lungs.

蝌蚪是有尾巴及肺的小青蛙，能透過肺呼吸。

■ The author asked for my email address in order that he can contact me.

作者為了跟我保持聯絡而向我要 e-mail 地址。

■ The solar panels are made thin for the purpose that they can be put in a bag or backpack.

為了能放進袋子或背包，太陽能電板做成單薄形式。

3.5.2 否定目的

■ You had better sign the contract with the seller as soon as possible for fear (that) he might one day regretit.

你最好儘快和賣方簽約，免得他有一天反悔。

說明 lest，以免，屬於舊式英文，近來英美人士較少使用。

3.6 結果：說明句子結果或因果關係的子句為結果副詞子句，連接詞以 that 為中心詞，多搭配 so, such。

■ The goat was so big that the snake could not swallow it.

山羊體積太大了，蛇吞不下去。

■ The scooter was damaged to such an extent that it couldn't be repaired.

機車損壞到無法修理的程度。

■ Nicole spoke such fluent French that I could understand what she meant.

妮可講的法文很流暢，我聽得懂她在講什麼。

■ The cellphone was very flakey, so much so that it couldn't adequately multitask.

手機不太好用，

■ Peter usually neglected his work with the result that he was fired.

彼得經常輕忽工作，結果遭到解雇。

3.7 比較：連接詞 as, than 引導程度比較的副詞子句。

■ Tigers are actually more muscular than lions.

事實上，老虎比獅子強壯。

■ It takes more time to go to Tamshui by bus than by MRT.

坐巴士去淡水比坐捷運還花時間。

■ The safe is twice as heavy as that one.
這支保險箱是那支的二倍重。

3.8 讓步：讓步是指「雖然、儘管、即使、無論」等語意。讓步副詞子句述及對主要子句未造成影響的狀況，常涉及假設語氣。

■ Much though I admire the candidate, I won't vote for him.
儘管我讚賞那名候選人，但我不會投票給他。

■ While Amy likes children, she doesn't want to bear her own.
雖然艾咪喜歡孩子，但她自己不要生小孩。

■ However hard you try, you won't get promoted in a family business.
無論你多努力，你在家族企業中是不會有前途。

說明

1. granted (that) 除表示讓步之外，還表示假設或原因，例如：
■ Granted (that) the rumor is not true, how will you deal with it?（假如）
即使謠傳子虛烏有，你要怎麼處置？

■ Granted that there were too many cars on the highway, we moved very slowly.（原因）
因為公路上車輛太多，我們移動緩慢。

2. 「granting that」較「granted that」罕用。
■ For that Chad promised so much, he did nothing.
儘管查德承諾這麼多，他什麼也沒做到。

■ Much as I am dead tired, I still need to complete the work.
= As much as I am dead tired, I still need to complete the work.
= Notwithstanding that I am dead tired, I still need to complete the work.
儘管我累癱了，我仍然需要將工作完成。

■ We need to fight for the goal, no matter how much price I need to pay for it.
我們需要努力達成目標，不論要付出的代價有多大。

■ While the leopard can run very fast, it cannot keep running for a long while.

儘管美洲豹跑得非常快，牠無法長時間一直跑。

★其他引導讓步副詞子句的連接詞：

as　像…一樣	when　當……時
if　even if　即使	whenever = no matter when
not but that　雖然	wherever　不管何時 = no matter where
whether...or　是 ... 還是 ...	whichever　無論哪個 = no matter which
what　…的事物	whoever　不管誰 = no matter who
whatever　不管什麼 = no matter what	whosever　不管誰 = no matter whose
however　不管怎樣 = no matter how	whomever　不管誰 = no matter whom

3.9 方式：方式副詞子句提供主要子句方式或對照的訊息，常見的連接詞有 as, according as, how, the way, what 等。

3.9.1 as：可代換為表示「猶如、好比」的「what」。

〔方式〕

■ Do in Rome as the Romans do.

入境隨俗。

〔對照〕

■ Air is to a human as water is to a fish.

= Air is to a human what water is to a fish.

= What air is to a human, water is to a fish.

空氣之於人類，如同水之於魚。

■ As you sow, so shall you reap.

= Just as you sow, so shall you reap.

種瓜得瓜，種豆得豆。

> 說明 as 表示「正如」，so 表示「也是如此」，整句意思是「如同
> 前者一般，後者也是如此」。so 引導的子句可不倒裝。

3.9.2 as if, as though：宛如，表示現在、過去事實相反，或未來可能發生。

■ The salesperson talks as if he obtained the contract.
業務員說得像是他拿到合約了。

■ The man has talked as if he had visited the place before.
男子說起話來就像以前去過那地方。

3.9.3 the way, how

■ The situation is going the way we are hoping.

= The situation is going how we are hoping.

現在的狀況就像我們所期望的

**3.10 限制：限制副詞子句表示限制的敘述內容，意思是「就…
而言」，常見的限制連接詞有「as far as, so far as（較不正
式）」, in as far as, in so far as 縮減形式。**

■ As far as I am concerned, what the astrologer said is nonsense.
就我所知，那位占星家的話都是無稽之談。

■ As So long as you pay me back as promised, I can lend you
some money.
只要你如期奉還，我可以借你一些錢。

**3.11 比例：比例副詞子句表示主要子句連帶變化的原因，as, the
引導副詞子句，in proportion to 引導名詞片語。**

**3.11.1 the：引導比較語詞，置於副詞子句首，搭配含比較語詞的主要子句。
副詞子句說明原因，主要子句表示結果。連接詞 the 可搭配名
詞、形容詞或副詞。**

■ The more orders; the more discount.

= When you order more, we offer more discount.

訂得愈多，折扣愈多。

■ The sooner you complete your work, the earlier you can leave.
= If you complete your work sooner, you can leave earlier.
你愈快完成工作，就能愈早下班。

3.11.2 as：隨著…愈…

■ Popcorn expands as temperature increases.
爆米花會隨著溫度升高而膨脹。

■ As the festival approached, the children became more excited.
隨著節日的到來，孩子們更加興奮。

■ As time grew from the husband's death, the widow became more calm.
隨著丈夫過世的時日增多，寡婦變得更為平靜。

3.11.3 in proportion to：按…比例

■ The suite is too long in proportion toits width.
以寬度比例而言，這間套房太長了。

3.12 對照

■ Americans prefer coffee, whereas the British prefer tea.
美國人偏好咖啡，英國人偏好茶。

■ Jordan invested his money in stocks, while his wife invested hers in real estate.
喬登投資股票，他老婆則是投資房地產。

4. 引導補詞子句的補語連詞：

一些形容詞或分詞搭配補語子句以提供相關訊息。引導補語子句的連接詞為補語連詞，例如 that, whether, if 等。補詞子句中的 that 可省略。

■ I'm sorry (that) I can't promise that to you.
很抱歉，我無法答應你。

■ I'm surprised (that) you didn't check the email.
我很訝異你沒有看電子郵件。

■ I'm afraid (that) I put too much detergent in the washer.
恐怕我在洗衣機裡放太多洗衣粉。

■ Be careful if you pull a horse's tail.
你拉馬的尾巴時要小心。

■ I am not clear who will substitute for my place.
我不清楚誰要接我的位置。

■ I am not sure whether I have done something wrong.
我不確定我有沒有做錯什麼。

5. 引導同位語子句的從屬連接詞：

除了 that, whether, how, when, where, why, what, who, whom 等疑問詞都可引導同位語子句。搭配同位語子句的名詞為先行詞，與同位語子句之間是同等關係，不同於形容詞子句與先行詞之間是修飾關係。

5.1 that：that 在同位語子句中沒有語意，也不是句子的組成成分。

■ Don't jump to the conclusion that all carnivores are not herbivores.
不要妄下邊論說肉食動物就不是草食動物。

5.2 疑問詞

■ There is a confusion about how the operating system works.
運作系統如何進行令人困惑。

■ It's an issue about how the government may react to the situation.
政府對局勢的可能反應是一項議題。

■ We should not make an assumption about what will happen next.
我們不該臆測再來會怎樣。

■ The question about who should be laid off required more evaluation.
誰該資遣的問題需要多加評估。

■ There is doubt about whether the fruit is from this year's harvest or last year's.
水果是今年或去年的收成令人懷疑。

■ The consultant raised an argument about where we should locate the business.
諮詢顧問挑起我們商模定位的爭議。

★常搭配同位語子句的名詞：

advice　建議	news　新聞
announcement　宣布	opinion　意見
belief　信念	probability　可能的結果
claim　主張	promise　承諾
decision　決定	proposal　提案
evidence　證據	remark　評論
explanation　解釋	reply　回應
fact　事實	report　報告
hope　希望	statement　陳述
idea　想法	suggestion　建議
information　消息	thought　想法
message　訊息	warning　警告

6. 引導分裂句中的從屬連接詞：

強調指定語詞而變形的句構為分裂句，強調語詞移為主要子句「It is…」的補語，即強調句型的先行詞，其補語連詞主要為 that 或 who，先行詞為人時，通常不選用 that。

6.1 that

6.1.1 強調受詞：

■ It was from an illegal bank that I borrowed the money.

我向地下錢莊借了這筆錢。

I borrowed the money from an illegal bank.
（底層結構）

■ It was on the Chinese New Year's Eve that the refinery exploded.

煉油廠是在除夕爆炸的。

The refinery exploded on the Chinese New Year's Eve
（底層結構）

■ It was an ancient painting that was stolen in the gallery.

美術館遭偷走的是一幅古畫。

6.2 who

6.2.1 強調主詞

■ It was an aboriginal guy who saved the drowning girl.

是一名原住民救了溺水的女孩。

An aboriginal guy saved the drowning girl.
（底層結構）

◆ 13-1 名詞子句

子句結構的名詞為名詞子句，具有名詞功用，扮演名詞角色。

1. 名詞子句的類型：

1.1 that 直述句

- ■ I don't doubt (that) the economic situation will remain difficult.

  我不懷疑經濟局勢會依然困頓。

- ■ My director told me that he was going to get a new job soon.

  我的主管告訴我他很快就會有新工作。

1.2 間接問句：疑問語氣的名詞子句為間接問句，由疑問語詞引導直述句型。

1.2.1 whether / if 問句

- ■ Many people question whether or not the new policy will be successful.

  許多人質疑新政策是否會成功。

- ■ I was wondering if you could send me a registration application form.

  我不知道你是否能寄一份註冊申請表給我。

1.2.2 疑問詞問句

- ■ I don't know when we will visit the distillery.

  我不知道我們什麼時候參觀酒廠。

- ■ I'm just looking for where the remote controller is.

  我一直在找遙控器在哪裡。

2. 名詞子句的功用

2.1 主詞：子句結構的主詞常移位置述語動詞右側，形成倒裝句型，這時 that 可省略。

2.1.1 that 子句

■ That the applicants' qualification will be cancelled is certain.
= It is certain that the applicants' qualification will be cancelled.
確定該名申請者的資格將遭取消。

說明 that 名詞子句作為主詞時，補語連詞 that 不可省略。

■ It's known to many people (that) Mozart's music helps intelligence and breathing.
許多人都知道莫札特的音樂有助於智力發展與呼吸。

2.1.2 間接問句

(1) whether / if 子句

■ Whether the rescue team can arrive as scheduled is a question.
救援隊伍能否按行程抵達是個問題。

■ It's still uncertain whether／if there'll be any seats left or not.
還不確定是否還有座位。

說明 if 名詞子句不可作為句首主詞，但可作為移位主詞，這時可搭配 or not。

(2) 疑問詞問句

■ It doesn't matter whatever the man claims himself to be.
男子宣稱自己是什麼不重要。

■ Whichever of you complete the task on schedule will receive a big bonus.
你們有誰準時完成工作的將獲得大筆獎金。

2.2 受詞

2.2.1 that 子句

■ The tour guide suggested that we (should) stay here another day.
導遊建議我們在這裡多待一天。

說明 假設語氣受詞子句的補語連詞 that 不可省略，述語動詞可搭配 should。

■ I think it's a pity that wealthy young man should do such stupid things.

我認為那名富少做這樣的蠢事真是遺憾

說明 that 子句常移至受詞補語右側，形成倒裝句型，that 不可省略。

2.2.2 間接問句

(1) whether/if 子句

■ I asked the company whether they would order any of our products or not.

我詢問那家公司是否要訂我們任何的產品。

■ I asked Bill if he would play hockey with us this weekend.

我問比爾這週末是否要和我們一起打曲棍球。

說明 正式用法中，僅 whether 子句可作為受詞補語，而 if 子句僅用於口語用法，且不可搭配「or not」。

(2) 疑問詞問句

■ The director inquired what had happened.

主管問發生什麼事。

■ The police inquired who witnessed the accident.

警方查訪有誰目擊意外。

說明 ask, inquire 等詢問語意的動詞只能搭配疑問詞引導的名詞子句。

■ The CEO hasn't made up his mind about who would be transferred to the Seattle office.

執行長沒有決定要調誰去西雅圖公司。

★常搭配名詞子句當受詞的動詞：

agree 同意	indicate 顯示
assume 臆測	notice 注意

當代英語用法指南

conclude　包括	predict　預測
decide　決定	prove　證明
demonstrate　顯示	pretend　假裝
discover　發現	realize　體會
dream　夢想	regret　後悔
guess　猜想	suppose　認為
learn　知道	suspect　懷疑
imagine　想像	wonder　想知道

2.3 主詞補語

2.3.1 that 子句

- The real reason is (that) the contestant lacks self-confidence.
  真正的原因是該名參賽者缺乏自信。

- Do you regard it as necessary that we should build a cat tree?
  你認為我們需要蓋個貓樹嗎？

2.3.2 間接問句

(1) whether/if 子句

- The problem is whether we have enough capital or not.
  問題是我們是否有足夠的資金。

說明 if 名詞子句較少當作主詞補語。

(2) 疑問詞問句

- That is just what we really need.
  這就是我們真正需要的。

2.4 同位語

2.4.1 that 子句

■ No one can deny the fact that drink and driving is a very serious offense.

酒駕是非常嚴重的違法行為，這事實無人否認。

■ He made a suggestion that the road (should) be widened by at least two meters on each side.

他建議道路邊至少拓寬兩米。

2.4.2 間接問句

(1) whether / if 子句

■ The issueof whether or notwe should build the nuclear power plant is still highly controversial.

我們應否蓋核電廠仍然是個具高度爭議的議題。

說明 if 名詞子句沒有同位語功用。

(2) 疑問詞問句

■ This might be the answer to the question why thousands of earthworms came out of the soil.

這或許是數千隻蚯蚓鑽出土壤的問題答案。

■ Here's a question, what has caused millions of bees to disappear from their hives.

問題在這裡，是什麼造成數百萬蜜蜂從蜂窩中消失。

◆ 13-2 形容詞子句

　　子句結構的形容詞為形容詞子句，後位修飾名詞，分為限定用法與補述用法二種。關係代名詞引介形容詞子句，指涉的語詞為先行詞，通常是名詞或先行詞所在的子句，也可能是該子句中的其他語詞。形容詞子句常因結構或語意關係而不與先行詞相鄰，這是遠距關係。

1. 先行詞的結構：

　　單詞關係代名詞的先行詞除了名詞或代名詞，語意上，也可指涉其他組成成分，但限於補述用法。

1.1 名詞

- The man who go this arm tattooed comes from Brazil.
  手臂刺青的男子來自巴西。

- Lions have very good night vision, which we humans don't have.
  獅子具有人類所沒有的夜視能力。

1.2 the ＋形容詞

- The rich who earned their own money appreciated more than those who inherited it.
  比起繼承來的財產，有錢人自己賺的錢更能受人重視。

1.3 代名詞

- God helps those who help themselves.
  天助自助者。

1.4 動詞

- Eric was caught cheating during test and, which was worse, argued with the examiner.
  艾力克考試作弊被抓到，更糟的是，還和審查員起爭執。

- Gina enjoys cycling but, which is very risky, usually goes cycling alone in the mountains.
  吉娜喜愛騎單車，但是非常危險的事，經常獨自去山區騎單車。

1.5 不定詞

- Sam was asked not to talk with his mouth full, which was very awful indeed.
  山姆被要求不要滿口食物時說話，那真的很糟。

- Kelly is planning to go on a working holiday in Australia, which sounds quite exciting.
  凱莉打算去澳洲打工度假，聽起來好刺激。

1.6 動名詞

■ My cousin is interested in bungee jumping, which I consideris too dangerous for me.

我表弟對高空彈跳有興趣，那對我來說太危險了。

■ Wally spent a lot of time playing online games, which is bad for his eyes.

瓦里花好多時間玩線上遊戲，那對他的眼睛不好。

1.7 分詞

■ Helen is addicted to smoked food, which is harmful to her health.

海倫愛吃煙燻食物，這對她的健康有害。

1.8 the ＋分詞

■ One of the wounded, who had been in critical condition, died this morning.

有名傷者突然陷入危險狀態，逝於今天早上。

1.9 形容詞

■ My roommate is able to sing on the moon guitar, which I am not.

我的室友會彈著月琴唱歌，這我不會。

■ Louisa is eager to learn English, which will leadto a lot of progress.

露易莎熱衷於學習英語，這讓她大幅進步。

1.10 子句

■ The man said he was not at the crime scene, which was not true.

男子說他不在刑案現場，那並非事實。

■ The budget was rejected by the committee, which was a big shock to the CEO.

預算遭委員會駁回，讓執行長非常震驚。

2. 形容詞子句的缺項：

語意上，先行詞指涉形容詞子句中的名詞缺項，結構上，關係代名詞填補此缺項。形容詞子句的缺項有主詞、受詞、補語、所有詞等。

2.1 主詞：形容詞子句主詞缺項由主格關係代名詞填補，不可省略。另外，主詞缺項的形容詞子句可縮減為片語結構。

- The animal that   which was first domesticated by humans was the dog.

  = The animal first domesticated by humans was the dog.

  = The animal first to be domesticated by humans was the dog.

  最先被人類馴服的動物是狗。

- The athlete who won the Marathon race is from Africa.

  = The athlete winning the Marathon race is from Kenya.

  = The athlete to win the Marathon race is from Kenya.

  贏得馬拉松比賽的選手來自肯亞。

2.2 受詞：形容詞子句受詞缺項由受格關係代名詞填補，前面沒有介系詞時可省略。受詞缺項的形容詞子句不可縮減為片語結構。

- The man (whom) you met at the press conference is my advisor.

  你在記者會遇見的男子是我的指導教授。

- I am not able to access the website (that) I am trying to get to.

  我無法連上我剛想進去的網站。

2.3 主詞補語：形容詞子句主詞補語缺項由主格關係代名詞填補，不可省略。

- Thank you for helping me become who I am now.

  感謝您的幫助讓我成為現在的我。

2.4 所有詞：形容詞子句所有詞缺項由所有格關係代名詞或「of which」填補，不可省略。

■ He's the man whose website has been praised by professional associations.

他就是部落格備受專業社群推崇的那名男子。

■ This is a house of which the doors are made of bulletproof material.

= This is a house the doors of which are made of bulletproof material.

這是一棟連門都是由防彈材質製成的房子。

2.5 介系詞受詞：形容詞子句介系詞受詞缺項由受格關係代名詞填補，介系詞未前移時，可省略。包含受格關係代名詞，且表示時間、地方、原因的介系詞片語省略時，關係副詞引導形容詞子句。

■ *"You may forget with whom you laughed, but you will never forget with whom you wept." -- Kahlil Gibran-*

「你會忘記誰與你同歡笑，但絕不會忘記誰與你同哭泣。」-- 紀伯倫 哈利勒 -

■ I'll never forget the place which I met my ex-husband at.

= I'll never forget the place at which I met my ex-husband.

= I'll never forget the place where I met my ex-husband.

我永遠忘不掉遇見我前夫的地方。

【比較】You can go wherever you like to go during your annual vacation.

年假期間你喜歡去哪就去哪。

說明 wherever 引導的子句無先行詞，屬於副詞子句。

■ Please tell me the exact time which I will be reconnected at.

= Please tell me the exact time at which I will be reconnected.

= Please tell me the exact time when I will be reconnected.

麻煩告訴我重新連線的確切時間。

3. 形容詞子句的用法：

形容詞子句有限定用法與補述用法之分。

3.1 限定用法：用以限定先行詞狀況時，形容詞子句為限定用法，與先行詞不以逗號相隔，關係代名詞受形容詞子句缺項的指涉限制。

■ People should care about all the animals that are endangered!
人們應當關注瀕臨絕種的動物。

■ The man who robbed a woman of her purse has given himself up to the police.
搶奪婦人皮包的男子已向警方投案。

3.2 補述用法：用以補充描述先行詞時，形容詞子句為補述用法，與先行詞逗號相隔，僅搭配關係代名詞 which／who。

■ That is my uncle, who will run for President in 2016.
那是我叔叔，他要競選 2016 總統。

■ The polar bear will become extinct, which is just a matter of time.
北極熊滅絕，只是時間問題。

4. 形容詞子句的遠距關係：

搭配形容詞子句的名詞組結構龐大，造成較小語詞置於句尾，不符尾重原則，因此形容詞子句常移至句尾而形成與先行詞的遠距關係。

■ The TV show has stopped which used to be popular with people at all ages.

= The TV show which used to be popular with people at all age has stopped.
曾經廣受歡迎的電視節目停播了。

■ My manager assigned a task which needs a lot of responsibility to me.

= My manager assigned a task to me which needs a lot of responsibility.

我的經理指派我一個責任重大的工作給我。

◆ 13-3 副詞子句

子句結構的副詞為副詞子句，僅修飾句子。

1. 副詞子句的位置：

副詞子句可置於主要子句前面、後面、中間。

1.1 主要子句前面：與主要子句逗號相隔，訊息焦點在後面的主要子句，形成掉尾句，符合語言邏輯。

■ Come what may, we must hold on straight to the end.
無論發生什麼狀況，我們必須堅持到底。

■ Seeing that the driver rejected to reconcile, we have no choice to sue him.
既然駕駛人拒絕和解，我們只好提告。

1.2 主要子句後面：與主要子句不隔逗號，訊息焦點在前面的主要子句，形成鬆散句。

■ The dissidents fled his country lest he be captured by authorities.
異議分子逃到國外，躲避當局的緝捕。

■ A pungent smell of incense overwhelmed me the instant I entered the temple.
我一進到廟宇，一股濃嗆的燒香味撲鼻而來。

1.3 主要子句中間：與主要子句逗號相隔，形成中間分支句。

■ Mr. Huang, since he has retired, is spending a lot of time traveling around.
自從黃先生退休，便花了很多時間到處旅行。

■ Albert, as the train delayed, didn't attend the wedding banquet.
因為火車誤點，艾伯特沒有參加婚宴。

2. 具有副詞子句功用的語詞

2.1 獨立不定詞：獨立不定詞與句中語詞無語法關聯，功用為修飾全句。

■ To give him his due, Leo is a little stubborn.
說句公道話，里歐有點固執。

■ To make a long story short, we need to cancel the project.
總而言之，我們必須取消計畫。

■ To change the subject, do you have any plans this weekend?
換一下話題，這週末你有計畫嗎？

■ To make matters worse, I was fined for parking on the wrong side of the street.
更糟的是，我因路邊停車的位置不對而被罰。

2.2 分詞構句：分詞構句或主詞為第一人稱且表示作說者的態度或觀點的獨立分詞構句都具有副詞子句功用。

■ Being caught cheating during test, the student was cited with a 1st Level Demerit.
被抓到考試作弊，學生被記一支大過。

■ Frankly speaking, our opponent is very much worried about the result of the election.
坦白說，我們的對手非常擔憂選舉結果。

■ Generally speaking, the harder you work, the more possibility there is for your success.
一般而言，你愈努力，你愈有可能成功。

2.3 形容詞片語：一些獨立構句的形容詞片語置於句前，表達對句子所述的議論或評述。

■ Needless to say, dogs need their owner to accompany them.
= It's needless to say that dogs need their owner to accompany them.
不消說，狗需要牠們的主人陪伴。

■ Strange to say, there came no students to the classroom during class time.

= It's strange to say that there came no students to the classroom during class time.

說來奇怪，上課期間沒有學生來到教室。

■ Contrary to my expectation, I failed the test.

與我的期待相反，我通過期末考試。

■ True, my Zwergschnauzer never eats meat.

= It's true that my Zwergschnauzer never eats meat.

老實說，我的雪納瑞從不吃肉。

2.4 副詞：修飾句子的單詞副詞常說明作說者對句子所述的觀點或感受，可視為副詞子句。

■ Obviously, the manager and his assistant are in a relationship.

= It's obviously that the manager and his assistant are in a relationship.

很明顯，經理和他的助理在交往。

■ Unfortunately almost all the seats have been taken.

= It's unfortunate that almost all the seats have been taken.

遺憾的是，幾乎所有的座位都被訂走了。

■ Financially, women spend more money than men.

在金錢方面，女人花的錢比男人多。

■ Theoretically speaking, no one can use my software without my permission.

按理說，未經我的許可，誰都不能使用我的軟體。

2.5 介系詞片語：一些介系詞片語置於句首，說明作說者的觀點或感受，可視為副詞子句。

■ As a rule,Mr. Wu is a competentdirector.

多數情況下，吳先生是一名稱職的導演。

■ All in all, things will work out for the better soon.

總之，事情很快就會好轉。

■ In a sense,your wife is the biggest part of your life.

就某種意義來說，你的妻子是你生命中最重要的部分。

■ As a result, the student was sent down from Cambridge University.

結果，劍橋大學將那名學生開除了。

3. 副詞子句的倒裝：

一些副詞子句的組成成分可形成倒裝詞序。

3.1 時間副詞子句：

3.1.1 hardly, scarcely, no sooner 等否定連接詞引導的時間副詞，助動詞可移至主詞前面，形成倒裝句型。

■ No sooner had the man arrived at the station than the train came in.

= The man had only just got to the station when the train came in.

= The train came in just after got to the station.

男子一到車站，火車就進站了。

> 說明 事實上，真實言談中，我們會先說早發生的動作，再提晚發生的動作，因此該句會這樣表達：

■ Leo had only just got to the station when the train came in.

里歐才到車站火車剛好進站。

■ The train came in just after Leo got to the station.

火車一抵達里歐剛好到車站。

3.1.2 until 副詞子句搭配否定語意主要子句時，until 副詞子句可移至句首，搭配否定語氣，形成倒裝句型。

■ The stray dog didn't leave until it ate up all the food.

= It was not until the stray dog left did it eat up all the food.

流浪狗吃完所有食物後才離去。

倒裝： Not until the stray dog left did it eat up all the food.

3.1.3 搭配 only 的時間副詞子句可移至句首，主要子句主詞與動詞詞序變換，形成倒裝句型。

■ You will realize how precious freedom is only when you lose it.

當你失去自由時，你就能體會到它有多珍貴。

倒裝： only when you lose freedomwill you realize how precious freedom is.

■ We will cancel trade sanctions only after the Government of the country makes a formal apology.

該國政府正式道歉之前我們不會取消貿易制裁。

倒裝： Only after the Government of the country makes a formal apology will we cancel trade sanctions.

3.2 結果副詞子句：

3.2.1 主要子句中的「so/such 形容詞」移至句首時，be 動詞移至主詞前面。

■ The heavy motorcycle was so expensive that the young student couldn't afford to buy it.

重型機車太昂貴了，年輕學生買不起。

倒裝： So expensive was the heavy motorcycle that Leo couldn't afford to buy it.

■ The situation was such that I couldn't continue working on the project.

情勢走到這地步，我實在無法繼續這份計畫。

倒裝： Such was the situation that I couldn't continue working on the project.

3.2.2 such 當主詞補語，表示程度，that 子句表示結果。such 移至句首時，be 動詞移至主前面。

■ The earthquake was such that it was felt from Hualien to Kaohsiung.

地震劇烈搖晃，花蓮到高雄都感受得到。

倒裝： Such was the earthquake that it was felt from Hualien to Kaohsiung.

■ The Rubber Duck was such that attracted millions of people to visit it in two weeks.

黃色小鴨好療癒，兩週內就吸引數百萬人前去觀看。

倒裝： Such was the Rubber Duck that it attracted millions of people to visit it in two weeks.

3.3 讓步副詞子句：

3.3.1 讓步子句主詞補語移至句首，主詞與動詞詞序不變。主詞補語為含冠詞的名詞片語時，冠詞應省略。

■ As he is a veteran sales representative, Tate is paid well.

身為一名資深行銷代表，泰特的待遇很高。

倒裝：Veteran sales representative he is, that is paid well.

■ Although it seems impossible, it is not false at all.

雖然似乎是不可能，但一點也不虛假。

倒裝：Impossible although it seems, it is not false at all.

■ Even as she is generous, the woman is living a simple life.

儘管慷慨大方，婦人過著簡樸生活。

倒裝：Even as generous as she is, the woman is living a simple life.

> 說明 as 連接詞可搭配副詞 even，主詞前也可加入 as。

■ Though he worked hard, the man could not support his family.

儘管努力打拼，男子還是無法支撐自己的家庭。

倒裝：Hard though he worked, the man could not support his family.

3.3.2 讓步子句不含主詞補語，也不搭配副詞時，以副詞 much 置於句首，主詞與動詞詞序不變。

■ Though I would like to go out for a drink of coffee, I'm really occupied with work at the moment.

儘管我想出去喝一杯咖啡，但一會兒我還要忙著工作。

倒裝：As much as I'd like to go out for a drink of coffee, I'm really occupied with work at the moment.

3.3.3 讓步子句的述語動詞為「may ＋原形動詞」時，原形動詞可移至句首。

■ Though you may insist, I still will not make a concession.

儘管你堅持，我還是不會讓步。

倒裝：Insist as you may, I still will not make a concession.

句子的分類

句子可依搭配子句的類型分為單句、合句、複句、複合句等四種。

◆ 14-1 單句

無搭配任何對等或從屬子句的句子。

■ Don't count your chickens before they hatch.
別打如意算盤。

■ Deep-sea fish may contain excessive amounts of mercury.
深海魚可能含有過量的汞。

■ The administration has listed Sabah as a travel warning area.
有關當局已將沙巴列為旅遊警示區。

■ Red eared turtles are semi-aquatic turtles native to the American South.
紅耳龜是美國南部半水棲原生龜。

◆ 14-2 合句

搭配對等子句的句子為合句。

■ *"Give, and it will be given to you."*（-Luke 6:38-）
「*有失就有得。*」《*路加福音：6:38*》

■ Hurry up, or you will be late for the concert.
趕快，不然你會趕不及音樂會。

■ Chris wants to sign up for the event, and so do I.
克里斯要參加活動，我也要。

■ You're smart, but you have to be more proactive.
你很聰明，但是需要更主動。

■ The trainee doesn't have much experience, yet he is eager to learn.
實習生沒什麼經驗，但他熱切學習。

◆ 14-3 複句

搭配從屬子句的句子為合句。

1. 單句＋名詞子句

■ I found it ridiculous that the gorilla picked up his own stool to eat.

我發現猩猩會撿自己的大便來吃,真是不可思議。

2. 單句＋形容詞子句

■ No one is so old but he can learn.

沒有人老到無法學習。

3. 單句＋副詞子句

■ Now that you mention it, I want to see the documentary even more times.

既然你提了,那部紀錄片我要多看幾次。

4. 單句＋分詞構句

■ There being so much noise, I couldn't fall asleep all night long.

這麼吵的噪音,害我整夜無法睡覺。

5. 單句＋補語子句

■ I'm astonished that the tourist from Taiwan was shot in the resort.

我很訝異來自台灣的觀光客在渡假勝地遭到槍擊。

6. 單句＋同位語子句

■ I just received the message that we will be performing from 7:00-9:00.

我剛收到訊息,我們的表演時間從 7 點 ~9 點。

7. 單句＋強調句

- Actually, it's only the female mosquito that bites humans.

  事實上，只有母蚊會叮人。

  Only the female mosquito bites humans.
  （底層結構）

◆ 14-4 複合句

同時搭配對等與從屬子句的句子為複合句。

- Please feel free to contact me whenever necessary and I will respond back ASAP.

  一有需要請儘管和我聯絡，我會儘速回應。

- I was shocked that the journalist suffered from a gang attack and her husband was killed during their stay in India.

  記者和她丈夫停留在印度時，她遭到輪姦，而她丈夫遭到殺害，這真是令我震驚。

- When Mr. Chen died, his son was in military service, and his daughter was studying abroad.

  陳先生去世時，他兒子在服兵役，他女兒在國外念書。

◆ 14-5 引介句

引介不定指事物的句子為引介句，結構主詞為虛詞 there，語意主詞位於 be 動詞之後，符合訊息尾重原則。面對面談話時，常以指示詞 this 引介訊息。

- Once upon a time, there were three little pigs.

  很久以前有三隻小豬。

- There was this prince who fell in love with this beautiful princess at the first sight.

  這裡有位王子對美麗的公主一見鍾情。

1. 引介句的語氣

1.1 直述句

■ There seems to be something wrong with the generator today.
今天發電機似乎有點問題。

1.2 否定句

1.2.1 主詞為不可數名詞：not any ＝ no

■ There is not any lubricating oil in the tank.

　＝ There is no lubricating oil in the tank.

油箱裡沒有潤滑油。

1.2.2 主詞為可數單數名詞：not a ＝ no

■ There is not a single passenger aboard in the tram.

　＝ There is no passenger aboard in the tram.

電車上沒有一個乘客。

1.2.3 主詞為複數名詞：not any ＝ no

■ There are not any seats available to assign.

　＝ There are no seats available to assign.

沒有可分配的座位。

1.3 一般疑問句：be 動詞移至句首

■ Is there any progress on this subject?
這議題有任何進度嗎？

　Yes, there is.　No, there is not.
有的。／目前沒有。

■ Are there any koalas in the zoo?
動物園裡有無尾熊嗎？

　Yes, there are.　No, there are not any.
有的。／沒有。

1.4 疑問詞疑問句：引介句可搭配 what, how many, how much 等疑問語詞以形成問句。

■ What is there in the cupboard?
碗櫥裡有什麼？

■ How many staff members are there in the organization?
機構裡有幾位員工？

■ How much juice is there in an orange?
一顆柳丁有多少果汁？

2. 引介句的數：

與主動詞相鄰的名詞為複數時，搭配複數形主動詞，其他形式的主詞皆搭配單數形主動詞。

■ There lies a shredder in the manager's room.
經理辦公室裡有一部碎紙機。

■ There was a microwave and a mini-fridge in the suite.
套房裡有一個微波爐與一台小冰箱。

■ There was a blackboard and some chairs for the students.
有一塊黑板及一些學生用的椅子。

■ There are ten minutes left.
還有十分鐘。

3. 引介句修飾語類型：

3.1 地方副詞

■ There go cockroaches everywhere!
到處都有蟑螂！

3.2 不定詞

■ There arises a new challenge to go through.
出現新的挑戰等著突破。

3.3 分詞片語

■ There appears a colony of ants nesting in the soil.
出現一窩螞蟻土裡築巢。

3.4 介系詞片語

■ There occurred an accident on the highway.
公路上發生一起車禍。

3.5 形容詞子句

■ There appears a Bigfoot that has been seen around central Washington State.
出現了曾在華盛頓州中部附近的大腳怪。

4. 引介句的主動詞：

除了 be，一些表示存在、位置改變或發生的動詞也可當引介句的主動詞。

■ There remain some problems to be solved.
還有待解決的問題。

■ There stands a chapel with a dome on campus.
校園內有一座圓頂的教堂。

■ There exist sharp contrasts between the two areas.
這兩個區域存在著強烈對比。

■ There emerges a new opportunity to avoid the crisis.
避開風險的新契機浮現了。

4.1 引介句的動詞可搭配其他動詞組，以呈現作說者的意念。

■ There is said to be a water sprite in the lake.
人家都說湖中有水之精靈。

■ There happened to be no plane tickets left for Singapore.
據說現在沒有一張機票能夠離開新加坡。

■ There used to be a movie theater in the town but now there isn't.
在小鎮有處被用來作為電影院使用，但現在已不見了。

5. 引介句的非限定用法：

引介句可以不定詞、動名詞、分詞片語形式呈現。引介句的不定詞、動名詞形式常扮演動詞或介系詞的受詞，分詞形式則常以分詞構句呈現。

5.1 不定詞

■ It's impossible for there to be any fish left in the pond.

= It's impossible that there are any fish left in the pond.

池子裡不可能有任何魚。

■ Employees expected there to be more bonus items.

員工期待更多紅利項目。

■ I really hate there to be long queues everywhere.

我很討厭到處都是大排長龍。

5.2 動名詞片語

■ They had no objection to there being a debate.

他們不反對來一場辯論。

■ We are grateful for there being a solution to the tough problem.

我們很高興有一個解決難題的方法。

5.3 分詞構句

■ There being a sudden rain, the baseball game was put off until next week.

= Because there was a sudden rain, the baseball game was put off until next week.

因為突然下雨，棒球賽延至下星期。

■ There being nothing else to do, the staff left earlier than scheduled.

= Since there being nothing else to do, the staff left earlier than scheduled.

因為沒有其他事情要做，工作人員較預定時間提早下班。

5.4 引介句可引介禁止或不可能的事情，搭配否定式動名詞。

5.4.1 禁止

■ There is no photographing in the museum.

= No photographing in the museum.

博物館裡禁止攝影。

5.4.2 不可能

■ There is no telling what may happen next.

= There is no way of telling what may happen next.

= No one can tell what may happen next.

= It's impossible to tell what may happen next.

未來會發生的事是不可能有人知道的。

6. 引介句的倒裝：

主詞結構較大時，主詞可移至副詞組右側。

■ There are a lot of athletes from many different countries in the gym.

倒裝： There are in the gym a lot of athletes from many different countries.

體育館裡有很多來自許多不同國家的運動選手。

◆ 14-6 強調句

為強調主詞、受詞、時間 地方副詞，而將句子分裂為主要子句與從屬子句的句子為強調句，又稱分裂句。強調語詞為主要子句的訊息焦點，其餘部分依尾重原則構成補語子句，置於句子後端。

1. 強調句的強調語詞

■ A wild cat ate two chickens behind the barn this morning.
今天早上野貓吃掉穀倉後面兩隻小雞。

■ An aboriginal found a Formosan bear beside the stream last night.
昨夜一位原住民在溪旁發現台灣黑熊。

1.1 主詞

■ It was a wild cat that ate two chickens behind the barn this moring.

今天早上是野貓吃掉穀倉後面的兩隻小雞。

■ It was an aboriginal who found a Formosan bear beside a stream last night.

昨夜是一位原住民在溪旁發現台灣黑熊的。

> **說明** 先行詞為人時，關係代名詞選用 who。

1.2 受詞

■ It was two chickens that a wild cat ate behind the barn this morning.

今天早上是穀倉後面的兩隻小雞給野貓吃掉了。

■ It was a Formosan bear that an aboriginal found beside a stream last night.

一位原住民是昨夜在溪旁發現台灣黑熊的。

1.3 時間副詞

■ It was this morning that a wild cat ate two chickens behind the barn.

野貓是在今天早上吃掉穀倉後面的兩隻小雞。

■ It was last night that an aboriginal found a Formosan bear beside a stream.

一位原住民是昨夜在溪旁發現台灣黑熊的。

1.4 地方副詞

■ It was behind the barn that a wild cat ate two chickens this morning.

今天早上野貓是在穀倉後面吃掉兩隻小雞的。

■ It was beside a stream that an aboriginal found a Formosan bear last night.

昨夜一位原住民是在溪旁發現台灣黑熊的。

2. 準強調句：

what 引導強調名詞或動詞的句子為準強調句，訊息焦點為主要子句補語。All 也可用於準強調句。

2.1 強調主詞：

■ My left leg hurts.

我的左腳受傷了。

What hurts is my left leg.
（強調句）

受傷的是我的左腳。

2.2 強調受詞：

■ I won a plasma TV.

我贏得一部電漿電視。

What I won was a plasma TV.
（強調句）

我贏得的是一部電漿電視。

2.3 強調動詞：

■ We played mahjong after dinner.

我們晚餐後打麻將。

What we did after dinner is (to) play mahjong.
（強調句）

＝ All we did after dinner is (to) play mahjong.

我們晚餐後做的就是打麻將。

說明 強調語詞為動詞時，補語不定詞可省略 to。

2.4 強調動名詞：

■ My godfather is interested in playing chess.

我義父對下棋有興趣。

What my godfather is interested in is playing chess.
（強調句）

＝ All my godfather is interested in is playing chess.

我義父感興趣的是下棋。

文法專用詞注音符號索引

ㄉ

文法專用詞注音符號索引

文法專用詞注音符號索引

文法專用詞注音符號索引

文法專用詞英文字母索引

文法專用詞英文字母索引

M

N

O

P

466

文法專用詞英文字母索引

V

Z

不規則動詞表

原形	過去式	過去分詞	中文解釋
bear	bore	born	生出，忍耐
beat	beat	beaten	打擊
become	became	become	成為
begin	began	begun	開始
bend	bent	bent	彎取
bet	bet	bet	打賭
bid	bid	did	吩咐
bind	bound	bound	綑
bite	bit	bitten	咬
bleed	bled	bled	流血
blow	blew	blown	吹
break	broke	broken	打破
bring	brought	brought	帶來
build	built	built	建造
buy	bought	bought	買
catch	caught	caught	捕捉
choose	chose	chosen	選擇
come	came	come	來
cost	cost	cost	值，花費
creep	crept	crept	爬行
cut	cut	cut	切割
deal	dealt	dealt	處理
dig	dug	dug	挖掘

原形	過去式	過去分詞	中文解釋
do	did	done	做
draw	drew	drawn	畫，拉
drink	drank	drunk	喝
drive	drove	driven	駕駛
eat	ate	eaten	吃
fall	fell	fallen	落下
feed	fed	fed	餵養
feel	felt	felt	感覺
fight	fought	fought	戰鬥
find	found	found	發現
flee	fled	fled	逃逸
flow	flowed	flowed	流
fly	flew	flown	飛行
forget	forgot	forgotten	忘記
forgive	forgave	forgiven	寬恕
found	founded	founded	建立
freeze	froze	frozen	冷凍
get	got	got	得到
give	gave	given	給予
go	went	gone	去
grind	ground	ground	磨
ground	grounded	grounded	使擱淺
grow	grew	grown	生長
hang	hung	hung	掛，吊
hang	hanged	hanged	絞死

原形	過去式	過去分詞	中文解釋
has	had	had	
have	had	had	有
hear	heard	heard	聽見
hide	hid	hidden	躲藏
hit	hit	hit	擊打
hold	held	held	抓握
hurt	hurt	hurt	傷害
keep	kept	kept	保持
kneel	knelt	knelt	跪
know	knew	known	知道
lay	laid	laid	放置
lead	led	led	領導
learn	learned	learned	學習
leave	left	left	離開
lend	lent	lent	借給
let	let	let	讓
lie	lay	lain	說謊
lie	lied	lied	躺臥
lose	lost	lost	說謊
make	made	made	失去，輸
mean	meant	meant	製造
meet	met	met	意指，意欲
mistake	mistook	mistaken	遇見
overcome	overcame	overcome	誤會
pay	paid	paid	克服

原形	過去式	過去分詞	中文解釋
read	read	read	付款
ride	rode	ridden	閱讀
ring	rang	rung	騎
rise	rose	risen	鳴，響
run	ran	run	升起
say	said	said	跑
seek	sought	sought	說
seek	saw	seen	尋求
sell	sold	sold	看
send	sent	sent	賣
set	set	set	寄送
shake	shook	shaken	安置
shed	shed	shed	搖動
shine	shone	shone	流出
shine	shined	shined	照耀
shoot	shot	shot	擦亮
show	showed	shown	射擊
shut	shut	shut	展示
sing	sang	sung	關上
sink	sank	sunk	唱歌
sit	sat	sat	沉下
sleep	slept	slept	坐
smell	smelt	smelt	睡覺
speak	spoke	spoken	聞，嗅
spell	spelt	spelt	說話

原形	過去式	過去分詞	中文解釋
spend	spent	spent	拼字
spin	spun	spun	花費
spit	spit	spit	紡
split	split	split	吐出
spread	spread	spread	裂開
spring	sprang	sprung	散佈
stand	stood	stood	站立
steal	stole	stolen	偷竊
stick	stuck	stuck	黏
sting	stung	stung	刺
strike	struck	struck	打擊
strive	strove	striven	奮鬥
swear	swore	sworn	發誓
sweep	swept	swept	掃地
swim	swam	swum	游泳
swing	swung	swung	搖擺
take	took	taken	拿取
teach	taught	taught	教導
tear	tore	torn	撕破
tell	told	told	告訴
think	thought	thought	思考
throw	threw	thrown	投擲
understand	understood	understood	了解
upset	upset	upset	推翻
wear	wore	worn	穿戴

不規則動詞表

474

原形	過去式	過去分詞	中文解釋
weave	wove	woven	編織
weep	wept	wept	哭泣
welcome	welcomed	welcomed	歡迎
win	won	won	贏得
wind	wound	wound	捲
wound	wounded	wounded	受傷
write	wrote	written	寫

參考書目

Cindy Hsin. Syntax Notes. 英檢 , 2000

Michael Swan. Practical English Usage. Oxford University Press

Victoria Fromkin and Robert Rodman, An Introduction to Language. Harcourt, 1998

吳炳鍾，吳炳文 . 實用英語文法百科 1：名詞 . 冠詞 . 代名詞 . 聯經 , 2007

吳炳鍾，吳炳文 . 實用英語文法百科 2：形容詞、數詞、副詞、比較 . 聯經 , 2007

吳炳鍾，吳炳文 . 實用英語文法百科 3：動詞、時態、語態、語氣 . 聯經 , 2008

吳炳鍾，吳炳文 . 實用英語文法百科 4：助動詞、不定詞、動名詞 . 聯經 , 2009

吳炳鍾，吳炳文 . 實用英語文法百科 5：分詞、連接詞、感歎詞、片語 . 聯經 , 2012

楊懿麗 . 現代英語文文法 . 國立編譯館 , 2006

蔣炳榮 . 簡明當代英文法 . 書林出版有限公司 , 2013

趙振才 . 英語常見問題大辭典 . 朗文 , 2006

陳新雄、羅肇錦、竺家寧、孔仲溫、姚榮松、吳聖雄 . 語言學辭典 (增訂版) . 三民 , 2005

蘇秦 . 圖解英文句子結構 . 人類智庫 , 2013

重要歷屆考題

( ) 1. _____ up to eight pounds.
   (A) Weighing a sea otter
   (B) A sea otter can weigh
   (C) The weight of a sea otter
   (D) As a sea otter can weigh

( ) 2. The scientific study of the motion of bodies and the action of forces that change or cause motion _____ dynamics.
   (A) call
   (B) is called
   (C) is calling
   (D) called

( ) 3. Did you feel _____ when Peter noticed your new hairstyle?
   (A) flattering
   (B) flatter
   (C) flattered
   (D) to flatter

( ) 4. Ticonderoga, _____ in 1775, was the first major British fort taken by the continental army.
   (A) captured
   (B) capturing
   (C) to be captured
   (D) being captured

( ) 5. Please wait here for a while. I'll have the documents _____ for you as quickly as possible.
   (A) prepare
   (B) prepares
   (C) prepared
   (D) preparing

( ) 6. Major newspapers have their Internet websites _____ daily, so their readers can get the latest information.
   (A) updating
   (B) updated
   (C) have updated
   (D) are updating

( ) 7. I _____ today. The stylist is professional and didn't charge me much.
   (A) cut my hair
   (B) had cut my hair
   (C) had my hair cut
   (D) had haircut

( ) 8. _____ the clues, can you predict the outcome of the story?
   (A) Acting as
   (B) Based on
   (C) Depended on
   (D) Feeding on

( ) 9. _____ the development of human civilization, it is plain to see that human beings are easily corrupted by power.
   (A) Give
   (B) Giving
   (C) Given
   (D) To give

( )10. Tom, _____ to retire in three months, was told that he could not get a penny because the company's pension fund just declared bankruptcy.
   (A) was planning
   (B) planned
   (C) to be planned
   (D) planning

1	2	3	4	5	6	7	8	9	10
B	B	C	A	C	B	C	B	C	D

(　)11. You'd better _____ Tim around.
    (A) get used to see   (B) to get used to see
    (C) getting used to seeing   (D) get used to seeing

(　)12. My father _____ hiking every Saturday, but after having a stroke some time ago, he no longer keeps this hobby.
    (A) is used to go   (B) is used to going
    (C) used to go   (D) used to going

(　)13. Although the city is relatively untroubled by crime in comparison with other cities, there is now more street crime than .
    (A) it used to   (B) there used to be   (C) was there   (D) it has been

(　)14. Mary keeps buying branded clothes, bags and shoes; I cannot help but _____ how she lives within her income.
    (A) to wonder   (B) wondering   (C) wondered   (D) wonder

(　)15. I haven't seen Jason for twenty years, so I very much look forward to _____ him next week.
    (A) visit   (B) visiting   (C) have visited   (D) visited

(　)16. I am overweight. So I try to avoid _____ any dessert after dinner.
    (A) eat   (B) eating   (C) to eat   (D) to be eating

(　)17. All you have to do is _____ the truth to the public about the company's wrongdoings.
    (A) reveal   (B) to be revealed   (C) revealing   (D) revealed

(　)18. Instead of hiring a repairman, Mrs. Smith made his son _____ the toilet.
    (A) fixing   (B) to fix   (C) fix   (D) fixed

(　)19. The approaching typhoon forced the organizer _____ the game.
    (A) to cancel   (B) cancelling   (C) cancel   (D) cancelled

(　)20. James Figg was the first boxer _____ as a heavyweight champion.
    (A) to recognize   (B) who was recognized
    (C) to be recognized   (D) that recognized

11	12	13	14	15	16	17	18	19	20
D	B	B	D	B	B	A	C	A	C

( )21. The wine _____ from rice. Add some to your fish soup, and it will taste better.

(A) is making   (B) made   (C) makes   (D) is made

( )22. The man protesters _____ with stones and sticks, ready for fight.

(A) armed   (B) to arm   (C) were armed   (D) were arming

( )23. Assault and homicide in Newtown are believed _____ a popular topic of common concern.

(A) that is   (B) to be   (C) being   (D) that

( )24. Professor Wu finds _____ that Tony didn't cheat in the final exam.

(A) to believe hard   (B) it to believe hard

(C) it hard to believe   (D) to believe it hard

( )25. Many artists considered him _____ a tasteless painter obsessed with the ugly.

(A) be   (B) was   (C) being   (D) to be

( )26. _____ their conclusions, the researchers matched the list of the most consumed foods with a list of black-hearted products and found an alarming degree of overlapping.

(A) Reached   (B) They reached   (C) Reaching   (D) To reach

( )27. After spending 5 hours in the interrogation room and conferring with her lawyer, the secretary eventually confessed _____ the money that had been earmarked for company travel.

(A) having stolen   (B) to have been stolen

(C) to steal   (D) to have stolen

( )28. _____ the traffic congestion on downtown streets, city officials are again looking at the possibility of establishing taxi stands.

(A) Facing   (B) Faced   (C) To face   (D) Face

( )29. The techniques _____ here are nothing more than special effects done by computers.

(A) using   (B) that use   (C) be used   (D) that are used

( )30. Not only you but also Michael _____ asked to participate in the annual conference.

(A) are   (B) has   (C) was   (D) were

21	22	23	24	25	26	27	28	29	30
D	C	A	B	A	C	D	C	D	A

( )31. Jack! How many times do I have to remind you _____ up your coat when you get home from school?

(A) hang   (B) hung   (C) hanging   (D) to hang

( )32. As Stephen entered his room, he found many books _____ scattered on the floor.

(A) lie   (B) laying   (C) lying   (D) to lay

( )33. The witness to the murder asked _____ in the TV news or newspaper. She wanted her name to be kept secret.

(A) not to be identified   (B) to identify
(C) not being identified   (D) not identified

( )34. The fierce typhoon is coming and it is time we _____ some food and bottled water.

(A) would buy   (B) bought   (C) will buy   (D) to buy

( )35. The problem _____ for three months now, and we need to find a quick solution.

(A) has existed   (B) existed   (C) is existing   (D) would exist

( )36. Michelle couldn't play yesterday because she _____ her ankle the day before.

(A) was spraining   (B) has sprained
(C) had sprained   (D) having sprained

( )37. I'm very sorry for not answering your call immediately. I _____ my hair when you called.

(A) washed   (B) has washing   (C) had washed   (D) was washing

( )38. The secretary opened the mail which _____ that morning.

(A) had delivered   (B) delivered
(C) had been delivered   (D) is delivered

( )39. Due to the economic depression, our sales _____ for months, so we are now in great financial difficulties.

(A) are dropping   (B) have been dropped
(C) had been dropping   (D) have been dropping

( )40. I _____ the beautiful Taroko Gorge in Hualien.

(A) have once visited   (B) have ever visited
(C) have been visited   (D) have to be visited

31	32	33	34	35	36	37	38	39	40
D	C	A	B	A	C	D	C	D	A

重要歷屆考題

(　)41. By this time tomorrow, she _____ the job.
(A) will finish　　(B) will have finished　(C) is finishing　(D) has finished

(　)42. Inside the heavy box are some love letters to my grandma. It _____ by my grandfather.
(A) must have been writing　　　(B) must write
(C) must have been written　　　(D) must have written

(　)43. I _____ the party earlier last night.
(A) ought to leave　　　　(B) should have left
(C) should leave　　　　　(D) supposed to leave

(　)44. The ground is wet. It _____ have rained last night.
(A) should　(B) must　(C) could　(D) would

(　)45. _____ got along well with my father before he passed away.
(A) If only I have　(B) I wish I had　　(C) If I had　　(D) Had I

(　)46. The director insisted that all the members _____ at the meeting time.
(A) are　　　(B) be　　　(C) would be　　(D) were

(　)47. Since Constanze had very little money, it was recommended that Mozart's corpse _____ the cheapest available funeral.
(A) was given　(B) be given　(C) given　(D) to be given

(　)48. The CEO demanded that all the letters _____ without delay by seven tomorrow night.
(A) were typewritten　　　(B) were to be typewritten
(C) would be typewritten　　(D) be typewritten

(　)49. It is imperative that the city council _____ in favor of the city renewal plan.
(A) to vote　　(B) vote　　(C) votes　　(D) has voted

(　)50. The manager talks as if he _____ mad at you, but this is just the way he talks to everybody.
(A) is　　　(B) be　　　(C) were　　(D) can be

50	49	48	47	46	45	44	43	42	41
C	B	D	B	B	B	B	B	C	B

( )51. _____ the GPS in his smartphone, the mountain climber couldn't be located so fast.
    (A) If it had not been for   (B) With
    (C) But that   (D) If it were not for

( )52. The work as a whole _____ carried through without Gibbon's insightful contribution.
    (A) should never be   (B) would never have been
    (C) would never be   (D) was never

( )53. If I hadn't slipped on the ice, I _____ my arm.
    (A) couldn't break   (B) couldn't have broken
    (C) shouldn't have broken   (D) might have broken

( )54. It's a pity that I failed again. If I had read the book carefully, _____ the test.
    (A) I shall pass   (B) I should be passed
    (C) I would have passed   (D) I would not have passed

( )55. It seemed that the walls _____ .
    (A) had repainted   (B) are repainted
    (C) have been painted   (D) had been repainted

( )56. I would not have finished my task so efficiently _____ _ you not _____ me a hand today.
    (A) if give   (B) had given   (C) have given   (D) if had given

( )57. The victims had hoped that the judge could right the wrong, but they saw their _____ with justice. They decided to take matters into their own hands.
    (A) dash   (B) dashing   (C) to dash   (D) dashed

( )58. When Joe came back to his seat in the library, he founded his wallet _____ .
    (A) steal   (B) stealing   (C) be stolen   (D) stolen

( )59. Soon after the robbery took place, two suspects _____ .
    (A) arrested   (B) were arrested
    (C) had been arrested   (D) had arrested

( )60. Mark _____ be a teacher, but now he is a CEO in an international company.
    (A) is using   (B) was used to   (C) is used to   (D) used to

51	52	53	54	55	56	57	58	59	60
D	B	B	C	D	B	D	D	B	D

( )61. I regret _____ the party last night as they had so much fun.
    (A) not to join   (B) didn't join
    (C) not to have joined   (D) not joining

( )62. My laser printer is not working properly. It needs _____ .
    (A) fix   (B) fixed   (C) to fix   (D) fixing

( )63. _____ , he left without saying a word.
    (A) Feel depressed   (B) He felt depressed
    (C) Felt depressed   (D) Depressed

( )64. Upon hatching, _____ .
    (A) young ducks know how to swim   (B) swimming is known by young ducks
    (C) swimming by young ducks   (D) knowing how to swim

( )65. _____ the way to take, the traveler went on his journey.
    (A) Telling   (B) Having told   (C) Have told   (D) Told

( )66. _____ English, many Chinese classical novels gain attention and popularity in the US.
    (A) Written in   (B) To translate into
    (C) To write in   (D) Translated to

( )67. The children of Israel, _____ the Ten Commandments, were still far from their promised land.
    (A) received   (B) having received   (C) receiving   (D) had received

( )68. I really _____ seeing you again.
    (A) would rather   (B) cannot but
    (C) cannot wait   (D) look forward to

( )69. The Kenyans have three runners in the 1500 meters, any of _____ could take the gold medal.
    (A) them   (B) which   (C) whom   (D) what

( )70. However hard we tried, we just couldn't find the person _____ car was blocking the driveway.
    (A) whose   (B) of which   (C) of whom   (D) who

61	62	63	64	65	66	67	68	69	70
D	D	D	A	C	D	B	D	C	A

483

重要歷屆考題

( )71. This is the college _____ I was graduated.
　　(A) that　　(B) in which　　(C) which　　(D) from which

( )72. The great Depression was an international economic crisis, _____ the unemployment rate rose to 25%.
　　(A) at which　　(B) during which　　(C) that　　(D) during that

( )73. The dog, _____ is a very popular house pet, is actually a very smart animal.
　　(A) what　　(B) it　　(C) which　　(D) that

( )74. The earth is becoming warmer and warmer. There are few countries _____ are concerned about the serious problem of global warming.
　　(A) which　　(B) not　　(C) without　　(D) but

( )75. _____ you are in the world of business or the world of social relations, the way you dress can make a tremendous difference.
　　(A) No matter　　(B) Whether　　(C) Although　　(D) If

( )76. _____ the senator could be elected for his second term remains uncertain.
　　(A) Whether　　(B) What　　(C) Which　　(D) That

( )77. To some people, Mickey Mouse is seen as the spread of American culture to other countries _____ he reflects American imperialism and ideas.
　　(A) which　　(B) when　　(C) where　　(D) from which

( )78. He started his own business five years ago. That was _____ he began to be independent of his parents.
　　(A) where　　(B) when　　(C) what　　(D) how

( )79. The doctor _____ was very gentle.
　　(A) examined who was sick
　　(B) who examined the sick child
　　(C) was being examined by whom
　　(D) examined the sick child

( )80. He who laughs last _____ best.
　　(A) laughs　　(B) laughed　　(C) is laughed　　(D) laughing

71	72	73	74	75	76	77	78	79	80
D	B	C	D	B	A	C	B	B	A

( )81. Kevin wouldn't tell me _____ she saw there.
    (A) where   (B) that   (C) which   (D) what

( )82. The manager made _____ a rule that all employees had to attend the company's events to show their loyalty and dedication.
    (A) what   (B) which   (C) it   (D) them

( )83. An achievement test should measure students' progress against their own performance and _____ of their fellow students'.
    (A) that   (B) most   (C) many   (D) much

( )84. There is a technical help-desk _____ dealing with any technical problem that may occur.
    (A) which responsible for   (B) responsible for
    (C) which is responsible for   (D) is responsible for

( )85. It was my grandfather's belief _____ women should stay at home and keep the house.
    (A) which   (B) what   (C) that   (D) who

( )86. _____ had they reached the other side than the fox tossed the gingerbread man up in the air.
    (A) Soon   (B) No sooner   (C) Soon after   (D) As soon as

( )87. _____ about the people who had inhabited in Taiwan before the current aborigines came.
    (A) Knowing little is   (B) Little known
    (C) Little is known   (D) Known little is

( )88. _____ you pay the bill, you cannot leave.
    (A) If   (B) As long as   (C) What if   (D) Unless

( )89. Wise men love truth, _____ fools shun it.
    (A) so   (B) therefore   (C) as   (D) while

( )90. The Human Comedy, a sentimental story of a family in a country at war, had special appeal because its principal characters are children _____ its perspective is adult.
    (A) when   (B) though   (C) where   (D) while

81	82	83	84	85	86	87	88	89	90
D	C	A	C	B	C	D	D	D	D

重要歷屆考題

( )91. My grandmother always talks to her cats _____ they were her kids.
(A) only if   (B) what if   (C) as if   (D) if only

( )92. Give me your telephone number _____ I need your help.
(A) whether   (B) unless   (C) so that   (D) in case

( )93. _____ I read the proposal _____ the budget was so high.
(A) Until   I realized   (B) Not until   I didn't realize
(C) Not until   did I realize   (D) Until that   did I realize

( )94. little girl was so shy and introvert _____ she was afraid to speak in public.
(A) when   (B) which   (C) but   (D) that

( )95. Some people think it's _____ late to do anything about global warming.
(A) so   (B) such so   (C) much too   (D) too much

( )96. _____ you purchase good tea, keep it in a dry cool place, avoiding direct sunshine. An airtight container is agood choice.
(A) After   (B) Though   (C) Before   (D) Whereas

( )97. When the 6.3 magnitude earthquake struck Taiwan, the railway administration immediately suspended trainservice _____ it checked for any possible damage to tracks.
(A) where   (B) that   (C) whether   (D) while

( )98. I have been taking the Yoga class _____ I came to this school.
(A) when   (B) for   (C) since   (D) before

( )99. _____ the economic situation is getting worse, some companies have no choice but to lay off their employees.
(A) Because   (B) Due to   (C) Even though   (D) While

( )100. _____ it was once a heavily-polluted rice field, it is now much cleaner.
(A) Because   (B) Whenever   (C) However   (D) Although

91	92	93	94	95	96	97	98	99	100
C	D	C	D	C	A	B	C	A	D

重要歷屆考題

( )101. Hawaii is a great location for all kinds of water sports. Some like to go windsurfing _____ others like to go water-skiing.

(A) despite of   (B) therefore   (C) whenever   (D) whereas

( )102. The city is going to hold a public hearing to discuss _____ the historical building should be torn down.

(A) whatever   (B) whether or not   (C) in case that   (D)no matter how

( )103. My mother found it increasing difficult to read, _____ her eyesight was beginning to fail.

(A) so   (B) or   (C) for   (D) but

( )104. Surf the Internet, _____ you can easily find the information you need.

(A) or   (B) but   (C) and   (D) yet

( )105. Diversity is the greatest asset of these regions, _____ people would be impressed by their shared characteristics.

(A) if   (B) so   (C) and   (D) but

( )106. _____ most of his time devoted to the extracurricular activities, Allen, one of the gifted students in my class, got only mediocre scores in his major studies.

(A) When   (B) With   (C) Despite   (D) Because

( )107. _____ no one living inside for long, that old building looked like a haunted house.

(A) With   (B) Until   (C) As   (D) Because

( )108. _____ , heat is produced.

(A) The mixing together of certain chemicals

(B) Whenever certain chemicals are mixed together

(C) Certain chemicals mixed together

(D) That certain chemicals are mixed together

( )109. Please wait for a while. The salesman will explain to you _____ .

(A) the machine works how   (B) the machine how works

(C) how does the machine work   (D) how the machine works

( )110. A historian does not only describe events, but tries to explain _____ occur in the first place.

(A) to what caused them   (B) what causes them to

(C) what they cause to   (D) what to cause them

101	102	103	104	105	106	107	108	109	110
D	B	C	C	B	A	B	D	B	

( )111. The parallax measurement is used in survey studies to tell how far away _____ .
(A) is an object distant
(B) distant is an object
(C) an object is distant
(D) a distant object is

( )112. This oral exam can be a challenge to those students _____ limited English proficiency.
(A) in
(B) with
(C) at
(D) for

( )113. A refractory is any nonmetallic material or object that can withstand high temperatures _____ becoming soft.
(A) and
(B) but
(C) or
(D) without

( )114. _____ , a television set is in use in every home for about 61 2 hours each day.
(A) It is averaged
(B) On the average
(C) The average that
(D) The average

( )115. It was the horrible traffic jam _____ caused the employee to be late for work.
(A) where
(B) that
(C) what
(D) in which

( )116. Bob went to Japan this summer vacation, and so _____ Bill. They both had a wonderful time there.
(A) is
(B) does
(C) was
(D) did

( )117. That shy girl always speaks quietly. _____ is not easy to hear what she says.
(A) What
(B) There
(C) She
(D) It

( )118. Fresh fruits and vegetables are healthier foods than canned _____ .
(A) ones
(B) them
(C) those
(D) these

( )119. _____ is always a lot of traffic during rush hour, and thus it will take longer to get to the airport.
(A) There
(B) It
(C) That
(D) What

( )120. The problem can be solved by _____ filling the order _____ refunding the payment.
(A) either or
(B) neither nor
(C) rather than
(D) too to

111	112	113	114	115	116	117	118	119	120
D	B	D	D	B	B	D	D	A	A	A

( ) 121. _____ does taking public transportation save money, but it also saves energy.

(A) Never   (B) Neither   (C) Not only   (D) Hardly ever

( ) 122. Not only _____ government patronage, we struggled to gain it.

(A) have we shunned   (B) did we shun

(C) we shunned   (D) had we shunned

( ) 123. Rather than _____ your children fish for survival, have you tried teaching them how to fish?

(A) to give   (B) giving   (C) give   (D) given

( ) 124. There are lots of toy balls in the pool. _____ are red, and _____ are white.

(A) Ones   the others   (B) Some   others

(C) Some   the other   (D) Some of   others

( ) 125. Individual differences in children must be recognized. While one child might have a strong interest in math and science, _____ child might tend toward artistic endeavors.

(A) one   (B) other   (C) the other   (D) another

( ) 126. Mr. and Mrs. Jones have three outstanding sons. One is a respected middle school principal, another is a famous doctor, and _____ is a talented music producer.

(A) others   (B) some other

(C) the other   (D) still another

( ) 127. This CD player is more expensive than _____ in the store.

(A) all together   (B) any other   (C) others   (D) all

( ) 128. A computer is usually chosen because of its simplicity of operation and ease of maintenance _____ its capacity to store information.

(A) the same as   (B) as well   (C) as well as   (D) but also

( ) 129. Everyone who went on that trip returned full of tales which were talked about for months _____ .

(A) latter   (B) latest   (C) later   (D) late

( ) 130. The Industrial Revolution created a great need for labor in the factories in and around cities; _____ , the population centers became less rural and more urban.

(A) so that   (B) consequently   (C) nevertheless   (D) otherwise

121	122	123	124	125	126	127	128	129	130
C	B	B	B	D	C	B	C	C	B

( ) 131. My sister has been learning English for ten years. She can speak English as _____ as a native speaker.

(A) best   (B) better   (C) good   (D) well

( ) 132. There's _____ highway traffic today than usual, and that's why we are late.

(A) most   (B) more   (C) much   (D) many

( ) 133. The harder you hit the ball, _____ .

(A) it will go farther   (B) the farther it will go
(C) the more it will go farther   (D) it will go as far as possible

( ) 134. It's often been reported that North Koreans are a few inches _____ South Koreans.

(A) the shorter   (B) the shortest   (C) shorter than   (D) as short as

( ) 135. Alice bought the house for eight-million dollars two years ago, but now it is worth _____ that amount.

(A) twice more than   (B) more than double
(C) double more than   (D) double

( ) 136. Premature infants have greater chance to become mentally retarded and need more care than _____ .

(A) do normal infants   (B) normal infants are
(C) that of normal infants   (D) there are normal infants

( ) 137. You sang well last night. We hope you'll sing _____ .

(A) more better   (B) still better   (C) very nicely   (D) the best

( ) 138. Only after he has acquired considerable facility in speaking, _____ .

(A) does he learn to read and write
(B) then he learns reading and writing
(C) finally comes reading and reading
(D) he began to read and to write

( ) 139. Finland is the least densely populated country on the continent and _____ its five million residents enjoy one of the highest standards of living anywhere.

(A) like   (B) then   (C) thus   (D) yet

( ) 140. My mom has often admonished me that we cannot be _____ careful in this world because there are lots of difficulties in front of us.

(A) too   (B) so   (C) very   (D) such

131	132	133	134	135	136	137	138	139	140
D	B	B	C	B	A	B	A	D	A

重要歷屆考題

( )141. Alone in a deserted house, he was so busy with his research work that he felt _____ lonely.
(A) nothing but
(B) anything but
(C) all but
(D) everything but

( )142. _____ does not circle around the earth was proven by Galileo.
(A) Since the rest of the universe
(B) as the rest of the universe
(C) The rest of the universe
(D) That the rest of the universe

( )143. _____ the ozone layer has already thinned to a dangerous point is a serious problem.
(A) That
(B) What
(C) It is a fact that
(D) Scientists know that

( )144. A man asked his friend about her trip to Bhutan:" _____ "
(A) How was the journey like?
(B) What the journey was like?
(C) How the journey was like?
(D) What was the journey like?

( )145. There are many things whose misuse is dangerous, but it is hard to think of anything that can be compared _____ tobacco products.
(A) in
(B) with
(C) among
(D) by

( )146. Those two families have been quarrelling _____ each other for many years.
(A) to
(B) between
(C) against
(D) with

( )147. It has always been very generous _____ you to assist us in arranging the meeting.
(A) for
(B) of
(C) to
(D) with

( )148. I will attend Mr. Wang's wedding _____ my father, who has gone to Hong Kong on business.
(A) on behalf of
(B) in terms of
(C) at the mercy of
(D) by means of

( )149. The project was a great success _____ the effort and commitment of everyone involved.
(A) except for
(B) but for
(C) thanks to
(D) in spite of

( )150. _____ that they were rewarded.
(A) Such great suggestion was
(B) So great was the suggestion
(C) However great the suggestion was
(D) The suggestion was great

141	142	143	144	145	146	147	148	149	150
B	D	A	B	B	D	B	A	C	B

( ) 151. Corn is, _____ , so highly bred, that botanists have only recently been able to track down the wild ancestors from which the Indian plants breeders developed it.
(A) such civilized a plant 　　　　(B) such a plant civilized
(C) so civilized a plant 　　　　　(D) so a civilized plant

( ) 152. If you think that skiing is so easy, _____ you should go to Switzerland and try to ski on one of the mountains there.
(A) then 　　　(B) but 　　　(C) though 　　　(D) and

( ) 153. The paper presents several findings, but none are explained in detail, as _____ in a professional report.
(A) they would be (B) they do 　　　(C) it would be 　　　(D) it does

( ) 154. Mr. Johnson rarely gets upset in the office, _____ ?
(A) does he 　　　(B) doesn't he 　　　(C) will he 　　　(D) won't he

( ) 155. If the weather is good, we _____ the company outing as scheduled.
(A) were to have (B) haven't had 　　　(C) can have 　　　(D) do have

( ) 156. I've had enough to eat. I _____ not have dessert. Green tea is all I want now.
(A) feel like 　　　　(B) prefer to
(C) would like 　　　(D) would rather

( ) 157. That he was shot _____ surprised everyone in school. We were told his funeral would take place a week later.
(A) dead 　　　(B) death 　　　(C) die 　　　(D) dying

151	152	153	154	155	156	157
C	A	B	B	C	D	A

國家圖書館出版品預行編目資料

當代英語用法指南 Modern English Usage Guide ／
蘇秦著；——初版 .——臺中市：晨星，2014.08
面； 公分 .——（Guide Book；347）

ISBN 978-986-177-812-9（平裝）

1. 英語 2. 語法

805.16   102026858

Guide Book 347

當代英語用法指南
Modern English Usage Guide

作者	蘇 秦
編輯	林 千 裕
封面設計	萬 勝 安
美術設計	張 蘊 方
創辦人	陳 銘 民
發行所	晨星出版有限公司
	台中市 407 工業區 30 路 1 號
	TEL:(04)23595820　FAX:(04)23597123
	E-mail:service@morningstar.com.tw
	http://www.morningstar.com.tw
	行政院新聞局局版台業字第 2500 號
法律顧問	甘 龍 強 律師
初版	西元 2014 年 08 月 15 日
郵政劃撥	22326758（晨星出版有限公司）
讀者服務專線	（04）23595819＃230
印刷	上好印刷股份有限公司

定價 450 **元**

ISBN 978-986-177-812-9

Published by Morning Star Publishing Inc.
Printed in Taiwan

◆ 讀者回函卡 ◆

以下資料或許太過繁瑣，但卻是我們了解您的唯一途徑
誠摯期待能與您在下一本書中相逢，讓我們一起從閱讀中尋找樂趣吧！

姓名：　　　　　　　　性別：□ 男 □ 女　　生日：　／　／

教育程度：＿＿＿＿＿＿＿＿＿＿＿＿＿＿＿＿＿＿＿＿＿＿＿＿＿＿＿

職業：□ 學生　　　　□ 教師　　　　□ 內勤職員　　□ 家庭主婦
□ SOHO 族　　　　□ 企業主管　　□ 服務業　　　□ 製造業
□ 醫藥護理　　　　□ 軍警　　　　□ 資訊業　　　□ 銷售業務
□ 其他 ＿＿＿＿＿＿＿＿＿＿＿＿＿＿＿＿＿＿＿＿＿＿＿＿＿

E-mail：聯絡電話：＿＿＿＿＿＿＿＿＿＿＿＿＿＿＿＿＿＿＿＿＿＿

聯絡地址：□□□ ＿＿＿＿＿＿＿＿＿＿＿＿＿＿＿＿＿＿＿＿＿

購買書名：當代英語用法指南 Modern English Usage Guide

· **本書中最吸引您的是哪一篇文章或哪一段話呢？** ＿＿＿＿＿＿＿＿＿＿＿＿

· **誘使您購買此書的原因？**
□ 於 ＿＿＿＿＿＿ 書店尋找新知時□ 看 ＿＿＿＿＿＿ 報時瞄到□ 受海報或文案吸引
□ 翻閱 ＿＿＿＿＿＿ 雜誌時□ 親朋好友拍胸脯保證□ ＿＿＿＿＿＿ 電台 DJ 熱情推薦
□ 其他編輯萬萬想不到的過程：＿＿＿＿＿＿＿＿＿＿＿＿＿＿＿＿

· **對於本書的評分？**（請填代號：1. 很滿意 2. OK 啦！3. 尚可 4. 需改進）
封面設計 ＿＿＿＿＿ 版面編排 ＿＿＿＿＿ 內容 ＿＿＿＿＿ 文／譯筆 ＿＿＿＿＿

· **美好的事物、聲音或影像都很吸引人，但究竟是怎樣的書最能吸引您呢？**
□ 自然科學 □ 生命科學 □ 動物 □ 植物 □ 物理 □ 化學 □ 天文／宇宙
□ 數學 □ 地球科學 □ 醫學 □電子／科技 □ 機械 □ 建築 □ 心理學
□ 食品科學 □ 其他

· **您是在哪裡購買本書？**（單選）
□ 博客來 □ 金石堂 □ 誠品書店 □ 晨星網路書店 □ 其他

＿＿＿＿＿＿＿＿＿＿＿＿＿＿＿＿＿＿＿＿＿＿＿＿＿＿＿＿＿＿＿

· **您與眾不同的閱讀品味，也請務必與我們分享：**
□ 哲學　　　□ 心理學　　□ 宗教　　　□ 自然生態　□ 流行趨勢　□ 醫療保健
□ 財經企管　□ 史地　　　□ 傳記　　　□ 文學　　　□ 散文　　　□ 原住民
□ 小說　　　□ 親子叢書　□ 休閒旅遊　□ 其他 ＿＿＿＿＿＿＿＿＿＿＿＿

以上問題想必耗去您不少心力，為免這份心血白費

請務必將此回函郵寄回本社，或傳真至（04）2359-7123，感謝！
若行有餘力，也請不吝賜教，好讓我們可以出版更多更好的書！

· **其他意見：**

晨星出版有限公司 編輯群，感謝您！

請填妥後對折裝訂，直接投郵即可，免貼郵票。

407
台中市工業區 30 路 1 號

晨星出版有限公司

更方便的購書方式：

(1) 網站：http://www.morningstar.com.tw
(2) 郵政劃撥　帳號：22326758
　　　　　　戶名：晨星出版有限公司
　　請於通信欄中註明欲購買之書名及數量
(3) 電話訂購：如為大量團購可直接撥客服專線洽詢

◎ 如需詳細書目可上網查詢或來電索取。
◎ 客服專線：04-23595819#230　傳真：04-23597123
◎ 客戶信箱：service@morningstar.com.tw